THE OLD CONTEMPTIBLES

Also by Martha Grimes

The Old Silent
The Man with a Load of Mischief
The Anodyne Necklace
The Deer Leap
The Five Bells and Bladebone
I Am the Only Running Footman
Help the Poor Struggler
Jerusalem Inn
The Dirty Duck
The Old Fox Deceiv'd

THE OLD CONTEMPTIBLES

Martha Grimes

HEADLINE

First published in Great Britain in 1991
by HEADLINE BOOK PUBLISHING PLC

Published by arrangement with Little, Brown Inc.

10 9 8 7 6 5 4 3 2 1

British Library Cataloguing in Publication Data

Grimes, Martha
The old contemptibles.
I. Title
813.54 [F]

ISBN 0−7472−0440−3

Typeset by Medcalf Type Ltd, Bicester, Oxon
Printed and bound in Great Britain by
Richard Clay Ltd, Bungay, Suffolk

HEADLINE BOOK PUBLISHING PLC
Headline House
79 Great Titchfield Street
London W1P 7FN

Acknowledgements

Fiona thanks Janine Adams for saving her skin; Alex thanks Chris Havrilesko for the track and the table; Melrose thanks Elise Kress for the poignance of the wine; and I thank, in addition to the works of the Lake poets themselves, Arthur Wainwright for his guides to the Lakeland fells; Don Gifford for *The Farther Shore*; and Richard Holmes for *Coleridge: Early Visions*.

Contents

PROLOGUE

It was a rainy day in Camden Passage, umbrellas tenting the smaller antique dealers who had set up their folding tables in the square, opened their trunks and cases and arranged bits and bobs of what was real or what was fake.

Jury and the beautiful second-floor tenant who lived in his terraced Islington house were searching for a gift for their mutual friend who occupied the basement flat.

'How much for these ones?' asked Carole-anne, holding out a pair of turquoise combs stuck about with bits of blue glass and scalloped on the edges.

The hustler in the fake lizard jacket had a smile to match. 'Two quid to you, love.'

It was worth two quid, thought Jury, just for a dekko at Carole-anne Palutski, standing there with her red-gold hair under a pink umbrella.

'Fifty p's more like it,' she said, holding out the coin.

'Them's real sapphire stones,' said the dealer, reknotting his purple polka-dot tie, shoving it up to his prominent Adam's apple. Then, with a leer, 'Just like your eyes, gorgeous.'

'My eyes ain't glass,' she said, holding out her final offer.

Jury drew back the hand that held the money and removed the bright combs from the other. He himself was inspecting a pair of jet combs that would look handsome in Mrs Wassermann's hair, once it was returned to its original style.

'Well, Super, but it's just to cheer Mrs W. up a bit. Awful down in the mouth she is about her hair. Always fiddling pins into it.'

'Her down-in-the-mouthness, love, is because she's been scrunched to death by Sassoon in one of your ideas of a Wassermann "do." ' Jury held out the ebony combs. 'How much?'

'Three quid, those ones. Pure jet.'

'Don't be daft. Seventy-five p.' Once again she held out the money.

As the lizard haggled, Jury looked about the Passage, almost automatically checking for a runner named Gladd who was a presence in the Passage. He'd been done twice for handling, and Jury was fairly certain whatever he'd brought today hadn't been purchased from dealers elsewhere. He also ran an eye over the crowd for Jimmy the Dip, one of his favourite minor villains. His glance came to rest on a woman in a white mackintosh on the other side of the square made by the arrangement of tables. She was studying either herself or the mirror of a small bureau-top dressing case. Very attractive, even in the damp coat and scarf. She had no umbrella.

'. . . and don't try and fiddle *him*,' she said, leaning towards Jury. 'He's a policeman.'

'One pound-fifty and that's my final offer.'

'A quid, then' said Carole-anne, for whom final offers were her provenance alone.

From the hustler came a mixture of grumbled acquiescence and lascivious looks at Carole-anne's jade green sweater that the first set of combs would have matched nicely, Jury hadn't failed to notice.

He also hadn't failed to notice that the lady in the white mac had moved on to a display of a delicate satin and lace negligee and had just cut a glance away from Jury as he looked at her again. Indeed, she seemed to be hiding a blush by putting her face very close to it. He smiled slightly. *Buy it*. It was dark gold, more gold than her brown-gold hair, but a material that would have enhanced both her hair and her eyes.

As the dealer was wrapping the black combs in tissue and trying to chat up Carole-anne, who merely twirled her pink umbrella, unmindful of the tweeds and eyes she managed to catch within its rib-ends, Jury noticed, at the end of the table, what looked like a coronet. Oh, Lord, don't let her see *that!*

The Lord met Jury on their usual terms and the next thing he knew Carole-anne was pulling at his sleeve. 'Wouldya look there, Super? A crown.' And how could she help but touch that hair of hers, clearly a crown's proper home.

'Forget it, Carole-anne.'

Which of course, she didn't. She thrust the baleful black comb package into Jury's hands and went for the coronet.

4

Even before she could put the question, the dealer in Crowns and Grails said, 'That'll cost you ten quid, beautiful. Look at them jewels.'

'I looked. Four quid.' She was turning the small coronet round and round.

'Carole-anne, for God's sake, you *don't* need a coronet. You look too queenly already.'

'I'll second that one, mate,' said the dealer.

Carole-anne glared at him. '*Superintendent*, to the likes of you.'

To the likes of others besides lizardy cut-rate dealers, Jury hoped. He had spotted Jimmy, who had nonchalantly bumped into a middle-aged woman who had thrust the antique bracelet she had just purchased into her bag (*why* would women push their bags out of sight behind their backs while looking at merchandise?)

The sly-smiling dealer said, 'Look, that coronet belonged to an Australian princess. Descendant of one of the czars — '

'Any particular one?' asked Jury, noticing the lady in the white mac smile. She seemed clearly to be delighted in the haggling.

The dealer pretended Jury wasn't there. 'Seven quid and we're square,' he said to Carole-anne.

'Five and we're crooked,' she replied and pulled a five-pound note from her little purse.

Miss Palutski was not born to sue, but to command. The head-gear was in place.

Jury noticed the attractive woman smiling again, flashing him another glance. Now she was holding up a yellow-stoned necklace, topaz also, like the material, holding it to the neck of the mackintosh and looking in a mirror. *Buy that, too.* It sparked her eyes, even in the gloom of Camden Passage.

Said Carole-anne, as the beleaguered dealer looked about for a wrapping for the crown. 'It'll just suit my new costume.'

'What costume? The Queen of Soho?' Jury had moved to the next table and was inspecting the supposedly 'antique' scrimshaw and ivory elephant tusks too new to be anything but illegally imported. From this collection of poacher's spoilage he divided his glances between Jimmy, the runner Gladd, and the lady in the white mac.

'Well, I'm tired of that Arabian thing. Anyway, Super, I've got to get to the Stardust.' She hitched up her shoulder bag. 'There's

5

a lady in a white mac over there been giving you the eye. About as much your type as SB-slash-H. Ta.'

No one, as far as Carole-anne was concerned, was or would ever be Jury's type. Carole-anne had turned all sorts of 'types' away from the Islington first-floor flat, the rental of which was in her hands; she had convinced the building's owner she was doing him such a favour by 'showing' it that he had even agreed to knock a few quid off her rent. Jury was not one to weep tears for a London landlord, but this one could wait until hell froze over before someone 'suitable' came along.

He shook his head and watched the men part for Carole-anne, their own dripping black umbrellas synchronizing to cover her bright pink one. It was like watching something from an old musical routine.

Jury wasn't about to nick Jimmy, who seemed to be apologizing to the middle-aged woman for bumping into her. Hell, it wasn't Jury's job and they were almost pals, Jimmy being a font of information about villains that did more than just work the Passage.

At least that was the way he put it to himself as the woman in white was getting closer to him, moving from table to table. And from 'The Lady in the White Mac' was an easy step to *The Woman in White*, except that Wilkie Collins's heroine had suddenly and mysteriously appeared in front of a carriage out in the middle of a dark and forlorn country road. And had as mysteriously disappeared.

It was pretty hard to square rainy, umbrella-laden Camden Passage with a ghostly figure on a foggy road.

They were now closing in on the same table and the same opportunity to examine, hold up to the tepid light, and make a casual remark about whatever-it-might-be's authenticity.

But the remarks had turned out to be even more banal: the weather, and neither of them with an umbrella. She had laughed and asked him if he'd ever been to the Lake District. *That* was rain and fog. They had moved off together then as if by mutual consent, and it was she, rather than he, who had suggested a drink 'before the pubs close'.

Jury had smiled. 'You're not from London, then? The pubs here are open all day now since the licensing laws changed.'

6

'Oh, I'd forgot. What a shame, really; it somehow makes a drink less appealing if you can get one anytime.' She paused and looked up at him. 'It's the end of something.'

Jury smiled. 'I hope not.'

The King's Head pub was never bright on the best of days; this afternoon it seemed as damp and pallid as the pavement outside. The ceiling fixtures cast bands of yellowish light across the polished bar like streetlamps in the mist; the coloured panes of the leaded-glass window by their table were tracked with rain.

Even the lank hair of the unhappy-looking girl who gave the wet-ringed table a wipe before transferring their drinks from her damp tray to the table looked rained on. 'Rotter, innit?'

As the waitress walked away, Jane Holdsworth smiled. 'She should live up North if she's put off by this drizzle.' She ran her hands through her hair, damp and curling at the ends where the scarf had missed covering it.

'Which part are you from?' asked Jury, raising his pint of bitter in a toast to their meeting.

'I? I'm not, at least not any longer. I have relatives there, though. A sister of my own and a few in-laws. I was married. I'm not, now. He's dead.'

'I'm sorry.'

She merely nodded. 'The relations are all on my former husband's side. Except for my one sister. They live near Wast Water — one of the lakes — in one of those old manorial houses the rich threw up in the last century after the poets and painters decided that mountain scenery was worth painting and writing about. I still visit. I have a son and it seems only fair to let his grandparents see him now and then.' She laughed.

But the hard expression in the eyes that regarded him over the rim of her glass suggested she didn't much care for the visits. 'I have a small house in the Lewisham road. It's near Blackheath. The unfashionable side of the Thames, according to my relations.' Her expression softened. 'That's all there is to me; what about you?'

'I doubt that's all there is. But me, I live here. In Islington, I mean.'

'Ah! *Very* gentrified and fashionable.'

'Not my digs; it's a terraced house. But only the ground-floor flat of one.' He signalled the waitress, who gave him a pathetic little look. Couldn't he see how rushed she was? All this custom? This rotten weather?

'I loved the coronet. That actress girl could have haggled him out of his whole tableful of wares.' She leaned her chin on her hands. 'Beauty drives a hard bargain.'

'Then you should have got that gown for very little yourself.' He looked at the brown paper bag. She would take it as a compliment, but he wasn't sure it was entirely one. It surprised him that he was annoyed by her comment about Carole-anne.

Jane picked the bag from the table, set it down again and laughed. 'How did you know about the gown?' She was rummaging in the outsized paper bag as happily as a child searching for a promised gift. The topaz satin wrap was resting over her finger.

'Ooh!' The wary waitress had just come up behind Jane. ''D'ja get that at market? You'll look a right treat in that. Two more, then?' She picked up the glasses. 'If only the bloody rain'd stop.'

Hastily, Jane had bunched up the paper bag and was gathering up her coat. 'No, thanks. I really must be getting back.'

'Suit yerself.' Almost as if the remark had wounded her, she walked away.

'In this rain? And south of the river?' But she had already risen and so did he to help her on with the white raincoat that she couldn't seem to get her arms into.

'I don't care much for pubs. It's more comfortable at home. Even in Lewisham.' Instead of looking at him, she started buttoning up the coat, shoving the top button in the wrong buttonhole.

Jury sighed and took her hands away. 'It'll hang all lopsided.' He rebuttoned the top ones.

She was tying on the scarf. 'In weather like this, what is there to do but go home and read a book?'

'Can't imagine.' Jury straightened her collar and they walked towards the door.

He closed the door of his flat and took longer than necessary to help her out of her coat, hoping it would give her a bit of time to examine the room and settle on something to say.

She settled on its neatness, which made him laugh. 'Carole-anne takes it upon herself every once in a while to play char.' He looked at the tiled hearth. 'I only have an electric bar in the fireplace, but your coat will probably dry out by the time you leave.'

'It's pretty wet.' She looked at him quite openly.

He had been about to say something suiting the occasion – *Perhaps you'll have to stay longer, then . . . How about the rest of your clothes? . . . Borrow a dressing gown of mine . . . Shall I put the kettle on . . .?* To delay the inevitable, however pleasurable; to increase the sexual tension; to put them at their ease. The variations on the theme were endless. He smiled slightly, looking at his old stereo, thinking there was always music, but thinking Kiss of Death (Carole-anne's favourite) might not be quite the ticket. She was always finding new groups – here was What the Cat Dragged In. And here was her favourite: Julio and Willie and all the girls they'd ever loved. He thought about those girls and their vulnerability and how chauvinistic that song was. Revolving doors full of women . . .

He felt Jane's hand on his arm. Her cough was light and she said, 'What are you thinking of?'

'Nothing.' He smiled.

'It was a long silence for a nothing.' Her own smile was unconvincing. She was nervous.

'Well, then, I was thinking of all the girls I ever loved before.'

Jane didn't seem to know where to look as her eyes roved the featureless (to him) room and she asked. 'Have there been that many?'

He put his hands very lightly on her shoulders. 'Practically none. It's the name of a song – my upstairs neighbour's favourite. But I'm sure the men don't send her out of their doors. She leaves them when she wants to.'

There was a silence as she seemed to be studying his shirtfront. 'It sounds awfully final, though.'

Jury smiled. 'Oh, she can always go back whenever she wants.'

'Lucky girl.'

He pulled her closer but not so close that their bodies touched. 'I can't promise an endless succession of afternoons, since this is the first one I haven't been working in God knows how long.' He smiled. 'But I might be able to do evenings.'

It happened so suddenly it amazed him, how quickly she put her arms round his neck and how tightly she held on, their bodies

9

more than touching, melting. His voice was very low when he said, 'Should I put the kettle on?'

His bed faced the window and through it, above the little park, he watched a flight of swallows rise; with the sun behind them they drifted up like burning leaves darkening, coiling. Suddenly, he rose up on both elbows, disturbing the drape of her arm. The swallows lifted, circled and then the dark *V* of them vanished. For some reason, he thought of a funeral pyre; he thought of Aeneas.

' "*Vestigia Flammae*," ' Jury said, without thinking.

She caught a laugh behind her mouth. 'Oh, dear. Not Latin. Not Latin, too, after everything.'

Her little laugh had struck the wrong note; not her fault, he told himself, but he felt absurd.

Jostled slightly from her comfortably dissolute position, she looked up at him. 'Did I say the wrong thing? What's the matter?'

In answer, he merely lay back, pulled her back again. But the note had been struck and it was false; a note that could become a false chord. When her face turned and burrowed into his neck, he felt himself mean for not speaking. 'It's what the Queen of Carthage said when she first saw Aeneas. "I recognize the vestiges of an old flame." '

He tried to shake it off, the sense of the wrong note, the feeling of foreboding. But the window was a blank square of white, the sunlight gone, and the park deserted.

PART I
OUR OLD FLAME

1

Feeling like Lambert Strether, Melrose Plant looked up over the edge of *The Ambassadors*, bought especially for the occasion, and toward the Adriatic.

Beside him, Trueblood snapped shut his own book and sighed. 'What a *yummy* novel!'

Melrose squinted his eyes nearly shut. 'That's the first time I've heard *Death in Venice* called "yummy". Wait until you get to the end, where Aschenbach is dying in his deck chair.' He looked at the colourful striped beach cabanas. No deck chairs.

'I have, old trout. Oh, I admit the plague part isn't much fun, but then comes that beautiful young man standing by the sea. All of that eloquent sunlit description.'

'Take off that tangerine scarf. It completely spoils the effect,' said Melrose. They were both dressed in white − Armani white. Thank the Lord the designer did white, since Trueblood had said he'd wear white over Melrose's dead body.

Fortunately, at the time of this whining argument, they'd been in the Calle dei Fabbri, behind San Marco. Suddenly Trueblood had stopped dead, causing a head-on collision between four old women, black-shawled, who babbled insults in Italian.

The Giorgio Armani shop. Trueblood gazed into its windows until Melrose felt like getting a prayer-rug. This holy icon had kept Trueblood buzzing round for well over an hour and Melrose saw the loose off-white silk and wool suit as Trueblood was taking out his traveller's cheques. It was the only way to get Trueblood into white.

'And roll down your cuffs. You look like you're at Wimbledon.' First, the tangerine scarf; *now* Melrose saw a jade-coloured handkerchief blossoming out of the jacket's pocket. 'And for the Lord's sake, get rid of that handkerchief. You're ruining the consumptive effect.'

'I don't see why,' said Trueblood, stuffing the jade silk down into the pocket, 'the Giappinos never become ill. Why does it always have to be *our* side of the family?'

Over the years of Vivian's engagement, these Italians, whom they had never met, had had so many stories woven around them, they had almost become Long Piddleton's second family.

'We aren't ill; we never were,' Melrose reminded him.

Trueblood insisted on sitting behind Melrose when they boarded the vaporetto.

Coming upon it across the water this way, Melrose thought that the city which floated there in the distance might actually have been — as the travel books said — the most beautiful city in the world. It was as if all the angels in heaven had fallen asleep at once and Venice were their collective dream.

'And don't forget to cough,' he called back to Trueblood as the vaporetto lurched and sprays of water hit him in the face.

'Cough? Why should I *cough*?' Trueblood yelled back over the roar of engines, slapping water, foreign tongues and dialectic babble.

The boat was jammed with Europeans (largely Eastern by the look of them) overflowing from Rome. It was surprisingly touristy for March.

'Because of the pneumonia, for God's sake! You're only just recovering!' Couldn't the man remember anything?

Marshall called back: 'That's *you*, old sweat. You're the pneumonia one. I'm the one who got hit by the lorry — '

Imprecations lost on the wind.

'Oh. Sorry.' Melrose felt abashed, but quickly forgave himself as he saw a rainbow wasting its palette of pale violets and pinks across the city that needed no further embellishment.

The trouble was, of course, that ever since Vivian Rivington had left Victoria Station that morning in January, Melrose Plant and Marshall Trueblood had been sitting around in Northamptonshire, either at the Jack and Hammer over Old Peculier; at Ardry End, family seat of the Earls of Caverness, over port; or at Trueblood's Antiques over Queen Anne and Lalique.

Hatching plots. Hatching plots to delay the wedding of Vivian Rivington to Count Dracula. Since Vivian herself had managed

14

to drag out her engagement to Franco Giappino for – how many years? three? four? – Plant and Trueblood had been sure a little help from Northants would not come amiss.

Vivian was a sentimental woman. She would not go through her wedding ceremony without her old friends from Long Piddleton gathered about her.

The alleged lorry accident to Marshall Trueblood had delayed the wedding for a good five weeks. Marshall had been in traction for four of them, and was still hobbling about on a cane. (He had grown stubborn, however, and refused to hobble in Venice.)

The complete physical examination Melrose had decided to have (after ten or more years of avoiding his doctor) turned up one shadowy lung (that was Melrose's rather poetic description of it) that the Harley Street doctor was not *awfully* worried about just so long as Lord Ardry had complete bedrest for several weeks. Which had taken care of the month of February.

No, no, no, no, Vivian! It's not necessary for you to come back to England. Honestly . . .

God help them if she had.

The third debacle that Plant and Trueblood had discussed was an accident to Lady Agatha Ardry. If necessary, she could break her jaw in one of the car accidents she was always having. And have to have it wired shut, Melrose had added.

The two of them had discarded that because it might speed up, rather than delay, the marriage.

Vivian was not a stupid woman; indeed Melrose wondered if she hadn't been suspecting something even at the beginning with the lorry accident. Trueblood, unfortunately, embroidered his tales as he did his clothes and a few unlikely threads had been woven in.

Thus, a little help from Scotland Yard (they decided) would not come amiss either.

But they weren't getting it from Richard Jury.

No, he would not make up some bloody cock-and-bull story about an axe-murderer slipping through a police cordon at Heathrow and hopping a plane to Venice . . .

'Why would I need to? You two just made it up yourselves,' Jury had yelled at them over the phone.

This had occurred three weeks before:

A conference call from Trueblood's Antiques in Long Piddleton. Marshall had every British Telecom convenience known to man and God − conference-calling, call waiting, call forwarding ('call-pretending,' Jury had offered) and the two of them had been sitting in the shop, punching buttons to New Scotland Yard.

'Don't you *care*?' Trueblood had whined to Jury. 'Don't you care if she becomes one of his brides and wanders round Venice in a white nightgown looking for victims?'

'Oh, shut up,' said Jury. 'Look, this is *Vivian's* life, not yours, although I'd never know it to hear you two talk.'

'We're trying to save her from herself; or from some idiotic-notion that just because she's been, well, going back and forth between Italy and England for all this time she's somehow obliged to marry the man.'

'Up to her, isn't it?'

Plant thought there was an uncharacteristic edge to Jury's voice.

Jury went on: 'And what about Ellen Taylor? Thought you were off to the States. New Yawk. Or Baltimore.'

'I am. As soon as Vivian's out of danger.'

' "Out of danger." God. Why don't you wake up?'

Trueblood lit a green Sobranie and stuck his feet up on one of his priceless fauteils as Melrose frowned. 'Wake up to what?'

No reply. 'Richard? Are you there?'

'Unfortunately, yes.'

'Good. Now listen. You're the only one who can stop her. For you, she'd come back.' For some reason, he hadn't liked saying that. 'Don't you remember that morning at Victoria?'

Pause down the line. 'Yes.'

'Remember how ravishing she looked? That creamy dress, that brown red hair − '

'Yes. And don't *you* remember when we all first met. Ten years ago that was. Long Piddleton. She was almost married then, too.'

'Well, good Lord, that's no compar − '

'You think she wanted to marry *him*?'

Melrose stared up at Trueblood's ceiling. Cobweb garlands held up plaster angels. 'I don't know what you're talking about.'

A long pause, long sigh from the London end. 'No, you're so blind you probably don't. Seen Polly Praed lately?'

'What the hell's she got to do with it?'

'I don't know.'

'We're talking about *you*.'

A chair creaked back in London. 'And?'

'Well, you must have been thinking *something* when the Orient Express pulled out of Victoria.'

Another long pause.

' "*Agnosco veteris vestigia flammae,*" ' said Jury before he hung up.

2

The Gritti Palace, although certainly a handsome hotel, was not as large or resplendent as Melrose had pictured it. The bar was empty but for one elderly lady whose powder was too white and cheeks too pink. She reminded Melrose of Mrs Withersby, given the way she slugged back her sambuca and tapped her glass on the table to get the bartender's attention. Between drinks she would stare out at the Grand Canal. A grey fringe of hair stuck out from under a brown hat with a moulting bird ornament on the band.

Probably a millionaire. Or a countess. Or both. Melrose thought if he and Trueblood sat there long enough for their hair to turn white and their teeth to fall out, everyone with any claim to fame would go strolling by.

Trueblood, usually fastidious to a fault, was stuffing nuts in his mouth. He did not give the impression of someone who'd just escaped from the Grim Reaper in an automobile accident.

Between mouthfuls he explored various possibilities: 'Good Lord, old sweat, we've got to decide on which story. I still favour the one about her being burgled − Vivian must have at least a million quid's worth of antiques in there.'

Melrose shook his head. 'Too big a job for us and we'd have to do it at night. People would talk. And, anyway, supposing we got her home, how would we get the stuff back?'

'I see what you mean. Well, then, what's wrong with Ruthven going mad and having to be put away? Vivian's always liked Ruthven.'

'She'd send her abject apologies, but I doubt she'd put off the wedding. It's not the same as you or I going mad. And we can't pretend anything more is the matter with us. And Ruthven couldn't do it, anyway, even if he wanted to.'

'Then what about making her think that Venice is a dangerous place to be?' Trueblood chewed another handful of nuts, his eyes

17

bright. 'Remember that business about the crazy dwarf? We might be able to convince her he or she's loose, running round stabbing people.'

Melrose shook his head. 'No, no, no, no! If a dwarf was doing that, it'd be in all the papers: "*Killer Dwarf On Loose*." Anyway, that was supposed to be Jury's idea — ' Melrose stopped. 'I've got it!'

'Here she comes!'

The Venetian Vivian stood before them looking gorgeous as she always did under the Italian influence: beautiful and awfully fashionable, her clingy, tiny-pleated dress seeming to have a mind of its own. Melrose preferred the good wool skirts and cardigans she always wore at home.

She embraced each of them, gave each a kiss, and sat down.

Said Trueblood, 'You took my advice and bought Utrillo! The lines are wonderful.'

'No, I took my own and bought a Dickens and Jones. In the sale.'

A look of loathing passed over Marshall Trueblood's face.

'Both of you are pale. Marshall has hardly any colour at all.' She frowned.

'We're much better, really,' said Melrose.

'Much.'

'You both also look guilty.' Vivian leaned across the table, eyes narrowed.

'Let's get you a drink, Viv-viv.' He caught the waiter before he attended to the elderly lady.

'If you've come all this way to see me, I'm certainly flattered. The wedding was put back another two weeks. A gin and orange, please,' she said to the hovering water.

'Well, if you *must* know,' said Melrose, 'there's something about Richard Jury.' Pause. 'He's getting married.'

Trueblood stuffed a few more nuts in his mouth as he nodded and nodded his head.

'*Richard*?' Vivian's eyes opened wide. She had a stricken look on her face as if the killer dwarf had just got her in the back. She opened her mouth and shut it at least three times before she could bring herself to utter a strangled 'to whom?'

'Her name is . . . I can't remember. Can you?'

18

Trueblood feined an effort at remembrance and shrugged. 'You don't know her.'

'Well, have you *met* her, then?'

'Oh, yes,' said Melrose. He turned to Trueblood.

'Good-looking, wouldn't you say?' Trueblood took another handful of nuts.

Vivian looked at the drink the waiter had set before her as if it were hemlock. 'He might have told me,' she said in a woebegone tone.

Melrose essayed the sadness and said, 'He wants you to be there.'

She looked up in surprise. 'When's this wedding to be?'

'A week.'

'Two weeks.'

Melrose and Trueblood answered together. Trueblood quickly corrected himself. 'That's it. In two weeks time.'

'But that's when Franco and *I* are —'

'Well, Franco wouldn't mind waiting just a bit longer. He's been so patient all these years. Must be a very understanding chap.' Melrose smiled brilliantly.

Vivian looked morose. 'What does this wonderwoman look like?'

'Auburn hair, hazel eyes and heart-shaped face.' He had just described Vivian, for God's sake.

'How did he meet her?'

Melrose thought. 'At one of my parties.'

'You never give parties.' Her glance was scorching. *Traitor*, said Vivian's eyes. 'What does she do, anyway?'

As Vivian seemed to be oozing farther down in her chair. Marshall Trueblood said, 'She's a writer.'

'A *writer!*'

'Um-hmm. Writes sort of biographical fiction, as I remember.'

Melrose looked doubtfully at Marshall Trueblood. He might be putting too fine a point on things. After all, one might easily make a mistake on the colour of a person's hair. But one could hardly manufacture a book.

Vivian looked more and more flattened by this news. She picked up her gin and drank half the glass at once before she banged it back on the table, bouncing the nuts. 'I expect she's famous?'

Just as Trueblood opened his mouth to embellish, Melrose said, 'No, no, absolutely not. You'd never have heard of her. As a

19

matter of fact, I'm not sure she's a writer anymore, is she?' He kicked Trueblood under the table.

'Definitely not.' Trueblood sniggered. 'Just one of those nine-day-wonder sorts of things. Think she might actually be on the dole.'

'She sounds,' said Vivian, 'just the ticket. Attractive, brainy and bookish. And in need of help. The perfect woman for Richard Jury.' Her tone hovered between sarcasm and despair.

Trueblood was now taking his own line. 'She likes Rimbaud. Or is it Verlaine?'

Melrose gave him a black look as Vivian sat up straight in her chair. 'Perfect. When she isn't sitting home darning socks she can visit you and talk about the French Romantics. Get another drink!'

Trueblood limped off to the bar.

'See, he's still favouring that right leg.' But Vivian didn't seem to care if it had been amputated at the knee.

She said nothing until Trueblood put her drink before her and (having had time to embellish the tale) said, 'To tell the truth, Vivian, about this woman's being "just the ticket" as you put it, well, we're not all that sure.'

'So what?' Vivian snapped. 'You're not marrying her.'

'The point is, we've been gently suggesting to him that she really isn't the right one for him.' Trueblood did not meet Melrose's eyes.

'You've just finished *describing* the right one.'

Marshall Trueblood extracted a pink Sobranie from his cigarette case, lit it and sat back. Melrose was stepping on his foot. 'This won't go any further, will it Viv? Both of us would be in the soup.' He put his hand on Melrose's arm.

What the hell was he doing? Vivian wasn't *that* naïve. On the other hand, when it came to Richard Jury, she'd probably believe stars had fallen in a fountain. At least, Trueblood had exacted a promise not to tell . . . tell what? Melrose was as curious as Vivian, now.

'The kiddies . . . ' Both Vivian and Melrose were hanging on Trueblood's every word.

'To marry a woman with three − or is it four? − children, two still at nursery school − doesn't seem realistic. And the teenage son . . . ' Trueblood studied the nut bowl. 'Did a newsagent's nearly landed in the nick.'

Vivian flushed and then went white. 'Is he crazy? He spends his life chasing crime. Does he have to marry it?'

'We've tried to persuade him, but . . . ' A sad little shrug said Trueblood too was at a loss.

Melrose gave his shin a kick. Good Lord, after all the stories they'd made up about the Giappino family, how could she be credulous enough to believe *this* twaddle?

Apparently she was. 'It's that saviour complex of his. For a detective he certainly gets messed up in other people's troubles!'

'The point is, we were hoping you might be able to dissuade him. You know how fond he is of you.'

'No, I don't.' She made wet rings with her glass on the table.

An uncomfortable, confused silence descended on the group, with Vivian doing what she could to keep busy — opening her bag, snapping it shut, taking another drink, going for what nuts were left in the dish. Then she said, her voice tight, 'All I can say is he must be besotted with her if he'd take on three or four children. All he needs is a teenager selling crack.'

Melrose and Trueblood laughed. 'The whole situation is beyond us. I can't think of anything worse than our superintendent's back bent under the weight — '

Melrose kicked him again.

'So he wasn't intending to come to my wedding?' The skin puckered between her eyes and she pulled at a thread from her Dickens and Jones dress. Melrose watched the hem of the sleeve unravel.

Trueblood said, 'Oh, I'm sure he was. With the family, of course.'

Melrose hid his eyes with his hand. The original pitch had merely been to get her back to Northants. Now Trueblood seemed to be breaking up a union between Jury and his intended — Oh, Lord, he was beginning to believe it himself!

Vivian didn't know where to look — at them? at the sleeve? at the ceiling? 'I've got to go. Franco's waiting for me.'

'It's been wonderful seeing you. You look radiant. Franco must be very good to you.' Trueblood smiled.

That would really throw her off guard, thought Melrose. Not once had they referred to coffins, Transylvania, sharpened stakes or mirrors.

'Oh. Yes, yes he is.' She looked puzzled by this new twist on the count. She rose.

'We're at the hotel on the Lido if you should change your mind,' said Melrose, looking downcast.

' "Change" it? I haven't even made it up yet.'

'All the better.' He held Vivian's hand in both of his. Watching them go would probably be more than she could bear.

They all left the Gritti Palace together. She looked pale and terribly confused. 'When are you going back?'

'In a few days. Not sure, really.'

'It was nice of you to come. And tell me what happens. You know.'

As they walked off in different directions, Trueblood said, 'That was quite brilliant.'

Said Melrose, sourly, 'The only problem is that he's *not* getting married.'

'Oh, that. By the time Vivian arrives, Jury, the woman, the tots and the druggie will all have broken it off.'

2

The boy in the tree had his high-powered Zeiss binoculars trained on a scene unfolding less than an eighth of a mile away from the Severn School grounds.

On another strap slung over his shoulder was a portable telephone.

The boy had climbed this tree in the school grounds many times, sailing above the high stone wall. He might have exulted in the feeling of elation that comes from such a perspective. He might have been moved to write a poem about what he saw.

He might have; but he wasn't. The boy in the tree was interested only in the perspective the tree allowed him of the racecourse out there and of the 'chasers pounding round it at this very moment. The second Rogue's Gallery hit the finish line at three-to-five odds, he spoke into the telephone.

'Number ten, Dusty Answer, thirty-to-one.'

'Got it, lad,' said his elderly companion, sitting in a bunged-up Land Rover outside the gates of Severn School. He hit four digits on his car phone and repeated the name of the horse, the number of the race, and the modest bet of twenty nicker to the person at the other end.

The turf accountant sighed. 'Have to time you, guv'nor, you know that.'

'Right,' said the man in the car, who then redialled to the boy in the tree. 'He's timing it. But I think we're wearing him down.'

The boy in the tree was sure of it. Over the last two months, their bets on long shots ranged anywhere from two to two hundred quid. They never won. That was the point.

The boy thought, *felt* with the confidence if not the prescience of teenage boys that today they'd hit it.

'Favourite, next race?' the boy asked the man in the car.

He sat behind the wheel with the racing form. The boy had one

23

too, but he was too taken up with the binoculars to give it a thorough study.

'Splendid Spring, looks like. Odds three-to-four . . . um, um, um. Several longshots, which one do you like? Shall we take one that'll make me look a little less like a total fool?'

'Yes. A little less.'

'Right. How about a ten-to-one named Cannibal Isle?'

The boy had raised the binoculars again, and was watching the horses get into post potion. 'Where do they get these names? Okay.'

'Will he ever fall for it, d'ya think, lad? We been at it now for weeks.'

'Greed. He thinks you're a fool that doesn't know horses; he's sick of hearing from you − hold on.'

The boy wished only he could hear it as well as see it. He had to use his imagination to hear the drumming of the hooves, the whish over hedges, the pulsing of the crowd, the wails, the screams − the victory. There! Not Splendid Spring but the third favourite, Gal O'Mine won. 'Gal O'Mine,' he said into his hand-held phone.

Again, his companion in the car hit the same digits, got the accountant. 'Cannibal Isle in the fifth. Fifty quid.'

'Jesus . . . isn't that like a twenty-to-one? . . . ' A huge sigh. No skin off the turf accountant's nose. 'I'll have to time it again.'

'All right by me.' To the boy in the tree he said, 'Skip the sixth. Give him time.'

'Uh-huh.'

They waited.

The bookmaker called, said to the man in the car. 'No. Both races already started.' The phone slammed down. *Don't waste my time.*

The man in the car called the boy in the tree. 'Surprise. We past-post again. Listen: in the eighth there's a horse I like. Really like. Give it a go? Nothing to lose.'

The boy thought about it. 'Is it favoured?'

'With me it is.' He checked the form. 'Second favourite, no, third. Odds are good − three-to-one. It's your horse, lad. Fortune's Son.' He laughed.

'I like it.' The boy smiled through the tracery of narrow limbs already coming into leaf. March had been warm. He picked off a leaf, looked at it, shoved it in his pocket. 'All right. Let's do five hundred. No, a little more. Seven. To win. That's real money.'

'If he takes it.'

'And if you're right.' The boy laughed. He took out a cigarette, lit a match, and sat there on the cool branch-bench, letting the next race go by. Then he snapped up his binoculars, watched the horses readying at the post for the eighth. He slewed the Zeiss along the line to number eight. She was on the outside. Still. Eighth horse in the eighth race. And he loved the silks, gold and blue. Fortune's Son.

They broke away and for a minute and a quarter the boy held his breath as he watched them leap hedges and ditches as if he'd actually put seven hundred quid on the line.

Fortune's Son came in first. 'Call,'' the boy yelled into his phone.

His friend in the car hit the digits.

The boy in the tree waited, binoculars still on the jockey's silks, the smashing bay horse looking as if he knew he'd won. He bet they did, the horses. He bet they knew.

The phone cracked. He held it to his ear.

A chuckle. 'Laddie, the damned fool fell for it. Couldn't resist that seven hundred. That's more than two thousand quid!' He let out a gleeful yell.

'Go and collect. And meet me here tomorrow. Say, during games. Three o'clock. And don't scarper.' The boy laughed.

'Not a chance, lad, not a chance.'

He shoved the phone in the belt at his back where his school jacket would cover it with hardly a bulge. The binoculars he didn't have to worry about. He was also studying bird migration.

He came down the tree most of the way before he dropped with a thud. Looking up as he brushed off his trousers, he saw his science master.

'Sir,' he said calmly and confidently.

'Hullo!'

The boy held up the new green leaf. 'If you look close, you'll see the striations are different.'

The master squinted. 'I don't really. But apparently you do. Interesting theory.'

'Thank you, sir. I'm finished now. I need to write up my findings.'

'I'll be interested to read them.'

25

'Sir.' He watched the science master walk off, hands clasped behind his back, musing. Nice man. Bit dim, but nice.

He looked at the leaf, tossed it aside.

One leaf looked just like another to him.

2

The boy sat at a round table in one of the rear rooms at the Rose and Crown. There were six of them playing straight poker. Ned Rice was one.

The other four were taking it as a lark that this lad apparently thought himself a first-rate player. He wasn't bad; he wasn't good. During the eighth months he'd been playing regularly (except for school holidays) he'd won maybe a dozen pots, all small.

He was brash; he liked to brag about the visits he's made to the States, always to Las Vegas (which he called 'Vegas'), where he had a rich uncle who was a 'high roller' in some club there called the Mirage.

And he played with U.S. dollars, never sterling.

Now, that had made them really wonder.

Allan Blythe, a National Health doctor who took private patients on the side and shoved the money in a drawer, had asked him why the bloody hell he didn't take the currency to the bank and exchange it for pounds sterling.

'Because the local banks here don't do currency. I'm supposed to go up to London just to exchange money? Don't make me laugh. I'm giving you a better rate of exchange than a bank, anyway.'

The first time he'd come round with his dollars and Ned Rice, the other four nearly laughed themselves sick. Frankie Fletcher knew a small-time counterfeiter and wouldn't let the kid play until he'd checked out a sampling of the bills. Frankie took the bills in his own winnings once or twice every month to his mate. They always checked out; they were real.

By now, the others were used to him. They got a kick out of having a public school boy at the table who'd come into town with the others once a week to go to the cinema. Only, this kid never saw the film. Since he wasn't a serious contender, since he didn't cheat (they'd watched him very closely) they began to treat him as a kind of mascot, this swaggering kid with his rich uncle in Vegas and his flashy Americanisms.

One thing they noticed: he always folded if the pot was small, saying he didn't play for 'chicken feed'. Frankie Fletcher snorted at that one. 'More like you didn't learn nothin' from that uncle.'

'He could wipe the floor with you,' said the boy, heatedly.

'Now, now, no offence, kid.' Frankie leaned over as the boy changed a twenty-dollar bill, drew out two five-pound notes and some American dollars. Then he raised Frankie a fiver.

Allan Blythe (the biggest skinflint at the table) kept track of the dollar-to-pound ratio, making sure the boy was giving them his promised better-than-bank rate. Allan Blythe even checked the currency fluctuations to make sure they were getting their five per cent higher.

Frankie won that hand with only a pair of tens. 'What the hell're you bettin' on, kid?' he laughed.

For another hour they played − no high rollers here, Ned Rice laughed − and he changed more money, at the same time calling. He put in a twenty, drew out some sterling and some American.

He lost again.

At ten o'clock the film was always over. The boy stood up, shoved his money in his pocket, either a meagre win or a meagre loss, and left, after smiling at Ned Rice.

This particular night was the night after the big win on Fortune's Son. It was fine with him that he was walking out of the side door of the Rose and Crown tonight with forty quid more than he'd walked in with, even though he hadn't won a pot. To that uncle in Vegas, sixty, sixty-five dollars would have been no more than cigar money. But he didn't have an uncle in Vegas. The boy grinned. Forty quid was nothing to sneeze at.

He turned up his blazer collar and went whistling down the alley between the pub and the cinema. Very convenient that was.

With his hand shoved in his pockets, he was practising his soccer, kicking a heavy wad of paper along the cobbles and onto the pavement by the cinema.

He kicked it onto someone's shoe.

27

The boy looked up into the thick, trifocaled glasses of his maths master staring down at him with eyes hard as rocks and arms folded. 'So.'

'Oh bloody hell,' the boy muttered.

3

When Jury walked into his office and said good morning, Wiggins was concentrating on the row of medications lined up on his dispensary desk. He responded with a bemused nod, his mind busy either trying to decide on what to take, or what ailment he was taking it for.

To Jury he said. 'You seem almost *hearty*, sir. You've been that way for two weeks.' His tone was accusing. 'Heartiness' was not on the superintendent's rota. Then he made a display of looking at his watch. 'It's only half-seven. You're not a morning person, sir.'

'I'm not?' Jury immediately started tidying up his desk, testimony to the refurbishing of his temperament. 'Am I usually in a bad mood, Wiggins?'

Wiggins thought this over. 'Not "bad" exactly. Melancholy, sometimes.' The sergeant pulled out his bottom drawer, the one that housed his collection of old herbal remedies for everything from bursitis to ooils to broken hearts. 'What I think is, you've not been getting enough sleep.'

'That,' said Jury, with a deadpan look at his sergeant, 'is the most accurate diagnosis you've ever made.' He had had, indeed, practically none for some days, at the same time he felt as rested as Rip Van Winkle.

When he went to Lewisham, which he had done every night for nearly two weeks, and Jane opened the door, they would embrace so quickly he'd kick the door shut with his foot. It made them laugh, realizing they couldn't keep their hands off each other. They were like survivors of a shipwreck who, once saved, could look back over the cold sea of their lives and wonder how they had managed to make it to the shore.

And when he wasn't with her, he still felt a contentment that made him invulnerable. It was as if she'd dressed him in invisible armour.

29

He knew from past experience he should not plunge headlong into a love affair. He should stand back, take the longer view, judge whether the land was truly safe, meet her, at least for a while, on other terms. But he could think of no other terms; he couldn't imagine their carefully stepping round one another, assessing the risks.

On his second visit to the Lewisham house, most of this had been going through his mind. They separated only when she said that dinner was burning. It was, but they were so reluctant to let go, the chicken turned black, the salad limp, the white wine warm.

When they finally broke the embrace, it wasn't to sit down to dinner, anyway.

'Do you know,' Jury had said, lying in bed, 'I've been coming here every night for nearly two weeks and I couldn't tell you what your living room looks like. I have vague notions about the kitchen, since we've eaten there, or at least I *think* we must have eaten something in the last two weeks, but if you put a gun to my head, I couldn't give a clear description of anything but the bedroom. What a rotten detective I make.'

She laughed and reached across his chest for three little vials of medicine. There was a carafe of water on the end table on her side. 'You know the only way to cure this myopic vision is take the time for a house tour.'

'What a waste of time. What are those pills for?'

She held them up each in turn and said, 'This one is for dropsy; this one is for the vapours; this one for bubonic plague.'

Jury made a grab for her hand.

Two nights ago he'd said, 'Let's be practical: I could move in. Or you could move to Islington.'

'Somehow, I *don't* think Miss Centrefold would appreciate that.'

It irritated him, these slighting references to Carole-anne. 'Her name's Carole-anne, not "Miss Centrefold!" '

'Sorry.' She'd turned away.

Jury turned her back. 'It's just that she's a good friend and has had a fairly rotten life.' Jury didn't actually know this to be true; he had to infer which of Carole-anne's stories were contrivances, which not. 'And if it hadn't been for her, we'd never have met.'

30

Jane smiled. 'How very true. Speaking of meeting – you have to meet my son.'

'Good Lord!' Jury pulled a pillow over his head. 'I'm going to have to pass the scrutiny of a teenager!'

'He's not your standard teenager.' She laughed.

As Jury chucked a pile of papers into the waste paper bin, Wiggins said, 'You ought to be careful; you never know but there might be something the guv'nor's routed to you.'

Jury squeezed his eyes shut. 'Wiggins, if I hear you call Racer that one more time, I'll take away your inhaler. There! All shipshape and so forth.'

Wiggins gave Jury's desk a baleful glance. 'You won't know where anything is, now, sir.' He pinched something out of a small tin and put it up his nose.

'I didn't know where anything was before.' Jury looked at Wiggins and looked again. 'What are you doing with tobacco up your nose?'

'It's not tobacco, it's rue.'

'Rue. Well, that explains it.'

'It's very good for bronchitis; Mrs Wassermann told me to try it. She's quite an expert about herbal medicines –'

'Mrs Wassermann? If you say so.' The only thing Mrs Wassermann ever prescribed for Jury was a hot broth that tasted vile. Perhaps it was full of rue.

When the phone rang, Wiggins came to attention and grabbed the receiver. 'Wiggins, here.' He relaxed. 'Oh, it's you . . . what? . . . but he's got to be around somewhere.'

Even from this distance, Jury could hear the wire throb with hysterics. 'What's wrong?' he mouthed to Wiggins.

'Yes, yes, yes! We'll be there in a tic.' He hung up. 'Fiona can't find Cyril.'

Jury was out of his chair. 'Let's go. But I'm not walking through the halls of the Yard with somebody who's got rue up his nose.'

Fiona, a towel pinned to hold back her hair, was tossing things about, looking in the waste paper bin, opening drawers. 'He's gone, I should known what was happening.'

Wiggins handed her the holy icon – his handkerchief – with which she wiped away the tears.

'He's probably just sleeping somewhere.'

Fiona wiped the back of her hand across her cheek and sniffled. 'He could be now he's had his tuna. He gets awful sluggish . . .' More tears fell.

'You know the way he likes to make himself invisible. Remember when he managed to get on the window-washer's scaffold that time? And all of those daredevil stunts like squeezing himself out on the ledge and smashing his face against the window with Racer looking every damn place he thought Cyril could be – '

All of this remembering only brought a fresh onslaught of tears from Fiona.

Jury himself felt his throat tighten, whereupon he turned and went into Racer's office to check up: he looked into the umbrella stand – an urn that Cyril was fond of as long as the umbrellas weren't wet; he bent over and opened the drinks cabinet; and he pulled out Racer's desk chair. Cyril was a master of hiding in plain sight.

Fiona was calling to him impatiently: 'Don't you think I've already looked in there?' Back in the outer office Fiona was snuffling and talking to Wiggins. ' . . . when he brought in that box, something was wrong. But he's always carrying things around. So somehow, he got Cyril into it!'

'Okay: assuming he took Cyril, where would he take him?' He was really talking to himself, but Fiona wailed an answer.

'Dropped him in Blackheath and the poor cat don't know where he is!'

Wiggins tried to soothe Fiona by bringing up a film he'd seen years ago: '*Incredible Journey* – that was about a cat and two dogs that somehow got lost when the family was moving and travelled *a hundred miles*, Fiona, and found their family.'

'But they *all* wanted those ones back.' She blew into the handkerchief.

Again Jury said, 'Where would Racer have taken a cat?' He was scanning the yellow pages. He found what he wanted in the telephone book, tore the page out and then in three pieces across, gave one to Wiggins, and one to Fiona. 'Let's start calling.'

'RSPCA? Animal shelters, sir?' He frowned. 'Superintendent Racer doesn't strike me as the man who would see to it an animal was taken care of. He's much more the shove-'em-in-a-sack, toss-

'em-in-the-Thames — ' Wiggins stopped midsentence when Fiona wailed again.

'Stop talking and start calling. I'll use Racer's phone.'

They were all talking at the same time and saying almost the very same things.

' . . .copper coat and he's very agile.'

' . . .kind of orangey. With white paws. Brought in probably this morning. . . .'

' . . .beautiful cat, intelligent . . . probably last night? No? All right, then, thanks.' Wiggins rang off.

'Stubborn? Hunger strike? Got the door of his cage open?' Jury was getting out of the chair while saying. 'That's him. My name's Richard Jury. That's J-U-R-Y. We'll be right over to collect him.'

Jury went to Fiona's office and smiled brilliantly. 'Got him, Fiona.' She banged down the receiver. Her smile was sunny. 'Get us a car; this shouldn't take long.' As he was going out of the door, he added, 'And send that tuna to forensics.'

One of the ladies minding the desk showed Jury and Wiggins to the rooms in which the cats were kept in numbered cages. Cyril was in cage eleven.

'Well. I'm ever so glad you've come to collect him. He sits that way all the time, hasn't touched his food and sometimes I think he hasn't slept a wink.' She moved to a cage on the end with mother tabby cat and one kitten. She shook and shook her head, sticking her fingers through the wire. 'These ones'll be put down tomorrow. When people bring in mother cats and kittens it's all I can do to hold my tongue. See, they've got less chance of being adopted because all people want is kittens.' She was trying to stroke the cat through the metal webbing. 'It makes me sick, it does.' When she turned back to Jury and Wiggins, she made quite a fuss over both the cat and his rescuers. Cyril watched them. 'You can tell he was feeling hopeless. But he's been putting up a good front.'

It was not a 'front'. Cyril's pose and slow-blinking eyes suggested that what the Fates had in store for him had better be reevaluated. And what the emphatic young woman had taken for stoic suffering Jury knew was simple disdain. Cyril was an adaptable animal, obviously, if he could put up with Racer. Even here he did not

33

appear unduly upset by his new, restrictive environment, for he knew rescue was at hand. He sat in that statuesque pose as cats do, paws neatly together, tail wrapped around him like robes of state. He yawned. It was only to be expected.

Deliverance.

4

They had returned Vivian-less.

Well, thought Melrose, so had Lambert Strether returned Chadless. Except that Strether had seen through a miasma of social pretension and moral decay. Melrose could not lay claim to any Jamesian refinement of sensibility. He found that, somehow, irksome. He'd told Ruthven to stuff that white Armani suit somewhere where he'd never see it again.

Still, it was heartening that Vivian would reschedule (yet again) her own wedding in order to come to London and talk Jury out of his. Trueblood had put on a first-rate performance, at one moment beating back real tears. The henna-haired woman was bad enough, given her seedy past. But the four children — well, that was not to be borne.

They had been back from Italy for two whole days before Agatha got wind of it, but here she was this afternoon jamming a scone while Melrose was trying to read his book and listen to his music.

The new sound system was wonderful, including a Meridian 208 CD player and Spica loudspeakers. He had listened all yesterday to Lou Reed ricocheting from windows to walls and back again while Lou really hammered on New York City:

Get 'em out
On the Dirty Boulevard

Occasionally, Melrose sang along with him, punching his fists in the air for emphasis, and startling Mindy awake.

Today, it was the Doors. Jim Morrison was a Rimbaud fan. Now, *that* was strange. Morrison's grave was in Paris and his death a mystery.

'Are you listening to that maniac again?'

'No. This is a different maniac.' Ah, it was to be yet another viva voce afternoon with Agatha.

35

'They all sound the same to me.' She was topping the jam with double cream.

He didn't answer. He was thinking again of *The Ambassadors*; Lambert Strether hadn't told Chad Newsome that he, Strether, had been hit by a lorry or that the young man's best friend had terminal pneumonia.

And Melrose and Marshall hadn't rung Richard Jury because they hadn't yet made up the story they were going to tell him. Melrose only hoped that Vivian wouldn't make a rash long distance call before they managed to disengage Jury from the woman and her intractable tots.

'I cannot *stand* all this racket!' Agatha was giving the silver tea service a rest by putting her hands over her ears.

Melrose reached over and turned the volume down. The speakers were adjusted so that music would explode in Agatha's face.

He returned to his book on Palladian architecture. Since his Venetian journey he had dipped into Ruskin, Henry James and several other writers on the subject of the buildings of that glorious city. Now, he was sharpening his knowledge with books on architecture in general. 'This is interesting.'

'What is?'

'Palladio thought that on every estate there should be an old ruin.' He stared over his glasses at Agatha.

'You look quite pale,' she said, by way of answer. 'I warned you about taking that trip so soon after that nasty bout of pneumonia.'

. . . the illness that never was. But Ruthven had done a masterly job of convincing his aunt of its existence during the two weeks when Melrose was supposedly 'laid up' before he'd gone to Italy.

How Melrose longed for those Agatha-less days: for two whole weeks he and Mindy had sat in front of the fireplace dozing, drinking port, eating. Melrose had directed Mindy's bowl be brought out so she wouldn't have the bother of taking the long walk to the kitchen. Both of them were besotted with the quiet, the fire, the drinks, the food. Ruthven was delighted to act as general factotum. He made it clear to Lady Ardry that His Lordship was to have no visitors.

'*Not even family? That's absurd!*'

'*Nonetheless, those are the doctor's orders,*' Ruthven had said with his foot in the door.

'What doctor? The one from Sidbury?'

'No, madam.' Ruthven paused. *'From London. A specialist.'*

Melrose didn't bother commenting; he continued reading his book.

'And with Marshall Trueblood, of all people, the silliest person in the village. He's a bad influence on you, my dear Plant.' She paused to defrock a fairy cake. 'He's making *you* silly. You with your aristocratic background —'

He sighed. 'Kindly *stop* introducing me as the eighth Earl of Caverness, fifth Viscount Ardry, et cetera.'

He raised his book so he wouldn't see her.

'You're just going through an identity crisis.'

That was a new one, he thought.

' — so you'd better take life more seriously.' She sipped her third cup of tea.

Hell's bells. He would have to take action just to shut her up. He rose, went across to his desk, took out his keys and used a very small one to open the middle drawer. Inside was a document. Melrose drew it out and returned to his chair, beginning to read the page intently. Occasionally, he would stop and purse his lips. It was a long and addlebrained bunch of nonsense drawn up by Melrose's ninety-year old neighbour (acres away) about the branches of His Lordship's beech trees straggling over the neighbour's stone wall.

'What are you reading?'

'My will.'

That stopped her hand on its way to the cake plate. 'What are you doing that for? Is something wrong? Was that bout of pneumonia more serious than we thought?'

Did she sound the least bit hopeful? 'You told me to take life more seriously; I assume that means death, too.'

'Really, Plant, you are a ghoul.'

Melrose frowned at the page. 'Humph!'

'What?'

'I don't think Ledbetter is right about that . . . ' He seemed to be speaking to himself.

'About what? Simon Ledbetter? The Ledbetters have been our family's solicitors for fifty years.'

Melrose loved that *our*. 'Precisely.'

'If I know you, Melrose, you're probably leaving something to Ada Crisp's rat terrier.'

'No. But I am to Ada.'

'Really, Melrose.' This was accompanied by an artificial little laugh. 'And that Withersby person, too, I expect. What are you writing there?' A hint of hysteria crept into her question.

'Rectifying Simon Ledbetter's error regarding the bulk of my estate.' He was drawing a cow on the paper.

She opened her mouth, but before she could gear up again, Ruthven swanned into the room with his whisky and soda tray and set it within easy reach of the wing chair.

'Thank you. Perhaps you could get Simon Ledbetter on the phone for me. Ring him tomorrow. Early.'

'Yes, My Lord.'

Melrose sipped his drink, said *ummmm* and went back to the cow's hooves. He studied the cow and started to draw in a nice shady tree.

'Why are you — and Simon Ledbetter — writing up codicils?' A sort of breathlessness accompanied this question as if she might strangle over the answer.

Melrose had drooped the branch over a stone wall. Before he could answer, Ruthven came back into the living room to tell him the superintendent was on the line.

'Jury?' Oh, my God! Here he'd been drawing a cow when he should have been thinking up a story.

Melrose's tone, naturally, was injured. 'I've been trying for two days to get hold of you. I had two or three interesting conversations with Miss Palutski, who wondered when I was coming to visit, told me about her job and asked me what sign I was born under. The Jack and Hammer, I told her, I *thought* you'd be eager to hear about Vivian.' He chewed his lip and hoped Jury wasn't.

'Of course I am. I've just been hard to reach. Is her wedding date stable yet? And did you see the count?'

'The Fanged One? No, but we did have a nice, long talk with Vivian —'

Jury broke in, 'Listen. There's a rumour going round I'm more or less engaged.'

Melrose was silent.

Trueblood had grassed.

Still, Jury seemed to be taking the little trick amazingly well, for he sounded quite cheerful. Said Melrose, 'I can explain about that. The children were, I admit, an exaggeration – '

'What children? There's only one.'

Melrose didn't know what to say. He scratched his ear. Ah, of course, Jury was being sarcastic.

'Well! That's marvellous! What's "more-or-less"?' Melrose grinned at the receiver.

'Oh, I don't know. Perhaps you and Trueblood can argue over it.'

Melrose sniggered. 'Be glad to help out. And what is your intended like?'

'Pretty, bright, wonderful sense of humour, about all any man would want. Though she's a bit changeable in her moods.'

Where had he got *this* description? Trueblood had forgotten the original story. 'She, ah, sounds quite wonderful.'

'She is. I can't say I'm not anxious – to the point of blind panic – about meeting her son. He's sixteen and he's been the man around the house for some years. He'll hate me.'

'Impossible.' Melrose frowned. He couldn't make all of this "going along with a joke" out. He said, 'Could you hang on just a second?' He put the receiver against his chest and stared in the direction of the sunburst of medieval swords on the wall without really seeing them. He shook his head back and forth like a bird dog with water in its ears. No, no, no. 'Ah, where did you meet her?'

'Islington. Camden Passage, to be exact.'

Would Jury stop sounding so damnably *cheery?* It didn't suit him.

'You'll like her. And her son. He's sixteen. Or did I already say that?'

Good Lord, when had Melrose *ever* liked anyone of sixteen? But that was hardly the point: this was no joke. Jury wasn't kidding. Melrose looked again at the swords and thought of falling on one. By some damnable coincidence, Jury really *had* met a woman. Well, the world was full of them, wasn't it? And most of them, from what Melrose had seen, were after Richard Jury.

How many more wedding bells would be breaking up that old gang of his? Next thing, Marshall Trueblood would marry that Karla person.

And Jury would bring his lady to Long Pidd and now they'd

have a perfect stranger hanging about the Jack and Hammer . . .
This *couldn't* be true! It was *too* much of a coincidence. Melrose
laughed. 'You're not serious.'

'Look, I know this is sudden – '

'Well, don't propose to *me*. Trueblood might have you, but I'm
– involved.' That should fix him.

'What's the matter with you?' Jury laughed.

'Nothing. Trueblood's obviously been on about what we said
to Vivian and so forth and now you're, as they say, taking the piss.'

There was a pause. 'I don't know what the hell you're talking
about. What did you say to Vivian?'

Melrose dropped the receiver in the cradle without realizing it
would crash in Jury's ear.

'He's serious,' he said to the swords.

5

Jury stared at the receiver, assumed either the connection or his friend's mind had broken and smiled. Plant's reactions had been a little strange, but then it was strange and sudden news . . .

Strange in a way to Jury himself, an announcement of an engagement that hadn't been settled, a proposal that hadn't even been made. And wondering if Jane would even *want* to marry him. Yet, given their relationship, she would at least take it seriously, he thought.

But the doubt plagued him, perversely making him decide he would go out now and buy a ring — not anything too frighteningly formal, just a ring. That she might refuse only made him more determined.

She needed him. After what she'd been through with her husband's suicide and was still going through with his family in Cumbria, she needed — well, if not a husband, certainly an ally, someone besides her son. He seemed to be her one source of moral support.

Whenever she talked about him, her mood, beginning blithely and happily, would shift to one either highly excitable or deeply morbid at the thought of the Holdsworths getting control of him, an idea that Jury told her was absurd. It would often provoke an argument, such as the one they'd had the night before.

He shouldn't have become so impatient, he knew. But her response to his own, as he thought, perfectly reasonable point that there could be no possible legal point that would permit the grandparents to take the boy from her, was to slam her hairbrush down on the dressing table, shivering the contents on top, every article of which he knew by heart. The little silver framed picture of her son jumped with the blow, as if he too were surprised at the fury.

'You don't *know* them, do you? Just because you're a

41

policeman, do you think you can predict *every*one's behaviour?'

Jury ignored that.

He had risen from the bed where he'd been sitting and come over to put his hands on her shoulders and look at her in the mirror. Everything about her presence seemed charged — her breathing, her eyes, the electricity that lifted a fine veil of hair. 'Janey, you're not thinking straight.'

'Thank you for *that!*'

Jury retrieved the silver-backed brush and went to brush her hair, thinking it might calm her, but she pushed his hand away. In a smaller voice and looking down at the table top, she said, 'A remittance woman, that's what Genevieve called me, oh, with a smile, naturally.'

'What on earth is that supposed to mean?'

Now she was brushing her own hair, furiously. 'That what I live on came from my family, and it's not much. That we live in Lewisham. That I don't have a job. That I've lost *four* in as many years, even if two were unfairly lost . . . Well, it's true, I have no head for business or money. That the next move will be into a council flat —'

'How about mine?' Jury reached down and kissed her cheek.

Then she started weeping soundlessly, tears running slowly down and splashing, one by one, on the glass-topped table as she raised her hand to cover his. 'Oh, Lord, I'm sorry. Why do I have to take it out on you?' And then she turned swiftly and grabbed him round the waist and clung.

'Take it out on me anytime, love. Anytime. And what on earth's wrong with this house? Two up, two down, perfectly respectable.'

He could feel her breath warm through his shirt as she said, 'How the hell would you know?' She laughed. 'You told me you couldn't picture anything but the bedroom.' She looked up at him and smiled, then leaned her head against him again. 'The thing is, it's the fourth move in five years. It makes me look unstable — that and the joblessness, and the way they say I bring him up. He's been expelled from school — the one I borrowed from a friend to pay for, but don't tell him — three times.'

'Sounds like you make a great pair. What did he do? Cheat in a test? Tell off the headmaster?'

'Him? He doesn't get angry. Or doesn't let it show. He's more stable than even you.'

'Impossible.'

'Probably cleverer too.'

'More impossible.'

She picked up the picture. 'Handsomer.'

'Now you're *really* being absurd.' Jury lifted her from the dressing-table stool. 'I'm afraid to meet this paragon.'

'Oh, he's not. I don't think he always tells me the truth, you know, about his activities. But one time the accompanying missive from the headmaster claimed he'd been caught with a deck of cards.' She was unbuttoning Jury's shirt.

'Keep going.'

Jury took the brush from her. He was relieved she was on lighter, airier ground, talking of her son.

'He paid for a lot of it, you know – the tuition – odd jobs, he claims. They must have paid well.'

Jury smiled. 'He doesn't sound like a kid in need of a change of venue.'

2

Left to himself, Jury would never have gone inside the little shop. It looked more like a costumer's than a jeweller's. Still, it had been recommended by a friend on the force whose wife collected antique jewellery.

Not much light was coming through the front windows, given the presence of soot and the absence of sun; the street was cobbled and narrow. The shop windows were stuffed with bits and bobs of jewellery, with sequinned and porcelained masks, antique clothes and feather boas.

Mr Cuttle was the name of the proprietor. (*'A bit stingy with words, but not with his wares; he asks ridiculous prices and knows you won't pay them, so haggle with him.'*) Jury was not a very good haggler, but he had decided he would buy the ring that day, after he left the office, even if he wouldn't be seeing her as they'd planned. He was still worrying it would seem too much of a commitment. How about an *old* ring? She could take it as a gift or a promise; it might not be threatening.

For at times she seemed to withdraw into some corner of her mind that he could not enter. Her face would shift and go slightly out of focus for him, like a face in water. She might stand at the long front window, holding back the curtain, looking out at the rain, almost as if she were looking for someone. Such moods made him feel anxious, excluded. He brushed this away, for much of the time they were like children sharing an enormous secret.

A few days after they'd met, and had been lying in bed, he'd put his arm round her, and asked, 'Have I blundered into the middle of something?' And he tried to make it mildly amusing. The answer was no.

There was no Mr Cuttle about, and only one other customer, a woman largely hidden by old velvets and beaded dresses, the boas and peacock feathers. One could get at them only by rummaging, which was what she was doing. Something about her struck Jury as familiar. He could see part of her back, and hair that curled up under a Liberty scarf.

A throat was being cleared. Jury swung around and saw that an elderly man had entered through a heavy curtain. He was a squat person who held his hands before him and his head down, staring up at Jury under heavy, wild eyebrows, as if sneaking a look.

'Mr Cuttle?'

The downturned head dipped a couple of times in a Cuttle-nod.

'I was wanting to buy a ring for a lady.'

The head dipped once.

The temptation to lean down and engage Mr Cuttle's eyes on his own level was strong. In the velvet ring tray, Jury had seen one he thought particularly lovely, a ruby set in antique gold, that looked as if it would not be too dear a price — worth haggling over, in any event. 'Could I see that one please?'

Mr Cuttle reached in and took it out. He stood there with it a few moments, and finally shook his head. 'Sold,' was all he said before he put the ring in his pocket.

'Oh. Well, how about the garnet — it is a garnet, isn't it? — with the tiny diamonds?'

The garnet went under the same scrutiny; a similar verdict was handed down.

'But, Mr Cuttle, why do you have rings already sold in with the ones for sale?' The buoyant mood that had set Jury forth on this mission was steadily deflating. 'Perhaps you could tell me which ones *are* for sale.'

Mr Cuttle took out the ring tray. Looked it over carefully, and extracted an onyx and silver filigree ring that looked heavy enough to drag Jane's arm to the ground. Mr Cuttle was looking up with a tiny smile on his face for any customer who might be silly enough to buy it.

'No,' said Jury.

While Mr Cuttle's fingers continued the search, a voice behind Jury said, 'Mr Cuttle, you'd better not play games with a policeman.'

Jury knew the voice before he turned. 'Lady Kennington!'

Smiling, she pulled off a glove and held out her hand. 'Superintendent.'

Jenny Kennington hadn't changed in the least, hadn't changed her hair, oak-coloured and shoulder length, and hadn't changed her wardrobe; Jury thought he recognized that loose, black sweater, shot through with tiny strands of silver. It was the scarf, he imagined, that he had tried to place. The lady had been wearing it when he'd first seen her, as she'd come running out and down the broad stone steps of her huge house, holding a sick cat wrapped in a blanket.

'Now, Mr Cuttle, we know you're just larking about; take those rings out of your pocket and show the gentleman.'

Grudgingly, he did. Jury picked up the ruby and asked, 'What do you think?'

'It's beautiful. I expect it depends on the person, don't you? And the occasion,' she added.

Jury said nothing to that, and then remembered he didn't know Jane's ring size. 'Stupid of me.' He looked at the hand holding on to the strap of her bag. 'Could I borrow your hand? It looks very much like . . . my friend's size.'

'Of course not; hands can be deceptive, though.' She put it out and Jury slid the ring onto her third finger. 'It looks just right.'

Jenny looked down at her hand and said, 'Indeed it does. Feels right, too. Anyway, Mr Cuttle will let you return it if it doesn't fit. Perhaps instead of trying to guess, you could purloin a ring she has now; that is, if the jewellery box is close to hand.' She smiled benignly.

'Thanks.' He turned to Mr Cuttle, who hadn't moved an inch or a hair. 'I'll have this one then.'

She put a tiny alabaster figure on the case. 'I'll have this. And, mind, the lady's gown is nicked and so's her arm.'

Mr Cuttle merely waved his hand, indicating clearly that she could have it as a gift.

'That's very kind of you.' She held it out for Jury's inspection. 'It reminds me of the courtyard at Stonington.'

'You're right. It does.' As he handed it back to her, Jury said to the old jeweller, 'The ring. I forgot to ask the price.'

Mr Cuttle gloomed over the ring; he scratched the grey tonsure of his head and then scratched his forearm. 'I make it a thousand.'

'What? A thousand *pounds?*'

Mr Cuttle nodded and inserted the ring back in the velvet tray. With the bare glimmer of a smile, come and gone as quickly as a wink of light on the ruby, he then put the tray back into its rightful place in the case.

Lady Kennington rested her arms on the glass display case and stared at him until Mr Cuttle had to look at her. He cleared his throat; he sighed.

'Mr Cuttle, Superintendent Jury could take away your licence, you know? You're . . . displaying goods under false pretences,' she said decisively. 'I've seen you do it again and again. How much were you thinking of spending Richard?'

She had never called him before by his first name. The mood of buoyancy was returning. 'Ah, somewhere between three and four hundred, I expect.'

'Now, Mr Cuttle, what price do you put on that ring?' She was staring him into submission.

He pursed his lips and looked up at the stained ceiling. He scratched his chin. 'Three hundred and fifty?' He looked blackly at both of them.

'Wonderful! Could you put it in a box for me?'

Without answering, Mr Cuttle shuffled through the dark drapery again, presumably in search of a box.

Lady Kennington said to him, 'I wonder why we're always meeting over jewellery?'

'Fate.' He felt he should explain about the ring. 'It's for a young woman who lives above me. She's done so many things for me.

Taken care of my apartment, cleaning, tidying it up; you know how it is with bachelor digs.'

'Lonely, I expect.' Her voice was quite serious.

Jury inhaled a lot of breath in order to set down more reasons for this ring. 'Her birthday's coming up and she loves jewellery but doesn't have much of it. So, for a surprise – ' He smiled winningly, and got busy writing a cheque for Mr Cuttle.

The man returned with a jeweller's box and removed the velvet tray. But he didn't hand over the ring immediately.

'Mr Cuttle?' said Jenny softly. He gave the box to Jury.

'Thanks. You've got some beautiful things here. I'll tell the men on the force.'

'Don't,' said Mr Cuttle. He went back through the draped doorway.

'He treats everything in that shop as if it were an old family heirloom,' said Jenny Kennington as they stood outside in one of the spidery streets of Piccadilly. 'You've a good bargain there; five hundred would be more like it.'

'Thanks for getting it for me. Look, are you busy just now?'

'No. Would you like to go somewhere?'

'The Salisbury's nearby.'

'Fine.'

He got their drinks and settled in the plush, red booth. 'Where are you living now?'

'Where we last met. Stratford-upon-Avon.'

'Sitting on packing boxes?' He lit her cigarette for her. 'You were always moving.'

She laughed. 'I'm sorry about that. The trip with my aunt didn't last long. She died in Paris, and I stayed. A place on the rue de la Paix. Rather sumptuous it is. I wasn't aware she had more than enough money for that last little fling. But if you come to Stratford again, I can offer you a chair, at least. That house I had in the old district came back on the market, and my cash flow – don't you love the way estate agents talk? – improved somewhat. Thus I acquired "a modern bath en suite companioning a luxurious dressing area which boasts a hundred and fifty cupboards," et cetera. Why do those agents think cupboards are so important? And the "luxurious dressing area" is about the size of an airing cupboard. It's a small place, really. But you remember . . . ' She paused. 'Is something wrong?'

He had been listening but not looking at her. Her face was tilted slightly to the side, inquisitively, with an expression somewhere between concern and amusement.

'No. Nothing's wrong. How long are you in London?'

'Until tomorrow. I'm at the Dorchester.'

Jury heard her, but he was looking again at her arm in the black sweater shot through with silver that reflected slightly only if hit by light at a certain angle. The arm was outstretched across the table, and in her upturned palm was the tiny statue, broken like the original.

He felt ill. His mental camera whirred backwards to the arm of his mother on the floor of their flat years ago, jutting from ceiling plaster after the bomb; and then moved in an instant to Lady Kennington's old manor house, and the ambiguous marble statue in the middle of the courtyard, the statue that one couldn't help but see, no matter which window served as vantage point.

If Jane had not had an "appointment", he would have been going to Lewisham later . . . no, he wouldn't; he had too much neglected work to catch up on. But he had felt a wash of fury when she'd said, no, she couldn't see him; she had an appointment.

And when she hadn't embellished, he'd asked her with whom, Godot? Why the secrecy?

'But I'm not *being* secretive. It's only someone you don't know.'

'I would if you told me.' Knowing, *knowing* it was wrong to push her.

'Good Lord, what difference does it make? Do you think I'm unfaithful? Do you think that? . . . You looked turned to stone.'

Jury's mind, which seemed to have ranged across forty years in the last four seconds, focused. It was Jenny who'd said that last part – *you looked turned to stone*

She wasn't smiling. 'What's wrong?'

'I'm sorry. I have to leave.' He pulled out money, put it on the table. He couldn't believe he was actually getting up, being so rude as to leave her sitting there.

'Do you always wear that sweater?' His mouth was as stiff as if he'd walked a mile through zero weather. 'Black doesn't suit you.'

He did not go back to Victoria Street to catch up on his neglected paperwork. Jury had no recollection of how long he walked; he simply walked from bench to bench, sat down, said either nothing or nodded or grunted if the bench was occupied; he walked deeply into the night, feeling ashamed he'd left someone just sitting there, especially her.

Finally, he ended up on a bench in Green Park with a mumbling drunk whom Jury was pretty sure he'd be able to compete with, given a few more years of feeling sorry for himself.

He was angry both about the self-pity and the awful rudeness to Jenny, whom he knew was easily put off, and who had been very kind. And that idiotic story about his reason for buying the ring . . . why had he lied?

6

She couldn't be dead.

Alex Holdsworth stood perfectly still in the doorway of her bedroom, the rucksack full of his schoolbooks dragging at his arm, and tracks of rain still running from his raincoat.

He could not force his foot across the doorstep.

He had taken the stairs three at a time, whistling between his teeth, swung round the post at the top, sure she would love the surprise of his appearing so unexpectedly. She would not be able to hide that before she was forced to got through the ritual sighs and head-shakes. *'Not again, Alex? You've not been expelled again?'*

Well, they both knew he'd been expelled again, but the game required this sort of thumping big surprise reaction that the headmaster had found yet another reason to send Alex home. A letter would follow, naturally, about the Rose and Crown.

Alex would, of course, appear properly humbled, abashed, pained that he was wasting her money and his time. And since (he had thought, whistling down the hall) she could never bring herself to send him to his room without stuffing him with a huge meal, he would take it upon himself to stick to a crust of bread and a glass of milk. There were times when he actually wished his mother were a little more hell-bent on discipline because he got tired of meting out his own. But there it was, then; as far as his mum was concerned, he could (no matter how many expulsions) really do no wrong.

The fatal step across the threshold was taken by another Alex. In order to keep from screaming the house down or throwing himself at that chaise longue where she lay, he had to split himself in two. He drew himself inward, inside a glass bell, and allowed himself, the one Alex, to descend into divers' waters.

The other Alex walked slowly, still dragging his book bag towards the worn green damask sofa. How had he known in that first instant that she wasn't merely asleep? For he couldn't have seen, twelve feet beyond him through the doorway, the pallor of the skin, the failure of the breast to rise and fall.

He knew because her breathing was in a sense his breathing, too. He knew because he had been beating back panic for the last eighteen or so hours, ever since he had woken very early this morning from a nightmare that left the sheets as wringing wet as his hair and his mac were right now. The dream was uncomplicated and came and went as swiftly as the birds that moved in it; it was a vision of the painting downstairs, the copy of a Van Gough whose name he couldn't remember, a picture of blackbirds flying across a darkening field. When he woke he lay there sweating. Before breakfast he had tried to call her. No one answered. Nothing unusual about that, he kept telling himself all through breakfast. He sat in the noisy refectory, stirring and staring at the bowl of porridge. The dream seemed to follow in his wake like a black ship, like the blackbirds. He had always been highly rational; he had never understood why he was given to complex and baroque dreams. Therefore, dreams (he had told himself) weren't portents.

While part of him stayed safely locked away in the dark silence of the glass bell, the other part stood in the middle of the room, unblinking and unweeping. He did not understand how he could cut himself in half this way; perhaps this was 'shock.'

Alex was almost ashamed that part of him was functioning, that half his mind should be able to look at this mother without flinching where she lay on that armless chaise longue, take in the swirling old pattern of its material and his mother's dress, every fold and pleat in the black velvet and chiffon.

It was her best, her favourite dress. No jewellery. Black leather and patent shoes sitting side-by-side on the floor, as if she were about to put them on, or had taken them off for a lie-down before going out. She must have been going out, or else why would she be wearing her black dress? Going out, or perhaps she'd had some people in. Rarely did his mother have people in.

His eye went to the little rosewood table beside the sofa that held a porcelain bowl and jug etched with a narrow wave of ivy, an ormolu clock and bottle of pills.

He was used to the pills — the tranks, the Seconal, the stuff for a minor heart thing, and he saw that the level in this vial was a quarter of what it was before. But she was supposed to take two of these a day, and he hadn't been home since Christmas. Something kept him from picking up the small bottle; instead he bent down and saw the date was the same. Same bottle, not refilled. Seconal.

He went into the bathroom, opened the medicine cabinet, checked those bottles. One had been changed; the others were the same dates holding lesser amounts. His mum didn't know it, but he kept track. There was nothing seriously wrong with her. She tended, though, to get extremely depressed.

He went back to stand where he'd been before. His other self was clamouring to get out of the bell, to rise from the safe depths of the water. Alex clamped his mouth and his eyes shut.

But not before every detail of the room was etched in his memory.

Then he picked up the phone and called an ambulance.

Name. Address. My Mother.

Alex was still standing there by the telephone when the double note of the ambulance filtered through the images that flickered in his mind: his mum kneading pastry for a tart crust, his mum bringing in a flat basket of wilting peonies, his mum in an old flannel dressing gown . . . a montage of little pictures, each sticking to the other, overlapping, crowding the album page in his mind, expanding infinitely until the rising-falling notes got closer, heard more clearly and must have stopped outside.

Pounding feet. Clattering doorknob. Alex didn't move. The feet came muffled up the stairs and people — so many of them it looked as if they'd brought people to view — burst into the room, white-jacketed, sweating, bearing a stretcher, unfolding a bed. Prepared for anything.

Not meaning to rough him up, they more or less knocked him out of the way and went to work.

He went to her bed and sat down heavily, half to watch, half to think. It was an old four-poster covered with a duvet. The bed, the chaise longue, the walnut bureau had followed them in all of their moves since his father's death, moving each time yet a little farther down the economic ladder. From the Hampstead house

53

to the semidetached flat in Knightsbridge to the huge flat in South Kensington and here to the terraced house not far from the Lewisham Road and Blackheath Common. Beautiful pieces — an Edwardian dressing table, a mahogany breakfront, a silver service, the heavy-plated silver cutlery as well — all had been sloughed off with the former lodgings.

They had never been absolutely poor, but they had never been absolutely well-off, either.

She'd insisted, though, on always keeping the snooker table, the sort of decision that had been his mum's own original way of judging priorities. It was during one of their games that the public school idea had been settled.

'Too expensive,' Alex had said about one she fancied.

She'd been chalking her cue; she hadn't even got to the table since he started his run. 'Well, then, what about Severn School? That's not "too." '

Alex was behind the balk-line, lining up the green ball. 'Anything's *too*, Mum. We haven't got the money.' He'd been fourteen just.

'We could take out a mortgage. On the house.'

That had been the Hampstead house. A fairly decent one.

'We've already done that. I don't mind the comprehensive.' He hadn't,really, as long as he'd let his attention wander from the pasty-faced maths teacher, the goggle-eyed languages lady, the awful square building with its dull masonry and puce-coloured paint.

But his mother had won the day. Severn School it had been, then, especially when he'd realized she was desperate to keep the loathed Holdsworth family quiet about how she was bringing him up. The only one he liked was his great-grandfather. The rest of them made him want to puke.

'I'm sorry, she's gone.'

A thin attendant in white was standing over him, refusing to use the word *dead*. Alex didn't look up.

'You her son? You the one who called?'

He nodded.

'Christ,' the fellow breathed. Behind the rimless glasses, Alex saw the pity. That a kid would come home, find his own mother like this. The man, perhaps unable to take Alex's steady stare, turned back to the others and gestured.

A young woman came over.

He was having a difficult time with the other self desperately wanting to get out of the glass bell, throwing himself round in it, trying to break out, to swim the dark waters. Alex looked at this one, who was (oh hell) *kneeling*, and willed her away. Should have been able to stare her straight to perdition but she just *knelt*.

'Now, we've got to do something about you, dear.'

Was she insane? He said nothing.

'. . . who should we call? Where's your father, then?'

Nothing.

With a vague gesture of impatience. 'Grandparents? Someone? Where's your family live?'

He thought for a moment. 'We don't have one. there isn't anyone.'

To her, clearly absurd. There was always *someone*. 'Oh surely . . .' And now, she thought, thought over the family she could drag in like new furniture. If there wasn't one, she'd set one up, chop, chop. '. . . cousins, then? Aunt? Uncle? Outside London?' The police would find out soon enough. Why help this one?

'A neighbour,' she ran on. 'Yes, a neighbour. To stay the night. Or you could go to their place.' She reached out, put one hand on each of his arms. 'Social services could come round –'

His other self clamoured, screamed. But he kept the diver down there, intact. 'No one's coming round. And get your fucking hands off me. You're not my mother.'

2

What first occurred to him was to get out immediately to avoid the police altogether. Then he thought that if he did that, they would only start a search.

So he stayed. He didn't want to answer the pointless questions and he didn't want their sympathy. The particular policeman asking the questions introduced himself in a diffident and soft-spoken voice as Detective Inspector Kamir: he was an Indian with brown eyes that seemed to melt into his face and might spill over at any moment with the tears that Alex didn't shed.

'It was a surprise, then, that you came down from school. Would have been, I mean,' he added apologetically.

Depending on the question, Alex either nodded or shook his head. The policeman assumed he was in shock. Alex could not afford that luxury: the mind had to keep working. Given the way the questions were going, it was obvious the police knew sod-all about his mother and wouldn't believe him, Alex, if he told them straight out they were wrong.

He knew where it was all going when the questions started centring on his mother's 'mental state'. Had she seemed, well, depressed lately? . . . Could you tell?

That made him wrench his face upward to stare into the inspector's weepy brown eyes. Mr Kamir lifted his shoulders in an apologetic shrug and asked him again: Did Alex know, could Alex tell, if his mother had been depressed?

Could he tell? Of course he could tell, he was her son. But then Alex thought of his friends at Severn School and realized most of them hadn't a clue what was going on inside their parents' heads, and didn't care. Not that some of the parents weren't bloody mindless themselves.

He looked down again. He did not tell Detective Inspector Kamir that his mother was depressed; you'd be depressed too if you had the Holdsworth family on your back.

Kamir did not persist for long with his questions because the boy was only sixteen and he was her son and had just been though the harrowing experience of finding his mother dead.

The policeman turned instead to the problem of Alex's care. To whom should the boy go? Your father? Alex shook his head. He's dead. What relations were there? Which of his mother's relations might he go to? No Galloways, Alex told him, his eye trained on the round bedside table with its flowery floor-length cover and its surface crowded with gilt- and silver-framed pictures of the dead. The grandparents on his mother's side; aunts and uncles; cousins, only two of whom were still alive and in Australia. Alex had never met them except for his Aunt Madeline, but *she* lived with the Holdsworths. There was a distant cousin to whom, at a pinch, he might have gone if he had any intention of going anywhere. Which he didn't.

The Holdsworths, then Inspect Kamir would not rest until he'd got the lad sorted out and safely in the hands of someone prepared to give him sympathy and a roof.

Alex shook his head. From the table he took a porcelain-covered box of tissues and rested it on his lap, as if he were going to need them.

The grandparents, you said they lived in Cumbria. Kamir seemed to find that satisfactory. Without any help from Alex, Kamir debated the problem of the boy's disposal . . .

At least this was what Alex imagined was running through the mind of Detective Inspector Kamir. He simply let it run, since it appeared to be doing the policeman some good; it certainly wasn't doing Alex any.

A police car would deliver Alex to the Lake District, or the Holdsworths might choose to collect him. Alex was agreeable to this plan, yes?

'Yes. Now can I go to the loo?'

The skylight in the bathroom was gummy with resin and soot. Alex pushed it open and looked at the splinter of moon above.

He removed the porcelain cover from the tissue box, pulled out nearly half the tissues and plucked up the small automatic and the cartridge clip, which he then covered in a few of the tissues, shoved the rest back in the box and replaced the cover.

The gun he dropped in his jacket pocket.

Then he hoisted himself onto the roof, highly practised in this manoeuvre. It was not that he'd ever needed an escape before; he had merely wanted to defy gravitational pull. This roof, like all the others, was steeply pitched and roughly slated. And tonight, also wet.

It had never occurred to him that the skylight escapades would be put to use for anything but clinging to the old chimney pot and staring at the stars. Alex did not commune with the stars or any other part of nature. He got his fill of that just from listening to his grandfather talking relentlessly about the Lake poets. Nature was something to be dealt with in practical terms, as in how his favourite would move on a muddy track at Aintree races. Nature was something to be overcome. Wordsworth had missed a lot of golden opportunities if all he could do was talk it to death.

Fifteen minutes later, having jumped two of the roofs in order to shimmy down the sturdiest of the drainpipes (it was copper and strong), Alex was sitting in the private park directly across from the house, watching the policeman up on the roof and two more running out of the front door. Three cars were angled up against the kerb, the front was now cordoned off, and at least a dozen people were standing behind the strip of tape, enthralled. There had probably been even more before the ambulance had done its run through the rain.

The rain had stopped now. Alex had taken off the mac and put on a cap to change his appearance slightly in case the eyes of the coppers grazed the park. The last place they'd look; the kid would have run down the street in one direction or the other, and this was where two of the cars were heading now, flashing lights rainbowing the slick pavements.

He lay down on the end of one of a pair of green park benches, the other already occupied by a slumbering drunk under a raincoat he must have nicked; it looked pricey.

Alex lay under his coat, the brim of his school cap pulled down on his forehead, but not too far down that he couldn't get a view across the street.

Just two old bums sleeping it off is what police would think, if they bothered looking into the park at all. Hardly worth investigating.

7

It wouldn't do his grandparents any good. Not unless they locked him up in that house they claimed was 'ancestral'. Did they really think he'd live with them?

Still, he could remember a summer's day in the Lakes and the lure of the spotted mare, the trout stream, the cascading waters, the incredible blue and glassy lakes and the whole wide northern sky when he had been — what? seven? eight? It was amazing how he could take off and run straight across the land with his arms stretched out, his eyes closed, a terrier at his heels, and no fear of running into anything, of smacking into fences or colliding into trees. It was the great emptiness of the place he loved, for it seemed to match something within himself, as if (he thought now, staring across the street) he had finally found a landscape out there to escape the one within. Out there was cool, dry, full of distant light, uncluttered. He could have run forever.

And there was his great-grandfather, whom he loved. And Millie...

Standing on the steps, Inspector Kamir was talking to one of the other policemen. He was looking up and down the street as if he expected Alex to come walking along. Another of the cars pulled away, so the one left must be the inspector's. The street had quietened; the thrill-seekers gone back to the telly or whatever. Alex looked down at his hands; he seemed unable to unlock them, as if he were handcuffed and needed a key.

The bundle of clothes on the next bench moved and moaned and cursed.

Why didn't they leave, the police? Get out and leave him to the empty house so that he could continue his own investigation. Take their stupid photos, markings, measurements, dustings, notebooks and conclusions away? He could see, in his mind's eye, the report of the doctor. Something that would have to do with ingestion of a high dosage of barbiturates. Suicide.

59

He looked away from the doorstep as the drunk sat up and wailed, 'Oh, GAWD.'

Alex saw the two heads across the street turn in their direction and whispered to his neighbour to shut the hell up!

He wasn't, the man whose head snapped round, the typical park-bench drunk, Alex saw, as newspapers rustled and the coat fell away. He was wearing evening clothes – a wreck of a dinner jacket, the black bow tie partly wrapped round his ear, the collar open.

'Been stood up, too, have you? I keep telling myself never to go to that fool's parties. What sort of getup is that?' He was looking at Alex's blazer and cap. 'Pretty young to be hanging about the boozer, aren't you? Got a fag? Or do you snort the stuff?'

Alex didn't bother answering. He watched as the two policemen came down the steps. They lacked the purposefulness they'd have had if they'd been about to investigate the park.

'But of course the boy must stay, Jane. He's looking so peaky.'

They had been sitting round the dinner table – his mother, his grandfather and stepgrandmother (whom he called 'Grandmum' to irritate her), his Uncle George and Madeline Galloway, his mother's sister.

'Don't you think so?' Genevieve Holdsworth's question had been put to the table in general. 'Alex really *must* get out of the city.'

He had sat there, five years ago, alternately looking down at his plate and shifting his eyes to the black terrier beneath the table.

'He doesn't look peaky to me, and heaven knows not thin. Not with all that black pudding he's been putting away,' his mother had said with absolute assurance.

She'd seen him reaching the horrible stuff down to the terrier. 'No,' he'd said to Genevieve. 'I have things to do.'

They occupied a special plane, his mother and he. It wasn't that there was no one else on that plane; he just didn't know them. Alex wasn't a Romantic: he'd trample a whole field of daffodils to get to a turf accountant. And he could certainly keep himself together for as long as it took to find out what had happened to his mum –

'Damn it.' Rooting through his topcoat pockets, the man on the bench cursed until he managed to drag out a mangled cigarette and an expensive-looking lighter. In the glow of the flame Alex saw he was middle-aged. Or at least twenty years older than Alex himself . . . Police were still there, leaning against their car.

'What's going on? What the hell are the police over there for?'

Alex wanted him to shut up, to stop invading his privacy and keeping him from thinking his problem through.

'What the devil are you doing sitting on a park bench at – ' He wrenched his wrist and squinted down at what looked like a Rolex. ' – one a.m.? My name's Maurice, incidentally.' His yawn was so drawn-out Alex thought he'd suck in all of the available oxygen.

Maurice upended a leather-covered flask, shook it a bit and sighed. 'Not a glimmer.' He turned. 'You've got a name, I expect?'

'William. Smythe.' Alex pronounced it with a long *i*; it was the name of one of his particularly revolting schoolmates. 'Well, good-bye.' Thank God the car was pulling away. But one uniformed copper was standing there still. Had they left anyone inside?

He crossed the little rear garden, let himself in with the same key that opened the front door, and sat down at the kitchen table. Alex stared into the dark, which his eyes soon penetrated so that he could see the outlines of fridge and cooker. He could find his way round in here like a blindman, anyway. He heard nothing.

Quietly, he pulled off his jacket, his cap and his shoes and slumped in the chair. Then he laid his head down on his folded hands. Afraid he'd doze off, he pulled his head up again, folded his arms hard against his chest.

His throat was killing him; it was as bad as the strep throat he'd had that one time. . . .

Don't cry. Think.

A coffee would help. Soundlessly, he padded to the cooker, pulled down one of the boxes of Rombouts and the white Rombouts cup his mum kept beside it, and lit the gas under the kettle. He picked it up before it whistled and carefully poured it into the prepacked coffee filter, then took the works back to the table and waited for it to drip through.

He decided his throat was not his own; it was William Smythe's. William Smythe would have got hysterical, would have screamed and kicked the cops, just the way he did when he missed the goal at soccer. Kicked the goalie.

William Smythe's mother and father were exactly like William. No matter what William did, it was the school's fault. Bricks flew out to hit William in the head; pavements flew up to flatten his nose; fists flew towards his face. (Well, *that* was true enough.)

And Alex's own mother was like *Alex*; *he* was goddamned if he'd let anybody − police, anybody − put it about that his mum had killed herself.

She hadn't; she wouldn't. He knew this as well as he knew the outlines of the cooker, table, fridge and the cup of Rombouts he was raising to his lips.

She simply wouldn't do it to him.

When he was certain that the police constable outside hadn't heard anything and didn't know anyone was in here, he would go upstairs again.

It was stupid speculating, but he couldn't stop his mind from going round and round. Would they say she'd died from an 'accidental overdose'? He dismissed this immediately. She wasn't careless. Certainly, she wasn't 'unstable', much as the Holdsworths loved to think she was.

That supposedly good-humoured yet long-suffering sigh from Genevieve . . .'*You just have such* bad *luck with jobs, don't you, Jane?'* His mother did not 'lose' jobs. If an art gallery closed, it was hardly her fault the gallery didn't need here anymore. If a temp sec employer tried to toss her in to bed (Alex knew what the vaguely mentioned 'trouble' meant), she could hardly be blamed for leaving his employment.

And then there was always the bit about his mum's own small inheritance: '*You've just run through your money, Jane, like some tout at Newmarket races* . . .'

If there was one thing Alex knew it was how hard she tried to budget the money so that it would last, and that she'd no head for figures. If there was another thing he knew, it was Newmarket races.

She wouldn't take money from his great-grandfather Adam, who had tried to press something, some little stipend, on her. He was the only one of them Alex liked and trusted, the only one who didn't somehow imply his mother was responsible for his father's death.

Alex couldn't think about his father. Not now.

Oh, fuck them.

He shoved the cold coffee away with one hand; his other went to the tissue-wrapped revolver in his jacket pocket. Taking the box from the bedside table had been a kind of reflex action; he hadn't known why he'd done it.

Yes, he did. He might need it.

His mum hadn't died of 'natural causes'; there was nothing seriously wrong with her. And she hadn't killed herself. That didn't leave much room for speculation.

8

Carole-anne Palutski took the call while she was doing a sausage, onion and potato fry up in Richard Jury's kitchen.

The voice at the other end was hollow, one of those voices that made you think the mouth was covered in cobwebs; but it still wallowed in officialdom.

Officialdom never impressed Carole-anne. On the contrary , it only tempted her to make clattering sounds with pans and spoons as the caller demanded to know who this was.

'*This* just 'appens − *happens*' (she snatched the *h* from the linoleum along with a wilted onion ring) 'to be Mr Jury's assistant . . . Well, *I* really don't know where he is, do I? It's not yet eleven, so the pubs're still open, and after all I expect he needs his bit of fun just like you and me. *We're* up, ain . . . aren't we?'

The demanding voice was replaced with a kinder, warmer one. It was important, you see. Although Carol-anne had every intention herself of giving the super what-for because she'd been planning to have him take her down the pub, to the Angel in Islington, still she wasn't about to let some stupid git of a copper jump all over Jury with his own problems − although she had to admit this one seemed much more pleasant than the chief superintendent, whom Carole-anne had decided was a pervert.

Holding the receiver on her shoulder, she picked up the pan, flipped the sausages with a spatula while the voice grew more insistent. He needed the superintendent straightaway and would she tell him to call the moment he arrived? The voice was so mellifluous it was almost weepy. Carole-anne wondered what a hound dog would sound like if it could talk. 'And *whom* might I say is calling?' She chewed a slice of nicely browned potato as she peered at her toes. She'd never go back to Pertfeet for a pedicure . . . 'What? Well just hang on a tic whilst I get . . .' She rummaged in a jam jar for a pencil. Honestly some people.

Thought you walked round all day with a notepad in your hand. 'Yes . . . yes. I got it. *Thank* you very much.' She rang off before he could and stabbed the sausages as she heard the front door of the Islington house open and shut.

Jury's ground-floor flat was seldom locked, a fact that the elderly basement tenant had often taken him to task for.

Carole-anne would only pick the lock, he'd said to Mrs Wassermann.

Mrs Wassermann never listened to criticism of Carole-anne. Such an example for a policeman to set, Mr Jury. She'd shaken and shaken her head.

This poor role-model of a policeman walked into his flat at eleven p.m. and tossed his keys on the table. He wasn't especially surprised to see Miss Palutski there; he hoped the building's smoke detectors were working given the apparent flammability of his kitchen — though he wasn't sure whether it rose from the frying sausages or Carole-anne herself, her red hair looking charged and her dress an electric-blue, out-of-fashion mini that would rush right back into fashion as soon as the men eyeballed its wearer.

He sniffed the air as he dropped his keys on the coffee table. 'Your own cooker break down? And why the hell are you cooking anyway at this hour?' he asked irritably. He was tired from too much walking, bench sitting, thinking.

'Well, *thank* you very much! And after I've gone to all the trouble of doing you a meal.' Actually, she was doing it for herself; she was starving after nothing but three half-pints and a packet of crisps at the Angel.

'Not for me, thanks,' he said as her saw her beginning to divide up what was in the frying pan.

'After all the trouble . . .,' she said righteously, shrugging her shoulders and sliding what was on his plate to hers. 'Probably had your dinner with JH, I expect.' She sat down in the sprung easy chair with her plate on her knees.

Wrong, CA. It was a drink with JK.'

Carole-anne looked up suddenly. All of the super's women were initials except for her.

He slid down on the sofa and clasped his hands behind his neck. '*Lady* JK. What's this?' He saw the message under the telephone.

'You got a call. *Who* is Lady — '

Jury frowned. 'I can't read this . . . Kahmur? Who's he?'

'Some copper. Wants you to call. You mean you gave JH the boot?' She was cutting sausage with a flourish; the news there might be a new woman was not, as he expected, bad news. She sighed as she watched him dial. 'I wish you'd get a push-button. Broke a nail on that dial, I did, last week.'

'Dial with your toe. Hello? Inspector Kahmur — '

'Ka-*mir*,' Carole-anne corrected him, as if he should, after all, be able to read minds. 'Sounded sad.'

'Sad?'

'I didn't know police had those kind of feelings.' She stared at him, chewing, ducking as he tossed a small pillow.

'Inspector Kamir? Richard Jury. You called — '

Kamir's voice was soft and plodding, having discovered *in the course of inquiries, Mr Jury*, that the woman was a friend of the superintendent. The inspector spoke each word slowly, as if it were a drop of oil falling into water to hang suspended before the next one followed.

But each hit with the force of a projectile as Jury moved the receiver away and stared at it, blinking. The voice, tiny now, kept on. He brought the phone back to his ear, said nothing into what was now a silence, heard the inspector ask if Jury could see him as soon as possible. Yes.

The receiver dangling from his hand, he hadn't known whether he'd spoken the word aloud, or that he'd said aloud *Jane's dead*. But he must have done, for there was a click at the other end and he saw Carole-anne's deep blue eyes widen, saw her rise from the chair, the plate sliding from her lap, but all in slow motion. Even though she must be rushing toward him, knocking over the table, it seemed more like an underwater propulsion. Swimming against air. His senses were so dulled he heard nothing, not the plate nor the cutlery clatter nor the table thud down.

Carole-anne was crying, her face baby-red and twisted and then thrust into his chest, her arms around his neck.

He just sat there, doing nothing, letting them drown.

And then the dulled senses became heightened and he realized she was on the phone yelling for Mrs W. to come, and what seemed vague and shadowy darkness broke into scorching light. Jury pushed Carole-anne aside and made for the door. Pulling open the door of his car, he didn't answer Mrs Wassermann, who was heaving up the steps from her basement flat.

What he saw in his rearview mirror was an elderly lady with her dressing gown clutched round her, standing in the middle of an Islington street.

9

Rain had started up again, a real downpour, while he'd been sitting at the kitchen table in the dark — for how long? Five or fifty minutes; he couldn't tell.

Alex put the automatic on the table and studied it. It was a Webley, small and snubnosed. His Uncle George had given it to her. *Given where you live* . . . Alex shook his head. You'd think it was Brixton.

They lived off the Lewisham road, near Blackheath. It was quiet, it was pretty, it was south of the river. Alex loved the vast green. Naturally, there had been repeated injunctions to keep the gun out of the boy's reach.

What a prayer. Alex was the one who'd sorted out the problem of where to keep it and where to keep the ammunition, too. Hidden, but within reach.

The slanting downpour changed to veils that rose and fell like delicate curtains and then hissed against the dark planes.

Alex jumped when he heard the front door open and close, heard feet pounding up the stairs.

They weren't back, were they? But it was only one person, one person who had run up the stairs and whom he could hear, now, moving about in his mum's room.

Alex stared up at the ceiling.

2

Jury wasn't expecting to find some telltale bit of evidence that had eluded Detective Inspector Kamir when he got to the house in Lewisham. Forensics would have gone over every inch.

The constable at the door had been surprised to see him, not so much him but the manner of his entrance, leaving the young policeman telling empty air, that, yes, sir, he could —

* * *

The dread of rooms from which someone had vanished was that they still clung to the presence of the one gone. The scarf draped round one of the bed's posts; the silver-backed brush, the spill of rosy powder on the dressing table; the slippers neatly aligned by the bed.

How could insensate *things* make the air swirl with such expectancy? That he could hear her step in the hall, that she would appear in the doorway . . .

. . .*an overdose.*

'*Have you every known anyone who could OD on one-a-day?*' she'd said, laughing.

'*Yes, My sergeant.*' More seriously, Jury had asked. '*Do you get them all from the same chemist?*'

'*No. I go all over London in dark glasses or disguised as a little lady in a shawl. Of course I get them from one chemist!*'

Jury had touched nothing in the room, only stood in its centre looking around him. Kamir did not think the overdose was accidental.

Yet, why suicide? She'd had every reason not to do that. There was her son; there was, he hoped, himself.

My God. Alex. He'd found her.

3

Alex sat in the dark listening to the silence. What was he doing? It wasn't, at least it didn't sound like, the policeman Kamir. That step had been light, almost lithesome. Inspector Kamir was not a big man.

Finally, he heard the person above move, heard steps descending. Heavy, dull, slow steps. It was, Alex thought, the way he himself had rushed up the stairs and would have been the way he'd come down again. Had this person run up, happily expecting to find his mum? Don't be stupid; there's a copper at the door.

And yet it had sounded like an echo, a ghost of Alex's own homecoming.

He sat with his chin on his chest, the gun on the table, trying not to fall asleep.

70

10

He was still sitting in his office as he had been just before dawn, pulling the little brass chain of his desk lamp on and off, absently. He'd turn from watching the shadows spring up on the wall to watching the grey morning light sift across the window.

Accident or design . . . he heard the voice of Kamir again and felt the man's voice and words had a strangely poetic quality, brooding words of an Elizabethan drama.

The thought of suicide was so unspeakable . . .

Say it; there was a part of Jane's mind to which he had never been admitted; a part she had held away from him, not, he thought, in the secretive sense of holding back – though, God knows, there could easily have been secrets. It was something isolating: a suggestion that he couldn't, in some things, be trusted.

He shut his eyes, hard. Anger and betrayal threatened to override grief and remorse. For a moment he hated her for so determinedly refusing to let him see the depth of her unhappiness.

Only a phone call away . . . that's all he'd been.

But perhaps that was a contradiction in terms for one set on ending one's life. Suicide was, after all, a closed world. If you could admit someone else into it, it would open.

He shoved aside papers and folders and put his head on the desk.

He realised he had dozed off only when he felt a presence above him, looked up and saw Sergeant Wiggins standing over him with a bag from Natural Habitat, one of Wiggins's new watering places.

As what Jury was sure must have been a bad dream turned itself into reality, he was at least thankful that he hadn't mentioned Jane Holdsworth to anyone around here. That was not because he couldn't take the sympathy of others; it was because the death and his part in her life were so utterly unresolved. He would simply not have know how to be.

'What are you doing here *this* early, sir? I know you've become a morning person, but not enough to beat *me*.' Wiggins's strangled little laugh was a relief from Islington's strangled cries.

Black coat, black hat, white face — Wiggins looked more like the Angel of Death rather than one who probably had in that bag enough benign chemicals to resurrect most of Scotland Yard's dead.

'Hullo, Wiggins.' Jury wiped his hands across his face and was glad he'd gone back to the flat. He'd certainly have gone back there anyway to let Carole-anne and Mrs Wassermann know he was all right. No stubble of beard or crumpled shirt to betray a mood.

'You always come in this early?'

'I do my best thinking in the morning,' said Wiggins, sanctimoniously. He emptied the bag, lined up some small brown bottles, a little tin of pastilles, a roll of antacid tablets, and one of those hideous containers of juice with a straw attached, the juice always hitting one in the face when it was prised open and freed of its bubble cover. Wiggins, however, was a master of this sort of exercise; getting cotton out of aspirin bottles, lining up white arrows on safety tops, pushing down with the thumb and turning. He should have been a safecracker.

'You look awful, if you don't mind my saying so, sir.'

'I feel awful, if you don't mind my dropping the subject.'

But a crisis on Wiggins doorstep was not to be discounted so easily. He had unstoppered one of the brown bottles, zipped open the juice container, poured some into a glass and carefully measured out drops (one, two, three, four) into the apple juice. It turned a sluggish shade of brown.

Jury shook his head. 'I'm not drinking that, Sergeant.'

Wiggins was already up and carrying the anodyne to Jury.

'No.'

'Fix you up in no time —'

'Fill it up with whisky and give it to Racer.' He was up and putting on his coat. 'If you need me, I'll be at CD.' Jury put a slip of paper on Wiggin's desk.

'Inspector — Kamir? What's this about, sir?'

'Case he's working on.' Jury wished he'd got out the door before Wiggins came in; his throat felt hot and raw. 'Possible suicide.'

Wiggins tapped a green and pink capsule into his hand. 'He caught the squeal, did he?' He tossed back some water.

'What?' Jury frowned.

'It's what they say in New York. "Caught the Squeal." ' Wiggins gave Jury a pinched smile. 'I've read it in books. Superintendent Macalvie'd like that, wouldn't he? It means –'

'I think I've managed to sort it out. Yeah, he caught the squeal.'

2

Detective Inspector Hanif Kamir had the doleful look of a policeman who had 'seen it all' and grown older, but not wiser, from the sight, for Jury wondered what wisdom was to be gained by viewing bodies in alleyways such as this one: an old lady, badly beaten but still breathing. A sour wind swept up the brick alley off Pembroke Villas, carrying with it the stink of dustbin refuse. It ruffled her lace collar as her nearly transparent, blue veined eyelids opened and shut, opened and shut.

They had taken her purse; she'd been able to tell them she was carrying only four pounds and change. As to wisdom, the old lady was not absorbing a lesson that she would, being the wiser, put to good use.

Neither was Kamir, Neither were the ambulance attendants who were carefully loading her onto a stretcher. Her eyelids fluttered and her thin lips moved, repeating that she'd only got the four pounds.

Kamir, his naturally soft voice further softened by the old woman's fear, murmured something to her that Jury didn't hear. His own state of mind was muting ordinary city-background noises, muffling the sound of the rear doors of the ambulance closing.

'They told me at headquarters you were here.'

'My sister – my older sister – died this way,' said Kamir, whose notebook's pages ruffled in that sour breeze.

Jury did not know what to say to this. Selfishly, he wondered if, in the chain of desolate happenings, he would be permitted to wedge in his own pain. 'Your sister.'

Kamir nodded. 'She was walking home, much like this old woman, to her little terraced house when she was attacked. It was probably because she was so beautiful that they did all their damage to her face. You know it is common practice, part of our religion, for a woman to wear a small jewel implanted in the nostril.' He

73

touched his own. 'It was a tiny diamond. I cannot believe they cut off half her nose to get that diamond. No.'

Jury heard as if from a great distance, the ambulance wailing in the Lewisham road.

They removed her sari, though not the undergarments. She wasn't raped or molested. But they took the sari, unwound it from her body, and that I found strange. Until I realized that they meant to denude her of her despised heritage.' He closed the notebook and said, 'I do not think I am cut out to be a policeman.'

'Who is?'

Kamir looked up at Jury, who was much taller, and nodded.

'From what I hear, you perhaps. You have the sixth sense, the intuition for it.'

'I doubt that.'

'Perhaps we could go somewhere else more conducive to conversation. There's a café round the corner.'

He went over to the police car, said something to the two men there and turned back to walk with Jury down the alley.

The café's fresh-cut sandwiches and buns beneath their plastic domes already looked stale and wilting and it wasn't yet ten in the morning. The same sour smell, now mixed with something sickeningly sweet — perhaps the sugary pastries — permeated the narrow takeaway with its single counter running down one wall at which Jury and Kamir sat.

Kamir kept his eyes on the cup of heavily sugared tea Jury had brought him and said, as he slowly stirred it, 'I'm sorry about your friend, Mrs Holdsworth.'

'Yes.' Jury's own tea remained untasted. 'How did you know she was?'

'Oh.' Kamir sipped. 'Address book. The number of your flat was also there.'

'Of course.'

'And the calendar. The one in the kitchen she must have used as a sort of engagement book. Appointments, dinner dates.'

Jury was surprised. He'd seen her just once scribble in a doctor's appointment there. But the excursions into the kitchen were rare. For one thing, she was a rotten cook. He started to smile, stopped. He'd stopped because the memory was painful, but now noticed that Kamir's eyes were fastened on his face. 'What?'

'There are two things,' said Kamir. 'One is, why would her son take himself off through a bathroom skylight? I was merely trying to fix up somewhere for him to go, or someone to come and stay with him. He found her —'

'I know.' Jury's tone was sharp enough to set the inspector back on his stool. More quietly, he said, 'I never met her son. But he sounded from the way Jane talked about him, very resourceful.' His smile was now unchecked. 'Skylight in the loo? And you couldn't find him?'

Kamir's smile was slight, a man not much used to smiling. 'At first he said they had no relations. Then he admitted that there were grandparents in Cumbria.' Kamir flicked through his notebook. 'A village called Boone, near Keswick.'

'I doubt he'd have made for there. He and his mother had a great deal of trouble with the grandparents. They wanted custody of the boy.'

Kamir had turned on the stool so that he could lean back against the counter. He was rubbing his shoulder as if the muscle there pained him. 'You have no idea, then where he might be, Superintendent?'

'I just said — wait a minute. You don't think I *know* and am refusing to tell you? Look, Inspector —'

Kamir's mouth tilted again in a ghost of smile.

'Just what *do* you think?'

Kamir left off kneading the shoulder and turned on his stool for another sip of tea, cold as tears by now. 'Would you mind looking at some police photographs of — the victim?' He was opening the manila envelope.

'Yes.'

Kamir said nothing, and after a short silence Jury put out his hand. The air felt so icy that he wouldn't have been surprised to see his breath like smoke in the café.

She was lying on the chaise longue in what he knew was her favourite dress. Black velvet. He shut his eyes briefly, blotting out the image and all the images and memories that trailed in the wake of seeing her in this special dress, dead. A recurrent dream returned, one of a black schooner cutting through an equally black sea. The water did not churn or curl or froth, but looked as if it were being cut by scissors and closing seamlessly behind the ship. Over the years, the portals had dimmed to pearls of light, the light shut out by shades; the rolled sails, once ghostly white in the moonlight, turned to dark sticks and the moon itself had gone. It was as if outline stitches in a piece of embroidery had been pulled, leaving only the background.

Jury said, 'She was dressed as if she meant to go out.' He handed the photos back, blank-faced.

'Yes. I wondered about this.'

'It was her favourite dress.'

Kamir was silent, considering, then he said, 'Then that perhaps explains it. It is not unusual for a person . . . in this frame of mind . . .'

Jury knew what Kamir was tactfully negotiating his way around the word. 'Who's suicidal,' he said, evenly.

'Yes. It is not unusual that such a person would choose to look . . . I don't know quite how to put it; I don't mean 'look her best', but perhaps imagine others looking at her and wanting to be seen in something she was especially fond of. In other words, not, for many, the tatty dressing gown, the uncombed hair. I expect that might surprise others. Why would one care, in that frame of mind? But I'm sorry; you know what I mean.'

'Yes.' It was near enough to the lunch hour for a few customers to be straggling in for the fresh-cut sandwiches, the takeaway, milky teas. To him they all looked the same, somehow, overtired, their faces blighted as the girl behind the counter dispensed the buns and teas. It kept his eyes away from the glossy photos beneath Kamir's arm. He felt completely selfish, self absorbed, and said, 'What about her son? She didn't know he was coming. Why was he there?'

'I can only assume that he had come down from school for some reason.' Kamir shrugged. 'It is regrettable.'

'Yes. What are you doing to locate him?'

'The usual. Wired a picture to provincial forces, especially in Cumbria. But he is probably in London.'

'Well, he wouldn't go knocking on the grandparents' door, that's for certain. Any results?'

'Again, the usual. A hundred calls at least from people who've seen a lad answering that description.'

'What about — ' Jury had to clear his throat. 'The post mortem? When's it going to be done?'

'I'm not sure. Tomorrow, possibly.'

'Look, would you mind very much getting either Dr Cooper or Dr Nancy? Do you know them?'

Kamir jotted down the names. 'Willie Cooper, yes. Not Dr Nancy.'

'Phyllis Nancy. I think they're the best we've got. And to be frank, well, I can talk to them . . . more easily.'

'Certainly.' Then he fell silent.

Kamir was silent in a certain way. It was a listening, expectant silence, thought Jury. And he imagined what Kamir was waiting for — something more than he'd got as yet from Jury. 'I was going to marry her. Or, I should say, I was going to ask her — ' He had not taken the ring box from his pocket; he had very nearly believed, before he saw the pictures, that its presence in his pocket had the potency of — what? Wiggins's belief in charcoal biscuits and rue. That at least broke some sort of spell. Jury put the box on the counter, saying, 'I brought this yesterday.'

Kamir, who Jury had come to realize had a great delicacy, made no move to touch it. He merely looked at the little burgundy box, its velvet rubbed from much handling, and finally said, 'I thought perhaps . . . well, since the calendar had your name written in so often, so very often . . . that the relationship might be very close. I can only repeat, I'm so sorry.' He rushed on. 'It amazes me that people seem to think of the suicide (at least if they can be sympathetic, and many can't) as a person who merely wants "to end it all", without considering the complexities . . . It is a very complicated act, I think. I wonder sometimes if the whole gestalt of the act does not encompass in the mind of the victim what he thinks to be the resolution of every conflict that has ever plagued him. Don't you think so?'

'Not in the case of Jane, no. She was too attached to her son, for one thing.'

Kamir looked up from his empty cup. 'And to you.'

Jury picked up the red box. 'Perhaps not. I might have totally misread her.' He could not keep the bitterness from his tone. He felt, he might as well admit it, duped.

'It's possible your anger is clouding your judgment.'

'I'm not . . . oh, the hell with it. Yes, I am angry.'

Kamir nodded in understanding. 'We were speaking of the dress. But I was wondering about the shoes.'

'Shoes?'

In his diffident way, as if not wanting to burden Jury with any more than he had to, he gently pushed one the of the photos towards him. It showed Jane Holdsworth stretched out full length on the chaise longue. Her feet were stockinged, but she was not wearing shoes. Jury remembered looking at the black pumps, set so carefully together beside the bed. 'I must be dim, Mr Kamir, but I don't know what you mean. If she took a handful of pills, it's unlikely she meant to go for a stroll.' Abruptly, he shoved the photo back.

'My point is that if she had imagined, before she took those pills, her own appearance — as we were remarking about the dress — then why did she not put on the shoes?'

Jury was silent.

'You had, or meant to have, dinner with her last evening?'

'Meant to have, yes. But she said she couldn't that she had another appointment. How did you know?'

A deferential shrug. 'The calendar. "R, din." was written in. And then crossed off.' Kamir shrugged. 'You don't know who it was she intended to see?'

Jury shook his head. 'No.'

'But you must have questioned —'

'*No*, I said. For some reason, she wouldn't tell me.'

Again, a silence fell. Kamir finally broke it. 'Who would have reason to kill her?'

11

Jury stared at Kamir.

'Do you think, Mr Jury, we could walk a bit, sit on the heath, perhaps? I'm finding this café extremely depressing.' Wearily, he looked at Jury. "I see you are too.'

Jury had more than the café to be depressed about, he thought, as he agreed.

They were sitting on a bench along one of the paths criss-crossing the common. When Jury was a boy, Blackheath had been more exciting a prospect of visit than the Tower. He could almost see the coaches, hear the horses' hooves, hear the thunder and yell of the highwaymen as they halted the great coaches.

He had told Kamir during their walk here that, unless one counted the grandparents, Jane Holdsworth had no enemies. Looking out over the enormous green, whose horizon had seemed endless when he was a lad, he told Kamir that Dick Turpin must have been on his mind.

Enemies. The word seemed to have no relation to Jane at all. And yet, she did not have particular friends, either; acquaintances, one or two of whom he'd met, but close friends, no.

Kamir was looking down at the spiral notebook, talking about the Cumbria family. In-laws, Jury reminded him. Except for the sister, she had no family. And Alex, of course. He seemed to have made up an entire family for her on his own.

'What I've learned about them,' said Kamir, 'You already know. You know far *more*, I'm sure. But I will tell you what I know. The husband, Graham —'

Jury felt an upsurge of jealousy.

'— is dead. The second Mrs Crabbe Holdsworth — Graham's father — Genevieve, who insists on the French "ve'*ev*"

79

pronunciation, seemed far more concerned about her grandson's whereabouts than about the death of the mother.'

'Hardly surprising. The death of the mother, as far as Genevieve is concerned would land Alex on her doorstep. I believe she's suffering under a misapprehension there, from what I've heard of Alex.' Jury was able to smile at that.

'There is the grandfather, Crabbe (what strange names you English have) Holdsworth, to whom I did not speak. There is his brother, George, unmarried; a painter-cousin who lives in a cottage on the grounds named Francis Fellowes; and, in addition to the servants, the sister. *Her* sister. I found it odd that Madeline Galloway was part of that household. She acts as Mr Holdsworth's secretary or assistant. I find this rather strange.' Kamir closed his notebook.

'It was through Madeline that Jane met her husband. Jane was visiting there.'

Kamir turned to Jury in surprise. 'But that would mean Miss Galloway had been in the household for, what? Certainly over sixteen years.'

'Eighteen or nineteen. She was in her twenties, I think, when she first took that job.'

Kamir frowned. 'But she looks so much younger than she must be.'

Jury turned quickly to meet Kamir's frown. ' "Looks"? How on earth have you had time to see her?'

'Just this morning, early. But she's here, Mr Jury. In London. At Brown's Hotel. And so is Genevieve Holdsworth. They've been here for two days; the sister came up to London to interview a few people for Mr Holdsworth. He wishes to have his library catalogued, or some such thing. Mrs Holdsworth came to shop, apparently. You didn't know they were here?'

To Jury, Blackheath's verdant green expanse and its far horizon were shrinking to little more than a stingy garden plot, the leaden sky closing in. 'I didn't'. Why in the name of heaven keep something as simple as the visit of one's sister a secret? *Its just someone you don't know.* He had been hurt enough to think that she'd needed to keep *any* visitor a secret. He leaned forward, his forearms on his knees and his head down.

Quickly, Kamir added, 'Her purpose in coming here was not to see Jane Holdsworth. Although she did say she had intended to.'

Jury looked up in Kamir's troubled face. 'Then it wasn't Madeline — or Genevieve — she was going to see last night?'

Kamir sighed. 'Not according to Miss Madeline.'

'What about these calendar entries?' Jury felt a fool. Her lover, and he didn't appear to know anything. 'We — ate out usually. I didn't see much of the kitchen.' *I hardly know a room in this house except the bedroom* . . . And then he looked at Kamir, hard. 'Hadn't she entered whoever it was on this damned calendar?'

'No. There was only your name.'

'Her sister. What was she like?'

'Pretty, in a thin rather nervous sort of way. Intelligent. Rather strange a woman like that would reach middle-age without marrying.' Kamir looked at Jury.

'I believe she thought she would. I believe she meant to marry Graham Holdsworth.'

Kamir held up his hands in a questioning gesture. 'We spoke of enemies?'

'Would she have waited eighteen years?'

'Some will wait forever.'

'Alibi?'

'No.'

'Would you mind if I spoke to her?'

'No. As I said, she is at Brown's. But I believe she leaves today on an afternoon train from Euston. Genevieve Holdsworth left early this morning .'

But Jury's mind was less occupied with them at the moment than it was with Kamir's earlier statement. *There was only your name.*

He rose and said, 'Perhaps I'll also take an afternoon train from Euston.'

Kamir turned his brown, searching eyes on Jury's face. 'If the situation were reversed, Superintendent — '

Jury half smiled. 'I know, your name on the calendar; your prints all over the house; you, the last one as far as I knew, to ever see her alive . . .' He paused. 'Oh, I'd tell you you wouldn't be taking the train from Euston.'

12

At Euston Station, Alex slipped four twenties on the turntable and asked for a single, first-class ticket to Windermere. Both ticket and change were spun back to him without the clerk's even looking up.

Perhaps it was a waste of money, he thought, stowing his rucksack and mac overhead in the empty compartment. He could as easily have paid for a second-class and then just moved along here once his ticket had been punched. But he was young. If you're young, you're expected to do something either illegal or rude. What he would have to do at some point was find an Eton jacket and school tie for use for British Rail rides.

Right now, though, it was more important to have a place to himself to think. He had managed, with endless cups of coffee, to stay awake. Sleep was out; he wouldn't dare. He would dream. He would dream about his mother and it would be one of those diabolically happy dreams that one never wanted to wake from even in the best of circumstances. And in waking, he would be totally vulnerable to the onslaught of feeling he had armoured himself to avoid. He remembered too many times waking up to misery (at the Holdsworths', in the scummy grey darkness of Severn School, at frozen points on a railway station when his father was coming to collect him long ago when he'd wake on the train . . .). If the dreams had themselves been miserable, it wouldn't have been so bad. But it was all a trick, wasn't it, life? Dream of a field grazed by sheep and wake up to wolves.

He took a small notebook and a pen from his pocket and held them, notebook open, pen unscrewed. HELL. He wrote it down. And then crossed it out. Why would anyone, any*thing*, bother to think up a Hell in the afterlife when all you had to do was stop awhile in this one?

Fields flew past, unremarked. All Alex saw was his own dim reflection in the pane. Occasionally a telephone pole here, a silo there. Farther along light shimmered over fields encircling some distant mirage of a village.

He leaned back. Money, fortunately, was no problem. Alex hadn't saved for rainy days; he'd counted on torrents, and one had come.

Some of the money he had just won on Fortune's Son was now on his person. For two years he had accumulated money to get him and his mum to some place the Holdsworths had never heard of — Lithuania, he understood, was pleasant. Fourteen hundred pounds. A hundred in his wallet (less the train fare), six hundred strapped in a small money bag around his ankle, four sewn into the lining of his jacket, the rest in an inside pocket of the rucksack.

Over four thousand quid had been accumulated during his business dealings at Severn School. Twice he had been expelled for card playing, although the headmaster could never understand why he played poker, since he never seemed to win.

When it had been decided that Alex *must* go off to private school, he had made the best of it. It wasn't that he minded so much going to Severn School — actually it made a change for a while from his comprehensive-school 'mates', whose idea of having a good time was spending Saturdays at the cinema, or going biking, or sitting about in some clubby way smoking and lying about their conquests with girls.

Alex certainly had nothing against girls, he just couldn't find one with any imagination. They turned out to be merely prettier versions of the boys; they went to the cinema and had overnight parties where they smoked and talked about the boys.

While his schoolchums were sneaking into X-rated films and leaving with only Parently Approved girls, Alex was studying racing forms, the stockmarket, and estate agents' brochures and adverts for properties in Ibiza. Merely for practice, he'd follow the gentrification of the London suburbs. He'd take the tube to Limehouse, Wanstead, even Bow — which was now trendy. Bow, would you believe it? Alex decided that once he got the stake he'd start a trend.

Alex studied demographics, not people. He knew about people

simply from listening in on conversations in tea rooms, on park benches, and in whatever pubs he could get into in dark glasses shoved on top of his head just to show he didn't have anything to hide. He was tall for his age and his voice, fortunately, had changed early.

But he couldn't get into the betting shops. Sitting on a park bench he'd found a seedy old con man named Ned Rice, a really convincing charmer with an uppercrust accent whom he'd taken on as partner. It was Ned who sat in the battered Land Rover and got a third. Alex got two-thirds; the ideas were his.

In addition, he'd take bets for a few, a very few, of his mates. When they didn't have two pence to rub together he'd tell them they could bet on margin. He tried to explain it was betting on the future, a concept they loved, since the unmoneyed future was abstract. Anyway, rarely did they lose.

As Alex looked at his reflection in the glass now, his head swaying dozingly with the motion of the train, he thought that was about as much as you could expect. Living on Margin.

He felt his shoulder being shaken, looked up, saw the youngish face of the conductor, heard him ask for the ticket.

Thank God it had only been a light doze, not the deep sleep he feared. He pulled out the ticket . . .

Jesus. The conductor.

Alex's mind flashed to the morning newspaper, not knowing whether her death would be of any interest to the papers or be merely a statistic. But what if the authorities wanted to get hold of Alex enough to put a picture in the paper. And why, anyway, was he so intent on keeping his whereabouts a secret? He didn't know. He merely pondered this with his face turned to the window image of himself as the conductor's punch bit onto his ticket.

The man might remember the face of the boy who got out at Oldham.

Now he was asking Alex if he was all right.

'Never better, guv.' Alex gave him a broad smile. 'Bored, is all.' Alex shook his head. 'School, bloody school.'

The train conductor probably wasn't too long out of it; his uniform and a complexion made pasty by his indoor work made his ferret-face look older. He had a thin nose and thin lips that tilted up in a smile now. 'Thought you'd be 'avin' yer 'olidays round about now.'

'Nah. Not till October.' Alex unzipped a pocket of his rucksack and pulled out a pack of greasy cards. 'You must get a bit of time off from patrolling them corridors. What d'you say to a game? Penny a point, odds against me, can't say fairer than that.' In one smooth motion he had fanned out the pack.

Challenged to a game he knew he'd be a sure loser; cards held no interest for him except insofar as they offered an opportunity for bluffing — for freezing the facial muscles, for hiding feelings. Anyway, he could only play if there was a lot of money in the pot.

The conductor's smile broadened. 'Not with one who handles a pack like that, mate. I've me wife and kiddies t'look out fer.'

He left the carriage.

In his mind's eye, Alex saw him looking at his, Alex's, picture in the paper. *Nah couldn' be 'im, cheeky young bastard. No one'd want to play cards with his mum just dead.*

2

Outside Windermere station there was a rack for bikes. Upon inspecting the four that had been shoved in, Alex found one that hadn't a lock on it. He looked it over carefully, decided it was worth maybe twenty-thirty pounds and left fifty in a grubby envelope he'd rooted from a dustbin. He hoped the owner of the bike would see the envelope forced into the slot where the bike had been.

As he wheeled away, alternately hopping up and pushing with his foot, he imagined this was how a fugitive must feel, guilty or innocent.

He couldn't get across the lake — he probably wouldn't have wanted to take the ferry anyway — but at least, on the bike, once he got to the other side of Windermere and to Coniston Water, he could find tracks inaccessible to cars and thereby get to Boone by a more direct route.

Direct. That was a laugh. It was teatime when he finally skirted the hamlet and dusk was coming on when he got to the Holdsworth property. In the distance he could hear water coursing. The countryside was full of becks and ghylls so that often, in spring, there were parts of Lake land that turned into ballets of water: tiny falls into larger streams; streams into great forces; water flowing into tarns and lakes.

Alex came to the corner of the long fieldstone wall that had once surrounded the house but now only managed to turn a rough corner before it began its disintegration, crumbling away to nothing. It served no purpose, anyway. He went off to the left and followed the wall for a quarter of a mile until it ended. Alex got off the bike and pushed it the rest of the way into the trees.

What he was headed for was the tree house. He and Millie had hammered the boards together three years ago, chiefly for a sanctuary for Millie, somewhere for her to go to get away from the family.

He walked a bit to a large beech tree and saw it. It looked just as he'd remembered. Not only was it well hidden because it was so high up, but even the leafless branches covered it, and the beech was also surrounded by conifers.

Alex laid the bike on its side in the moss and blanketed it in lichen, twigs and dead leaves. Then he walked over to the beech, upended the ladder and started to climb. He was amazed it had all held together for this long. The ladder hadn't rotted and the house itself, when he was up far enough to see inside, looked clean. He wondered if Millie still used it.

Food. Lord, but he was hungry. He dumped his rucksack in the corner, took the gun and ammunition out of his pockets and shoved them into the sack. He tore the wrapping from a cheese and cucumber roll and gulped the sandwich down in four bites. The milk was warm, but he drank the whole container.

He fell asleep still holding thc milk carton.

13

Jury liked Brown's, a hotel that could easily have been missed in the street in Mayfair because of its unpretentious façade. It had always been a favourite place for afternoon tea, with its firelit lounge and tiered cake plates, which was what Madeline Galloway was looking over now.

'You look like your sister,' he had said when he first seen her.

'We've been told that,' she answered, offering him tea.

'I could use a cup, thanks.'

He could not tell whether the next few moments of banal conversation implied relative indifference to death or was a way of avoiding it.

She poured another cup of tea for herself, held the pot aloft by way of question, but Jury shook his head. 'Haven't finished the first.'

'Haven't *started* the first,' she said. And then, 'Did you know Jane well?'

'Well enough,' he responded a little tightly. He did not care what she inferred from that.

'Oh.' She looked into her cup, not at him, kindly.

'You've been working for the family more-or-less as an assistant to Mr Holdsworth? Inspector Kamir wasn't quite clear as to your duties.'

She laughed, and then perhaps thinking laughter was out of place, cut if off. 'More-or-less is right. He's been writing, for years, a study of the Lake poets, though I don't think he's seriously thinking of getting it published. Since he writes from inspiration, very little actual writing gets done.'

'The Inspector said you'd been interviewing people for a librarian's post.'

She sighed. 'No joy there. Who'd want to come to a remote area in the Lakes for the small salary he's offering? And for something as dull as cataloguing books? I should have been more specific in my advert, I expect. It's an enormous library, floor to ceiling, and I can barely reach the top even on a ladder. He thought at first I might as well do it, but, thank you, no. I told him I couldn't especially the foreign-language volumes; and that it would take Lord knows how long at the rate I'm going.'

They were skirting, Jury knew, and thought she did, the issue.

'What would have caused the suicide? Any ideas at all?'

Madeline shook her head. 'Only that the Holdsworths were continually harassing her about Alex. And she wasn't at bottom a happy person.'

'I know, I think, what you mean. There were times when she could shut a person out.' Times he remembered Jane staring out of the window as if she were waiting for someone or something. She was miles away from him. For what? For what was she waiting.

Madeline merely shook her head. 'I thought she loved her son too much to put him through something like this. I can imagine her not being able to go on if something happened to Alex − if he died, say, or went missing for years. I can imagine that. And now he *has* gone missing.'

'No, I wouldn't say missing. "Escape" is a better word. Apparently, through a bathroom window.'

Her laughter released some of the tension. 'That sounds like Alex. But why would he?'

'I don't know; perhaps you can tell me. You just said it sounded like Alex.'

'I mean only that he, well, gets up to all sorts of things.'

'Such as?'

With a shrug of impatience, she asked, 'Does it matter?' She peered inside the teapot, looked as if she had not found what she wanted, and put the top back.

'It might explain . . . something about him. How many children could you imagine finding a parent dead without their breaking down, going into shock − those are the usual reactions.'

'How many times have you had cases where children discover parents dead?'

Had her tone been less hostile, he wouldn't have said it: 'My own. I found my mother dead after a bomb had gutted our house.'

She looked off into the fire, said only, 'I'm sorry.'

'The point is that police at the scene said the boy was like ice;

90

he didn't cry; he was as hostile as you just now; he wouldn't answer questions, or when he did he lied. He told the inspector he had no other family.'

Her head came up and she said, 'That's not a lie.' The words came out flat, uninflected.

'What about you? You're his aunt, you're fond of him, and you don't appear to share the opinion of his grandparents.'

She had taken one of the several scatter cushions on the sofa and was holding it against her like soft armour. 'There is another family member Alex likes. Adam, his great-grandfather.' She smiled. 'To tell the truth, that's who Alex reminds me of. Adam's a curmudgeonly old man who prefers to live in a swank retirement home and make *visits* to his *own* home. It's all his, you know.'

' "All his"? The house, you mean?'

'*All* of it. Tarn House — the estate — and the money. The lot.'

'You say "the lot" as if there were a great deal of it.'

'Well, good heavens, there is.' She looked at him squarely, not dropping her eyes, not attempting to distract him with the pot or the plate from the inference he might be drawing. 'It's hard to know what goes on in Adam Holdsworth's mind; he undoubtedly likes it that way, you know, to keep people on edge. He certainly does not appear to hold his son and daughter-in-law in high regard.' She smiled slightly. 'That Person' is how he refers to Genevieve.' She reached for a small meringue, inspected it, put it on her plate, untasted. 'Whenever Alex and Jane came down from London, Adam always made a point of being on hand.'

She let that hang. Jury said, 'In other words, Adam Holdsworth liked them.'

'Especially Alex. I've seen the two of them, Alex pushing the wheelchair, escape to some part of the grounds and have everyone looking for them. They plotted, I think. There's nothing that man likes so much as a trick.'

'Then Alex, perhaps his mother, would have expectations.'

She lit a cigarette with a porcelain lighter and sat there, her knees together, leaning forward, looking thoughtfully into the fire.

'To be sure.'

'And now its just — Alex? That is, for most of this "lot".' He thought perhaps the smile would draw her out. It didn't.

'I don't understand what anyone's expectations have to do with my sister's death,' she said frostily, as she flicked ash into a floral tray.

'I'm sorry.' He had seen her, sized her up somewhat, which was all he could do at the moment. 'Could I take you to your train?'

She had put out her cigarette and risen, looking down at him speculatively. 'I've ordered a taxi. I've still got over an hour.'

Which she didn't want to spend with him, clearly.

Jury pulled out one of his cards and handed it to her. 'I'd better be going. Please ring me if you remember anything.'

'What is there to remember?'

A great deal, thought Jury, as they rose. 'Incidentally, I think I know someone who might just fit that librarian's position. He's good with languages. I wouldn't worry about the salary end; he's just scraping by as it is.'

'I'd be eternally grateful.'

'I'll ring him. He's quite brilliant, really. Eccentric. Likes to do odd things.' Jury studied the cake plate. 'Anything to get away from the family.'

14

'If Yngie J. Malsteem can't drive her out, no one can.' said Melrose, as much to the stuffed cheetah Scroggs had dragged in to the Jack and Hammer as to Scroggs himself.

Dick Scroggs turned to another page of the *Bald Eagle*, whose paper wings he always managed to spread all over the bar.

'Would that be one of your guitarist friends, my lord?'

Melrose sighed. 'Get me another half of Old Peculier.' He shoved his glass forward.

'Yes, My Lord.'

'Oh, for heaven's sake, stop calling me that and stop talking down your nose. Ever since you painted 'saloon' over 'bar' on the door you've been doing it.' *Saloon* had been scrolled in white paint on the frosted glass; it was part of Dick's campaign for a stylish new decor. 'It's all because of the Blue Parrot. We told you Sly's place was too far outside the village to be giving you competition. Though God knows his camel looks better than your cheetah. It's moulting.'

Dick knifed off the collar of foam and said (still looking over half-glasses he'd also taken to wearing), 'I find it lends the place a bit of style, even if some don't.' The big stuffed animal, poised to strike, was crouching by the huge fireplace. Its fur was rubbed, even bald in places, and its front teeth were missing. It bore an eerie resemblance to Mrs Withersby, who had come to char, stayed to drink and was now snoring beside the cheetah, an objet d'art that had been part of some hunting buff's estate that Trueblood had bought up. There were a few other objets d'art, also, deployed about the Jack and Hammer, such as the monkey hanging from a vine of rope.

Melrose pointed out that Dick's new menu had several oddities on it that it could do without.

'Well, I'm sure my wife's every bit as good a cook as Trevor Sly,' said Dick, huffily shaking out the *Bald Eagle*.

'*Any*body's as good a cook as Trevor Sly. That's not the point.
I don't see why you have to try to change the old pub. I don't
like change.'

'You mustn't be so upset Miss Rivington's gone, sir.'

'I'm upset that Mr Jury might go the same way,' muttered
Melrose.

'What?'

'Nothing.' Melrose stabbed his cigarette into the ashtray, felt
the chill air as the 'Saloon' door opened. 'Hell's bells, its six p.m.
where *is* everyone?'

'Right here, old sweat,' said Marshall Trueblood, Long
Piddleton's Everyone.

It did at least give Melrose a certain satisfaction to be able to
wipe the smile off Trueblood's face. 'I have news for you.'

'Interesting?' Trueblood nodded to Dick; 'My usual, Mr
Scroggs.' As Dick drifted over to the optics, Trueblood called,

'And if it's watered down like last time, I'm going to the Blue
Parrot.'

'Ha! As if Sly's *ain't*.'

'Well, his water comes from a well. What news?'

'Jury's getting married.'

'Of course he is. We haven't settled definitely on a date, though.
Vivian –'

'I don't mean *our* version, I mean *his*.' Melrose raised his glass,
disgusted.

'He doesn't have a version, don't be silly.' Trueblood refused
to be ruffled. 'Who the hell would he marry anyway?'

'Look, there *are* women in London.' The distant *brr* of Scrogg's
telephone sounded as Trueblood waved the suggestion aside. 'I
can't imagine what you're talking about.'

'For you, My Lord,' called Scroggs. 'It's Mr Ruthven.'

'Why must people be bothering me here?' He marched heavily
round to the public bar.

. . .And returned like a sleepwalker. Melrose sat down and stared
at Trueblood. 'She's dead.'

'You mean Agatha *finally* – ?' He was absolutely gleeful. Then
his face darkened. 'Still, it won't be the same here without the
old finagler.'

'Not her. Jury's lady-friend. And he's been suspended.'

Trueblood was tapping a pink Sobranie on his polished thumbnail and raised an equally well-manicured eyebrow when he looked from Melrose to Dick Scroggs. 'He's really gone round the bend this time, Dick. Give him a drink.'

'Just did,' said Scroggs, sharing Trueblood's opinion of the report on Jury.

A new voice chimed in, although the sound was far from bell-like; it was more a rusty clapper hitting dull metal. Mrs Withersby, whose glass was as empty as the plate she passed at Sunday service (there's some ain't any more Chris'en than . . . she'd tell the vicar), came down the bar to utter her dark prognosis, which would become darker the longer she had to wait for a refill. 'Fam'bly allus 'as been a bit, you-know — ' Here she made small circles round her temple with her finger and circles with her glass on the bar. She had a cigarette behind the ear but she meant to hang on to it, asking Marshall Trueblood for one of his 'fag ends,' and laughing uproariously at her own joke. 'Look at 'im come all over white, 'e 'as. Stout's not good fer that . . . ah, thankye, thankye,' she concluded as Melrose shoved the untouched glass towards her. Happy now with her fag and her half pint, she shuffled away.

Melrose's eyes were still glazed over. He shook his head, quickly, trying to clear it.

'Listen, old trout, you need a holiday.'

'We just got back from Italy, you idiot.' He was so upset over the news he actually took a green Sobranie when his friend offered it. 'I'm going to the Lake District.' He drew in on the cigarette, coughed.

'Don't be ridiculous.' Trueblood shuddered.

'Southey?' The name seemed to taste, in Melrose's mouth, as unfamiliar as the bright green cigarette he dashed out.

Scroggs shook his head, his eyes still clamped on his paper. 'Cumbria, My Lord. North.'

'Is Theo still open?' Melrose checked his watch.

'Why? Yes,' said Trueblood. 'That money-grubber stays open every night until seven, seven-thirty. You're not going *there?*'

Melrose didn't answer as he hurried out of the door.

The door of the Wrenn's Nest Book Shoppe stood open, all ready to admit March winds of gale force so long as they blew a customer in.

Theo Wrenn Browne, proprietor, sat like a hawk atop his library ladder marking up the price of a first edition. He declared himself an antiquarian book dealer, but Melrose generally found him either deep in some American bestselling woman author's décolletage (the picture on the back) or deep in his cash drawer as if he were robbing his own shop.

This evening, however, he was up at just the right height to look down on Melrose Plant, whom he disliked intensely, although not so much as Marshall Trueblood, whom he absolutely loathed, most probably because Trueblood's sexual persuasion, despite his flying the colours that Theo loved to see, was actually in doubt; whereas there was no closet stout enough (in a manner of speaking) to contain Theo Wrenn Browne, even though he thought he was hiding from everyone back in the cobwebbed corners. Theo Wrenn Browne was such a screaming queen he would have stood out at the London Silver Vaults.

Any way of demonstrating his superiority over Melrose Plant (Long Pidd's most popular citizen) or Marshall Trueblood (the village's most colourful one) made him nearly choke with pleasure. Thus finding out that his own knowledge of the Lake poets surpassed Plant's made Theo almost swing on his perch. 'You mean Robert Southey, I take it.'

'Well, are there any more Southey poets?' asked Melrose innocently.

Sniffing sarcasm (where none was intended), Theo's *no* was as snappish as the book he snapped shut. He came down and rolled the ladder along to the far side of the shelves and was annoyed that he hadn't a Southey edition. 'Here's a *Collected Works*. Wordsworth, Coleridge, De Quincey, Southey.' He handed down the heavy book.

'It's not the poetry. I've read *Lyrical Ballads*. Something on their lives, in addition to all the usual gibberish about Dorothy and William. And don't you have anything shorter? I've only got till tomorrow morning to bone up. How about one of those A-level booklets?'

Theo Wrenn Browne looked shocked. 'Don't tell me you'd stoop to a student's crib-manual.'

'Yes. Do you have one on the first half of the nineteenth century?'

'I don't have *any* of them. I don't encourage that sort of thing.

Here.' He handed Melrose a small book. *Guide to the Lake District* by William Wordsworth. 'One of the better-known volumes on the Lakes.'

'A guide? Do I want a guide?'

Said Theo, prissily, 'You obviously need one.' He returned his eyes to the shelf. 'The West is here. That's Thomas West,' he said, looking down at Melrose and mouthing the name as if his customer were retarded. 'But I believe Wordsworth refers to it in his own book.'

'Give it to me. Might as well. There's one on Dorothy's letters. Might as well let me have that too.'

Theo pursed his mouth. 'The West is rare. Expensive.'

Melrose sighed and got out his chequebook.

PART II
FAT MAN'S AGONY

15

'I'll put my teeth in when I damned well feel like it,' said Adam Holdsworth to one of the tastefully dressed nurses who comprised part of the Castle Howe staff.

No uniforms here, but they still talked nurse-talk. 'Come now, Mr Holdsworth,' Miss Rupert said in her best wheedling voice, 'we're *ever* so handsome with our teeth in.' Miss Rupert did her best to keep the ends of her mouth tucked up in a tiny smile.

'You may be, Miss Rhubarb, but not me.'

'Ru*pert*, as you very well know.' The smile-tucks vanished. 'Your teeth, Mr Holdsworth – '

'For Gods sake, woman, I'm eighty-nine and look like Alas poor-Yorick, fresh from the grave. Now, get that blood-pressure cuff off and get out of my way!' Stringy as a runner-bean she was, but when she clamped your wrist it was the same as wearing manacles. He pushed the lever on his electric wheelchair and Miss Rupert had to jump back.

Castle Howe had nothing appended to its name (such as 'nursing' or 'retirement' home) that would tarnish the image the brochure meant to convey of grand vistas and luxurious appointments. It was, of course, both, in a sense, there being several nurses, two doctors who came in part-time and two resident doctor-psychiatrists who lived in the gatehouse and got more business than all the rest of them, entertainment opportunities being otherwise negligible. None of the staff wore uniforms, however; their clothes were simple but expensively tailored. Everything was done to keep the 'guests' (never 'patients', whether they fell face down or died 'quietly' in their sleep) – to keep their minds off illness, mild or terminal.

Those who took up residence at Castle Howe were merely coincidentally sixty and up, or as Mrs Colin-Jackson, the owner manager, put it, in their 'golden years'. This was the phrase she used to describe Castle Howe's prospective 'guests'. And the residents lived not in mere 'rooms' but in 'suites', the difference being that the 'suites' had a small alcove in which there was a fridge, a Teasmade, and a kettle. The 'suites' were not numbered but named with any name that might fit the Lakeland heritage: the 'Wordsworth', the 'Coleridge', the 'De Quincey' (which was Adam Holdsworth's, who tried to live up to the name by filling the room with cigar smoke, since opium was at a premium), and other poetical names, reaching even into Scotland for 'Burns' and 'Scott'.

It was very difficult to describe Castle Howe without a fulsome use of italics. Adverts in *The Lady, Country Life*, and occasionally in the *Times* assured the prospective client of its *wondrous* scenery and its *splendid* appointments. All words that bore the stigma of nursing or retirement homes were avoided. Both ads and brochure were artfully composed by Mrs Colin-Jackson, obviously aimed at the well-to-do who wanted to dump their rich old mums and aunties and grans who might hang on for two more months or two more decades.

The colour brochure displayed a living room and a music room stuffed with antiques and dressed in William Morris wall-paper complemented by gorgeous mouldings and silk curtains. It also showed a candlelit dining room worthy of an expensive hotel, with its linen and white-jacketed waiter apparently taking the order of two men and a woman who looked rich enough to spend their time in takeover bids for airlines and computer companies.

The advert, with its pen-and-ink drawing of the manor house certainly did not draw attention to the small-print stipulation that prospective residents must be 'largely ambulatory' and must have a 'clean psychiatric record', both phrases so ambiguous that they could be translated in any way that Mrs Colin-Jackson wished. Thus, she was in a position to decide for herself whether the elderly prospect would be suitable, a decision taken on the basis of money only.

It was troublesome to Mrs Colin-Jackson that there were, among the *middle*-class (rather than the upper to which she really catered), daughters and sons and nephews and nieces so self-sacrificing that they would spend their last penny to see that Mummy or Uncle John could live in posh surroundings. Last pennies held little interest for Mrs Colin-Jackson. In a case such as one where bequests would be unlikely and the children were intent upon walking around and actually assessing the accommodation, Mrs Colin-Jackson would explain that 'largely ambulatory' allowed for a cane or two and their mummy could make her way round only with a walker. If all else failed, there simply would be no suite available, but, yes, the name could be added to the list after the names of the Duchess of Wanderby and Viscountess Stuart.

If a resident became especially troublesome, Mrs Colin-Jackson would kick him or her out by ringing up the family and telling them that their golden oldster had suddenly become unmanageable — throwing bits of food or making advances to the doctor; she would apologise profusely but insist the resident be removed. A week's grace was permitted, or if the relations were willing to pay half-again the cost, a month's notice could be managed.

Adam Holdsworth knew all this, of course. He was the only resident there who had chosen to come, and chosen it over the protests of his relations, made nervous by the thought of money walking out of the door, perhaps to end up as a bequest to the dear woman who had overseen Adam's golden years. There was an irony in all this, thought Adam: the residents were treated far better by owner and staff than they would have been at home, where they would have been ignored unless a change in one's will was mentioned. Mrs Colin-Jackson's money-grabbing didn't bother Adam at all since she had to pay dearly (in time and in patience) for things like Mr Wynchcomb's planting his bowl of Weetabix on one of the Dunster sisters' heads. Not only put up with it, but smarmily, as if she thought them to be quite the pranksters, but they wouldn't do it again, now would they? If poor old Wynchcomb had pulled that prank at home, he would have been locked in the attic.

None of this was illegal or even by a stretch of the imagination, dishonest. The rooms pictured on the brochure did indeed exist, although the angle of the camera might have been wrong; and the food was extremely good, for all that it was served up by people who knew only four words of English.

Adam had got Millie Thale to wheel him up to Castle Howe, where his interview with Mrs Colin-Jackson had been satisfactorily concluded by the exchange of several thousands of pounds to stretch the interpretation of 'Largely ambulatory'. She had smiled and smiled and said that she would need time to converse with her 'staff' and Adam had said, *Go on, I'll give you fifteen minutes.* And still she smiled smarmily.

He knew the only person she wanted to converse with was his banker at Lloyds'. And since Adam had chosen the place himself, he clearly wasn't being tossed aside. Not only that, his home was so near that he would (he said) be visiting his relations quite often.

Then he had rolled himself into the brochure-pictured high ceilinged and silk-draped library where an old girl in handsome tweeds, holding a Bible, was ministering to a nonexistent audience. *Don't bother about Miss Smithson*, Mrs Colin-Jackson had told him, *her family is coming to pick her up. We really can't have this annoyance in Castle Howe.*

Thus it was that Adam had moved into the De Quincey suite.

Mummy is so independent; I know she couldn't abide the restraints of a nursing home.

Over the two years he'd been living there, it always amazed him that the scenario was so predictable. He enjoyed making his unambulatory self highly visible when he knew an 'interview' was coming up because it drove Mrs Colin-Jackson to distraction. Through gritted teeth she would point out that 'our Mr Holdsworth can get round in that wheelchair faster than a marathon runner' and then bray with laughter.

She had several times requested that Adam make himself scarce (not to put too fine a point on it) while she was talking to prospects. Naturally, he didn't; he would sit in the wide door of the Southey Room with the stocking cap on and his teeth out when the pigeons were in that lushly furnished drawing room being bilked for two thousand a month to take on Mummy.

To hear that 'Mummy' or 'Dad' or 'Auntie' *had* to have their independence and then to see the old frails practically brought in baskets was testament to the small print of Mrs Colin-Jackson's contracts. Actually, though, after they got to Castle Howe, they began perking up, tossing the Weetabix and duelling with canes in the lush environs of the conservatory.

And there was the brochure's much-touted freedom of the grounds. Anyone was free to leave at any time. Given a two-thousand pound security deposit and a waiting list, any guest was free to fall off the ramparts or into the pond as far as Mrs Colin-Jackson was concerned.

Indeed, it was considered quite a social plum to have one's barmy old relative in Castle Howe (*Auntie Florence? Oh, yes, after that hectic world cruise she felt she* must *have a bit of a rest and was quite* mad *for the chance of living at Castle Howe*; when in reality — a scarce commodity at the Castle — Aunt Flo had never got nearer a cruise than her rear garden pond where she screamed obscenities to any luckless person who was taking the public footpath).

So he had moved in to thoroughly enjoy a number of 'annoyances' — if one considered things like the flaming and long-standing row between the Dunsters or Colin-Jackson's sidekick, Miss Maltings, who sat near the entrance, eternally knitting black wool. Adam catalogued such incidents in a leather notebook with a Mont Blanc pen held in a hand that was just a little trembly, something like the idling of a motor engine. He could still write, although sometimes he thought the result looked a little like a page zipped off one of those electrocardiogram machines.

He had an electric wheelchair with which he would, when things got dull, race about the grounds to see how many residents he could tumble or autos he could bring to a screeching halt. It had almost as many gears as a motor car. Once in a while he would ring up the house and ask for Millie to come round and give him a ride outside, through the grounds and garden. He liked Millie's company. The only ones at the house he trusted unconditionally were Millie and her cat.

His time at Tarn House was spent largely in the kitchen which was warm and cosy and delicious-smelling and where he was welcome but not fawned over. On many of these visits he insisted on a staring contest with the cat Sorcerer. It annoyed him no end that he, Adam, was always the first to look away. That cat was almost enough to make him believe in reincarnation. In one of the cat's former lives, he must have been Rasputin. Mrs Callow, when she wasn't imbibing (with the butler), cooked the vegetables, and Millie always had something simmering in a pot. Like her mother, Millie was a born cook. He liked to wheel about in the kitchen hiding pence and pounds in the crockery for her to find later. He wasn't concerned about Callow's finding it; she couldn't see straight for the port.

Finding very *large* sums in the crockery (so to speak) was, of course, what the rest of the family was waiting for. He couldn't live forever, but he could do long enough to make them question mortality. He often felt sorry for Crabbe and could hardly blame him for retreating into his world of poets and painters. Why was it so many decent people made such messes of their lives? Coleridge, De Quincey — not, of course, Wordsworth. But Adam imagined if he himself could zip round the hills and vales with a loving sister to hang on to his every proclamation, well, he'd feel like rattling off an ode, too.

Jane. He frowned. He had liked his grandson's wife merely for having a son like Alex.

Genevieve was not saddened by Jane's death but furious with Alex, who had claimed he had no family.

Damned right, thought Adam Holdsworth, sadly.

2

Lady Cray had been one of those who came *with* her wardens: her daughter and son-in-law. With her little black hat and large black bag, dressed in the finest silk, Lady Cray was all vague smiles, as if she couldn't remember why she was here or with whom she had arrived.

She walked away while Mrs Colin-Jackson was selling the young Crays a bill of goods. Adam, who'd been sitting just outside the doorway of the lounge, thought there was more here than met the eye and followed her down. Lady Cray seemed to be wandering aimlessly in and out of drawing room, games room and library and finally found what she wanted in the dining room. She picked up the silver place-settings from a table for two and put them in her black bag, which she closed with a satisfied little snap. When she turned to leave and saw Adam, she simply smiled her dimpled smile, opened the bag again and brought out a wad of notes as big as a fist. Peeling off a fifty, she offered it to him, 'if you can keep your mouth shut'. Her voice was so softly decorous, she might be offering him a glass of sherry.

'Generous of you, but I've got too much money already,' said Adam.

'Ah. Then would you care for a spoon? The silver's surprisingly good.'

'No, thanks. I've got my own.'

He was hoping that Lady Cray would take up residence here. *She* certainly needed her independence. She didn't seem to mind if he wheeled right beside her as she made her way farther along the sumptuously decorated hallway.

Adam took out his precious Mont Blanc pen and made an entry in his dairy. As he wheeled along beside her, he filled her in on Castle Howe. Good accommodation and surprisingly good food. You could eat in the dining room or in your own room. Nothing was bad as long as you knew they were all great nits who ran the place. Colin-Jackson always disappeared at the cocktail hour with a bottle of gin and she'd come to the dining room and have a rave-up with the guests.

'How nice,' said Lady Cray as she entered the library and looked around, brow furrowed.

'There're some bits of ivory over there on the shelf if you fancy it.'

She sighed and turned away. 'Tusks of elephants.' She shook her head. 'Isn't it dreadful, the poaching?'

Adam agreed, and since nothing else interested her, they turned and left. French doors lay at the end of the hall, leading to the gardens, and he suggested they take a 'walk'. 'I hope you decide to take up residence here, Lady Cray. Be nice to have a kleptomaniac.' He stopped. 'No offence. I just assumed you weren't a collector.'

They went down the path into the gardens and Lady Cray began gathering flowers. Soon she had quite a little bouquet, which she put in the bottomless bag. 'I'm quite deft, you know. I'm used to much chancier places. Harrods is a favourite. A dreadful place if you take it seriously. I believe it's Harrods my daughter and son-in-law have requested to arrange my funeral.'

'Didn't know Harrods did funerals. I'll have to tell Genevieve.'

'Genevieve?'

'My daughter-in-law.'

'Oh. Well, I'm sure I shall enjoy it here,' said Lady Cray, picking a bloom near the wheelchair. 'Anything to get away from my family.'

'Can't say I blame you!'

'Oh, do you know them too?' she asked absently, her grey eyes looking about as she seated herself on one of the wrought-iron benches placed among the box hedges.

'No, but I know mine. Just send for your solicitors and watch them hit the whisky!'

'Absolutely, Mr Holdsworth. All I have to do is mention my will and Beau — he's my son-in-law — gets the shakes and rattles the glass against the vodka decanter. I do believe its making him an alcoholic. I only hope he doesn't break the decanter. It's Lalique. Look, there's a robin.'

He wagged a finger at her. 'Don't open that bag.'

She laughed. Lady Cray had quite beautiful skin, he noticed. 'One feels at times a bit sorry for them.'

'This one doesn't.'

Again she laughed. 'Ah, you know what I mean. My daughter Lucia is not a bad person at all. But so *weak* that she lets that husband of hers breathe for her, nearly. I wonder sometimes if that's why I do it — take things, I mean. To justify my child's own weakness.'

'That's certainly a charitable way of looking at things. Kingsley would like to hear that bit of insight. He's one of the resident shrinks.'

'How is he with the "whilst balance of mind was disturbed" gambit? Or the "undue influence" ploy? Lord knows what they'll do when my will is read.'

'Hmm. Don't think it's ever come up here. Oh, people *die* here, don't get me wrong. People *die* here, naturally. But I can't remember anyone contesting wills. Kojak probably keeps that mum.'

'Kojak?'

'Short for Colin-Jackson. As long as she gets her bequests, police could drag every lake around for bodies, she wouldn't care.'

Lady Cray had by now another little bouquet, which she arranged while she asked, 'You mean no one's been murdered here?'

Damn! but he wished he'd got his teeth in because his mouth dropped. 'The way you said it, and with your nose in those flowers, you'd think it was a daily happening.' Adam rubbed his hands together. The arthritis was acting up. 'Not a bad idea, come to think of it, as long as it's not me.'

'Doesn't it bother you someone might? I'm quite sure one or two little attempts have been made on me. There!' and she drew the little stem of a winter daisy though the buttonhole of his jacket.

This time he remembered to keep his mouth shut when he registered his astonishment. 'What? How?'

'Oh, nothing significant — and certainly not successful.' She brought her gloved hand up to her lips as if to hold in the little laugh. 'I believe I was pushed into the path of a London bus. Not hurt, just a little dusty.'

'Good God . . .' Adam grew thoughtful. 'You know, we've had a recent, well, tragedy, I'd call it. Suicide. Especially tragic because it was my great-grandson's mother. He's an ace and was very attached to her, and in my family, love isn't something you come by every day.' Adam told Lady Cray the little he knew.

'You think it was murder, then.' She plucked from the flower a dead petal and blew it from the tip of her finger.

'What? I didn't say that! Look, they might all be a bunch of horses' arses — pardon the language — but I don't think they'd stoop . . .'

She sighed wearily. 'Really, you know perfectly well they'd stoop until they crawled.' Lady Cray's brow furrowed. 'But why her? Did she have expectations — oh, how unmannerly of me. To ask about one's will is as tasteless as asking about one's politics.' Adam was following his own line. 'Can't picture my sons trying it. George is an idiot and Crabbe's been writing this voluminous account of the Lake school for a hundred years. Genevieve, though, you've got to watch out for. She married my son for the money, naturally, and she's a good twenty years younger. Probably came out of the chorus line of *Cats*. Trouble is that if I leave *him* half a million, *she'd* be running his show. So you know what I've done?' He leered and cocked his head.

'What?'

'The money's his only if he takes a trip round the world. Alone.' Adam sniggered. 'The way I see it, if he takes off the manacles for a year and is off meeting new people — women, I hope . . . Those cruises are sexual orgies, I've heard, and the man's only sixty.'

'No one that young should be stuck for the rest of his life in an unhappy marriage.'

'And if being away from her doesn't wake him up, well —'

'That's quite clever of you.'

'Glad you think so.'

'If only *I* could think of something like that! My problem is that if I don't leave them most of the money, Beau will certainly contest the will, and since I have wandered from the straight-and-narrow, if you know what I mean . . .'

Adam lowered his voice and looked about. 'Ever been caught?'

'Oh, yes. It was my grandson, Andrew, who came down and bailed me out. He's my favourite person in the world; naturally, I'm leaving the large part of my money to him. Well, he would come to the station looking very serious —' Here Lady Cray put on a mask of sobriety. — and as soon as we got to the car, he broke out in peals of laughter. Like church bells. It made me feel as if there was hope for humanity.'

'Right. what does he do?'

'Andrew's very bookish. He got a first at Cambridge and his parents were absolutely furious when he opened a bookshop. I visit frequently but don't take anything.'

'Sounds like Alex. He's *my* person. My great-grandson, sixteen years old. What his mother's death will do to him . . . he's not easily broken, though.' Adam brightened up when he said, 'The boy's been expelled from school three or four times.'

'How delightful. What did he do?'

'Playing the ponies — he concocted an elaborate scheme and even let his mates in on the betting. And once for fighting.' Adam drove pretend-punches in the air.

'He sounds lovely.' Lady Cray's expression changed. She looked off in the direct of the Castle and sighed. 'They're signalling.'

Adam saw the relations waving frantically, as if she might be taking off on a voyage from which she'd never return. 'Too bad.'

'We'll have time to clear it up, I expect, the suicide or the murder.' The black bag rattled as she lifted it.

'What've you got in there besides the silver? A gun?' He chuckled at his little joke.

'Yes. People in our position can never be too careful, can they?'

Adam nearly fell out of his chair. 'Didn't Kojak frisk you? Let me see it, let me see it.'

'No.' She put her hand on the arm of his chair, indicating they really must go. 'We'll have time for a chat. If we're still alive.' She looked at him brightly. 'Come on, then. They're getting hysterical.

'Tell me,' asked Adam, wheeling back down the garden path, 'are you a *real* kleptomaniac, or is it all an act?'

She laughed. 'There *are* a few things I feel compelled to take. For the rest, yes, it *is* an act. But one has to do a bit of larking around or go crazy. Old age, if it's nothing else, should at least be theatrical, don't you know?'

'What are the few things?'

'Hair ribbons and chocolate.'

'That's damned interesting. Listen, can you pick pockets too?'

In answer, she handed him his Mont Blanc pen.

Adam Holdsworth nearly strangled with laughter.

'Did you think I was fooling with the flowers for nothing?'

He was *damned* sorry he hadn't put in his teeth.

But he was glad he'd worn his bright blue sweater.

16

There was one thing he had to say about Wordsworth, Melrose thought, as he sat in the Swan having coffee and reading the poet's *Guide to the Lakes*, William Wordsworth had his priorities straight: the man had an eye for an Inn. Oh, not just the venerable Swan with its old beams, comfortable floral-chintz armchairs and sofas encircling a roaring fireplace – not only this one, but a compendium of others. Wordsworth, teetotaller that he was, was also a man who knew that tourists to the area, having viewed the scenes he told them to view, and from heights that Melrose had no intention of familiarising himself with – Wordsworth knew these walkers among the fells would be dying for a drink. He was, therefore, quite scrupulous in pointing out to his reader that there would be, near to hand, following one or other transcendent walking-and-viewing experience, an Inn where they could partake of rest and refreshment.

Some of these Inns were named – such as the Larches, at the foot of Windermere; but for the most part they were simply called Inns. What, he wondered, was the modern penchant for referring to *all* houses open to the public as 'pubs'? Wordsworth called them Inns. The Saxons called them Inns. Could one possibly look at the White Hart in Scole or the New Inn in Amersham or the Old Silent in Stanbury and think only of a 'public house'? Did that famous little band of storytellers leave the Tabard 'pub' behind them as they made their way to Canterbury? Did thirsty Salopians, he wondered, say of Ludlow's lovely, half timbered Feathers, 'Let's go down the pub . . .?'

These reflections led him back to Long Piddleton's old inn, the Man with a Load of Mischief, sadly untenanted for over ten years. He would cycle up there occasionally, giving Mindy (who was once the proprietor's dog) one of her infrequent forays into the world of exercise, remove his bicycle clips and walk around. In winter snow sometimes drifted to window level; in autumn, a dead leaf would skitter like steel across the cobbled courtyard. Mindy would sniff round the drains and the crusted duck pond, and Melrose wondered if animals remembered.

Sometimes he wished he couldn't but, then perhaps Wordsworth had something. Perhaps memory was invention. Or, perhaps, as with Proust, once could absolutely lay claim to the past, could reconstruct it, call it back.

He went back to Dorothy's rather amazing descriptions of the surrounding fells and her commentaries on her and William's walks. His sister constantly referred to him as 'Wm':

> Wm. and I returned from Picnick on Scafell . . . Coleridge wants to walk to Helvellyn . . . Wm very tired.
>
> I walked with Coleridge and Wm up the Lane by the Church, and then lingered with Coleridge in the garden. John and Wm were both gone to bed . . .

Wm, Wum . . . It thrummed pleasantly in Melrose's ear as he snapped shut the book.

Melrose paid his bill, walked from the lounge and saw, in a glass case in the entry-room, a china plate round which was printed a line from one of Wordsworth's poems, a question, Melrose vaguely remembered from his reading, that Wordsworth had put to Coleridge or De Quincey, having met up with him on one of his walks:
'Who hath not seen the wonderful Swan?'
Who, indeed?

Earlier, he had overshot Ambleside and the road that would get him over to the other part of the Lakes and Boone. Thus, he had stopped off in Grasmere at the tourist information centre and been told by the helpful lady there that, yes, certainly Wry Nose Pass and Hard Knott would be far more direct way to Wasdale Head and Wast Water; but it was quite an 'iffy' little road. Fortunately, the weather was fine, he and his car wouldn't have to contend with snow and ice.

Melrose didn't care for the sound of that, but since the

alternative was to drive back to Windermere and take a circuitous route from there, he decided to take the 'iffy' road.

It had been a little after one o'clock when he left the centre and he thought it might be helpful to poke about Grasmere, Wordsworth's old village, picking up what he could, taking in the sights. It was a lovely place, despite its commercial bent. The car parks, taken together, were nearly as large as the village itself. He stopped in the perfumery and sent toilet water to Agatha and Ada Crisp. He made sure Ada's was slightly larger than Agatha's, in case they met. He also sent the gentleman's version to Marshall Trueblood. The mingled scents in the Jack and Hammer might cover those of the cheetah and Mrs Withersby.

He stopped in the book shop and picked up a copy of one of Dorothy Wordsworth's journals.

He stopped in a tiny little place that made gingerbread and shipped a smallish quantity to Agatha and a larger to his cook, Martha. To Martha's order he added a container of rum butter.

He stopped in a little tea shop and bought a bun, which he ate standing up while reading a bit of a 1733 edition of *The Kendal Weekly Courant* that was hanging on the wall: *'Sir, though I am but a woman (and upon that account apprehenfive of being laughed at for appearing in your Courant), yet I can't help telling the author, whoever he is, of the last copy of Verfes you made publick, and he abufed QUADRILLA after a very scandalous manner.'*

Melrose munched on his bun and mediated on this letter, sleepily. It had been a harsh and unbroken drive from Northants and he decided he needed more than the bun for sustenance, went to his car and headed back towards the Swan.

Now, having had his lunch in the venerable Swan, he knew he was going to have to face that further drive if he meant to get to Boone by late afternoon. Still, when he saw Dove Cottage, on the road back to Ambleside, he decided he must see it. A guided tour would give him a quick fix on the Pond poets, and, besides, he was beginning to feel a certain camaraderie with Wum.

Dove Cottage had once been a pub called the Dove and Olive Branch. He learned this from the young man who faced his little group of tourists in a very small room of dark burnished floor boards and timbers. It was the main room. Altogether, Melrose thought, Wordsworth and Dorothy's home was more the size of a Wendy-house than a real one. And the poet was hardly a tiny man. Yet, for all its petite structure, Dove Cottage struck Melrose as the paradigm of the English cottage, that amalgam of opposites: how could a house be drafty and cosy at the same time? Sparsely furnished and pleasantly cramped?

. . . and, good Lord, the young man was telling them that it wasn't just the poet and his sister who occupied the house; the Coleridges, the Southeys and their various children had *all* free-loaded here, and *all* at one time.

Melrose looked about him. The little place had at one brief period housed thirteen people? *Thirteen?* And at one point De Quincey, too? Sitting here having a smoke, no doubt.

Then he thought, Well, it wouldn't seem any more crowded than having tea with Agatha in Plague Alley.

His small fund of knowledge about one of the greatest of his country's poets embarrassed him. Oh, yes, he admired *The Prelude* and 'Ode: Intimations of Immortality.' He'd have to be an idiot not to.

Melrose had to admit it, though.

He preferred Sam to Wum.

Coleridge was a *voyant* somewhat in the manner of Rimbaud, although not so conscious of it and certainly not so extreme. As Melrose hit the narrow road in the Langdales called Wry Nose Pass, he thought of Jim Morrison, mysteriously buried in that grave in Paris.

And he thought, most of all, of his friend Jury. How had he stood it? To be on the point of actually marrying and to have the woman either kill herself or be murdered? To come under suspicion *oneself* as the killer?

As he negotiated a bend, Melrose tried not to think of himself and Marshall Trueblood doing their silly act in Venice, making up that absurd story . . .

Perhaps it was as well that he was driving on a killer road. It stopped him thinking about anything but getting off the damned thing.

Once out of danger, he pulled his Japanese car into the car park of one of those Inns mentioned by Wordsworth, and simply let his head fall against the steering wheel.

That was the lady's idea of 'iffy'?

The Swaledale rams he'd passed, smitten with blue blobs, would have had even more fun staring if he'd been driving his Bentley.

2

What car to take had presented a problem. If one were applying for post of librarian, one probably wouldn't arrive in a Bentley or Rolls. He supposed he should be grateful to the Japanese, even though he couldn't get the damned thing up much over ninety on the M6. And it made noises. But it hugged the road like the fell sheep.

His clothes had presented another problem. Last evening, he had instructed Ruthven to pack old clothes, tatty ones.

'My Lord, you do not own any tatty clothes.' the butler had replied, seeming offended that he might allow His Lordship's suits and sweaters to stagger downward, like old drunks, into the gutters of pulled threads and pills.

'Hells bells, there must be something that would make me look like an out-of-work librarian.' Melrose was inspecting one of his hand-sewn shirts; he tossed it on the bed in disgust; it was a masterpiece of tailoring. Why was he so self-indulgent? Why hadn't he bought from the Oxfam shops, like a sensible person.

Ruthven pursed his lips and ran his fingers over jackets, trousers, robes. He pulled out a suit, holding it away from him with a frown. 'This one might do, My Lord. It's all shapeless. Deconstructed, I'd say.'

Melrose heaved a sigh. 'Ruthven, that's *Armani*.'

Ruthven, a disciple of Savile Row and Bond Street, was not about to be awed by some foreign tailor. He gave a few little tugs to sleeves and long lapels, as if by way of improving the cut, shrugged, and stuck it back in the wardrobe. 'Here's one of your blazers, sir. Double-breasted and ten years old. This might do.' He held it up for inspection.

'It doesn't even look ten *weeks* old. I always knew you took good care of my clothes, but this is a revelation.' While Ruthven simpered with pleasure, Melrose said, 'Nothing to do but rub some life out of this Harris tweed.' He tossed the jacket to Ruthven. 'Get Martha to pull out some threads and put patches on the elbows. And I'll take the Armani and hope the Holdsworths aren't fashion freaks.'

Ruthven walked out starchily, chin up, but holding the Harris tweed as if it were a dying baby.

3

He needed a drink, and here finally was Boone, and here was a small pub whose overhanging sign he might kill the owner for, so that he could nail it outside of Agatha's cottage: the Old Contemptibles.

It was a sign in every sense of the word. It whistled to him , called to him, crooked its wooden finger at him, drew him like a magnet.

There appeared to be only the one bar, entered by way of a darkish hall with a thread of oriental carpeting far more rubbed than the patches on his sleeves. A desk in the hall beneath some dusty prints of geese and pheasants held a registration book and a sign above that said *Accommodation*.

The public bar would have been as dark as the hall except for the bonze-shaded fixtures and the shaded fluorescent light above a long, gilt-framed mirror in need of resilvering, overly oranate for such a simple room of deal tables and hardwood benches.

A framed document on the wall just inside the door announced that one O. Bottemly was licensed to serve alcohol and food.

It must have been O. Bottemly who came down the length of the bar, for he swaggered towards the newcomer with a proprietorial air. Sorry, sir, no Old Peculier, but there's Jennings, very nice and rich that is, O. Bottemly assured him.

Obviously, such an out-of-the-way pub got few transients, for the half-dozen people rooted to their bar stools were certainly getting their fill of this one. Given the villagers he had seen outside on his way down the street (three of them bent over walking sticks) and the ones seated here, Melrose wondered if there was anyone in the place under fifty. Age was an epidemic in Boone for which no one had found a vaccine.

Not even the woman who came in through a curtained doorway had been successful if creating the illusion of youth. But she'd certainly tried hard enough, with her plump breasts and buttocks

stuffed into a frilly, flowered dress, her beads and bangles, rouge
and carmine lipstick overflowing the natural line of the mouth.
She turned to the optics and drew off a glass of sherry, at the same
time introducing herself over her shoulder as Connie Fish.
Manageress, she made sure to add. O. Bottemly harumphed and
sucked a toothpick.

'The old Con,' said one the regulars, lifting a near-empty glass.

Melrose looked at the row of faces and smiled brightly. One
of them had his head on the bar, asleep and snoring, but the other
five smiled back, including Connie Fish, who really put her heart
into it as her fingers went to her overmoussed and colour-leached
hair. It looked like bleached grass.

The gentleman sitting next to Melrose said, 'Hoo do, squire?'
and inspected him carefully.

Melrose returned the greeting and asked if he lived in the village.

This man nodded and then asked, surprisingly, 'You be police?'

Melrose was surprised. 'Not at all. Are you expecting police?'

When they all started talking at one, it was as if waters suddenly
foamed in forces and ghylls down craggy slopes. He all but
drowned in their rush of words.

An old, wet-eyed man, called 'Rheumy' by the others told him,
'There's that bairn gone missin' . . .'

'. . . Holdsworth. Mum murdered.'

'. . . London, 'twas.'

The fattish woman named Mrs Letterby leaned across three of
her compatriots and called to Melrose, ' 'Twarn't murder. The
mum done hersen in.'

A bag of bones in a brown suit shook his head. Melrose couldn't
tell whether this was in disagreement with Mrs Letterby or the result
of the palsy that also inhibited him from lifting his pint. The hands
couldn't make it to the mouth. The straw went back in the glass,
making bubbles in its emptiness.

Suicide and disappearance didn't quench their thirst for
excitement. They also wanted something liquid. They turned their
heads rhythmically in his direction and fondled their empty glasses.

He ordered drinks for all and after they arrived, asked, 'When
did all of this happen?'

'Few days ago,' said a man named Billy, hoisting his fresh pint
to toast his benefactor.

'It sounds very bleak for the family. I expect you know them?'

119

Melrose took out his cigarette case and motioned to Billy Mossop to pass it along the row.

'The Holdsworths?' asked Connie Fish, beads dangling over the bar, sherried breath wafting over Melrose. 'Tragedy, they are. Something always happening. Lost their son, isn't that so Mrs Letterby?'

'Aye.' She made a gruesome gesture with her two hands curved round her throat and her tongue stuck out. ''Ung up, 'e was. From a beam.'

17

A careful assessment of his clothes had been made before he left
the pub; Melrose wanted to make sure he looked properly seedy.
The elbows of the tweed jacket were rubbed and the cuff was
darned — nearly invisible, but you could still make it out. The
freshly polished shoes could not hide the scuff marks on toes and
heels. And the collar of his expensive white shirt was almost, not
quite, frayed. But the new handkerchief in his jacket pocket showed
that he was keeping up appearances, this aristocrat fallen on hard
times.

He had decided to leave the car at the pub, and to walk to Tarn
House.

The corner where stood a little post-office store appeared to mark
the end of clustered cottages and he kept on walking and trying
to breathe deeply in this rarefied and cleansing air with the glorious
views of fells and mountains. But he didn't feel nearly as healthy
and robust as he would have sitting in his chair at Ardry End
smoking and drinking Graham's '44.

Melrose passed, about an eighth of a mile farther along, a walled-
in drive that swept in and out of deciduous trees up to a turreted
and towered building on a high rise of ground and with a backdrop
of misty fells and mountains that the Lake poets had loved but
that made him feel agoraphobic. At first, he thought he must have
finally come to Tarn House a (Poe-esque name, he thought), but
a brass plaque embedded in the stone announced this to be Castle
House. *Refined Retirement*. Translation: Rip off the Relations.

According to his new drinking companions, this was the place
where Adam Holdsworth had chosen to live, rather than in his
own home, so that must say a lot about *his* relations. Melrose struck
out again down the road. At least that was the picture he would
have liked to present, himself the country gentleman with knobbed
stick and trusty dog. He should have brought Mindy. Mindy? She

would have taken one step and crawled back into that rattletrap Japan called a car.

He sighed and looked down the narrow road. Not a house, a cottage, a smoking chimney pot in sight. But there were signs of life coming towards him in the persons of three, no, four, back packing tourists who, as they passed him, waved and gave him the thumbs-up sign as if they had met on one of the poles and lived to tell about it. One of them looked twice his age, her leathery skin set in deep crevices, and smiling (smugly, he thought) because she was walking faster than the whippet she had on a lead.

That thumbs-up sign was the giveaway: just who did they think they were kidding, all of these people who came up here to this area known for its execrable weather, its dozen lakes, its smoking mountains, its fells full of sheep? He was not passing judgment on the place, merely thinking that it really would take a person of a poet's or painter's sensibility to appreciate it. But for some reason or other, droves of tourists would race up here in the summer, slog about in waterproofs and wellingtons, and give you the thumbs-up sign of pantheism. That lot he had just passed had probably just had high tea up the road somewhere, talking six-to-the-dozen while the poor whippet twitched beneath the table. Oh, he was sure that there really were those few who blew cold breath in caves and cabins, wrestled crocodiles, let the North Sea spray them in the face while they crested mile-high waves and truly communed with Nature. But he thought there were very few of them and, looking at the enormous peaks of Scafell and Great Gable ringed in mist marvelled at Wordsworth and Coleridge's interminable walks.

He finally caught a glimpse of the house. Within less than five minutes he was there and wondered why Jury hadn't told him it was a good mile from the village. Of course, how would Jury know, since he'd never seen it?

How could he know that Tarn House, from its surrounding wall to its main structure, was a mysterious mass of dun-coloured and weathered stone that had found an expedient setting in a large expanse of weedy, boggy, vapour-covered ground with those mountains as a backdrop. Melrose had to walk across peaty ground through dull brown bracken for some little distance on an old footpath after the proper driveway stopped. Wheeling above him were what he wanted to believe were peregrine falcons but which he knew were buzzards. Waiting.

The old iron gate was flanked by stubby pillars (fortunately unlioned) and he had passed a gatehouse, apparently tenanted. The main house was manorial, but not at all as impressive as Refined Retirement back down the road. Tarn House had taken its name from the dark pools — lakelets? — of water that sat on either side of the overgrown drive. The grounds were not impressive, merely brooding, nor was the house — a flat fronted, slate roofed, dark structure whose tall windows were neither leaded nor firelit, nor hung with any curtain that drew back and quickly fell again at the sight of him. He knew his problem: free association. It should have been the House of Usher, and E. A. Poe, and Baltimore in Maryland where Ellen Taylor was zipping through rain-darkened streets on that damned BMW. Or the setting for a Praed mystery. When had he last seen Polly Praed? Not that *she* cared.

Melrose sighed heavily, pushed the uncreaking gate closed, and walked towards the house. How much he would have preferred to be back at Ardry End, ah! That fire, that Graham's. That aunt. Forget it.

Someone must have watched his approach, for the door was opened almost before the knocker fell.

Melrose quickly drew in breath at the sight of the little girl and sent up a prayer to Samuel Taylor Coleridge. She seemed proof of the positive alchemical interchange of magical transposition or whatever was going on in 'Kubla Khan'. It was as if Ardry End appeared before him in human form. Plain dress of green and hair the colour of Graham's '44, irises in which tiny coals burned and at her feet the blackest cat Melrose had every seen, a cat from Hell.

The girl looked up at him. Unfortunately, she was probably no more than eleven or twelve, which would put her entirely outside his conversational jurisdiction.

And that tilt to her mouth was not a smile, but a study in exasperation mastered. She then turned and went, apparently to summon an older person. When he didn't follow, she stopped and put her hands on her hips.

No thumbs up here, he thought.

*   *   *

'That was Millie,' said Madeline Galloway, as if that explained all of Melrose's questions.

Madeline Galloway was attractive, a look heightened by her nervousness; it was as if it were she, not Melrose, who was seeking this modest employment.

They were in the much-touted library, and Melrose had to admit it was quite impressive. As if she wanted to get the bad news over first, she plunged right into an accounting of the position of librarian, saying, 'I'm awfully afraid the pay isn't much.'

'I really wasn't expecting much.'

There was a tapping at the door before Millie entered with a tray on which there were a decanter of sherry and two glasses. Silently she looked at Madeline.

Why, Millie. Where's Hawkes?' She explained to Melrose that Hawkes was the manservant. She smiled. 'We can't exactly call him a butler.'

Judging from Millie's face, they certainly couldn't. Millie turned to leave.

'But you haven't said where he is. This is his job.'

Millie chewed the inside of her cheek and said, 'Down the cellar. With Cook. Looking at wine.'

Melrose thought he detected in those pauses something that suggested butler and cook were doing more than looking.

Millie left; Madeline turned to Melrose. 'Your friend Superintendent Jury said you sometimes picked up a job here or there that suited your interests.'

Derelict Plant, apparently, shuffling about in baggy trousers tending to the philodendron cuttings or searching the dustbins. He'd have preferred, if not a nobler, at least a more mysterious cover . . . and now she was saying something about 'eccentric', lifting an eyebrow, smiling as if they shared a secret, Melrose, Madeline and the Superintendent.

Eccentric. He was tempted to remove the silk-fringed lamp-shade and put it on his head.

'We've known each other for a long time.'

'Yes, Well, the job won't last very long, I'm afraid. Of course, it depends how fast you can do the cataloguing. Since you were a librarian, I understand, it should go very well.'

A down-at-heel, eccentric librarian. 'Not for very long.'

'I hope we can find arrangements that suit you. You're welcome to live at Tarn House or if you prefer I could find a room for you in the village. The Old Contemptibles does rooms, I believe.'

'I'd much prefer the house.' He rubbed his hand over his knee and thought of Crutch and Cripple. 'Bit of a gammy leg, so I avoid doing too much walking.' He had forgotten the car.

She looked down and frowned. 'I didn't notice anything.'

'Comes and goes.' He wanted to get off gimpy legs and pursue more interesting paths; he picked up the picture and waited for her to comment but she had walked over to the mantelpiece and picked up a Staffordshire figurine, a shepherd leaning on his staff, looked at it blankly and held it probably without knowing she held it. Obviously, she had other things on her mind.

'May I?' As she turned, Melrose indicated one of a pair of leather Queen Anne chairs that stood on each side of the table on which rested the silver tray.

'Oh! I'm sorry. Yes, please sit down.' Madeline stopped fidgeting with the china shepherd lad and set it on the table before pouring the sherry, a very fine amontillado. Her own glass now in hand, she sat in the other chair. 'I'm afraid I'm pretty rotten at this interviewing business. Mr Holdsworth seems to think that simply because I like to read' — and here she looked round the noble library — 'that I must be bookish enough to know whether you'd make a good cataloguer and indexer. Or whatever he wants.'

'But, then, why isn't *he* doing the interviewing? He's the one I must suit.'

She shook her head. 'Shy, I expect. Well, that's not true, really. He's probably out there waiting in the wings for the right moment to come wandering in, looking terribly preoccupied. It's his little, oh, pose, I expect. He's such an admirer of Robert Southey that he apes his posture and attitudes. From pictures and portraits. I'm sure he'd love nothing more than to wear a high collar and tie a cravat rather carelessly. As in one of the portraits. At times I believe he thinks he *is* Southey.'

'Inconvenient, Robert Southey being dead.'

Her smile was a bit forced. The fate of her sister would hardly leave her in a mood for a bad joke. 'Should I explain your duties?'

'That sounds appropriate.'

'Your being a librarian, you'll understand better than I. Crabbe wants his collection indexed and cross-referenced. You know —

subject, author, title, and so forth. Have you been to Greta Hall yet?'

'No, I haven't. Just arrived.' Attendance at the Southey shrine would no doubt be one of his duties. Why Southey, for God's sake? If one had to get into this so-called Lake school of poetry, why not Coleridge? Because he was demonic, probably; whereas, Southey was a gentleman.

Her eyes took in the rows and rows of books. They were so perfectly arranged, so beautifully bound in tooled leather, that Melrose wondered if they were actually being read. 'Crabbe's library is nearly an exact copy of Southey's,' she said. 'His library was his absolute pride and joy, and he loathed having people muck about in it, especially Wordsworth, who was a gobbler of books . . .'

Madeline Galloway's voice trailed off, lacking interest, clearly, in her subject. 'I'm sorry, but I saw you looking at my sister's picture.' She picked it up. 'I should tell you something because it's cast pretty much of a pall over the house. She's dead; it happened three nights ago.'

Melrose replaced his glass gently on the tray. 'I'm terribly sorry. I can see why you'd rather not be doing — can't understand why Mr Holdsworth wouldn't have time.'

When she looked up at him, her eyes were wet. 'Don't be sorry on my account. It's all — very complicated. Very.'

The voice trailed off again as she held the silver frame. 'It's terrible. Overdose of barbiturates.' She added quickly, 'An accident, it must have been. But the police won't let us claim the body until the post mortem's done.' She paused. 'I expect there's always got to be one in cases of suspect deaths.' Her fine-boned hand gripped the chair arm and she looked at Melrose as if he might ease her mind about what sort of suspicion might have attached itself to her sister's death.

'I think it's routine, yes.'

In a brief silence that followed, he studied Madeline Galloway, finding her rather conventionally pretty, with her wide eyes and dark hair held back by a velvet band — a rather childlike look, though certainly not insipidly so, but a woman of blurred outlines. She did not appear to have great strength of will, although her slightly diffident air might have been a posture struck for the benefit of the Holdsworths. It was strange that she would want

126

to stay on it a place that must have been a constant reminder of humiliation.

'The police were here. I can't see why it's a matter for the police.'

Melrose shrugged. 'Again, routine, I expect.'

But when she looked round at him, straight in the eye, he readjusted his former opinion of spinelessness.

'I don't think so.'

Having forgot her mission, she was taking about the sister, her death at a young age, her son, the tragedy of it all.

'It was indeed,' said a male voice, and Melrose turned to see a tall thin man with a small book in his hand, and his head lowered over it, come into the room. He was introduced as Mr Crabbe Holdsworth, Melrose's future employer.

Crabbe Holdsworth sat, still with his book, on the little sofa facing them. 'Devastating, that death,' he said, snapping the book shut. 'And so young, yes.' He looked in a slightly unfocused way at the Staffordshire figurine, picked it up, stared at it, set it back. Apparently, Madeline having already appeared in his stead to verse the new librarian, Mr Holdsworth thought further introduction superfluous and continued his line of thought: 'He was only twelve.'

Melrose and Madeline exchanged slight frowns that Crabbe Holdsworth took in. 'Henry. Southey's boy.' He nodded towards the book.

Was the man really so dense? wondered Melrose. Dense and insensitive? Quickly, Madeline rose and went to lean her hands against the mantelpiece as if, in not so engaging them, she might hit him. 'We were speaking of Jane, *not* Southey.'

'Oh. Oh. I'm terribly sorry.' But his slight frown seemed more puzzled than sorrowful as if he were attempting to place this 'Jane.' No, apparently he was aware of the 'rotten business.' as he termed it. 'Rotten,' he repeated, turning to Madeline, who then returned to her chair.

Crabbe Holdsworth had a long face, a sorrowful face that probably stood him in good stead when he couldn't actually work up appropriate sympathy. 'I was, as usual, preoccupied. You're Mr Plant? Well, what do you think of the library?'

Death (except for the Southey family) held few terrors for Crabbe Holdsworth, it would seem.

While Madeline Galloway pleated her skirt and fumed beside him, Melrose mumbled words of appreciation, accolades being too difficult. 'I think I could take it on.'

'Fine.' He picked up the shepherd lad again and, again, replaced it. 'It's a largish house but a small household. There're just the four of us, my wife, my brother, Madeline and myself.'

'You're forgetting Adam.'

'Oh. Yes, there's father. But he doesn't actually *live* here, Madeline. My father's . . .' He seemed to gloom about over this person, trying to think of some way to describe him . 'He actually lives at Castle Howe; that's a retirement home. Tarn House belongs to my father, actually, but he seems to think it a lark to live down the road in that overpriced home.' He still held on to the figurine. 'My wife would like to meet you,' he said as if speaking to the figurine.

And then what Melrose had taken for, at best, absentmindedness over the tragedy of death; or, at worst, cold-bloodedness in Crabbe Holdsworth's concern over a century-old death when such a recent one stared him in the face – was suddenly and surprisingly explained:

'We can't find Alex.'

2

'My husband's grandson,' said Genevieve Holdsworth. 'For some reason he got out of the house whilst police were trying to locate his family. Why on earth would he do a thing like that?' She was not asking; she was merely speculating, looking past him. And she sounded more irritated than concerned.

Genevieve Holdsworth was sitting in the chair vacated by her husband. He was, apparently, to be interviewed by all of the household, taking turns. Then she said, 'Disregard gossip, Mr Plant. You'll certainly hear enough of it if you befriend the denizens of the local public house.'

He wondered not only why 'gossip' would be a high priority, but also why she used the stilted language of a Victorian housekeeper, given her feline look. Perhaps the elevated language was meant to create some bridge between the highbrow mind and low cut blouse.

Melrose had formed no clear picture of the second Mrs

Holdsworth. If he had, he would have expected more the female counterpart of the husband with the possible addition of more hardmindedness. Good tweeds and sensible shoes, at least. Instead, she gave off the pure and unadulterated scent of sexuality. There was something oddly enticing in her cool manner of address that contrasted sharply with the heaving sense of her presence as she fingered a narrow gold chain whose cross lay strategically placed in the neckline of her silk blouse. At the same time, she was adroitly making little circles with her ankle as if taking the opportunity to turn a leg already done by a master craftsman.

For some reason, Melrose noticed with a slight smile, none of them seemed able to avoid handling the Staffordshire shepherd, still sitting on the table. But whereas Madeline had fingered it nervously and Mr Holdsworth had picked it up absently, Genevieve dallied with it.

'I don't pay attention to gossip.' He added nothing, hoping his lack of curiosity would prompt her to assuage it.

'I'm sure Madeline told you about her sister,' adding nothing either.

'I'm very sorry.' He would hardly have called this tragedy 'gossip'.

'Yes. Her death was a great loss.' As she rose, so did Melrose. 'We dine at seven-thirty.' Death and dinner sharing equally in her thoughts, she walked out of the room.

18

A new one, thought Millie Thale.

Now there was a new one. Another place to set, another bed to make, another early morning tea.

Millie Thale slapped back another page of the 'These Glorious Lakes calendar, trying to decide where to drop another drowning figure. She took a watercolour pencil from the tin on the huge chopping -block table and studied Wast Water. That was the deepest. No, she was definitely saving that for Mrs Holdsworth. She turned back to February. Derwentwater. Nurse Rhubarb was already in that one: there were her shoes sticking out of the lake's blue surface over to the side and almost hidden by some bracken in the foreground.

Mille smacked back March and looked at April: Buttermere. That would do; it quite fit him, since his hair was a sort of darkish-buttery colour. Well, no *so* yellow . . . oh, no! Daffodils. Over to the right of whole breezy bunch of them. If William Wordsworth (whose name she was sick of) was such a great poet, why did he have to write those old, overused lines?

As Millie licked her pencil preparatory to crowning the centre of Buttermere with a half-moon of head, Mrs Callow shouted in from the butler's pantry: 'Millie, you done them fritters?'

'Yes,' Millie lied, shouting back, pencil poised.

'You know how Mr Holdsworth likes his bit o'fritter!'

Millie stuck out her tongue at the butler's pantry as a peal of giggles (from Cook — as she was wrongly called) and a few duck honking, indrawn breaths that passed as laughter erupted from Mr Hawkes, the so-called butler. They had, she supposed, found something rude in the comment about the fritter. They should talk, back there drinking up the port they'd brought up from the cellar and leaving her (as usual) to cook the dinner and lay the table. Oh, Mr Hawkes would take in the cocktails — he was good at

131

that – and announce dinner; he was also good at that, even if he was woozy by the time seven-thirty rolled around.

Her pencil hadn't touched the paper yet. She was a bit undecided about Buttermere. Millie sighed and looked at August. Patterdale. That was her favourite; it sounded like rain and the Raindrop Poets. But she was saving that one for herself, so she couldn't use it for him.

'Millie! Remember to put more oysters than mutton in that pie!' And here a low murmuring, punctuated by an *oops!* and glass breaking, followed the command.

She didn't bother answering as she turned to September. Dove Cottage. She held her nose and rustled the pages back to February. She studied the dark skies above Coniston Water, the mist and low cloud, the slightly shimmering pewter-coloured lake. Not bad. Buttermere was more like him, though.

'I don't smell them fritters, miss!'

This was the place for Him. And *here* was a bit of poetry she loved:

His flashing eyes, his floating hair

'Well, its hardly gone six yet and they're supposed to be hot. Anyway, I'm counting out the oysters.' She hummed lightly as she considered this, her favourite poem. It was true. He *did* have 'flashing eyes'. They were as green as the grass beside Buttermere from which daffodils were always springing. She gold pencilled in a little hair floating and then thought: it would hardly be fair not to put in the flashing eyes. From the can she drew a lime-green water colour pencil and wetted it. Millie was no good at faces, she knew, so the head she made was a little lopsided, and she dotted in a bright green eye and a lot of gold hair. She frowned. He was going down and she didn't *really* know him. She tossed down the gold pencil, took an ordinary lead one and quickly pulled an arm and hand out of the water.

A larger hand slapped the calendar shut. 'Just as I thought! Thought I didn't know you wasn't doing nothing?'

Millie lurched back in her chair as the shadow of Mrs Callow fell across her calendar and the figure of Mr Hawkes lounged against the doorjamb, port glass in hand.

'Here, let's see this –'

'*No!*' Millie yanked her calendar from the thick hand of the cook.

Mrs Callow withdrew, pinning up some stands of hair that had loosened from the rollls on each side of her elderly face. 'Well,just see you do the Guiness pie proper tonight.' She straightened her apron, leaving the field to the victor.

Millie was the victor by virtue of being the best cook (except for her own mother) the Holdsworths had ever had. Of course, they didn't really know an eleven-year-old was doing most of the cooking, but that made no odds to Millie, who quickly opened the calendar to Buttermere and finished drawing the hand, fisted round the rope.

It was her own mother's death that explained this obsession with the lakes. It had happened five years ago when Millie was only six. Her mum had been found on the stony shore of Wast Water, half in, half out of the lake. No one had seen what happened, but what Millie was told was that her mum had fallen from the rocky cliff outgrowth on the property onto the shore.

Millie had come to know this had to be a lie. It would have been almost impossible to *fall*. Yet she had never been able to sort out what actually had happened.

The Holdsworths had wanted to send her to London and live with her only relations, her Aunt Tom. Thomasina, her name was, but Millie called her Aunt Tom. It made her sound as hard as Millie claimed the woman to be, and she had told Alex's great-grandfather that she didn't want to go to London. She hadn't told him why, though: that she'd stay and stay until she found out what really happened to her mother.

So Millie had stayed.

From the time she was tall enough to see the top of a cooker Millie had been fascinated by cooking, and had learned so much that when Ma would be sick with 'cramp' and didn't want the Holdsworths to know, Millie could prepare whatever meal her mother told her was expected, and no one was the wiser. After her mother had died, of course the family had got Mrs Callow, who was, at best, a mediocre cook, and who'd left more and more of the actual cooking to Millie.

More giggling from Cook and the butler, who was reaching over the cooker to grab at something. The rich aroma of Guiness pie came from the oven, but Mrs Callow hadn't remembered that Millie had only just said the oysters weren't in it yet.

Millie had cleared up her calendar and watercolour pencils and sat with the heels of her palms pressed against her eyes.

19

He dreamed about his mother. They were walking along a narrow road straight through a landscape so barren it was blank, as if the road itself had no verge but melted into the outreaching land. It was the very opposite of the English Lakes, the fells and dales, becks and waterfalls. But this did not seem to bother them; they were holding hands as tightly as if the fingers had been welded together. And the blankness of the land was not their concern, for they were walking towards a horizon of such breathtaking loveliness that the dream-Alex felt it was the only thing worth reaching in the world, full of rainbow lights, pale colours melting into one another and a light so glorious that it was less seen than felt. He supposed that that was God up there.

Except that as far and as long as they walked, they did not get closer to the horizon. The coloured light did not dim, did not recede; it was just that the distance between them never shortened. The horizon was always *out there*, but they drew no closer to it.

Then Alex became aware of something heavy he was carrying in his other hand. He felt its heft and weight more and more, and the more he tried to drop it, the more it stuck. When he finally raised his hand, he saw a pack of cards Sellotaped together. But his mother, although he did not look at her, was unaware of the pack of cards; he knew she was smiling and that her face was aimed towards that horizon and did not seem to know that they never drew closer.

He could not take his hand from hers because he was afraid she would disappear if he didn't hold on; so he could only get at the Sellotape by picking and picking with fingers of the hand that held the cards. He was terrified; he was terrified that what he had been 'getting up to' all these years would keep them from getting to the end of the road. He wanted to get rid of the cards. And magically, the cards separated and he fanned them out with his one hand. Their faces were blank, all blank except for one: the Queen of Hearts. His heart turned to ice, and when he looked at his mother her face was draped in a kind of cowl, her features similingly rigid — the Queen of Hearts.

The cards, tiny bits of confetti, were swirling away towards the horizon , still full of all that pale, coloured light, and his hand, both hands were empty. Alex screamed.

And woke up, fearing he was screaming, moving his hands before him trying to part the darkness like a swimmer trying to part water, and was as drenched with sweat as if he had been dropped in one of the lakes. His heart was pounding; he was gasping for breath, hunched up into the corner of the hut, wondering if he could get to a phone to call his mother.

What he had been fearing happened. Full consciousness and the reality it brought with it returned. He squeezed his eyes shut, put his hands over his ears and knew he would scream, for real. The glass bell had surfaced, finally, up from the bottom of the lake and here he was, unprepared, unarmed. Before whatever animal feeling sound could reach his lips, he heard a rustle and opened his eyes.

The verdigris-green eyes of Millie Thale's cat pinned him to the wall. There was a message in them. The message was *No*.

Alex slowly relaxed. 'Hullo, Sorcerer.'

The cat blinked slowly.

Millie had found him five years ago. Or, rather, the cat had found Millie. He had appeared from nowhere, down by Wast Water; she'd seen him through tearful eyes, sitting there as if he'd been expecting someone. Later, she had looked for (with a lack of thoroughness that had made Alex smile) but could not find the cat's owner.

His name was Sorcerer. She had told Alex this as if the cat had informed her of it.

Millie had hung on to Sorcerer over the objections, though not violent ones, of Mr Hawkes. Hawkes didn't really care much about anything if it did not interfere with his own business. Sorcerer did interfere, appearing as if out of nowhere when Hawkes and Mrs Callow were having a 'conference' in the butler's pantry. He got a proper kick, of course, but kicks only made the cat more determined. And the only person Sorcerer would pay any attention to, anyway, was Millie.

Alex looked at his watch and saw he had been sleeping the entire afternoon. He looked again and saw by the tiny calendar insert that the day had changed. It was Thursday. *Thursday*. He had been sleeping the clock round. Drifting in and out of his long, long dream since yesterday evening. Sorcerer, who seemed to have stared him out of oblivion, apparently satisfied he was awake, now lay down and curled his paws beneath his chest. But he still stared.

No wonder he was hungry, Alex thought, looking in his rucksack and finding nothing but a couple of Wispa bars. He opened his mother's black leather telephone book, the one she had always kept in the nightstand drawer because she didn't want to carry it for fear of losing it: *all* the names and numbers of the people she knew were in this little book. The one the police had found was the one she carried with her. It had only the numbers she called most frequently. It had no history.

He considered each name. There were a few he wasn't familiar with, probably people she'd worked with over the years. The relations were all there. The number of Castle Howe, where his great-grandfather stayed most of the time. Her friend, the doctor, Helen Viner. A Mauriuce Kingsley whom Alex had never met. A few unfamiliar names, unlikely to be important, acquaintances, probably. His headmaster. Oh, yes, his headmaster. Underlined twice. Names of two other masters — maths and history — who didn't count Alex amongst their favourite students. Had they called his mother? Anyway. At the end and not under its proper letter *J* there was a new name. She had used blue ink; the others were in black. And the tiny ballpoint pen in the book contained blue ink. 'R. Jury.' Who was he? 'Supt.' Supt.? It was a London number.

Alex frowned. It seemed vaguely familiar. Had he heard her say it? No. Seen it? He frowned, not liking it. He thought it was probably a man, because of the initial for the surname. For a woman friend, it was the oppositive. 'Helen V.,' for instance. Supt.
Superintendent?

Alex shut the book and said to Sorcerer. '*A policeman?*'

137

2

Melrose wondered, sitting amidst the gloom of the shadowy dining room and that of the diners, how they managed to get through this nightly ritual. For it was hard to believe, from the little conversation he'd had with at least three of these five people, that their sombre mood was caused only by a fresh tragedy in their midst.

The intermittent outward and inward swing of the door between dining room and kitchen permitted him a glance now and then into the Stygian depths of the connecting passageway and butler's pantry. Dishes were replaced by other dishes; one cheery note about this dinner was the quality of the cooking. A pie of oysters, meat, and stout! The only slight improvement that could have been made would have been the use of Old Peculier instead of Guinness.

'He'll turn up. Bound to,' said George Holdsworth, who seemed less interested in Alex than in there being only this oyster-and-mutton pie for dinner instead of the pheasant he'd shot just that morning. George was the younger of the two brothers, but looked older, perhaps all that time spent in the outdoors having weathered and lined a face that only slightly resembled the smooth, high-foreheaded one of his elder brother. 'Amnesia. Shock. Something.' George went on as if he were periodically shooting at an unidentified object that had come with his line of vision.

'Don't be absurd, George,' said Genevieve, in what sounded like a knee-jerk reaction to whatever George might suggest. 'Alex never forgets anything,' further suggesting she only wished the boy would.

Crabbe was helping himself to peas and roast potatoes served by Hawkes, who struck Melrose as sneaking up on one with his silver dishes and murmured *sirs*. 'But George might have something there. Alex is like his father, a bit.' Placing the spoons in the dish so that Hawkes could retreat into the shadows again, he said, 'My son, Graham, Mr Plant —'

Quickly, Melrose looked across at Madeline Galloway to catch her expression; her head was bent over her plate, but she had stopped eating.

' — was a poet. And, I think, would have been a great one, if he'd — lived.'

Melrose could have sworn he heard coming from George, in two murmured syllables, Rub. Bish.

'But I expect, living here in the Lakes, it would be difficult not to be a poet.'

On the contrary, thought Melrose, it would be difficult to *be* one without feeling a little silly. 'I'm sorry.' He felt he had been spending the entire evening proclaming his sorrow. 'How did he — ?'

Instead of answering, they all kept their eyes on their plates. George was about to say something, but was forestalled by his brother, who said to Melrose, 'An accident.'

Given he had got his job through a policeman-friend, Melrose thought it would be best to ask as few questions as possible, hoping that amongst them would supply information. He wondered, though, how unlucky a household could be. This one had certainly had its complement of 'accidents'. He trotted out the reliable cliché. 'You've certainly had your share of grief.' He hoped George's insensitivity was as reliable as he thought it was.

It was. 'Virginia. Don't forget dear old Ginny.'

Melrose watched as Genevieve stubbed out a cigarette she had been impolitely smoking as the others ate. 'Oh, shut up, George. Don't you think we've had enough on our minds?'

George ignored her. 'Awful, that. Bad fall. Hawkes. Wine.' He thumped his glass.

Melrose was surprised that Crabbe Holdsworth's complexion could pale any more than it already had. The hand that held the fork trembled.

20

Melrose's appearance in the Old Contemptibles was a signal for the regulars to empty their glasses quickly.

'Hoo do, skip?' Billy Mossop called over, wiping his mouth on his sleeve.

Mrs Letterby was launching into a lengthy description of 't'wedder' as O. Bottemly came down the bar, also prepared for good custom. 'Evening!'

Melrose ordered a pint of Jennings and also gave the nod to refill the others' glasses, including one for the proprietor. O. Bottemly smiled and took his beefy self back to the beer pulls.

After the relieved sighs — what would they have done had he not appeared this night, he wondered? — Mrs Letterby started up some largely indecipherable monologue about the family at Tarn House.

'Aye,' put in Rheumy round the phlegm in his throat as he picked up the dirge. 'Unhappy place, it be.'

Melrose commented on the apparent 'accident' suffered by the first Mrs Holdsworth.

The three of them argued the fate of the first Mrs Holdsworth: it was Mrs Letterby who decided with assurance that she'd 'went down t'gill off Scafell. Neea doot,' she added, turning, as usual every syllable into two.

The door to the public bar opened, blowing a cloud of rain and another customer inside. From the greetings, Melrose realized that this was the painter-cousin, Fellowes, who must have been another regular, although not a dispenser of largesse as was the recently arrived Mr Plant.

Francis Fellowes shook the rain from his coat and ordered a whisky. For himself alone, so others went back to their now half-full glasses.

Melrose introduced himself and, after exchanging the polite and

141

banal remarks of the newly met. Fellowes nodded towards a table.
'Let's sit over there.'

'You were missed at dinner.'
  'Hmm, I usually am. Did you enjoy it?'
  'Well, it was a bit sombre. Apparently there's been a recent death
in the family.
  Francis Fellowes had taken out his sketchbook and pencil;
Melrose had the feeling Fellowes was holding back some response
that he thought inappropriate. He made some swift strokes and
then said, 'Jane, the son's wife. Very unfortunate.' His tone gave
no indication of just how unfortunate he thought. 'Police have
been round, did they tell you?'
  'Her sister did, yes' When Fellowes merely studied his drawing
and chewed on his pencil stub, Melrose when on. 'Some notion
that it might not be suicide.'
  'They always have 'some notion' or other, don't they?' He held
his drawing away from him, brought it back. 'Pure hell for her
son, poor kid. Apparently, he went into a flap and scarpered.
Expect he thought he'd wind up here otherwise.'
  Melrose tried to keep his voice as matter-of-fact as he could.
'His father's dead, too, I understand.'
  'Ah. Graham. Yes. Did Crabbe give you all that poet-in-his
prime stuff? Graham wasn't much of a poet, but he was a fairly
decent type. Never worked, of course, but do any of us? To listen
to his father, Graham was the paradigmatic poet struck down
in his youth. Except he wasn't "mildly consumptive". That's
the only part of the stereotype that's left out. Mildly suicidal,
however.'
  'What?'
  'No wonder no one mentioned it. Hanged himself right there
in the gatehouse. By his belt from a crossbeam in the parlour. I
live there now. You looked shocked. My goodness, do you think
it ends there? The "li'l berran" they were speaking of,' – he
nodded towards the huddled group at the bar who occasionally
cast glances over their shoulders to see when these two would stop
their infernal crack and buy some more drinks – 'Millie. It was
her mum who found him. Graham, I mean. After which –' His
eyes were still on the people at the bar, his pencil still moving.
' – she apparently jumped from a sort of little cliff at the edge

of the wood. Her body ended up down on the edge of Wastwater. It was given out as an "accident".'

'My God.'

Connie Fish was behind the bar now, making a theoretical stab at calling Time, but her heart wasn't in it. Fellowes held up their glasses. When the drinks came, he reached for some change, but Melrose was quicker.

'Ah, thank you. I'm the stereotypical starving artist, distant cousin. I should feel grateful to them, letting me have that gatehouse for my use, but somehow I don't .' Fellowes held up his glass. 'I wonder why one of them doesn't just pass round the cup of poison and do us all in in one go instead of this piecemeal stuff. Cheers.'

2

He had to see Millie.

Perhaps it was cold comfort, but Millie would understand how he felt since the same thing had happened to her.

Not exactly, of course, for he knew his own mother hadn't killed herself. Annie Thale had. Although no one had ever talked to Millie about it, not even the police, as anything other than an accident. Millie knew differently.

It was too much. His father's suicide, Millie's mum only three weeks later, and now the police obviously believed his own mother had done the same thing. It was just too much.

Alex remembered five years back to when they had told her, Millie, that her mother was dead. Such a confusion of people, coming and going, of hushed voices and raised voices. He could still see Millie, standing in a far corner of the kitchen, six years old and with an apron on, shaking. Her mother had been cook to the Holdsworths and taught Millie. Millie had the wooden tasting spoon in her small hand, for stirring the soup. No one had wanted to go near her, as if her shaking presaged, like a flawed foundation, the collapse of the house. Alex had not reacted nearly so strongly to the death of his father, whom he had loved but never been terribly close to. He had felt that death at a distance, as if his own feelings had filtered through his mother's. She had shielded him against the worst of it.

143

Millie had had no such shield. She had had no father, no other relations except for an 'Aunt Tom' whom (she had told everyone) she didn't want to live with. She had told Adam Holdsworth (when the others were secretly planning her quick removal to London and Aunt Tom) that this woman was dreadful and would beat her. That was the end of Millie's leaving. His great-grandfather was very fond of Millie. When he'd heard Hawkes make snide references to Millie's being illegitimate, Adam had snapped that he'd never seen Hawkes perform one legitimate pursuit, and to shut up.

Annie Thale had been depressed for weeks after his father had died. She had (his mother had told Alex) been very fond of his father and it had been Annie who had found him — that terrible 'accident'.

The family, the servants, everyone seemed actually frightened of Millie's reaction. One would have thought the little girl was capable of visiting some horrendous doom upon the people there, blaming them for the death of her mother. It was Wast Water. That horrible lake. It had been deep summer and the lake then had been very blue, as blue as Coniston and Ennerdale, almost. Millie had come to hate *all* the lakes.

And she had (like Alex) disappeared. Two days later they had found her at the bottom of the trod, a poor rutted path leading downwards, there near the lake, her hands, her face, that same white apron stained yellow. Millie had pulled up all the daffodils she could find, pulled them up and apart, torn them to shreds. It had been George who had found her.

With that, he'd said, pointing to the black cat. *Feral animal, it must be*. The cat had been rushed at him (he claimed) and then gone to sit silent as a statue beside Millie, who herself sat on a carpet of crushed daffodils.

Millie would know how he felt.

It was past eleven o'clock, dark as ink, and he could make his way to the house. The problem was Hawkes, who stayed up drinking until early morning sometimes. Pebbles tossed against windows would do no good.

But he had to see Millie.

Alex opened his eyes and looked in the corner. Sorcerer was gone.

3

Melrose tried to contain his shock at this unexpected revelation of Francis Fellowes'. He forgot himself and offered the painter a cigarette from his solid silver case. 'What in heaven's name are you suggesting? It sounds as if you think somebody is trying to pick off the family one by one.'

'Wouldn't be at all surprised. Nice this,' said Fellowes, looking from the case to Melrose, the poor out-of-work librarian.

Melrose snapped it shut and quickly returned it to his pocket. 'Aunt gave it to me. A bit of money, but I'm not a favourite.' Actually, it was all he could do to keep 'Aunt' from nicking it. 'One of those distant, dotty relations.'

'Like Adam, you mean?' asked Fellowes. Oh, but I rather imagine they all wish he *was* dotty.

'But the cook, that is, the one who committed suicide – she wasn't part of the family.'

'No, But she was well liked by Adam. So was Graham. Even though he didn't amount to much, he was a kind boy; he was thirty-five, but I could never think of him as anything but a "boy". And he was, after all, the only grandchild. As far as his own sons are concerned. I don't think Adam cares for either one. Crabbe and George are both fools in different ways. And Genevieve. Well, Genevieve . . . Oh, of course Adam'll leave them something, as I expect he might even leave me enough for paints and brushes. But it's the ones he truly likes who'll get the spoils. Such as Jane would have. Very fond of Jane, he was. The ones he likes seem over the years to be dropping dead.'

'How did you come to know Madeline, did you say?'

He'd asked it rather overcasually, Melrose thought. Hell, he wondered if Francis Fellowes believed for a moment he was a simple librarian. Certainly a simpleminded one, he thought, with irritation. 'Oh, I didn't know her. She just happened to be in London interviewing people who answered adverts for the post.' Let him think he'd been one of them; he hoped Fellowes wasn't interested enough to check with Madeline. Perhaps he might confess something to Fellowes, something he hoped his new friend would keep to himself. Confess what? Confess he did not hold with cherished beliefs about the Lake poets. Actually, he thought he was right. 'Look, don't let it get back to Crabbe Holdsworth, but frankly, Wordsworth was exploiting Coleridge . . . at least *I* think he was. The fabled friendship might have started well, but it certainly ended with Wum — I mean, William — blasting poor Sam out of the water. Well, perhaps that's a *bit* strong. But Sam got understandably down because 'Christabel' never made it into *Lyrical Ballads* . . . and you know who did all the editing on *that* lot, don't you? So there was Coleridge, being upbraided for all the supernatural stuff in his poetry and that was the very *reason* Wordsworth ostensibly wanted him in on the game in the first place. Coleridge might as well've been a book-cataloguer, for all the thanks he got!' Melrose said this heatedly, stubbing out his cigarette in the tin tray. 'Chap's got to make a living, though.'

Fellowes laughed. 'You're one of the few people in that house who does. And you appear quite an authority, to boot.'

Just a fast reader, thought Melrose. 'You don't honestly think all of that codswallop in *Lyrical Ballads* is true?'

Fellowes frowned. 'What's true?'

'The similarity of purpose. That "seeing the mystical in the ordinary" stuff? Wordsworth simply couldn't deal with snakes and albatrosses, that's all. Poor Coleridge. Y'know he suffered excruciating pain for a large part of his life. Neuralgia.' Why was he tenderly feeling his own face? Melrose wondered. Quickly, he lowered his hand and continued his lecture. 'Don't you know the name "Lake School" was a sarcastic assessment by the *Edinburgh Review*?' Melrose polished off his bitter and thumped the glass down. Instead of thinking about some obscure nineteenth century essay, he should be working on a way of getting information to William, ah, Richard Jury, shouldn't he? He couldn't ring Jury from Tarn House. Fellowes was often out . . . 'Are you on the phone?' he asked, rather overcasually, considering the recent hectic of his stinging appraisal of Wordsworth.

'The phone?' Fellowes frowned. 'I've an extension, yes.'

'You mean of the Tarn House main?'

Fellowes nodded. 'Why?'

'Oh, no reason. Just wondered how the service was here.' Could he make up some reason for visiting Adam Holdsworth? Use the line at Castle Howe? He could hardly stand about in a call box with a bucketful of change. He looked at their glasses. 'Care for another?'

'Good idea. 'I'll buy.' Fellowes started up, but Melrose waved him down.

'My turn.'

As he walked up to the bar and plunked the glasses down he thought of his problem. Actually, with his thorough note-taking — well, he *imagined* himself to be thorough — there would be too much material for a call, anyway.

Rheumy nodded to him in the mirror, his large Adam's apple shifting up and down as he drained his pint. Sadly, he regarded the cavernous emptiness of his glass.

Melrose signed to O. Bottemly to take care of the empty pint, saw dawn break in Rheumy's smile, and asked, 'You on the phone?'

Rheumy stared at him and shook his head as if British Telecom were something he'd had a brief flirtation with ages ago, but had long since left in the lurch.

Absently, Melrose gathered in the two full glasses for his table, as he said, 'How the devil does anyone get information out of this village?'

'Over t'post office.' Rheumy lifted his glass.

'Letters take too long.'

'Fax it, Squire.'

4

The cat had appeared in the kitchen suddenly, out of that nowhere that only cats have discovered. The kitchen door was latched; the windows were shut.

Sorcerer kept getting in her way. He was standing between Millie and the cooker, staring at her, moving as she moved, forward, left, right, blocking her way to the pan on the stove. Millie could never sleep well; she always came down at night to make herself cocoa and usually Sorcerer slept right on top of the pillow above her head. But he hadn't been there tonight.

He was here now, though. *What's wrong with you?* she asked wordlessly, irritably, as she reached again for the pan. Of course, she could have shoved Sorcerer, but she never did that. Not after that horrible time five years ago when the cat had appeared magically and watched her and stayed with her.

'What's *wrong*?'

Sorcerer raced to the kitchen door and sat, tail twitching.

When she continued to dip the spoon in the cocoa, he came back sat down between her and the cooker again.

She frowned. Back to the door. Back to Millie.

Millie walked over to the inside door that opened onto the cloakroom. She switched on an electric torch that Hawkes kept on a shelf. Nothing. Before she could turn and close the door, the cat was through it and sitting at the outside door. When she didn't move, it ran between the two doors, going cat-crazy. Millie opened the door and Sorcerer made a dash for the field.

She took an old jacket from a hook and shoved her feet into the wellingtons she always kept there. Through the darkness, she could see Sorcerer's eyes staring at her over the broom and tall weeds, eyes that seemed disconnected, floating above the grass. Millie aimed the torch downwards to keep the lane of light as short as possible. You could never tell who might be watching from that house. Mr Hawkes's light was on; as long as there was light inside, he couldn't see outside.

The grass was long, the ground peaty. Near the wood she ran the torch along the edge and saw Sorcerer clambering up the rotting ladder that led to the tree house.

Alex heard her climbing and saw here eyes come up over the edge of the floorboards. 'It's me, Millie,' he said.

She opened her mouth but nothing came out. Millie was not given to physical demonstrations, but now she was speechlessly hopping from one foot to another as if she had to pee, her small hands fisted against her temples. Finally, she sat down, still without saying a word. She sat in the other corner, opposite him, her arms twined round her updrawn knees.

At last, she said, 'Police are looking for you. They were here asking questions. They even asked *me* questions. I told them you had amnesia. That you were wandering in London and didn't know who you were. I told them you did it before. Had amnesia.'

Alex laughed. She like the sound of the word on her tongue. Millie had heard someone use it, perhaps even in relation to his disappearance, and had taken it up. Millie loved words, certain words. When she heard one she liked she would use it in every possible circumstance, whether it fit quite perfectly or not. *Debauchery* was a favourite. When she was able to talk about her disappearance after mother's death, she said she had pulled up the daffodils in a fit of debauchery.

Alex wanted to say to her now, about his mother, *she didn't do it*. But that would have been terrible, because Annie Thale really had. She must have thrown herself off that grassy promontory to lie, with her broken body, in the lake below. Wast Water was the deepest lake in all of England. 'Fickle blue,' Millie called the lakes.

It was Millie who said it: 'I don't believe it.' No need to define 'it'. 'You can cry if you want,' she added, in that businesslike manner of hers that put people off the scent, that made them think the little girl was uncommonly cool and adult.

'I already did. You know, I must've been here a whole day and a half, asleep. What's been going on? What did the others tell the police about — Mum?'

'That they couldn't believe it and they didn't understand it and she was . . . "neurotic." ' Millie was fooling with the rucksack.

'Worse than that, I'll bet. The usual stuff about her not being a good mother and not being able to hold a job and so forth and so forth.' He hadn't had to ask, really. 'What police were here?'

'Oh, that constable from the village. But he just came along with the one from London. Cramer, or something. He looked foreign.'

'Kamir?'

'That's right, with his sergeant. And your granddad was here' — meaning his great-grandfather, Adam — 'Telling police that all the rest of them were crazy, that there was nothing wrong with your mum, and anyway why were they asking questions as if it was —' She stopped.

'It's okay. As if it was suicide, you mean. What'd they say?'

'Nothing. They didn't say nothing, except that it might be a "suspicious death". I expect it's different from a sudden one. Then everyone had to tell them where they were on Monday night. Did you know your aunt Madeline and Her' (meaning Genevieve, whom Millie loathed) 'were in London, and had to admit it? They went up on Sunday.' Millie's smile was more than a little mean.

'For what?' Alex sat up; the steel band had loosened its grip on his chest. 'Why?'

'Your auntie had to see people about getting a person who does books to help Mr Holdsworth. *She* went like She always does, to buy clothes. I'm surprised there's anything left in the shops.'

'Were all the others here? Was Francis?'

Millie shrugged. 'He always leaves after dinner, when he has it. I didn't see him. Only your uncle George and Mr Holdsworth had dinner. I had to cook rabbits. Yuck.' She screwed up her face.

'If he kills them, he ought to have to cook them.'

Alex sighed. 'I expect I'll have to show my face. I can't learn anything sitting in this tree.'

Millie gave him a look of disgust. 'You can think, can't you?'

He lowered his head. 'I had a terrible dream.' Millie was very good with dreams figuring them out. Sometimes he was amazed at her sensitivity, the way she could feel things that normally passed other people by, the way she could work her way into other people's feelings. It was almost as if she *became* the object. *Too close to the ground, Millie is,* his grandfather, Adam, had said once.

'The pack of cards,' he said. 'It kept sticking. I didn't believe before she'd really – ' He stopped. 'I wonder now if I had something to do with it; I was always betting. Just before it happened I was playing poker and got expelled'

'No!' she raised her head and thrust her legs out violently. 'Your mum would never have killed herself and anyway it wasn't a pack of cards.' Again she drew up her legs rested her chin on her hands. 'Things never are what they look like in dreams.'

'But she turned into the Queen of Hearts. It's as if she was stuck, stuck with me in that pack of cards – '

'Alice-in-Wonderland.' Millie shut her eyes and rocked back. There's a Red Queen. The Red Queen is riding a horse but she never really gets anywhere. Where'd you get this?' Millie held up the automatic she'd rooted from the sack.

'Put that down, for God's sake! You could get hurt!' Even Sorcerer jumped.

'If it's loaded, I nearly sat on it.'

'Of *course* it isn't. You think I'm crazy? It needs the clip.'

'How do you do it?'

Alex took out the ammunition clip and smacked it into the handle with the palm of his hand making sure the safety was on. The gun gave off a slightly oily smell.

Millie studied the gun in his hand. Thoughtfully, she said, 'Maybe that's the pack of cards in your dream.'

Alex blinked at it, laid it on the boards, Then he remembered: 'Something was missing from my mother's room. But I can't remember what.' Like Millie, he grew thoughtful. 'Do you think it's safe to talk to Dr Viner?'

'I don't think it's safe to talk to *anybody*. I'll make you some sandwiches and Sorcerer can bring them back.'

'How can Sorcerer carry them? — Put that down, Millie!' Before he could stop her, she'd picked up the gun and pulled out the ammunition clip. 'It's not to play with.'

'I wasn't thinking of playing.' She put the gun and clip in the rucksack. 'There's somebody new here.'

'Who?'

'His name's Mr Plant. He's the one that your aunt hired to do something with the books.' She studied the hole in the roof of the tree house. 'At least that's what he says he's doing here. I don't believe him.'

21

The Dunsters were feuding again.

Their feuds did not take the form of baleful glances, spiteful silences or vitriolic remarks about appearances. Had the fights been mere vituperative name-calling, Mrs Colin-Jackson could easily have stepped in with here smarmy manner and wheedling voice, promising extra sweets.

Sweets were the reason for the fight, as a matter of act, a whole two pounds of them which each claimed their niece had given to her.

Unfortunately (for Mrs Colin-Jackson, if not for their fans) the Dunsters had turned to other outlets for their mutual dislike and were going at each other with cane and rolled umbrella in the solarium, moving about with sure-footed agility amongst the silk trees and spider plants.

One hand on her waist, the other holding her umbrella, elbow crooked, Juliette suddenly shot it out and flicked off Elizabeth's velour hat. A ripple of applause. Elizabeth, equally well trained, swished the cane about, but could not dislodge Juliett's own hat.

The Dunster girls had been fencers in their youth, practising their thrusts and parries when their friends were slumped before their pianos, making sounds as discordant as Mrs Colin-Jackson's present demands that they *stop it this instant!* That brought only more noise from the gallery, so to speak, boos and hisses and honks from Mr Bannister (a sound he made with his hands tented over his mouth and that was, he claimed, the mating call of the mallard).

The girls were not about to be intimidated by threats of no crème caramel for dinner (probably because each expected to get the box of sweets), and were also highly excited that they were attracting more fans than the film being shown in the screening room: *One Flew Over the Cuckoo's Nest*.

Adam and Lady Cray had themselves watched half of it, Lady

Cray remarking that it was not the most appropriate film to be shown in Castle Howl (as she called it after only twenty-four hours there). Adam saw Mrs Colin-Jackson march out. 'Kojack's gone to fetch Kingsley, probably. Spoils all the fun.'

'Who's he?' Lady Cray lit a cigarette as Elizabeth made a dandy thrust and nearly raked the umbrella from Juliette's hand.

'Psychiatrist. There are two of them: Viner and Kingsley, though Kingsley doesn't do as much work as she does. A soft berth for him. Then there're two general practitioners, but they don't live in the grounds; only come around if somebody falls on his face.'

Lady Cray smiled at this, blowing perfect little smoke rings in this room where smoking was not permitted. A woman who strode with some authority made her way through the assembly. 'And who's this? Nurse Ratchett?'

Adam Holdsworth wheezed with laughter. 'Dr Viner.'

Helen Viner was as far a cry from the custodial type as one could get. For one thing, she was a dauntingly lovely woman with a warm (*Ingratiating, Adam ingratiating,* Lady Cray had later said) smile; for another, she was on the side of the 'guest'-patients, often taking up their causes and bringing their needs to the attention of Mrs Colin-Jackson; for another thing, she didn't believe in the use of force, not where negotiation was possible. And Helen Viner was a well-trained, clever negotiator. She could thrust and parry as well as the Dunster Dualists.

'Elizabeth,' she called out, 'Flèche'

Elizabeth broke all out in smiles and took some running steps.

Juliette glared at Helen Viner. 'Taking sides?'

'No, Juliette. You haven't been keeping your guard up.'

Both of them went at it again, this time with a clearly different attitude. It had now become a fencing match.

'Ah,' said Lady Cray, 'Douglas Fairbanks, Jr.' She was within easy earshot of Dr Viner and she allowed her clear, bell-like voice to carry.

Helen Viner turned, slightly surprised, and when she saw the new 'guest', smiled. 'Thank you.'

With an advance-lunge, the tip of Juliette's umbrella was straight into Elizabeth's frontage. 'Touché!' cried Juliette.

There was applause all round, and both sisters took bows. When Alice Dimpleton started to hand over the prize to Juliette,

Elizabeth's face clouded over again and Helen Viner took the chocolates.

Adam couldn't hear the exchange, but apparently Dr Viner had mollified the two of them by holding the box herself.

As the Dunster sisters and Dr Viner walked past Lady Cray and Adam, Dr Viner said hello to him and held out her free hand to Lady Cray. 'I'm Dr Viner. We haven't met yet, I'm sorry.'

All Lady Cray said, looking at the box in the doctor's other hand, was 'Cadbury's Opera Assortment. How very nice.'

22

Considering the Constable on the wall behind them, Melrose was hard put to listen to Crabbe Holdsworth holding forth on the painting on the wall before them by Ibbetson.

'Quite beautiful, isn't it?' said Crabbe of the Ibbetson, a painter that Melrose had never heard of and hoped never to again after his indentured servitude at Tarn House.

No, thought Melrose, as he *hemmed* his response, trying to look appreciative.

'Probably the most painted view of the Lakes. Only a copy, of course. But it's a fine example of that particular school.'

Melrose sighed. He had always been suspicious of 'schools' and 'genres'.

The painting showed fells that looked as warm and brown as huge loaves from an oven; they were reflected in a glassy lake that looked no more real than the rounded peaks themselves. In the foreground were two young ladies, a man, a child, and a dog, very close to a group of cows who had decided, apparently, to sit down and join them. This happy scene was framed by willowy trees and, on the opposite side, a boat with furled sails. The sky was a shading of pastels.

That Crabbe Holdsworth could enjoy this sampling of the so called picturesque school was a total mystery to Melrose. One had only to look at the Constable to see how ludicrous the Ibbetson was — how unreal, how lacking in perspective. Constable's peaks looked like peaks — difficult, remote, unreachable beneath a smoky sky.

In this grouping there was a watercolour that Melrose thought fairly decent — honest, at least, as the Ibbetson certainly wasn't — but found that his opinion was disputed by the received wisdom of Crabbe Holdsworth, who made a gesture that as good as waved it off the wall. 'My cousin Francis considers himself a painter.

157

So did Ibbetson, so that made no impression. Crabbe continued. 'My son, Graham, was a far better painter than Francis. There's a small scene Graham did of Rydal Mount out there in the gatehouse.' Crabbe Holdsworth gestured down the drive. 'Perhaps you'd collect it for me sometime. I keep meaning to ask Francis to bring it up to the house. But he's always out and about with his easels and brushes.'

Melrose smiled. 'That's the way with painters, isn't it?'

'In all weathers.' His sigh was martyred, as if the cousin were constantly dragging Crabbe along with him.

They had been discussing – rather, Crabbe had been soliloquizing on – Robert Southey that morning while Melrose had been working over file cards. Indeed, Melrose wondered if he had been hired not really so much to catalogue the books in this library (which smelled so pleasantly of old leather and beeswax) as to provide an untutored ear for Mr Holdsworth, all other ears in the family having turned away.

Although the Southey-talk might have seemed cold-blooded to someone else in light of his daughter-in-law's death and his grandson's disappearance, Melrose imagined that it might be a case of what a psychiatrist would call 'displacement', a mental leap from his grandson to Southey and the death of that poet's little son. No, Melrose didn't think that Alex Holdsworth was far from his grandfather's mind.

'I've always thought that Southey was an especially underrated poet, don't you?'

'Not really.' Melrose had replied, noting the title of a volume on his index card. His index cards were a mixed lot. Most of them were filled with information on the Holdsworth family, cards which he slotted in with the others until he had enough for a 'report' to Jury. Thus he always appeared to be working on his indexing when he was doing little else than making notes on current events. The cards were either in his pockets, or locked in the desk. No one questioned this, since he doubted that anyone really cared. He imagined his presence here was really more to keep poor old Crabbe company. The man was a pleasant but dim companion. His wife certainly wasn't listening to his monologues. Melrose's difficulty lay in finding a way to get this information to London. He sighed.

Since his knowledge of the Southey ménage was pea-sized, he

had decided that what might increase his credentials (if not his popularity) would be to disagree.

Crabbe Holdsworth blustered about, walking up to a reproduction of the famous painting of the poet (as if Southey might furnish him with a rebuttal) and then turning to Melrose again. 'Mr Plant he *was* poet laureate.'

Now Melrose could drag in his own little be of erudition. 'Only because Walter Scott turned it down, remember.?'

Diane Demorney. Melrose never would have believed the woman would bring a genuine smile to his lips. When he realized that he was supposed to be something of an authority on the entire Lake School and further realized (after Jury had called him) that he had only overnight to become one, he had actually called on Diane Demorney. Diane had cotton bunting for a mind, but she had stuffed it with facts just as Agatha had stuffed her cottage with treasures from Ardry End. Diane's little secret was that she kept the facts limited so that she could converse on any subject. Not 'converse' as much as 'stump' her listener.

'The Lake District, Diane,' Melrose had said.

'I think I might be ill. Come over for a martini.'

Melrose had drunk her martinis once. He hadn't appeared for two days. 'Don't have time. Not the area itself, just the poets'

'Not Wordsworth. I don't bother with the ones *everyone* knows about.'

'Robert Southey, how about him?'

'Well, naturally, I've never read any of his writings. Let's see: Robert Southey was made poet laureate in nineteen-o-something but only because Sir Walter Scott refused it. That's all, except I think he was another of them who freeloaded on Wordsworth . . . or was it the other way round? Oh, I do know *one* thing about Wordsworth. He wasn't famous during his lifetime. Most people think he was being read six ways from Sunday, but he wasn't. Not even after *Strange Interlude*.'

Melrose had squeezed his eyes shut. 'Diane, that's a play by Eugene O'Neil.'

'Really?' Total indifference.

'You're thinking of *The Prelude*.'

'Never heard of it. How about — ?'

'You come trailing clouds of glory behind you, surely . . .!'

'I do, don't I? How about that martini?'

'Later. Thanks.'

Though considerably more beautiful, Diane Demorney was Long Piddleton's answer to the Wizard of Oz. All curtains, pulleys, wigs and puffs of coloured smoke.

Although Crabbe had to admit that Scott had been offered the laureateship first, he still felt he had to prove to Melrose that Southey was treated most unjustly. 'Byron was especially sneering.'

'Byron wore a perpetual sneer.' That was probably a safe bet. But Crabbe was conditioned to uphold the southey honour and so took from the shelf a copy of *Thalaba*.

Even though Melrose's ears were ready to drop off from boredom, he still didn't mention the freeloading. He said only, to keep his hand in, 'He was a better proser than a poet.'

Genevieve Holdsworth was giving plenty of thought to the disappearance of Alex.

It was teatime, and they were gathered in the drawing room at the rear of the house. Millie Thale had brought in the tray, Mrs Callow following with the sandwiches and cakes. It was a small five-tiered table that Agatha would have died for. Millie stayed to pour the tea and drag the table from one to another.

Disdaining tea and cake, Genevieve had earlier poured herself a double whisky and was smoking cigarettes. 'I've called that policeman half-a-dozen times. You'd think that after three days they'd've found him.'

'Not if he doesn't want to be found, Genevieve,' said Madeline. 'His mother's dead, my sister, in case you've forgotten.' She sounded more angry than sorrowful.

'Of *course* I haven't forgotten, but please don't put on that injured air — ' Without looking at Melrose, she must have remembered that they had a stranger in their midst and asked Millie to pour some more tea. Holding out her glass, she asked her husband, please, for another whisky. 'Sorry.' Her slight laugh was feigned. 'I'm so upset I'm not sure just what I'm saying.' This was directed at Melrose; her adjustment of her position on the sofa suggested that she did indeed know what she was saying, at least in the legs department.

'Would you like a fortune cookie?' asked Millie of Melrose, staring at him in a manner that said he'd better.

'Millie makes them, if you can imagine,' said Crabbe. I'll have one.'

Melrose reached for one and she turned the plate ever so slightly. He took a cookie and she passed the plate to Crabbe. 'I hope it's cheerier than the last one, Millie. Oh, have one, Genevieve,' he said as she waved the plate by in the same way she'd declined all other sustenance that wasn't liquid. Crabbe read from a narrow strip of paper: ' "Alex will be here soon." Well, thank you, Millie. That's very encouraging. I'm sure you're right.'

'What does yours say, Mr Plant?'

Melrose grinned. 'You're not a poet.' He looked round the assembled company, at Crabbe smiling smugly, as if Southey had been vindicated. 'There's a lot of truth in that.' Actually, there was more truth in the message than they knew. In extremely tiny letters she had written: *You're not what you say.*

'Ha!' said George. 'I'm to win at Braitherwaite Races, Whitsun, according this.' He wagged the bit of paper at Millie and said, 'Just see Hawkes gets that feed mixed right this time, will you? Thin as gruel it was yesterday. And don't trust him to feed them, girl; do it yourself.'

His tone was not nasty. They all appeared to think of Millie as one who could be sent here and there on whatever large or small errands they deemed necessary. To none of this did she make verbal answer. She merely looked her reply or nodded — except where Melrose was concerned. Him she ignored utterly, apparently quite sure that he would find a way to talk to her.

When she'd left the room, Melrose gazed after her. 'Is that little girl from this area? She hasn't a Cumbrian or Lancastrian accent at all.' He thought of the guttural stops and elided *l*'s of the regulars in the Old Contemptibles.

'No; her family's from London. Well, what's left of it. One aunt,' Crabbe said, 'who is not, we understand, a very good sort.'

Madeline smiled slightly. 'Aunt Tom. Hard to believe any woman would let herself be called "Aunt Tom".'

'Thomasina, probably,' said Genevieve, absently, interested in little but the gold bracelet on her wrist.

'Why is it that Millie isn't living with her aunt?'

Crabbe bit into his fortune cookie. 'As I said, a bad sort.'

What Melrose wondered, did *that* mean? Prostitute? Terrorist? Moors-murderer?

'Millie didn't want to go to her; she begged us to let her stay. We had not intention of doing so,' Genevieve was saying, 'but *Adam* insisted. *Adam* thinks Millie is *grand*.' The emphasis made it clear that Genevieve thought neither of them so.

Madeline said, 'The aunt apparently would have made the girl's life hell because this person's got no patience with . . . you-know.'

Since no one had mentioned a father, Melrose inferred that 'you know' was a sexual reference and that poor Millie was illegitimate.

'Beats her, the girl said. We did send her to stay with this Aunt Tom right after her mother's, ah . . .' Crabbe looked down at his cup.

'Suicide,' said Genevieve impatiently. 'Call it what it was.'

'Yes. and when she came back Adam insisted she come to us; there were, you know, bruises . . .'

'Horrible,' said Madeleine. 'We wanted to call the police, but Millie got hysterical, even defended the woman, said she — Millie, I mean — just had a bad fall. So we did nothing. And to think this aunt could do that after what the niece had been through.'

'Sex.' George offered his opinion abruptly. ' "Tom" indeed. Victorian. Repressed. Pretty sister. Jealous. Dr Viner knows. Tart?'

Melrose declined. He was more interested in finding Millie.

23

Which he did, after tea, when she was feeding the hounds. As the cage of the kennel clicked shut behind her, the raucous outcry he'd heard in the distance had died; hounds were gobbling down their glutinous feed and slurping at their water.

Mist had rolled in across the cobbled yard and covered their feet, Millie's wellingtons squelching as she walked over to the wall to set down the empty buckets. For all the attention she paid, he might have been invisible. Then, with a feigned little start, she said, 'Oh, hello,' as if she hadn't noticed until that moment his approach through the rising ground mist.

'Don't sound surprised. You knew I'd wonder just who I am, if I'm not what I say I am.'

She looked up at him, chewing at the inside of her mouth, as if now that he was here, she wasn't too sure. 'Oh *I* don't know that. I only know you're not a book-cataloguer; you're not really here to work on Mr Holdsworth's library.' Then she waited out the ensuing silence.

'Just how do you know that?'

'You told me.' She walked with her buckets through the door to the kennels. The hounds sounded as if they were rioting.

Melrose called after her, 'What the devil's that supposed to mean?'

She came out into the cobbles and stared up at him. 'If you *were* what you said, you'd have looked at my message, frowned, looked peculiar and read it out to everyone.' She shrugged. 'But you made something up to say.'

He wouldn't have minded so much being found out by Fellowes, or Madeline or *any* of them. But this eleven year old child with her witchy cat (Sorcerer had just emerged from the gloom) was really too much. 'So you weren't sure until then. Well, what would have happened if I *had* read it out?'

'I'd have said it's a Chinese saying. Want to go for a walk?'
She was buttoning up an outgrown overcoat, short in the sleeves
and not as long as her dress.

Melrose winced. 'Are you sure you feel *safe*, walking about with
a person who's not what he says he is? I could be dangerous.'

'No more than anyone else around here. I want to show you
something.'

'They told me it was an accident,' she said, as they stood on a
small shelf of cliff surrounded by conifers that overlooked the foot
of Wast Water. The three of them (Sorcerer making a third) had
walked for perhaps ten minutes through the deeply wooded land
and come out here, not far above the lake. 'Come on,' Millie
commanded, making her way down the rocks. Melrose followed.

It was not a cave, exactly, but another mass of lichen-covered
rocks with the shelf above serving as a roof. Sphagnum moss
dripped down from the rocks above. The overlapping flattish stones
on which they stood, Millie pointing downwards, were slippery
with cladonia. 'They said she slid and fell down onto the lake shore.
See that sort of path?'

Not a path to walk down, certainly, more of a gully beside which
ran a narrow beck. The path was an obstacle course of rock, roots,
bracken and bog-myrtle. It would have been, as Millie was certainly
smart enough to tell, hardly possible to *plunge* downwards and
into Wast Water. Too many things would have impeded the fall.

'Anyway, I tried it out. A person can't.' Millie sat down and
pulled up her knees.

Tried it? What on earth do you mean?'

'To fall. You can't do it. I got some cuts, but that stump there
stopped me after I'd gone a few feet.' She looked up at him. 'Mum
was unhappy. She killed herself is what happened. You'd have
to *walk* into that lake, anyway, to get deep enough.'

Melrose lit a cigarette. 'I'm sorry, Millie.'

She was silent for a moment. 'She found his body. I expect they
told you that.'

You mean Alex's father.'

Millie nodded, her chin rubbing her knees. 'Was that what made
her unhappy?'

Melrose honestly thought she believed he knew. Because he
wasn't 'who he said he was' and was therefore a mystery, he was

fast gaining omniscience, perhaps, in her mind. 'I didn't know your mother; I can't say; but something like that, finding someone you're . . . fond of, dead. It could be terrible enough, I'd certainly think.'

'But it didn't make Alex's mother kill *herself*.Because it was years ago. Then maybe she didn't care as much as mine did.'

Melrose said nothing, the coal-end of his cigarette as he dragged on it sparked the blue dusk. He looked up, suddenly; he thought he'd heard something like the crack of twigs. 'What's that?'

'What? I didn't hear anything.'

'You must be deaf. It was loud as a pistol shot.'

'You've just got this big imagination. It's from sitting here in this fog.' She sighed. 'Alex knows his mum didn't kill herself. All he wants is to find out who did.'

Melrose turned to her. 'What do you mean? Why would he think someone actually killed his mother? And how do you know, Millie, *what* he thinks?'

She stared off towards Scafell, its eastern slope beginning to purple in the failing light, and asked, 'Do you live with your mum?'

The question startled Melrose. In her mind, if you had a mother, you'd naturally live with her, no matter how old you were. 'No. She's dead.'

'Were you there?' Millie reached down to place her hand on the cat's head, to still what was already stone-still.

'Yes.' He remembered the heavily curtained, medieval bed, his mother's luminous skin, humorous eyes − as if this were only one more hurdle to get her jumper, Isis, across. The letter she had left with their firm of solicitors was not given him until he was thirty. It had taken him a long time to absorb its contents.

He looked down at Millie, who was looking up at him, her urgent little frown suggesting she was desperate for details from someone who had, actually, been there. He told her about the room, and how his mother had looked, and remembering the barren look of the room, cluttered though it was, for three or four minutes told Millie what his mother had said to him, what he had said to her. Melrose invented the dialogue; they had said none of it. After the stroke, his mother had been unable to speak, but had managed to convey a great deal with her eyes. Pale golden hair, pale green eyes. He had tried to say something to her and could think of absolutely nothing to say.

165

Millie seemed somewhat comforted by this conversation between Melrose and his mother. They had even had a laugh together over the cats chasing each other across the bedclothes (or so Melrose told her). Millie wanted to know what colour they were, the cats. Black, both of them, he said, looking at Sorcerer.

No one said anything about anybody's father for a long while.

In the deepening night and silence, finally Melrose asked, 'Was his father fond of Alex?'

She nodded.

Melrose thought for a moment. 'Did they fight? I mean his mother and father?'

'Mrs Callow said they did. So did Mr Hawkes. He said he'd pass by the gatehouse and hear them. That's where they lived, where Mr Fellowes does now. Railing, Mr Hawkes said. But you can't believe much of what he says because he's always drunk.'

'Where did Mr Fellowes live, then?'

'Oh, I think in the village. I can't remember. Anyway, Alex's mum was always going off to London or somewhere.'

'Then where was Alex? Did he stay behind, here?'

She lowered her head, pulled at a tuft of dry grass. 'Sometimes. If it hadn't been for me he'd probably have run away. He hated them.'

'Even his father?'

'No, he liked him, but not as much as her. Did you see his picture? He was handsome, like Alex. They said she went to meet someone. You know.'

In the gloom, Melrose couldn't see her face, but he knew what she was implying and that she didn't know how to talk about it. Jane Holdsworth had had a lover? 'You mean Hawkes and the cook talked about it?'

Millie shook her head. '*She* did.'

She, of course, being the nemesis, Genevieve Holdsworth. Was there, Melrose wondered, any truth in this — that Jane had a lover? And would she sacrifice what would surely have been a fortune by involving herself with someone else?

'It's time to go!' Millie jumped up.

'Time to go where?'

She didn't answer, but turned and started to scramble up the rocks.

There was nothing to do but follow. He had been so absorbed in their talk he hadn't realized that darkness had fallen.

'I've got to get back to cook. It's already gone six. You go that way.' She pointed off to another stand of trees near the cliff's verge. 'Good-bye.'

'Wait a minute! Come back here! Where am I going?'

'To that big tree over there. Sorcerer knows.'

Sorcerer sat his ground, staring up at Melrose.

'Well. go on, *go* on!'

The cat turned and started through the trees.

It was dark, clouds scudding across the moon. In that way trees do in dreams, they seemed to take on human shapes – crooked backs, stretching arms, twiggy, skeletal fingers.

Out of the corner of his eye, he could have sworn that beech he'd just passed separated, divided.

A voice, not loud, but clear. 'Just stop there.'

He turned slowly. 'What – ?'

The slim boy standing there who had been until now part of that tree – how could anyone stand that still? – had a gun in his hand.

'You must be Alex.'

24

'No. I'm not holding a conference in a tree house.'

Alex was already halfway up, and indicated, with a nod of his head that Melrose should follow. Sorcerer flew up the ladder, his paws barely touching the wood.

Across the long field of bracken and bleached grass, Melrose could see the lights in the kitchen and on the first floor, where a figure moved before the window and then out of his line of vision. Madeline's room, Melrose thought. He looked up the tall tree; Alex was sitting in the makeshift doorway beside Sorcerer. 'Come on. Uncle George might be out there somewhere.'

Melrose gave in and grudgingly climbed up the rotting ladder, sure it would give way under him. 'What would George be grubbing about at night for? And what are you doing with a gun?'

'He's laying drags, maybe.'

There was no explanation of the gun. Melrose squeezed through the opening. He felt ridiculous. Still, as he looked round at the battered boards, the roof of tin, the few implements, such as bedding and books to make it habitable, he felt a wave of nostalgia.

'Besides,' said Alex, striking a match into flame and cupping his hands round a cigarette, 'we can smoke up here.' He tossed a packet to Melrose.

'Great. Can we say swear words and look at dirty pictures too?'

Alex grinned. 'Sorry. Don't have any. So you're the librarian?' Alex looked him over as if to say his grandfather surely could have done better. He took a drag, exhaled slowly, studied the librarian.

'You know damned well I'm not if you've been talking to Millie.' Melrose took out his own silver case.

'Flash that about in the house and people'll know you're not some seedy book person.'

Must he take lessons from a *boy*? 'I don't "flash" it about.' And then he remembered that this particular boy had only days

169

before found his own mother dead in their house. He did not know what to say that would be at all affecting, considering the horror of such a discovery. So he smoked and looked at Alex. Handsome, indeed. Eyes so dark he could hardly distinguish the iris; dark hair, slightly long but that was probably because the barbers weren't always available in tree houses. It had just begun to curl above the cable-knit sweater.

'Tell me what's going on in the house. Millie has, some, but she can't be hanging round the way you can. How are they taking it?' He'd lifted his chin slightly when his eyes had started to glisten, as if to keep any tears from spilling over.

'I'd say more angry than upset.'

'That's what I thought the reaction would be. Even Madeline? Even her own sister?'

'Madeline seems disturbed, yes. But over what I can't ascertain. Nervous is perhaps a better word. Tell me if my information's right: your aunt was at one time thought to be going to marry your — father.' Melrose studied the tip of his cigarette. How could a child stand losing both parents, *both* by suicide? This one seemed to be handling things very well. Businesslike, straightforward. Alex swallowed hard. He nodded.

'It just seems strange to me she could stand to live in the house after her sister had, well, taken away her fiancé.'

'Not fiancé. Lover.' he said with cool directness. 'Money.'

'She's not even a relation.'

'Probably wouldn't make much difference to Granddad.'

'Alex, why are you hiding, acting like a fugitive?'

'Because I've already talked to the police and they're on one of Uncle George's aniseed scents. They're dragging the wrong part of the wood. My mother didn't commit suicide.'

'There's a good bit of speculation that she was murdered, Alex. By a policeman. He's a friend of mine. He's also been suspended pending, as they say further investigation.'

Alex frowned. 'R. Jury, S-U-P-T?'

'Superintendent Jury, yes. How did you know?'

'Her address book. The one the police didn't take away.' He got it out of his rucksack, thumbed to the entry. 'It's a fairly new name. You can tell by the different colour. And, anyway, if she'd been friendly with a copper, I expect I'd've known. She didn't know him long, right?'

'Two weeks, perhaps. No, not very long.' Melrose reached out to rub the cat behind the ears, something to distract himself. Jury suspended. God's in his bloody heaven. 'The way I sort it out,' said Alex, 'Is the Seconal was dumped from the capsules into a drink. Several drinks. Mum liked whisky. His tone was not apologetic, not defensive. 'Obviously, no one could stuff pills or capsules down your throat.'

'But she *could* have done it herself.'

'Well, she didn't. I kept tabs on her medicines. The amounts, the dates. She didn't know it; it worried me.'

'And the ten or fifteen barbiturate capsules couldn't be accounted for; is that what you mean?'

'Oh, I can account for them. At Christmas we were here. She lost an entire bottle − she'd just had the prescription filled. She searched all over.'

Melrose ground out his cigarette, rubbed the ash with his shoe. 'Alex you've *got* to talk to the police. It's just the sort of thing you'd know; they wouldn't. Look, I can understand how you feel −'

'Oh, really?' The boy's smooth dark eyebrows rose and drew together into a single line. There was just the edge of sarcasm; he was incredibly cool. His effort to distance himself from his feelings (and Melrose had no doubt that his feelings were strong and deeply buried) so that he could remain objective was remarkable.

'My mother died when I was your age.'

'But not like this.' He kept rocking slightly on his buttocks, forwards and backwards, one leg drawn up, the hand with the cigarette thrown over it.

'No, not like this.'

'And you were there.'

'I was there, yes.'

'There was nothing you could do about it.'

'No. But neither could −'

'There's no way of knowing for sure whether I could.'

'If a person's set on suicide −'

'Thought we just canned that. Mum didn't kill herself.'

'You could hardly have stopped a murder planned three months ago, if you're right about those pills.'

'You don't think people can save each other?'

171

'Hard enough saving ourselves.'

'Then why are you here?'

'This is different.'

The boy merely smiled.

Melrose said, 'For God's sake. This is all *your* responsibility? What about the person who killed your mother?'

'It's a point.'

'I'd say so, yes.' Melrose felt vastly relieved. And he wondered if he'd taken Alex through this catechism for both their sakes.

They were both silent then, wondering the same thing: *Who? Why?*

'There are really only two motives for murder. Love and money.'

Alex shook his head. 'You forgot revenge.'

'Well, if you're thinking of Madeline Galloway, that's part of the 'love' motive, I'd say.'

'And what about silence?'

Melrose frowned. 'Meaning?'

'Silence. Keeping someone quiet. Like my mother.'

'About what?'

'No idea. But it's a motive, isn't it? Enemies: no, none I know of. Money: in this family, that's a fairly safe bet. And then of course there's me.'

'You.'

'Me. My grandparents have been trying to get me to live here for years. Or tried, until I got too old. Genevieve hated Mum.'

'I'd say that fits the enemy category; but killing her wouldn't get you, obviously.'

'Maybe she thought there'd be no where else to go.'

'I have a feeling your grandmother —'

'Genevieve's not my real one. That was Virginia. Virginia died in a fall.' His eyes blazed darkly. 'A lot of accidents right?'

'Yes. Too many. Your uncle?'

'Oh, I'd discount him. He's not bad, really. Just a bore.'

'Francis Fellowes? I've talked with him a few times.'

'He seems . . .' Alex shrugged. 'He seems interested in painting, full stop.'

Alex hadn't mentioned his father, and Melrose simply hadn't the heart to ask him, not now. 'Fellowes implied people were being killed off one by one.'

172

'Probably being dramatic. He likes to get a rise, you know what I mean.'

'But you said something of the same thing: a lot of accidents.'

'That's true. But *some* could have been.'

Alex didn't look at him; Melrose knew he was thinking of his father. And then he started and changed the subject.

'There was something missing.'

'What?' asked Melrose.

'I've been racking my brains, trying to remember.'

'Perhaps your unconscious mind has. Millie said you'd been dreaming the same dream every night.'

Alex told him the details. 'I know why the landscape was so empty.' Alex broke the twig, searched for another word. 'More than empty.'

'Sere?'

The boy frowned. 'Seer?'

'No, "sere". S-E-R-E. Blighted.'

'Tell Millie that word; she'd like it.' Alex smiled.

It was the first spontaneous smile Melrose had seen.

'Millie likes words.'

'Like "exercise". She wanted to take me to the place overlooking Wast Water to "exercise" ghosts.'

Alex laughed. 'Sounds like her. She thought the Red Queen had something to do with Alice-in-Wonderland. But the Queen there wasn't any help to Alice. She was a pretty mean person. Not like Mum.'

'You're being too literal.'

He scraped the hair back from his forehead.

'Millie thinks it's the gun.' He put the gun in the rucksack.

'Like *spellbound*. Did you ever see it?'

'Ingrid Bergman. She was a psychiatrist, wasn't she? There was a gun in there somewhere — '

'In the dream it was a wheel the killer was holding. Rolled in the snow. Ingrid,' Melrose smiled, 'saved him by working out that dream. Have you thought of talking to a psychiatrist about yours?'

'I'll have to see Granddad first. Adam. Then I'll do what you say; I'll go to the police.'

Melrose felt his backbone creak as he got up. 'I'm too old for living in tree houses. Although, when I think of my aunt, it might not be a bad idea.'

Alex laughed and started down the ladder. Melrose followed. The cat followed Melrose, slipping from rung to rung, past him. when they got to the bottom, Melrose brushed off his sleeves. 'Does the cat stay? Or go?'

'Depends where he thinks the action is.'

'Not with me, certainly. After you see your great-grandfather, Adam, get word to me.' He held out his hand. 'It's been — an event, meeting you.'

'I'm sorry about your friend. The superintendent.' Alex paused, looked off towards the lake. 'I don't know . . . was he, well, a particular friend of my mother?'

Melrose hesitated, not knowing whether now would be an especially good time for her son to think he had competition. 'Yes. Very special. I think he wanted to marry her.'

'Christ,' breathed Alex. He looked round, baffled, like one of his uncle's hounds that had lost a scent. 'Christ. And instead they're telling him he killed her?'

Melrose looked at him, thinking that Jane Galloway had been lucky to have such a son — bright, inventive, bold, caring (so much he checked her medicine), and still with compassion left over for someone he didn't even know. Had he, Melrose, been anything like that at that age? He doubted it. Maybe a little, but he doubted it.

'I'm not worried. The whole charge is too absurd. He's innocent.'

Grimly, Alex said, 'I never knew that to do much good.' He sketched a little salute. 'Good-night.'

Melrose nodded and turned towards the field.

Behind him, the tall grass separated magically. Sorcerer had decided where the action was.

25

'They think I should avail myself of psychiatric assistance,' said Lady Cray, sitting in Adam's room. 'And pigs might fly,' she added, exhaling a delicate ribbon of smoke. 'Must breakfast be served at the revolting hour of eight?'

Everything about her, from her hair to her clothes to the way she held her cigarette, simply reeked of breeding. Adam sighed and tossed a handful of salted almonds in his mouth. He always had his teeth in these days. 'So do it. Probably make a change, be fun.'

'Um. I think, actually, it was *more* than a suggestion. Mrs Colin-Jackson, although her tone bowed and scraped to me, made it sound as if I'd get tossed out on my arse if I didn't comply.'

'Hell Kojak doesn't really run the place. Helen Viner does. She's the only one with any sense. So see her; she's interesting.'

'It's *I* who am supposed to be "interesting", in this case. I wish Andrew were here.' She sighed and sipped her coffee. 'I did see her when I first got here. "Routine investigation", as the police love saying.'

'She always vets the guests.'

'It isn't *really* a retirement home, is it? Isn't that just a euphemism for "mental"?'

It's anything you want it to be if you have the cash. You want Andrew to spring you? You just got through saying you thought you'd get the boot. Listen —' Adam leaned towards her and whispered. '— why don't we both escape? I've worked out a really crackerjack way to do it.'

'I've heard about your escapes.' She smiled. 'Since we're free to walk out of the front door at any time, isn't it rather redundant?'

This rankled. He would have thought she'd have appreciated escape plans. Testily, he said, 'Well, Kojack — or rather Dr Viner

175

– wouldn't have said anything about shrinking you down it if hadn't been for the silver, damnit.'

'I *did* replace it. It was Miss Rupert who squealed.'

'Some clever replacing. You let Rhubarb catch you setting the table. You want to be caught, cleansed of your incorrigible, insatiable desire to satisfy your lustful cravings –'

'Oh, do shut up. Have you been reading Judith Krantz again? Have some more coffee.' She held up the silver pot she'd taken from the dining room sideboard.

'Not supposed to, so I will. Thanks.' She poured. 'Chocolate and hair ribbons. Bet Helen saw you giving that box of Cadbury's the eye.'

'Oh, she already knows about my 'lustful cravings'. *They* told her about my entire infamous history.'

'Daughter and son-in-law, eh? Family. Naturally, they would. So have you got an appointment to see Helen?'

'No. She wants me to see Dr Kingsley.'

'Maurice?' He frowned. 'That's strange. Thought she just kept Kingsley on out of generosity. He's an alcoholic. She must not think you're in such bad shape, then. Nice fellow, but more of a playboy than a doctor. Medication-orientated, Helen says. Wait'll you see the pills he's got lined up behind him.' Adam checked his bedside clock. 'Hell, he'll be in here checking up in five minutes.'

' ''Checking up''?'

'Oh, they do it with certain people. They like to see if I'm still here or if I've wheeled myself over the hill.' Adam wheezed with laughter. 'I can do it, you know. Have done, as a matter of fact.'

She looked round his room. It was choice, a corner room with tall windows overlooking the courtyard, the dry fountains, the wide grassy slope and the maze. 'The windowsills are low, yes. But still, you'd need your chair.'

'Feel that bicep. I've very strong arms.'

Lady Cray looked at his extended arm and made a moue of distaste. 'No, thank you.'

'The chair's collapsible. Did Rhubarb tell you about the night they spent hours looking for me? I was in the maze.' He nearly choked on his almonds. 'I'm the only one –'

Lady Cray, who was looking out of the window Adam had

indicated, sat up suddenly. 'Adam, someone's out there.' She'd heard what sounded like footsteps scraping across the courtyard.

Alex didn't know what to do, not with a stranger in his grandfather's room. Now she'd seen him, or heard him, before he'd seen her. He flattened himself against the wall to the right of the window as it opened and this woman — an older woman clearly unafraid of intruders — asked, 'Who's there?'

He said nothing. And then his granddad's old, familiar head jutted out, muttering imprecations, and Alex decided, Oh, all right, if Adam likes her, she must be okay.

'Alex!' The bright blue eyes of Adam Holdsworth teared over as he embraced his great-grandson. 'For God's sake, you can come in the front door, but I'm glad you didn't. This is my friend, Lady Cray.'

She held out her hand. Alex thought she was really — elegant. *Elegant* was the word. And her grey eyes had that sharp, steely look that he often saw in his grandfather's. She was rich, you could tell.

'Don't cry, Granddad.' Alex put his arms round him again.

'Oh, he does that all the time, young man. He's a regular dungeon-ghyll, a veritable waterfall.'

'Am not!' he yelled at her. 'My God Alex! You disappeared. Everybody's looking for you.' He seemed to crumple right there in his chair.

'Granddad?'

Adam looked up at him, sadly. 'Your mother. What can I say? What can I say or do?'

Alex looked away.

Lady Cray raised her chin a bit. 'Nothing. There's nothing anyone can say or do. I doubt he came here to cry on your shoulder. He doesn't look at all the type. He's like Andrew.'

Whoever Andrew was, Alex smiled at her businesslike manner. Somehow, it took the sting out. She said she was very happy to meet Alex and then was quickly gone.

'She's nice. Who is she?'

'Just some woman.' Adam waved dismissively. 'Now tell me what the hell's happened.'

As Alex told him, he though his great-grandfather seemed to age visibly, a bit more and a bit more, as if a special effects expert were working on him for a film. Alex knew he was also thinking of his father; his father had been one of old Adam's favourites. Two suicides.

'It's unthinkable,' said Adam, as if he'd been following Alex's thoughts. 'Jane'd never have done that. Not to herself, and not to you.'

Alex relaxed, took a cigarette from the lady's packet. After he'd drawn in deeply, he told Adam about the 'new one'.

'That librarian-fellow old Crabbe hired?'

Alex liked that 'old Crabbe'.

'Only he's not a librarian.' Alex told him about the talk in the tree house. 'So I've *got* to go to the police, don't I? I'm the only one — except whoever did it — who knows about those pills.'

Before Adam could answer, the door opened and Maurice Kingsley entered, smiling. 'Glad to see you're here, Adam. Who's your company and whoever he is, I presume he came through the window. Looks like you, must be another Holdsworth. Don't Holdsworth's *ever* use doors?' He put out his hand.

Automatically, Alex shook it.

He was the man on the bench outside their house in Lewisham.

26

'Crinkle Cottage,' I call it,' said Fellowes, once they were inside the old gatehouse. 'I named it after Crinkle Crags, that wavering line of fells. You been up there?'

Been up there? Was he joking? 'No. Remember, I just got here. Haven't had much time to do any exploring.' Never would, either, if Melrose could help it.

'I always feel it's a good metaphor for my mind, Crinkle Crags.' Paintings were stacked five, six, seven deep against all four walls, and Francis was pulling them out, shoving them back, making various sounds of displeasure in looking at his own work. 'Damned if I know where it is. Here somewhere.

Crabbe had released Melrose from his relentlessly boring discourse on — what was it this morning? — Rydal Mount — to send him along to see if the cousin could locate Graham Holdsworth's painting of a view of the famous Wordsworth-Southey place. Melrose knew he'd have to visit it. Sometime.

'Here's one. Not bad.'

'Graham's'

'Of course not. All of his were bad. Mine.'

It was yet another view of Wast Water and Screes and was, indeed, 'not bad.' 'Your ability to handle lights and shades is impressive. That sounds pompous.'

'Hell, who cares. I can use all the encouragement I can get.'

Melrose picked up a largish painting of a lakeland scene. 'Whose is this? Not Ibbetson or Graham Holdsworth's.'

'That? That's a Thompson. He's very good. The colours are so thick you'd think it's an oil. But it's watercolour. Look at *that* lighting. Look at the green. Viridian.' Fellowes's thick finger made a trail across the horizon.

'Looks like Sorcerer's eyes.'

179

Fellowes had again turned back to the collection. 'Ah! Here's an Ibbetson. Take it.'

The view of Greta Hall was, Melrose thought, saccharine and unimaginative. It made no difference whether one had seen it; the painting had no more character than the others on the library walls.

'Just for the fun of it, I tried aping his style. Thought perhaps I could pass it off to Crabbe.' He sighed. 'But I hadn't the heart, in the circumstances.'

'What circumstances?' There were two paintings, one a downward-looking view at a bit of Wast Water and Wasdale Head. The other a tedious look at crags, a high-walled mountain with a large crevice, clouds like flakes.

'It was the day Virginia died. I told you, she fell when she was climbing Scafell. Broke her neck on the rocks below. I told you I came in for some heavy questioning. She liked Scafell too; she wanted to make the ascent from Borrowdale because of the magnificent scenery, but I insisted going up by way of Brown Tongue. I told her I wasn't killing myself just to — sorry, no pun intended.' Francis was sitting in the single stuffed chair packing down his pipe.

Melrose stared. 'Just a minute. You mean you were *with* her?'

Francis looked up, drawing hard on the pipe. 'That's right. That's why the police were so interested in me.' He shrugged. 'But one needs a motive, after all, and I certainly hadn't one. Except perhaps I was very fond of Ginny and they tossed about the idea of jealousy. That was nonsense.' Fellowes smiled and puffed.

'Where's the site?'

'You mean where Virginia had her accident?'

'Where you did the painting.'

'Some yards down the Eskdale side of Scafell. Virginia was determined to get to Mickledore by way of Broad Stand. That's the tricky rock-face that bars it. Otherwise, you have to double back and go round another way.'

Melrose ran his hand through his hair. He was thinking of Alex last night, how he had separated himself from that tree, how he had been all but invisible. 'Why were you suspected at all?'

Francis laughed. 'Like Hilary, because I was there.'

'But that's ridiculous. someone *else* could have been there.'

'But that's the point: someone else *couldn't* have, or I'd have

180

seen them. Anyone else would have had to go past me, unless the person was a very experienced climber.'

Melrose frowned. 'How could you have seen anyone? You were painting this view of Wasdale Head. Your back was turned.' Melrose frowned. 'Unless you were looking directly at the mountainside, here.' Melrose indicated on the second watercolour.

'I forgot; you don't know the way Ibbetson painted.' Francis walked through the clutter of canvases, papers, jars to a battered desk, opened a drawer and tossed something to Melrose. 'It's a Claude glass.'

From a leather wallet Melrose drew a small convex mirror that fitted the hand. He looked questioningly at Fellowes.

'Claude Lorrain, like Salvator Rosa, influenced a whole way of seeing and painting. One of the worst perversions of "seeing" I've come across. It reminds me, sometimes, of the way people "see" a photo; a snapshot, that is. I've watched tourists do it. Snap their friends in front of Dove Cottage, say, then gather round to see what they look like in the picture, instead of looking at the real thing.'

'What's that to do with this?' Melrose held up the mirror.

'That device was very popular with painters of the "picturesque" school. You paint what's behind you, not what's in front. The mirror acts as a "framing" device. Claude believed in painting exactly what you see. You don't "interpret" — although, obviously, it's impossible not to — so that what you paint supposedly duplicates what's actually there. It's extremely artificial and as close to a mirror-image as one could get. It's the same as Ibbetson's idea of "framing" the painting with trees, for example. In addition of course to tossing in sentimentalized people and animals in postures more lugubrious than the regulars at the Old Con. How many times have you ever sat down with a cow, for God's sake?'

Melrose tried not to think of Agatha.

'So you hold this Claude glass thing in your hand and look at what's behind you.'

Fellowes nodded. 'It would make a poet like Wordsworth die a thousand deaths. To him, perception was actually creation.' He knocked his pipe against the pottery jar. 'Ever read Thomas West?'

'Oddly, yes.' He hadn't finished his acquisition from the Wrenn's Nest, however.

'Then you know he believed tourism should be a set of perfectly arranged pictures or settings. It's the start, in a way, of Baedeker and all of those guides. You're told precisely *what* to look at. Tourists come here to see Dove Cottage, Grasmere, Hawkshead Church, Coniston Water, Ruskin's house, Beatrix Potter's cottage, and so on. A set of perfectly arranged pictures. And this school loved Gothic elements, too. Ruined castles, twisted trees. You know, one of my favourite writers is Jane Austen, and one of her best characters is Edward Ferrers, who was really taking the piss out of the heroine's sentimentality. "I do not like crooked, twisted, blasted trees. I do not like ruined, tattered cottages." '

Fellowes laughed. Melrose thought for a moment. 'If I wanted to get up to this spot where you did your painting' – he shuddered at the thought of climbing anything higher than the stairs of Ardry End – 'which route would I take?'

'You? Pardon me, but I somehow can't imagine you kitting yourself out for a climb up Scafell.'

'Neither can I. But which?'

'The easiest. The one I took, or we did. From Wasdale Head, the other end of West Water. You'd begin at the Wasdale Hotel –'

Melrose would just as soon end there, too.

Ah, Wordsworth! Ah, Inns!

27

Dr Maurice Kingsley had appeared not to recognise him.

Alex couldn't be sure. The only light on that night had been the reflected one from the open door of their house and the spurt of a flame as Kingsley had lit a match. And certainly the doctor had been drunk enough not only to have forgotten the face of William Smythe, but to have forgotten the whole evening. Blotto, he'd been.

Or had he?

The doctor's expression showed nothing but concern. 'I'm sorry, Alex. About your mother. I liked her,' he said simply. Kingsley looked away and back. 'Look, come round and have a talk sometime if you feel like it. It helps talking – '

'You should know, Kingsley, ' said Adam. 'You do enough of it.' Adam took out his teeth and dropped them in a tumbler by his chair.

Kingsley laughed. 'Oh, come on, Adam. Break out one of those cigars you keep squirrelled away that you smoke against orders.'

Prissily, Adam mimicked Nurse Lisgrove: ' "Oh, Doctor, he'th been thmelling up hith room again." Bloody hell, she's got a case on you. God knows why. Though I expect all the women round here do . . . except Helen Viner. She's got too much sense.' Adam bent over, rooting round under his bed. He brought out a box of hand-rolled cigars and tossed one to the doctor.

'Undoubtedly, she has.' His smile was enigmatic. 'Thanks.'

All the while this exchange was going on, the doctor was watching Alex. It was true, Kingsley did strike Alex as a sort of ladies' man, but he also looked like a man who'd be running to fat in ten years. From booze, probably. Would his mother be attracted to him? He was friendly, but glib. Shrewd, Alex thought.

Whether his concern was feigned, Alex didn't know any more than whether the boozy drunk had been an act. The trouble was,

Alex was having a hard time of it seeing the truth in *anyone's* face, except for his great-grandfather's and Millie's. This policeman's friend, Mr Plant. He saw truth there and was surprised he was so convinced of it. He was momentarily comforted by having the man around.

It made him feel, even, reckless.

'What happened to you Alex? Your family's been beside themselves . . .' Kingsley stopped.

The 'Family'. Alex wiped all expression from his face. Kingsley certainly knew from someone – his granddad, Dr Viner, someone – how much Alex would believe the family had been worried about his welfare. 'I was in London. I holed up in an hotel. I didn't want to be badgered by the police any more, or anyone else. What'd they ask you?'

The cigar still unlit, the hand holding it dropped to Kingsley's side. ' "They"?'

'Police.'

Adam was saying nothing. His grandfather could 'Seize up' with stillness, nearly vanish from the scene, if he thought the occasion warranted.

Kingsley frowned. 'Police? Why, nothing. I mean, other than asking me if I knew Mrs Holdsworth. Should they have done?' He smiled slightly.

'Mrs Holdsworth.' Not 'Jane.' That, thought Alex was a nice touch. Kingsley wasn't on that bench in evening clothes waiting for any 'Mrs Holdsworth'. He was thinking hard, half hearing Dr Kingsley talking about police always asking questions . . .

' . . . in cases of – sudden death.' Discreetly, he looked away. 'Dr Viner can tell you more. She knew your mother far better.' He paused, looked from the blank face of Adam to the blank one of Alex. 'Listen, are you saying the police suspect something else?'

Tonelessly, Alex replied, 'No. I'm saying I do.'

Maurice Kingsley broke the silence finally by saying, 'Trauma often results in – fantasies, strange thoughts, Alex. I'm not, for God's sake, saying you're *wrong*. But I wish you'd come and talk to me about it.'

It's a wager, thought Alex, like the track, like cards, like any wager. If he remembers me or suspects I was the William Smythe on that bench, he'll do something.

Let him.

'I've an appointment, sorry.'

'We're not,' said Adam, giving him a toothless smile. 'Better get to your office before Lady Cray cleans it out.'

Kingsley gave Alex a good-humoured smile that said *I'm used to it* and left with his unlit cigar.

'What the hell was *that* all about?' asked Adam, plucking one of his cigars from the box and trying to gum the end off.

'He was *there*, Granddad. Outside our house on the night – ' Alex stopped, utterly befuddled now. 'Sitting on a bench in the park, drunk as a lord, mumbling about being stood up, asking me for a fag.'

'What were *you* in the park for?'

'I'll tell you later, never mind,' said Alex impatiently.

Adam said, round a damp and shredded cigar, 'You mean . . . bloody hell. It was *after* the coppers got there.'

Alex nodded. 'You're not going to say it could have been a coincidence.'

Adam said, 'I'm saying tell the police. Your aunt and Genevieve were in London that night too. That makes three.' Adam puffed, stared out of the dry fountains, the misty day. 'Three we know about.'

2

He had told his great-grandfather he was going straight to Tarn House (with his story of trauma, amnesia, or whatever his mind kicked up like pebbles along the way), but Alex lingered in the grounds of Castle Howe.

He no longer understood himself. What he had discovered about Dr Maurice Kingsley should have sent him right to Melrose Plant or to the telephone to ring up Inspector Kamir because now they had a person who could be absolutely placed at the scene of the crime. Whether they believed there *had* been a crime made no difference to Alex. He knew.

Yet he lingered. He walked though the gardens, looked down the long lawn towards Dr Viner's office in the little stone house, watched two elderly women (rich to their earlobes, just look at those diamonds) walking arm-in-arm and speak intimately. One gave the other's arm a bit of a squeeze and the other laughed.

They seemed so carefree. In his mind he repeated the word again and again. It sounded hollow, false, a word without meaning. Down the path edged with early primroses he walked, eyeing the beds of daffodils and thinking of Millie. Was there no end to it, this feeling of desolation.

He came to the entrance of the maze (his granddad's favourite place) and stood there staring in. If he went in, could he get out? Did it make any difference? Alex looked up at the leaden sky. Feelings like this were totally unlike him, and even his mother's death couldn't explain this thing that went beyond depression. He felt dried out, shrunken, much like some of the feeble old people at Castle Howe. And yet most of them seemed to have more life to them in their craziness, more energy in their madness, if it be madness. A few of them like to wander in here, get lost, and start crying out *Help Help*. Kojak was always complaining; she wanted to level it to the ground, but his granddad wouldn't let her. And he was Castle Howe's biggest benefactor.

Anyway, someone looking down from the upper floor, or from the parapet, could track the person's movements. There was no danger of a 'guest' dying in here.

It put Alex in mind of the tree at Severn School, the binoculars, the racecourse. All that seemed years ago, continents away, something lost.

He entered the maze, walked a bit and sat down on one of the wrought-iron benches placed at intervals in little nooks.

The horses, the card games, the scams. They seemed to belong to a past he remembered only mistily.

He had changed; he was frightened.

'Alex!'

When he saw her, he sprang up, surprised his body had the energy left for such a precipitate rise or his mouth the means to smile. But there was and had always been something about Dr Viner that made his blood run quicker.

He even blushed as she came towards him from the opening a few feet away. He forgot to say hello.

'Alex.' She put her hands out, put them on his arms, made no move to embrace him, to crowd him. Her eyes, without seeming to move, searched his face. For signs. Signs of strain, signs of struggle.

And he could only just barely keep his expression controlled. As if beneath the tight skin, bone was cracking, muscle loosening — it was becoming the face of one of these old people. But it didn't. He kept still, looking at her. And it wasn't easy to look at her because she reminded him of his mother. Same sandy-coloured hair, goldish eyes. Or hazel, he supposed that was what they were, fretted with different colours — brown, green, topaz, blue. Worse, she had his mum's sympathetic expression. No wonder they'd been such friends; no wonder Dr Viner was such a good psychiatrist.

All of this went through Alex's mind as he finally said hello to her and as she sat down on the bench and pulled him down beside her. Though it didn't feel as if he were being pulled. It was more like a magnetic force. He looked away from her, his glance straight ahead, because he felt in her presence, some new gravity, as if he would fall not down but sideways, but towards her.

He almost, right then, told her about Kingsley. But that was news only for police.

'You don't agree your mother killed herself, do you?'

She was so direct. Looking him right in the eye like that, naming the unnameable.

'I wonder, too. No matter what troubles she was having, no matter the depression, the pressure from the family, it's too hard to believe she'd have done that. She loved you too much.'

What he had said to himself, what he had known all along still sounded sweet to his ears coming from someone else.

'The police said it was an overdose. They asked me how anyone could be given a fatal dose of Seconal without the victim's knowing it.' The contemptuous expression wasn't meant for Alex, when she looked at him. 'As if their own pathologist couldn't answer that question. I told them obviously all anyone had to do was empty the capsules into liquid, and whisky would hide the taste. Especially several whiskys. They thanked me and went away. That is, after they'd talked to Maurice Kingsley. He's in —' She sighed. '— a bit of a spot.'

Alex looked at her quickly.

'Maurice went to London that night. But you only just met Dr Kingsley, didn't you? He knew your mother. I'm honestly not sure what this inspector from London believes. He gave very little away. I was probably her best friend; Maurice less so, but a man.

Jealousy, there, perhaps. I don't think they'd worked out a motive for me — '

'*You?*' Alex stared. 'You're the *last* person — '

She smiled. 'One has to be careful about the *last* person. The thing is that any doctor would have access to prescription drugs.' She shook her head, lowered it. 'I'm sorry, I'm sorry, Alex.' She put her face in her hands. 'Oh Lord, *I'm* the doctor and I'm crying on *your* shoulder.'

It made him feel somehow better that she was, the way he'd often felt with his mum. He felt he could return the confidence. He told her about the dream. The pack of cards wrapped in tape, the blighted landscape, the Queen, Millie's notion. He didn't tell her about the gun, though.

'Let's walk,' she said. 'I think better.'

'Will we get lost?' He tried on a smile.

'We're already lost.' She stuck her hands in the wide pockets of her white coat.

'A desolate landscape contrasted with a beautiful horizon: Heaven and Hell, perhaps.' was her comment on the dreamscape.

'It's the pack of cards I don't understand.'

'You're quite a cardsharp, Alex.' She smiled. 'I've heard.'

'Don't compare me with the Vicar and Mrs Bradshaw. I could beat them blind.'

She turned to look at him. 'Apparently, you did.'

'They couldn't count. But the cards in the dream — '

'Mean more than that, I know.' Dr Viner was silent for a while, walking slowly. 'What're your associations?'

'Nothing. None.'

'Oh, but that's impossible. Your mind can't be a blank. Look at it from another point of view. For instance, the word *card* could refer to a person. A *pack of cards*, then, might be a group of your friends, tricksters, something like that. I'm only giving you that as an example.'

'House of cards?'

She said nothing, letting him think it through.

'My family. Take away Mum, and the whole thing comes tumbling down. As if she was the foundation.'

'Well? Does it seem to fit? It's your dream.'

'No.'

188

Abruptly, she stopped. They were near another white bench, or perhaps it was the same one. How could he tell?

'You think its important?' she asked.

'I know it's important.'

'Why?'

Now they had come to another opening, which presented them with a blind wall of boxwood hedge.

'It's the something missing.'

'What do you mean?'

'From Mum's room. There was something missing. Whatever it is, it registered and got turned into the cards. Someone reminded me of that film *Spellbound*. Where a wheel in the dream is really a gun in reality.'

She smiled. 'I saw it. Ingrid Bergman solves the puzzle. I only wish I were Ingrid Bergman.'

Alex broke off a bit of twig from the hedge. 'Oh, you're all right as Dr Viner.'

'Thanks for that. Who else did you tell the dream to?'

'Who?'

'You said someone reminded you of the film.'

'Oh. Millie. She loves films.' She might find it odd he'd tell the new cataloguer of books, a perfect stranger. 'I have this dream every night. I'll remember at some point.' They had come to another hedgewall. 'Right or left?'

'Left. I've memorized this maze. I had to; the Dunster sisters like to play hide and seek here.' As they neared the opening that would at last allow them to exit, she said, 'It's like sleight of hand, isn't it? Or a good card trick?'

'Except this pack was Sellotaped together. And my mother had something to do with it.' They were standing now on the stone path where the line of primroses began, and daffodils. 'Then the bits blew away in the wind.'

She frowned, buttoning her coat against a chill in the air. For a moment she looked off towards the manor house. 'I've got to go. I'll see you at dinner tonight. Your great-grandfather asked me and Lady Cray. Will they escape in the delivery van or simply leave through the front door?' She laughed and walked off.

He watched her go, thinking still of the confetti-like bits of the pack of cards carried away in a swirling wind.

The expression came unbidden to his mind. *Pack of lies.*

28

Lady Cray gave a bright, birdlike look at the pill in Dr Kingsley's outstretched hand. 'If you feel you really need it, take it.'

'That's very funny.'

'*I'm* expected to swallow it?'

He nodded.

'For what?'

'It'll calm your nerves.'

'I'm so calm I'm nearly comatose.' She took out her gold cigarette case. 'A cigarette will do far better. Please remove your hand from my face.'

'Tell you what. Take the pill, you may smoke.'

'What is it? Truth serum? Insulin shock therapy?'

Kingsley sighed. 'For God's sake, Lady Cray, It's a mild tranquillizer.' He reached to the shelf behind him, along which sat a row of vials, and picked one up to show her.

'Oh, very well.' In the corner of his book-lined office — very psychitastry, she'd thought, when she'd seen it (they all want you to think they can read) — was a water cooler. 'Well, get me some *water*.'

'Oh sorry. I take them dry.'

She took them no way; the pill went under her tongue. When he brought back the little paper cup, she gulped down the water and pushed the cup towards him in the manner of a shipwreck victim. 'More.'

As he returned to the water cooler, she plucked out the pill and tossed it in his wastepaper basket. 'I just love to see the bubbles pop, don't you?' She nodded towards the glass tank, in which the water sucked down, came up and bubbled. She crumpled the cup and tossed it away too. Probably a behaviourist, she thought. Handsome, but doesn't look smart enough for Freud or Jung. She smiled widely enough to show her dimple. She loathed dimples, but for some reason men thought one on a lady of a certain age to be absolutely disarming. Thus she smiled charmingly when he handed her the second cup.

'So. What do you do to keep busy?' Lady Cray looked round the office. Big picture -window behind, so that one could turn in the leather chair and view the artifacts of the Stonehenge days making their way about with sticks, walkers, Nurse Rhubarb, Lisping Lisgrove and the younger helpers. There was the Vicar (with what Church he had once been connected, she had no idea, but it must have had wealthy patronage) slowly moving along the side of the beechwood hedge, thrashing at it with his cane. And far in the distance, Wast Water. Very far. So far, indeed, no one could see it except with binoculars up on the ramparts. The brochure was really stretching things to have its greensward rolling right to the lake's shores. It was, she thought, a cold, unforgiving looking body of water. Not like the other lakes. It was the deepest in all of England.

'What are you thinking about?' he asked.

'Wast Water.'

'Why?'

'You tell me.'

'Why do I think you're not going to cooperate? He smiled, taking Adam's cigar from his pocket. 'I knew he kept them under the bed.'

'I've never been under it, so I wouldn't know.' She took her slim gold cigarette case from her creamy leather bag and extracted a Black Russian. Beneath some papers, Dr Kingsley found his lighter − equally slim, an elegant black Porsche. He lit his cigar after her cigarette.

'You doctors must make a packet out of this place. That's a handsome lighter. I have one just like it.' She rooted a bit in her bag. 'You psychiatrists, you're truly clever at seeing things. You could see a cigar from the top of Nelson's Column.'

Actually, it was she herself who could do that. Her vision had always been superb, a point she prided herself on. It was marvellous watching youngsters have to take out their glasses to see the Tower of London, when she could pick out one of its ravens from half a mile away. Well, a *bit* of an exaggeration. Oh, dear, now he was talking about the silver. Perhaps he wasn't a behavioural psychologist after all. It was sounding much like the Freudian primer.

'. . . the need to supplant some loss in your childhood.'

She winced. The very *word* 'childhood' made her want to rip apart every book in the cases — of which there were plenty. Three walls of them. So psychiatristry and he probably hadn't read one. Beside one of the filing cabinets was a dainty table with a hot plate and things for tea-making. 'It was the tea set,' she said, looking up at the ceiling. 'You see, Mummy gave me this wonderful doll's tea set. Little spoons and all. My brother smashed it. I still think about it. Mummy was usually entertaining on-the-dole 'artists' or actors 'resting between roles' at one of her 'salons '. Mummy drank her gin neat.'

Maurice Kingsley was puffing and smiling. 'Got to do better than that, Lady Cray.'

'I do?' One enamelled-looking eyebrow shot up. 'Why?'

'You don't have a brother.'

'I could have sworn . . .' She shrugged. 'Perhaps I'm mistaken. It must have been one of Mummy's lovers' kiddies. She had simply dozens. I was always left out. . .' His head was moving from side to side. No good, that, either. 'Do you read?'

Poker-faced, he said, 'No. They're all hollow. Just rows of fake spines.'

She tried not to smile, but couldn't help it. 'At least you've a sense of humour. Her gaze netted the rows of books. 'More or less.'

'Look, Lady Cray, we know perfectly well that you're not a compulsive thief, although your family appears to think so.'

' "Family". Have they the gall to call themselves that? My lank, greedy son-in-law and my wimpish daughter?'

He sat back. 'Perhaps we've arrived at some sort of truth.'

What was he saying? And why taking notes? 'You've obviously *not* talked to my grandson. Andrew.' She could feel herself beam; blood suffusing her fine narrow frame. 'He's the only one worth tuppence. You know, he might be twice that boy's age, but Andrew, and Alex Holdsworth would truly hit it off.' He'd stopped taking notes. Or doodling.

He looked up at her under his thickish eyebrows. 'You've got to know Adam well, haven't you?'

'It's where I stash the swag. His room.' Doodle, doodle.

Silence. Had she struck a nerve?

'The reason you want to be here is because you loathe living with your daughter. But why do you? You're obviously independent. You're rich. Gold silk and pure cashmere.' He nodded at her suit.

'I've never head of impure cashmere, but I'm glad you like my outfit.' She looked down at her blouse, her lightweight suit. It *was* stunning. 'My daughter and her husband do give people the false impression that *I* live with *them*. It is, in fact, the other way round. It is *my* house, although I occupy my own quarters, separate entrance, separate everything.' She sighed. 'It was quite nice whilst Andrew was living with them. But he left and took the best of the fun with him. A friend showed me a brochure, several brochures, of retirement homes, nursing homes, mental homes.' She smoked and smiled. 'I'd say you've all three here.'

He put down the cigar and flipped to another page of her file. 'You've been arrested, let's see − '

'Three times. *I* can tell you that. What other interesting titbits did your Dr Viner include after she vetted me?'

Again he ignored her comment. 'Mrs Barrister claimed you took the candlestick from her table in the dining room.' He chewed his lip.

'Oh, my *God*. Now I'm to be accused of *everything* that goes missing. Why would I bother to take a candlestick?'

'Why would you bother to take a silver place-setting?' His eyes were round, innocent, feigning wonder.

'Mrs Barrister shouldn't even *have* a candle on her table. According to Adam, she set her hair on fire. Looked like the burning bush, he said.'

'Lady Cray, we can't have our guests complaining all the time about their things being taken.'

' "*Guests*"? Most of them are totally bonkers. Just have a look out of the window. The Vicar is thrashing the life out of the rose-bushes again.'

Kingsley shook his head, rose and went to the window where he observed the old gentleman hacking away. Lady Cray's hand flashed out and deposited the lighter in her bag. Kingsley turned. 'Admittedly, some of them are very elderly and not quite in full command of their faculties.'

'Loopy, scatty, round the twist. Don't talk nonsense.'

'*Not* the majority.'

'Oh, all right, I will agree with that. Most of them are perfectly civilised and relatively sane. Why do you have books with fake spines?' She flexed her neck, indicating the bookcase to the left.

'You don't miss a thing, do you?' Kingsley walked over, pulled down a 'book' and, as she watched, he drew from its hollow core a bottle of a rare Lindisfarne mead.

'Your private stock! How wonderful! I could use a cordial.'

'No.'

'How dreary. You're worse than the police. Don't drink on the job.' His head, she thought, came up rather quickly when she mentioned police. That was interesting. But he said nothing, merely bent over his appointment book.

'Ten o'clock all right with you?'

'That depends. For what?'

'It might be tough,since cooperation will be minimal, but I'm good, you know. I could help you. Unfortunately, I think you enjoy your little illness all too much.' He was observing her over tented fingers, smiling.

Outwardly, she smiled. Inwardly, she shivered. He was wrong. Wrong, at least about the things she did feel compelled to take. The chocolates and the ribbons. Red ribbons, especially. To avoid meeting his eye, she let her own trail again over the rows and row of books.

That one, there behind him. By itself and three shelves above the one on which he'd just replaced the liqueur-filled book. Dr Kingsley's eyes were quite bad; she knew also that he must be a trifle vain, for his glasses — bifocals — rested on his desk. This particular 'book' also had a fake leather spine, and in it was a marker, one of those one sees in especially nice old volumes, a ribbon. She could see it clearly. The colour of blood.

'You know, dear Dr Kingsley, I think it might be even better if I could see you again today.'

He looked up, totally surprised.

'If you have a free hour. Threeish, fourish? I feel that we get on rather well.' She hoped her dimple was showing.

'I'm amazed, but, yes. Three?'

'Wonderful.'

She watched as he stuck the cigar back in his mouth and searched for the black lighter.

'Oh, do allow me. I found mine.'

She reached over and lit his cigar and he thanked her.

195

29

Alex put on his best call-to-bookmaker voice and, when Hawkes answered, he asked to speak to Mr Melrose Plant.

'It's your solicitor, Mr Plant,' said Hawkes, refusing to look directly at Mr Plant, whom the butler had found in the library.

Melrose , sitting round-shouldered and nearsightedly over his index-cards, looked up over his gold-rimmed glasses. 'Solicitor? There must be some mistake.' Did nearsighted, droop-shouldered librarians on the brink of poverty *have* solicitors?

Hawkes, investing the repetition of the message with as much boredom as possible, added, meanly: 'You may take the call in the kitchen.'

Why, wondered Melrose, would Simon Ledbetter be calling him *here*? Walking through the dining room to the kitchen, he suddenly thought: Agatha. She's managed to get to the firm about his will.

But the voice at the other end wasn't Ledbetter's.

'Listen,' said Alex, 'and don't say anything.'

Both Mrs Callow and Hawkes, although feigning indifference, were all ears. 'Mr Ledbetter? It's been years since we've talked. Well, hardly anything to talk about, was there, considering the money's gone.' Melrose laughed weakly.

'Is someone listening?'

'Obviously. That's why I find myself in a rather difficult position.'

'Then stop talking. It was Dr Kingsley. Maurice Kingsley. You don't know him. He was the man on the bench. You know, outside Mum's —'

The voice broke off.

Melrose himself could think of nothing to say. Another suspect, a *real* one, no smoke and mirrors. A man who had been at the scene of the crime and Alex could prove it. 'Are you, ah calling from your offices, Mr Ledbetter?' That was stupid. Where the hell would a solicitor be calling from? A newsagent's? Hawkes was staring at him.

'From the Castle. Granddad's room. You'll meet him tonight.' The line went dead.

Meet who? Kingsley? Adam?

'Renovation all done, is it? Fine . . . No, I really can't help you out about those particular papers . . . Yes, I'm sorry.' He hung up, debating.

Under the insolent stare of Hawkes, there was no way he could make a call, much less a call to London, from here, although several cleverly coded conversations raced through his mind. And any call made from Tarn House would have to be made where he could keep Mrs Callow in view, having been advised by Millie that she'd pick up when she saw one of the phone's red snake eyes blink on.

He would include this new information in the typed-up report he had been about to take to the post-office fax machine.

Madeline was studying the painting by window-light.

When Melrose returned from the kitchen to the library (where he'd left pillars of books stacked in front of the partially empty cases to simulate hard work), she started.

'Oh! I didn't hear you.' The watercolour left her hands, drifted to the floor as if it were a large feather. She reclaimed it and put it back on the desk.

'I got it from Francis, if you're wondering.'

'I wasn't wondering anything, really. I'm surprised he'd have it; he hates that style.'

'Oh, he didn't just "have it"; he painted it.'

'Francis did?' She appeared genuinely surprised.

'The day that Mrs Holdsworth died, the day of her fall.' Melrose had moved round to his chair at the desk to stand beside her. Madeline was tense, her hands clasped behind her, looking down at the view from Scafell toward Wasdale Head and Wast Water. He was about to comment further, but stopped. He did not want to appear the confidant of Francis Fellowes after only having just arrived within the week. He left it to Madeline. Better anyway.

He found it odd that her proximity to him − the touch of her shoulder, her hip nearly grazing his − called up no response, not the slightest tingling, warmth, or feeling of arousal. And she was certainly not an unattractive woman with those tilted eyes, that soft hair that feathered about her face. 'He said he was with her. That he and Virginia Holdsworth had walked up Scafell together.'

'Yes. Francis was question in such a way you'd think he might have had something to do with it. But I expect it was only because he was at the scene.'

If her sister hadn't come along, Madeline might have married Graham Holdsworth. And she had stayed when (Melrose thought) another woman would have absolutely run from the scene of such humiliation.

'Have you every climbed it?'

Madeline's face grew rosier at the same time that the bridge of her nose showed that telltale band of white. White anger. At him? At her dead sister?

She said nothing in answer to his question except, 'Alex is back.'

At Alex.

'Alex is back.'

In the sort of watery, superimposition of faces one sees sometimes in films, Madeline had been replaced in the library by Genevieve, who carried the same news.

Bad news. No matter how she tried to arrange her expression, the eyes flared, the smile looked stitched in place and soon vanished as she walked from rosewood end table to Chippendale sideboard, picking up her fashion magazines, riffling pages, thrusting them down. Terribly careless (he thought) of the impression she was making on Melrose, her pink-varnished nails lay on the silken sleeves of her blouse as she tapped her foot and stared out of the french windows.

'That's wonderful,' said Melrose, rising, he hoped, to an occasion no one yet seemed eager to celebrate.

'Crabbe's in Keswick; George doesn't know yet, either. He's out with the dogs.'

From the tone, one might have thought that if George *had* known, he'd have set the hounds yapping at the boy's heels.

'Of course, Alex went along to Castle Howe and saw Adam first.'

He thought she'd tear the copy of the Harrods catalogue to pieces. Melrose suppressed a smile. Her manner suggested a future of looking at shop catalogues, rather than buying out the shop itself. It would be a bit like Marshall Trueblood having to pin up the latest wardrobe by Armani on his walls rather than settling it on his person.

'Adam and two or three others are coming to dinner.' Her head was still bent over the slick magazine. Finally, she threw it down and it slid from table to floor. She didn't bother picking it up. That was for others. 'Drinks at seven. Dinner at eight.' She swung round and started for the library door, turning to announce, 'A party for Alex.'

Melrose stared at the door that had come close to slamming.

Alex. It was all Alex. No use killing off Adam; he was an old man, anyway. To get to Adam's millions, one would have to get over the hurdle of Alex.

Melrose looked down at the painting of Scafell. It would be about as easy as getting to Mickledore by the hurdle of Broad Stand.

30

'I don't see why Hawkes has to pick us up,' said Adam. He had reworded and repeated the complaint several times as he tried unsuccessfully to do his black tie.

'Do stop whining.' Lady Cray sat in the chair beside the window in a gown of that strange hue of Waterford crystal, greyish blue in its depths, a nearly invisible hue. The gown was cut straight from straps to hem, on the bias, unadorned. The only piece of jewellery she wore was a smoky, square-cut diamond nearly the shade of the gown itself. This ensemble brightened her silver, large-pupiled eyes. Her fingers drummed on her evening bag, made to match the gown. Drummed and drummed in what would have been a tattoo if the silky material hadn't muted the fingers' touch.

'Not whining. Carstairs makes its deliveries here right about now — ' Adam checked his bedside clock. ' — and after it leaves the Castle goes straight past Tarn House on its way to Boone. It'd be no trick at all, when the driver's inside — ' Here he pecked his head in the direction of the kitchens. ' — to nip up the ramp of the lorry. You don't even have to push. This thing's electrified, remember?' He patted the wheelchair's arm affectionately.

'And just how do you plan on getting the lorry to *stop* on the road in front of the house?'

He was pulling the end of the tie this way and that. 'Oh, make a rumpus,' he said impatiently.

'A rumpus. How do we do that? By tossing lettuces out of the slats? By hurling cabbages against the cab? Is it articulated, this lorry? That would be even a greater exercise of skill — '

'Shut up and help me with this damned tie.'

'I prefer to drive, as per plan, in a chauffeur-driven Daimler.' Her fingers tapped the bag again.

'Sissy.'

'Adam, "make a rumpus" has little finesse. I heard about your excursion in the laundry van. That one apparently you thought through to its rather absurd end.'

He wheeled round to face her and gave his version of a giggle. 'Got me to Boone, didn't it? Got me to the Old Contemptibles.' He wheeled back again to face the tie.

'You're not a prisoner. You could zip out of the front door.'

'Who wants to? Why should that toby jug of a Maltings see where I go. In that black dress and with her knitting she reminds me of the little ladies who guarded the door in *Heart of Darkness*. Two of 'em make a good team: Kojak and Kurtz. Now *there* was an adventure for you. Wouldn't you love to go straight down the Amazon in some little tug, far as you could, and fight cannibals?'

'No. I can simply go to the Swan and fight the tourists for my tea.'

'I'd have thought *you* of all people would have more taste for adventure. Does this look all right, this bloody tie?'

It was lopsided. She didn't care. She smiled at him in the mirror. 'Ah, you think I have none?' She opened her purse, drew out what looked, in the mirror, like paper squares, and tossed them right into his lap.

'What the hell're these?'

She sighed. 'What on earth do they look like?'

'Letters.'

'You're bright.'

He forgot about the tie and wheeled over to her. 'They're to *Jane*.' He stared up at her, his mouth working. 'Where in God's heaven did you get letters to Jane?'

She lit a Black Russian with her lately acquired black lighter. 'I wouldn't call it God's heaven, actually. On Dr Kingsley's shelves. In a hollowed-out book. A fake book. He has several where he keeps his booze.'

Adam could only gawk, look from her to the small pile of letters clamped together with a large clip. And shake his head. And splutter. 'Eh . . . but . . . well? Did you read 'em?'

Her eyes widened. 'Certainly not. I might be a thief, but I am not a nosy Parker.' She snapped her bag. 'I don't believe in prying into others' affairs.' Her eyebrow arched. 'I'm glad you've got your teeth in because your mouth is open. Please close it.' She stubbed out her cigarette.

'How?' It came out in a sort of squeak. 'How'd you find these in his office? Why were you going through his things?'

She sighed in exasperation. 'Adam, I do not go through people's things. You recall I had an appointment with him this morning? Yes. Well, I spied — something — then. When he told me he wanted to see me again tomorrow at ten, I was only too willing to agree, but suggested we begin immediately, this afternoon. It was during this second appointment that I managed to get at the hollow book. Oh, never mind. It was scarcely more clever than your laundry van trip.'

'Well? What did you "spy"?' She checked her circlet of a watch. 'Isn't it time for that Daimler?'

'You can't see *through* spines, at least I don't think you have x-ray vision. So how'd you know?'

Distant footsteps reached them. 'That's probably Mrs Colin-Jackson coming to —'

'Forget Kojak. How?'

'They were tied up.'

He leaned forward, waiting.

'Oh, very well. You get the letters, but I —' She opened her bag again. '— get this!' It was a length of narrow red ribbon, creased where it had been clearly tied, as around a package.

Now he was open mouthed again, staring at the ribbon that curled round her finger and dangled down. There was a heavy-knuckle knock at the door.

'Put them away.' said Lady Cray. 'In a drawer, somewhere —'

'To hell with that. I'm not leaving them here.' He thrust them back at her. 'In your bag. Go on!' He cleared his throat. 'Come!'

Mrs Colin-Jackson opened the door and stuck her flushed face round it, gave a wide, lipstick-smeared smile and said, 'Car's here!'

The announcement was as smeared with gin as her mouth was with lipstick. Letters popped into bag, wheelchair aimed at door, Adam Holdsworth and Lady Cray followed a weaving Mrs Colin-Jackson down the carpeted hall, past the Wedgwood-blue dining room, the richly painted walls, antiques and portraits — through the splendid ambience of Castle Howe.

31

It was Alex's night.

Everyone deferred to Alex except for a few who fortunately had remembered that the reason for the boy's return was not the reason for the return of the Prodigal Son. And that the lavish dishes served were really the funeral baked meats, although the funeral was yet to come.

Drinks had been taken in the library, where Crabbe Holdsworth had held forth on Southey and Company. The disarray — the stacks of books off the shelves and on the floor — only seemed to whet his appetite for discourse on the Lake poets.

Hawkes had moved amongst them with plates of skewered oysters and sweetbreads on cocktail sticks, which were utterly delicious. Crabbe Holdsworth was an oyster addict, apparently. Melrose remembered there had been many plump ones in the delicious mutton and oyster pie served previously. Millie would one day be chef at the Dorchester or Ritz if she kept this up.

Melrose wondered who had chosen the wine and wouldn't have been surprised to find out this was Millie's duty also. But apparently the key to the cellar was held in the large hand of Hawkes, and he chose himself or followed Genevieve's instructions. There were three wine glasses — one white, one red, one dessert — suggesting a decent meal, which it indeed was, though the amalgam of dishes was unusual: the guests were being treated to anything that had once swum, leapt or flown.

There had been potted Silloth shrimps to start, followed by a game mousse that simply misted on the tongue, it was that light. George Holdsworth assured them that the pheasant had been hanging for some weeks, the duck had been shot out of the sky only yesterday, and the guinea fowl's neck wrung just this morning (or that's the way he made it sound). They washed down the mousse with a superior Chablis Grand Cru.

They were now onto their jugged hare and the story that went with the stalking of this wily animal. Melrose was happy to miss most of this account, since his concentration was fully on the vintage accompanying the dish. It was a Château Lafite-Rothschild, '55. If this didn't attest to the wealth of the Holdsworths' cellars, nothing would. Polite attention was paid George, his turgid accountings met, even, with relief. Kingsley and Fellowes had been half drunk upon arrival; Kingsley was getting drunker and Fellowes soberer.

Madeline sat beside Melrose taut and smooth. She joined in without much enthusiasm when the talk got round to Crabbe's book.

The seating arrangement had presented Genevieve with a problem, there being more men than women. She had at least had the sense to seat Alex next to his great-grandfather, whose wheelchair had been placed strategically to her right. But she was having precious little luck drawing either Alex or Adam into conversation and doing little better with Adam's friend, Lady Cray, who seemed to want, judiciously, to hold her tongue and listen to others.

Adam Holdsworth's friend fascinated Melrose. He thought her an altogether singular − and secretive − woman. She was elegant and extremely intelligent, attested to by her holding her tongue amongst strangers. She had an odd gesture of raising her arm across her breast so that the hand fell slightly over the opposite shoulder. It was as if she were handing back information to some messenger who would spirit it away. He could barely see the silvery irises of her eyes in the light from the candelabra; it was the jet beads of her pupils that looked as if they were boring straight through him. Lady Cray would look, look away, look, look away. It occurred to him that she (like Millie) knew he was not what he said he was.

Melrose had been surprised to find himself allocated the seat on Genevieve's left, he, bespectacled, cramp-necked cataloguer of books until he realized during the mousse course that she apparently found him if not absolutely attractive, at least new. It next occurred to him that Genevieve might be on to him, too, for she had raked her eyes more than once over the grey-green suit. You could take the label out of Armani, but you couldn't take the Armani out of Armani, and Genevieve Holdsworth was anything but blind to fashion. That cream-coloured viscose gown she was wearing hadn't come off the rack, that was certain. Why had he thought that going northward meant he was going frump-ward, to a place where all the women knew only muslin and macs and wellington boots? Or that a comfortably loose cut would be taken as a baggy old suit? He made a rotten mole.

His only dissatisfaction with the seating was that it put Dr Helen Viner on the other side and at the other end of the table next to Crabbe Holdsworth. They had had an interesting discussion about the creative process (a spin-off from Crabbe's brief commentary on 'Kubla Khan') that Melrose had only half heard because his mind was so busy with trying to sort out what it was about her that so attracted him. Genevieve was far sultrier, Madeline far prettier. But Dr Viner was one of those people one felt one knew instantly − at first glance or first touch, the rare sort one met as one meets an old friend.

In an odd way, she was, since Alex had told Melrose about his talk with her in the maze. That he, Alex had felt upon watching her walk away a sense of unease. Had Alex thought she was *lying* to him? No. Well, she could have been, couldn't she? What had they talked about except (the absurd, to Alex) notion of her as a possible suspect and then about his dream. She had an alibi, Melrose told Alex. Indeed she was the *only* one who absolutely did.

Melrose could understand how Alex felt drawn to Helen Viner. So did he. She was more than receptive; she was a receptor, a receptacle into whom one could pour one's thoughts with no fear that one would neither quantify or qualify; she would not make one feel one should be more, or less, or other. He felt, when he suddenly thought of the phrase 'ideal mother', a terrible jolt. It felt like aftershock. She reminded him of his mother and he felt ashamed. But when he looked over and met Alex's eyes, the feeling passed and the blush receded. And there was Millie. He was furious that someone could possibly have been the cause of their losses.

The featherweight wineglass broke.

He had been increasing his hold on both bowl and stem to the point that the stem had snapped, making a straight shallow cut across his two fingers. Never had he done anything like this before; he laughed and responded to the several concerned voices that it was nothing as he wrapped his napkin round the fingers; Hawkes was sent for sticking plaster; good old George bellowed down the table that not a drop of wine was spilt — ah, that was the thing!

Did anyone else but Melrose see that Lady Cray turned chalk-white? Her own fingers, as if in sympathetic response, tightened on the edge of the tablecloth as if she'd pull the whole lot to her lap and the floor. It took her less than five seconds to regain her composure completely, for the colour to return to her cheeks, for the hand to cross over her breast and rest on her shoulder handing back that message to the past.

Melrose saw that Helen Viner was looking at him, and even from this distance he could read her expression. *Never mind. We all do it.*

Although two doctors were present, Genevieve delighted in playing nurse and applying the sticking plaster. The tiny line of blood had been so thin, the cuts had all but disappeared anyway. The little accident was forgotten and conversation resumed over the citron soufflé and Sauternes.

But if the talk seemed fairly ordinary, dinner-table talk, underlying it all through the meal had been a pervasive sense of dread. Not even the half-dozen bottles of wine they'd consumed eased the high-wire tension round the table.

Melrose saw that everyone was watching everyone else. Only Crabbe and George were truly finding themselves more interesting than they found the others. Whatever Kingsley, Genevieve, Madeline, Helen Viner, Fellowes — and especially Adam and Alex — made a remark, Melrose felt small *frissons* of anxiety, as if a little tearaway spark from a log hitting the carpet had caught fire to each of them, which took another dull anecdote from George or Crabbe to stamp out.

Naturally, there was a lot of conversation about nothing at all to avoid the *something* on everyone's mind: there were an uneven eleven of them; there should have been twelve, there should have been Jane.

When he shifted his eyes from Alex to Adam to Lady Cray, their own eyes responded. Ever-so-slightly, they nodded. Melrose could have sworn the three of them were in collusion.

Banquo's ghost could appear at any moment and bring the house of cards tumbling down.

2

He did not have to rout her from the middle of the coffee and port and walnuts in the drawing room after dinner. To what he thought was his great good fortune, Helen Viner approached him.

She did it adroitly, in a slow movement from Francis Fellowes to old Adam, and seemed to end up at Melrose's side merely by accident. He would not have called it 'adroit' had he not noticed that Lady Cray was following Dr Viner's movements. And his. Although she appeared to be listening to Madeline Holdsworth, she was watching them as she lit a cigarette with a black lighter.

'Mr Plant, could we talk for a moment?' Helen Viner had a lovely smile.

He would have liked to have been able to help her into this new dimension of their relationship; he found, however, that she was perfectly capable of handling it on her own. She even suggested that they go for a walk. 'You'll need a coat,' he said.

'I need nothing.'

He wondered if she ordinarily used this elliptical or ambiguous way of talking. Perhaps it was the psychiatric training, the listening ear that resulted in this moderation of her own speech.

There was no patio, only a few steps leading down from the french windows to the wet grass. Their feet were lost in ground mist as they walked the weed-choked path towards the kennels.

'It's about Alex,' she said.

'Oh? What about him? It's tragic about his mother's suicide, but he seems to be handling it remarkably well,'

'Yes. Too well, perhaps. He's only sixteen. I'm sure he's convinced his mother was murdered.'

Melrose made appropriate sounds of astonishment.

'Oh, but you know the police have been asking questions, certainly. Anyway, for Alex this is especially terrible. Because of his father. His father killed himself, too.' When he nodded, she said, 'You knew about that?'

'Francis Fellowes told me.'

She pulled her sweater more closely about her. 'God, he's a worse gossip than the regulars at the Old Contemptibles.'

Melrose laughed. 'Well, he *is* a regular, isn't he? But this wasn't gossip. Graham Holdsworth *did* kill himself — didn't he?' Their approach to the kennels had set hounds barking, but sleepily. Then all was quiet. 'Look, I don't understand, quite, why you're talking to *me*. I don't think this boy is about to have a heart-to-heart with *me* about his mum; I only met him this afternoon.'

'No, you didn't,' she said, evenly, as if she were disagreeing about the weather.

'I beg your pardon?' If Alex had told her, Melrose wished Alex had told *him*. They were leaning against the gate to the courtyard. Melrose turned up his jacket collar, shivered and wondered what the hell was going on. He said nothing.

'When I saw him at Castle Howe this morning, he said the first person he'd come to see was Adam. Yet he mentioned that there was a new "librarian" at Tarn House.' Her white teeth glittered as she smiled. 'And, anyway, you just referred to his mother as "mum". You know you'd have said "mother" or "mummy". Alex uses "mum" merely to annoy his grandparents. It's rather lower class word, they think.'

'You should have been a detective.'

'Or a psychiatrist. They are some similarities. Anyway, Alex told me a dream that he's been having repeatedly.' Pulling at the sweater again, she moved closer to him. 'He said he'd told "a friend" about it, the dream. Since the only friends he has here are Millie and Adam, and he'd have named them, I expect it was you.'

Melrose saw no point in denying it. He took off his jacket and draped it about her shoulders. She seemed very surprised by this attention and he wondered when last she'd got some. 'Go on.'

'You'll freeze −'

'Just go on about Alex.' He was rather sorry, when he saw her pull the sleeves of the jacket about her, that his arms weren't still in it.

'It chilled me. Something sinister in the symbolism. That Queen of Hearts image − the one he seemed 'glued' to. Well, one can't appropriate another's dream, or tell the dreamer what it means, still . . .' She paused.

'You're not suggesting *Alex* might make a suicide attempt.'

Her hands were clasped beneath her chin as she thought. 'I don't know. Some sort of therapy might help him.'

'With you?'

'No!' Her voice rang through the night. 'Not I. Alex wouldn't do it anyway. The important thing is —' She looked hard at Melrose. '— that he have a friend. I don't know precisely why you're here, and it's none of my business. I don't care —'

(He could have done without *that*.)

'— but he has no friends in this family except for Adam. Adam can't watch over him. He needs someone totally unconnected with the Holdsworth ménage, someone with no interest in the money. There are too damned many "accidents" in this family.'

'You don't believe in accidents.'

She thought for a bit. 'Graham's death was suicide, that was certain. He left a note . . .' She paused. 'Could I have a cigarette? I stopped two months ago and my willpower has about given out.'

Melrose lit it with a scratched aluminium lighter he'd found in the desk drawer.

'Damn!' she said. She raised one fisted hand to her cheek, turning from him. The tears were spasmodic and over in a few seconds. She gulped the air. 'He was a patient of mine for a short time. That's no secret. Graham was having a hard time about the divorce.'

'You blame yourself?'

'I should have seen it coming. It wasn't his first suicide attempt; years before he'd tried to cut his wrists. He was simply a self-destructive person. Still, I feel I should have been able to do something. I can tell you one thing: it was something else that broke up his relationship with Madeline. It wasn't Jane.' She was smoking in angry little jabs. 'I'm sick of that particular myth. I expect Madeline believes it.'

'There's no point in asking you what it was.'

She shook her head.

'You know, you probably have information that would help the police.'

Again, she shook her head.

Melrose sighed. 'This is going to seem impertinent coming —'

'I'm used to impertinence.' She laughed. 'I'm used to far more than impertinence.'

'You said there were too many accidents in this family. Besides the first Mrs Holdsworth —'

'Virginia? The police were satisfied that was. Unless Francis pushed her.' She half smiled. 'I can't imagine Francis doing anything more violent than running from one canvas to another.'

'Annie Thale.'

Helen looked at him through a tendril of smoke. 'Annie Thale wasn't a member of this family.'

He was silent for a moment. 'Is Millie?'

Her look cut like the crystal stem of the glass. 'You're speculating that Graham was Annie's lover and Millie's father? And that she was disconsolate about his suicide she took that way out herself?'

'Obviously, you've thought of it.'

'No. The police did. It isn't true.'

'How can you be sure?'

She dropped the cigarette in the mist. 'Because I am.' She sighed. 'When Annie "fell", and so soon after finding him in the gatehouse, well . . . if you put two and two together then you can imagine that police might suspect that, too. If I could be accused of destroying doctor-patient confidentiality, to hell with it. I wasn't going to have that rumour circulating, and it was. If they'd been lovers, I'd have known. He talked about her, yes. The sexual attraction was only on her side. Graham was a generally unhappy man, but also a very appealing one. He was sweet and gentle and extremely upset about wanting to get out of the marriage. I've told you nothing at all that everyone didn't know. Except about his relationship — or lack of it — with Annie Thale. And that's really a negative, isn't it? Not something he *did* tell me but something he didn't. I *am* a responsible doctor. I've built my life around it.'

'You don't have to justify yourself, certainly not to me.'

Her downturned face came up; she pulled a strand of hair behind her ear. 'Thank you'.

'Do you trust Kingsley?'

It seemed to hit her out of the blue. 'Why on earth shouldn't I?'

He smiled and shrugged. 'Just wondering.' Did she know he'd gone to London? 'Was he a friend of Jane Holdsworth?'

Helen looked puzzled. 'Yes. Why?'

'Again, just wondering.'

Defensively, she said, 'Maurice drinks to much. But he is, actually, a very good doctor. Let's go in shall we? Thanks for this.' She slipped the jacket from her shoulders, handed it back.

They walked in silence for a few moments, and then Melrose asked, 'Do you think Alex is right?'

'About his mother's death?'

They had reached the steps leading up to the french windows.

212

Melrose saw that coats were being delivered by Hawkes. 'Yes. That it was murder.'

'It probably was,' she said, stepping into the light.

That stopped him.

3

I've hardly a moment to talk with you, Mr Plant,' said Lady Cray. 'You're quite a popular young man.'

'Not popular, not young, but thank you anyway. I noticed you've had me in view all evening. Was there something in particular?'

The guests were shrugging into coats, keeping up that good-bye conversation that people do when they're leaving but don't go. Lady Cray had swept towards him in a cape that matched the gown, ready to leave, except for her 'word' with him. She had slipped her arm through his and manoeuvred the two of them towards the fireplace where now he stood, his back to it, she facing.

'Yes, there's something very particular.' She started to cough. She coughed several times, opened her cream-coloured bag, and searched for a handkerchief. 'I can't find mine. May I use yours?'

Her eyes kept flicking up and over his shoulder. 'What? Certainly.'

'Thank you.' Opening the handkerchief, she dipped it into her bag, quickly brought out some papers and raised the handkerchief to her mouth.

Melrose's own mouth fell open.

She smiled. 'Please don't do that, Mr Plant. Look blank. Dr Kingsley and Madeline Galloway are staring right at us.'

'How – ?' And then he remembered the large mirror above the mantel.

'The mirror. They can see us, but no one can hear us. And put your handkerchief in the pocket of your jacket. Lovely suit. Armani, isn't it?'

He sighed. 'I'm not much of an undercover man.'

'Oh, you do quite well. I wouldn't know except Alex told Adam and Adam told me. Now, that's right, keep your face blank – '

'Do I do it well?'

'It looks quite natural. You may smile, but don't react otherwise. I've just given you five letters that were written to Jane Holdsworth.

213

Please – ' She anticipated a question. 'I'll explain later. For the moment let me just say that they were hidden in Dr Kingsley's office.'

'You astonish me, Lady Cray.'

'I'm sure; but kindly don't show it.' Her eyes flickered again, moving up to the mirror. 'We haven't read them.'

' "We"?'

Impatiently, she said, 'Adam and I. We thought they should go straight to the police.'

'Through me.'

'Through you. You don't have to look quite so stupid. Just don't ask questions, as I've no time to answer. Good-night, Mr Plant.' She was smiling wonderfully, holding out her hand.

He returned her smile, although he was having a bit of trouble doing it. 'It's been maddening, Lady Cray.'

'That's just what my family thinks.'

He watched her intercept Genevieve, who'd been coming towards them, watched her say her gracious farewells, watched her leave.

PART III
KILL ALL THE
LAWYERS

32

Pete Apted, Q.C., was sitting with his feet on his desk, finishing off a sausage roll and frowning over the file on his lap, when Jury walked in.

Received wisdom was that Pete Apted, Q.C., got the highest fees of any advocate in the City. Clients didn't complain. He didn't lose cases.

But because of the high cost of living, raised even higher by Apted's services, Jury wondered how the man had been retained to represent him, Jury. He had been told to come in at the daunting hour of 7:00 a.m. by Apted's instructing solicitor, a young man named Burley who had questioned Jury two days ago. Not until such preliminary groundwork was done did Apted ask to see him. What amazed Jury was that it seemed to have taken precious little time for the solicitor and Apted's junior to assemble statements from (presumably) witnesses. It had been only two days before (one after he'd been suspended) that a Mr Burley had rung Jury up and told him he'd call immediately. Which he had done, at the Islington flat.

'I don't understand. I haven't engaged a solicitor. Why are you here?'

'Because I was sent,' was the only explanation.

And he had questioned and taken cramped little notes for over three hours. Mr Burley definitely fitted the office, if not the name. He was narrow, owl-eyed young man with a tall brush of hair and a parsimonious way of speaking.

Apted's assistant, a woman, had questioned Carole-anne. A woman who was unimpressed at finding out that she was (according to Carole-anne) in the wrong profession. (*'Her being a Virgo and all.'*)

And when Melrose Plant had sent in the second report to Jury, he had immediately related the information about Maurice Kingsley to Mr Burley. It was the first break they had had, Jury had said. The solicitor had merely thanked him and hung up without further comment.

Pete Apted scrunched up the greasy paper bag and chucked it towards the waste paper basket. 'Sit down, for Christ's sake,' he said, as he started polishing an apple on his shirt.

Jury had been standing watching Pete Apted chew and slap back one page after another in the file propped up on his thighs. He did both with equal ferocity. Jury sat, as commanded, on one of the two wood and leather chairs across from this barrister who must be older than he looked, but still too young-looking for his office. Except for one tall narrow window curtained in some heavy, fusty material, the office was dark and somehow crotchety. Books had been shoved and wedged into shelves; stacks of papers were crammed into pinched containers; chairs were spindly and narrow. Staring from portraits on opposite walls were angry-looking men in silks. Standing with one hand tented over a stack of leather volumes, or seated stiffly and heavy-lidded in a medieval chair, both looked as if they'd prosecute anyone to within an inch of his life.

After another moment or two of silence broken only by the crunch of Apted's apple, Jury asked, bluntly, 'Who's paying for this, Sir Peter? You're not taking on this case out of sheer love for the Met.'

Apted winced. 'Sir me no sirs and my name's "Pete", not "Peter". Actually, "P-I-E-T", – Dutch – but I finally gave in to Fleet Street on the spelling. No, I'm not doing it for love; I'm doing it for money. I've never done anything for love in my life, a rule you might do well to follow in future, considering where it got you. As for who's paying, that person wishes to remain anonymous.'

Jury was astonished. It couldn't be Plant; he wouldn't bother with anonymity; he'd just not be argued out of it.

Who? Vivian Rivington.

Vivian was a rich woman and the news had certainly hit the papers. Someone in Long Piddleton could have got the information to her. Lady Ardry had probably shot that news straight across Europe.

It was a stupid gesture, but Jury made it anyway. 'I'd prefer to pay you myself.'

'Out of what? I'm not on hire-purchase, two pounds a week. Stop feeling sorry for yourself and be grateful. Some hack down the Old Bailey, and this heap of rubbish would wind up in court.' He tossed the thick file on a desk dominated by a hooded bronze figure and a framed photograph that Jury couldn't see.

Jury could not believe that eyes the shade of weak tea could be so electrifying. His hair was the same colour, his mouth thin, and his frame wiry — taut and wiry; Jury thought he was the type of barrister who would spring from his seat to confront witnesses.

'Wait a minute,' said Jury. 'What do you mean *would*? This heap of rubbish *will*.'

Apted shook his head, not, apparently, so much in denial, but at Jury's dull-wittedness. 'Mr Jury, there's only one thing I believe in.' He'd nibbled the apple down and now shied the core towards the same basket. He looked pleased that he'd hit it.

The silence that hung there implied that Jury was supposed to fill it by telling Pete Apted, Q.C., what the one thing was.

'Truth?'

Apted slewed a disbelieving glance towards Jury. 'Winning. Unfortunately, the truth has a way of screwing that up. So, naturally, I have to know it before I can take on a case. If you *tell* me you're guilty, I can't defend you. But you're not, so you won't, so I will.'

'Then you know I had nothing to do with Jane Holdsworth's death.'

'No. I don't know you "had nothing to do with Jane Holdsworth's death".' His tone stopped just short of mimicry. 'I only know you didn't kill her. I'm amazed that this Detective Inspector —' Again, he slapped though the file. '— Kamir thinks there's any chance you did.' He tossed the detested brief back on the desk. 'You want to sue the department for suspending you? That might be fun. Higher fee, of course.' Pete Apted had a lightning smile; it struck and left.

The lawyer's confidence in himself (legendary) flooded Jury with relief. 'You read Mr Burley's report on Maurice Kingsley.'

Apted nodded.

Jury waited. Apted said nothing. 'You think it might have been Kingsley, then? He was there.'

'Well, he's not my concern, but offhand I'd say, hell no. He does in this woman, goes out to sleep — assuming he was sleeping — on a bench and then strikes up conversation with a kid he might or might not have recognized as her son, makes no difference, so he'll be sure to be remembered.'

Apted had said it flatly, almost by rote, a man reciting an alphabet of common sense.

Jury was deflated. 'There might be reasons for that behaviour.'

Pete Apted seemed to be thinking, deeply. 'Yes. He could be a cretin. All right, we don't know all the specifics, but I repeat: I'm not defending this Dr Kingsley. I would, however, still consider suing the Metropolitan police.' Again that flash of a smile. He sat now with one shoe *plunk* up against the edge of the desk, rolling up his tie from the bottom like a schoolboy who wasn't used to ties.

'I don't want to sue the Met, and Kamir's no fool. And please explain the difference between "having nothing to do with her death" and not murdering her, I expect I'm just dim.'

Apted flashed him another one of those looks that said *no doubt*, and Jury remembered then (from accounts of barrister's courtroom manner) that it was one of the man's tricks: he could shoot those looks at an adversary who had presented a perfectly cogent argument, and if the sheer weight of the expression didn't reduce that argument to utter rubble, it at least left a large crack in it.

'Sorry. Did I say something stupid?'

'Oh, don't apologise. I'm sure your ordinary sharp mental processes' (there was no sarcasm) 'have been dulled by an involvement with this woman. *Especially* this woman.' He did not, as Jury had seen him in his mind's eye, spring from his chair. Pete Apted rose slowly, as if he had a great weight on his shoulders, and walked over to the window, where a weak glimmer of sun showed the dust in the material's folds. Apted shoved his glasses on top of his head and stood in the wavering light. Without the glasses and with his profile turned that way he looked ten years younger. Or perhaps he *was* ten years younger than he'd appeared, seated and frowning over his apple and open file.

He narrowed his eyes again the morning light coming through the window as if it were intruding, cutting across the light of his own mind. 'No point in going over the obvious,' he said.

'I'm not sure what you think is obvious.'

'Same things you do,' he said, walking back to his desk, dropping himself into his chair and the glasses back over his eyes, 'Or they wouldn't be obvious, right?' He realigned the large photograph on his desk with an expensive pen set Jury doubted the man ever used.

'You haven't answered my question about her death. What's the difference?'

'You didn't kill her. That doesn't mean you didn't, oh, perhaps invite her to kill herself.'

Jury stared at him.

'For God's sake, don't look like that. I'm not saying you did. I merely wanted to point out how circumlocution can lead to errors of thinking.'

'Please skip the legal lecture, Mr Apted. If I didn't —'

Apted interrupted. 'You know, in all of your talk with Detective Inspector Kamir — which, incidentally, is one of the "obvious" reasons for concluding you yourself were not the perpetrator; is there anything you *didn't* tell him? — in all of this injudicious account of your own actions over a two-week period, without benefit of counsel (I might add), you didn't once mention the calendar.'

Jury hesitated. 'Calendar?'

Apted sighed. 'Superintendent: the one with your name and or initials scribbled into tense little squares. The times she saw you. Dinner. Bed. Et cetera.' Apted brought his chair down with a thud and crossed his arms across the pile of papers. 'If you were crazy enough to buy her a ring, you certainly thought your affections were returned. Or to put it another way: if I were fucking a lady, I *damned* well wouldn't expect her to have to make notes on a calendar for future fucks.' He stopped and got up again and walked over to the window.

It was like a body blow. 'It had occurred to me.' He had tried to keep the doubts at bay. But during those hours after buying the ring, after talking with Jenny, walking through the park, sitting on the bench, he had wondered. Or tried not to wonder. 'Why?' He was hardly aware he'd said it aloud.

From the window, Pete Apted answered. 'She needed a cop.'

Jury looked up, surprised. 'What?'

'A policeman. Someone who was thoroughly trained in investigation. So she picked you. And writing your name in on

221

the calendar would assure her that you'd be in on the investigation, if not in charge of it.'

'She didn't even *know* me. She didn't know I was CID until the second time we'd been together.'

'Yes, she did.' Apted came back from his desk. 'You really did blank it out, didn't you, Mr Jury? And I don't think your internal affairs people are as thorough as they could be. For example: interview with Miss Palutski. Definitely a hostile prosecution witness type.' Apted smiled over the report. ' "I don't have a clue what you're talking about. *Who* was in Camden Passage? Never saw her." Et cetera'

'She was telling the truth. If she did see Jane Holdsworth, it didn't register. She was too busy playing with a crown.'

'I sent my junior, Kath. Kath could run rings around some of you people. She smokes to much, drinks too much, lives like — ' Apted shrugged. ' — impossible to describe. But, oh, is she bright. The idea was to get Carole-Anne Palutski — quite a charmer, according to Kath; she said the young lady wanted to tell her fortune, read her stars, read her mind, et cetera. Kath got Miss Palutski to *replay* the Camden Passage scene, which she did, good as any actor.'

'She thinks she is.'

'Well, she certainly got an actor's recall. Ran right through it, the whole scene with the Camden Passage Fagin, dealer in antiquities fallen off backs of lorries, no doubt.' Apted *hmm*'d and *da-dah*ed his way through part of it and then said, ' " . . . so I says to him, "Don't try and fiddle the police . . ." and down a bit, yes, here: ". . . a *superintendent*." ' He looked over at Jury. 'All within earshot. You think Ms Holdsworth "accidentally" happened to work her way round those tables?'

Jury answered quickly, 'She knew someone was going to try to kill her; she knew it would be made to look like suicide.' Jury was trying. He was trying like hell.

'You were set up.'

'Don't tell me she wanted it to look like I'd done it. That doesn't make sense.'

'I didn't say that.'

'Whoever was coming to see her that night — '

'The mysterious visitor? It was this Kingsley's misfortune that he got the wrong night.'

'Then who –'

Pete Apted lowered his head and squinted across at jury. 'What's wrong with the most likely explanation?'

'Which is?'

'She killed herself.'

Jury sat, staring at Pete Apted, who seemed already to be getting onto another case. His glasses came down, he pulled over a brief.

Jury reviewed the conversation with Kamir – the speculations, the arguments. They looked even weaker. But he resorted to 'Listen. Why would a woman who was passionately happy kill herself?'

Apted shoved the glasses back up as he tossed down his pen. 'Mr Jury, if it waddles like a duck and quacks like a duck, let's say it *is* a duck.'

Jury repeated the weakest of the arguments. 'She was dressed to go out; she was meeting someone.'

Apted rolled his eyes heavenward. 'That's what she told *you* Probably deliberately.' His pale brown eyes burned as he leaned towards Jury. 'And as far as her son is concerned, wouldn't murder, horrible as it is, be less painful for him than suicide? Remember, "passionately happy" is the way *you* saw it.' the glasses came down again; he picked up the pen. 'Frankly, I don't think you really believe that.'

Jury shifted in his chair. He didn't, of course. 'And she implicates me.'

Slapping new pages over now, Apted said, 'Right. But not intentionally; I'd guess she thought no one would take the implication seriously. You *were* bedmates, after all.'

Jury was silent, watching the lawyer jotting down notes. Then he said, 'Why?'

Apted looked up, suddenly. ' "Why?" ' Again, he put down his pen and leaned across the desk. 'My job is to protect you, Mr Jury.' He pointed his finger directly at Jury's chest and silently mouthed the word again: *You*. 'And *you* were set up.'

Jury rose wearily. 'Anything else?'

'No,' Pete Apted looked up and smiled. This time the smile lingered. 'But I think you can consider yourself back on the job. No one wants to prosecute you; you're too well liked. Apparently.'

That seemed to be an afterthought. Jury smiled. Somehow, he

couldn't imagine this man taking silk, going through the ritual, the pomp and circumstance. 'You're pretty good,' was all Jury said.

Pete Apted, Q.C., didn't even raise his eyes.

'What if I need you again, depending what I find out?'

'I'll be here.'

33

When he walked into Racer's office at eight-thirty, Fiona jumped, jiggling the tiny squares of paper plastering her face. 'You!'

'Me. Good morning.'

Fiona immediately attempted to switch to the cool pose, extremely difficult when one was looking at a man one especially cared for at the same time as one was wearing a glutinous-looking mask of paper on one's face.

One could only try. Fiona casually picked two tiny damp squares from nearest her eyes, balling them up as Pete Apted had his sausage roll wrapper, looked at them as if this familiar accoutrement to beauty was mildly annoying (but then what wasn't?) and flicked each tiny ball towards the waste paper basket, just as Apted had.

Cyril, already fascinated by the skin-thin squares, was now sliding down air from the desk to the basket. Surely, more would follow.

No. Instead, Fiona fiddled a cigarette from her packet, asked Jury for a light, recrossed her legs, and draped one arm over the back of her secretary's chair, which movement tightened the black blouse across her breasts. 'Knew you'd be back in a tick, we did. Al was just saying yesterday, "They'll have him back here in a tick." ' Fiona was the only person on the face of the earth (Jury bet) who called Wiggins 'Al'.

Cyril sat at the ready near the waste paper basket, staring up at those little thin squares.

Rotten as Jury felt, there was a part of him that could barely keep his face straight. 'What're you doing, anyway?' he asked. The kettle whistled.

This was fortunate for Fiona, for it gave her something to be busy about. 'Whatever do you mean?' She looked at him blankly, and then, as if surprised, said, 'Oh, this? Well, it's the newest thing,

225

innit?' She looked at him with some disdain as she popped the tea bags into cups. 'But I expect you don't follow Fergie's and Di's beauty routines, do you?' She grimaced, trying to make a joke of it.

Solemnly, Jury shook his head. Fiona might be dying one thousand deaths, but she was a stand-up woman. Fiona was — he had never thought of it before — an inspiration to anyone in an impossible situation.

'It's a collagen treatment. Does wonders for the skin. Tea?' she asked calmly, as the tissue-thin paper shifted round her mouth.

'Absolutely. Where's our chief?' He sipped the milky tea, watching Cyril who, apparently realizing no more paper wads were coming his way, swayed off towards the 'chief's' office.

'Ever know him to be here before nine? Ha! Not that one.' It was difficult drinking with the paper squeezing round her mouth, but she managed. 'Not since we had that redheaded typist.'

He remembered. The poor girl had lasted a week and spent most of her time walking quickly down the hall away from Racer.

'Think he had a casting couch, wouldn't'ya?'

Jury watched as Fiona brought out the heavy ammunition: mirror and makeup kit. She extracted from the kit about the same number of items Wiggins had from Natural Habitat. Only with Fiona, Nature could go hang; she herself had a much finer hand. She sat smoking her cigarette; she couldn't peel off the paper mask with Jury sitting right there.

'I think I'll have a word with Cyril. Haven't seen him for several days.'

Fiona called to Jury's departing back: 'Mind you don't let him make a right mess in there!'

All Jury could see of the cat Cyril were his eyes and ears projecting above the top of Chief Superintendent Racer's desk, which denied, as always, that anyone worked here. No messy papers or files. Pristine pen in shining holder. Pristine blotter with another travel brochure wedged into one of its corers. Racer, of course, accounted for this near-virginal state of his work area by dwelling on organisation. Organisation was something Jury didn't understand (according to Racer). The organised man looked as if he hadn't a thing to do. In Racer's case this was true.

Cyril looked at Jury, blinked lazily and returned to his morning job of emptying Racer's middle drawer of its little belongings. It hadn't taken much practice for Cyril to learn how to fit his paw in the brass ring and pull. This once done, he could set about the inside.

'How're things, Cyril?' Jury heard little rasps and lisps of what were probably clips and pins, and then Cyril raised his head, blinked again at Jury in a gesture of camaraderie before the head disappeared once more.

From the six little nooks in the front of the drawer, Cyril was dishing out paper clips, pencils, Sellotape, drawing pins, and other oddments. Then there was the rattle of paper, which Jury knew would be pushed over the lip of the drawer to flutter to the floor.

Cyril had apparently finished, for he raised his head, yawned as if the task were boring, slid down and reappeared, blinking at Jury.

For all of this work, Cyril expected at least an inspection of the damage.

Jury went round to the other side of the desk: drawer open, everything out except for the mousetrap Racer had fitted with a sardine. Oil stained the wood.

'Great job, Cyril. Smells, too.'

When the outer office door opened, Cyril's ear pricked up and he make a hasty move to the urn used for holding umbrellas. From this vantage point he could observe without being observed. Racer stopped long enough to vent his spleen on Fiona for making tea bag tea.

He marched into his own office, took one look at Jury and said, 'You're a mess.' Sartorially perfect in his silk shirt and hand built suit, Racer doffed his outerwear and walked round his desk, where he saw a far greater mess. As if he meant to smash it to pieces, Racer hit the intercom and yelled, '*Miss Clingmore! Get in here and clean up the carnage and if the rat-catcher does this one more time it's not only his life but your job!*' He glared at Jury and said, 'Every effing thing except the damned sardine.' He tossed the mousetrap on his blotter. 'And you, you've probably been sitting here watching all the time. I swear I'm getting a couple of priests in here for exorcism.' His head swivelled. 'Where is that ball of mange? *Where?*'

A completely refurbished Fiona Clingmore sighed her way into the office and set about collecting the clips and pins.

Totally rattled, Racer went to his drinks cabinet for a reviver, 'That damned cat is pure distilled cathood. He's one hundred and ninety per cent proof. He's the only animal Noah let on the Ark by himself.' He slugged down a finger of Rémy.

Said Jury, 'I believe I'm being reinstated.'

'Sir Peter-bloody-Apted called the Commissioner.' Racer was still scanning the room for Cyril. 'If I see those yellow splinter eyes just one more time . . . Haven't you cleared up, Miss Clingmore? Get out and look for him.'

Fiona winked at Jury as she walked past the umbrella urn.

'Pete, not Peter,' said Jury.

Racer caught Jury in his cat-scan and went on. 'So now I expect you'll want to stick your nose into "P" Division's case.'

But he didn't appear to be as massively irritated with his nemesis, Jury, back on the job as Jury would have thought. Indeed, Jury thought he detected some relief. 'Well, it's caused *me* a lot of personal grief. It it's all right with Kamir, yes, I'd like to talk to the Holdsworths.'

Jury rose.

Racer waved him down. 'You could do with a bit of patience, Jury. The world doesn't step to your time. If it weren't for you, this mess wouldn't have landed on my plate.

'Sorry about that. But it's made a bigger mess of *my* plate wouldn't you say?'

Hell, of course he wouldn't say.

'All right if I take Wiggins?'

'Take him.' Racer smiled meanly. 'The weather up there might clear his mind.'

Sergeant Wiggins, although delighted to see Jury back in their office, didn't agree. Worse than Yorkshire, it'd be. Rain. Wiggins fiddled with his pills, washed down several just thinking of bogs and mosses and wet as Jury was stuffing Melrose Plant's faxed reports and his own notes in a case, and talking to Wiggins about Wordsworth, about his heavenly walks across the heavenly fells, soaking up blue lakes, daffodils, mountains, and even reciting 'I wandered Lonely as a Cloud'.

'Do I look like a cloud, sir?' Grimly, Wiggins shovelled a dozen vials of something into a bag.

The Wiggins suitcase, clothes be damned.

34

It was true that Thomasina Thale lived in a 'grand' house – at least it was a formidable brick residence in one of the better squares in Earl's Court – but she didn't own it. She did not even own the small part of this house in which she lived, a second floor flat.

This was not the only part of Plant's report that diverged from the truth: 'Aunt Tom' was not an elderly, 'Victorian' lady. She was probably in her mid-thirties, with a pretty unmadeup face, lovely chestnut hair and (Jury saw when she preceded them down a short hall) a leg in a brace. She had to drag it.

People called her 'Tommy'. As she indicated chairs for Jury and Wiggins to take in her front room, whose windows over looked a little park, she laughed at the sobriquet her niece had chosen.

That was not all she laughed about. When Jury (truly dumbfounded) reiterated the description Plant had put in his report – a description of a starch-bosomed, flint-eyed old lady who had (literally, it seemed) a whip hand . . .Tommy Thale laughed even harder. It was a rich, honestly rollicking laugh, wonderful to hear coming from someone who must be facing a life of denial and privation. Yet, as Jury looked at the room, the warmth that came from the fringed-shaded lamps and the two-bar fire, the embroidered cushions and needlepointed chairs, he thought that Tommy Thale was one of those people not easily disheartened, one who would see the glass as half full and be happy simply not to die of thirst.

She was wiping the tears of laughter from here eyes with the heels of her palms. 'Well, she had to, I expect. *They'd* certainly have sent her up. To London, you know, to live with me. It was a story invented for old Adam's ears, probably. Millie's favourite, perhaps second only to Alex. He'd never let *them* lay a hand on her.'

'The Holdsworth family. Have you met them?'

She laughed again, her hand twisting the stick back and forth, and said, 'I couldn't have done, could I? Not without my high buttoned boots and whip. Sounds a bit S-and-M-ish, really.'

'I beg your pardon, miss?' Wiggins looked puzzled.

'Sadomasochistic, Sergeant.'

'Oh, yes. Being homicide, we're not much into that.'

'I hope not.'

Jury smiled at her attempt to keep her own face straight. It was, he thought, the first time in days he honestly felt like truly smiling. Her own refusal to give in to her fate diminished his own unhappiness.

She went on: 'But I know about all of them from Millie's letters. She's quite a letter-writer — who knows if they're the truth? — and from Annie. When she was alive.' Tommy looked considerably sadder, as if there were other fates much worse than hers.

'Why wouldn't she prefer to live with you, though?' asked Jury. 'Why want to stay in a place where she does all the work — at least according to what my friend tells me — and is treated rather basely by the rest of the staff, *and* has no affection for the family. Except for the old man and . . . Jane Holdsworth's son. Alex, I think his name is.'

'That's why you're here, I expect. About Jane Holdsworth? I read about it and, pardon me, but hadn't you something to do with her?'

'Yes.' He couldn't keep the blunt, hands-off edge from the word.

Wiggins looked up rather sharply, then returned to his notes.

Tommy Thale gave him a long look. 'Sorry, I expect you should be asking the questions, not I. Millie, then. Millie stays because of her mother. My sister, Annie. You know something about that, I expect?' Jury nodded, and she went on. 'Everyone told Millie it was an accident, that drowning, though I doubt anyone, including the police believed it. Millie's determined to stay.' Her eyes flicked over to a picture-grouping on a round table covered with a lace cloth. 'Poor thing. Like a little ghost who haunts the place of suffering. Still, I think her reason is more than that; I think she's determined to find out what happened.'

'Do you think it was suicide?'

She did not answer immediately; she was thoughtful. 'It's hard to believe.'

'Was your sister like you, temperamentally?'

230

'I'd say so, yes.'

'Then it's very hard to believe.'

Tommy smiled at him. 'That's a compliment?'

'Absolutely. But that leaves only murder, Miss Thale.'

'Tommy. Yes, I expect it does. And *if* anyone did that, and *if* Millie finds out, that person had better watch out. My niece is ferociously loyal. Quite fierce. I sometimes think of her as sitting in the eye of her own storm. She can give the impression she's cool, quite calm. She isn't calm; she's braced. Braced against whatever particular horrors come her way.' Tommy smiled again. 'And a first rate cook, like her mother . . . Oh! Wouldn't you both like some tea? I forgot . . .' Laboriously, she made to rise from the sofa.

'My sergeant is a first-rate tea-maker. And I'm sure he'd love a cup. Right, Wiggins?'

Wiggins rose quickly. 'Are the things ready to hand?'

'Yes. The kitchen's just through there. 'To Wiggins's retreating back she called, 'Tea's in a canister, so's the sugar, pot's on the counter.'

Wiggins was, Jury imagined, dying for his cuppa.

'What does Millie know about her father?'

Tommy shook her head. 'Nothing, except she hasn't one. Nor do I know anything, if that's what you're hoping.'

'Did you ever speculate that it might be someone up there? In the family, perhaps?'

'Oh, yes. But I doubt it; Annie went around with one or two men here in London.' She leaned forward, her hands cupping the stick's handle. 'There's one person I know it *wasn't*: Graham Holdsworth. Annie was terribly upset when that rumour got started. The thing was, you see, I think she was really in love with him. But he wasn't with her. He'd talk to her, though. Quite a lot. They'd be together, alone, say, in the kitchen, or even out walking on the property, and people knew it.'

Jury paused. 'Can you be sure? I mean, perhaps she only wanted to protect him.'

'Then she wouldn't have gone so far as to tell me he was gay, would she?'

Jury did not so much sit back as fall back against his chair. And what else did Jane not confide in him, if this were true? 'Graham Holdsworth was homosexual?'

231

'Yes. Annie couldn't believe it. She said she'd simply never had guessed, never thought that — well, isn't there some sort of chemistry? Can't a person *tell*?'

'Sometimes, sometimes not. Go on.'

'He told her it's what broke up his marriage. He was finally getting some therapy, apparently. He told Annie it was what probably kept him from marrying Madeline Galloway in the first place. For some reason though, he seemed comfortable enough with Jane . . .' She shrugged. 'It's complicated. Of course, this is hearsay, but, believe me, Annie never lied, never. She was afraid that realizing this about himself was what made him do it. Kill himself, I mean.'

'In these times? My God, the closets are nearly empty.'

'Not for the Graham Holdsworths. And he'd tried before, you see, when he was twenty or so. Some people just aren't on the side of life, are they? He'd had a hard-enough time accepting himself, Annie thought, without these feelings surfacing. He was — she said — rather weak; that sounds cold-blooded, but you know what I mean. After all, he'd been coddled all his life, never had to work, not really, and treated as a "poet" and "painter" with the attendant privileges for a special gift.' Again, she shrugged. 'But he was very nice and kind, Annie said. Gentle.' Her smile was the mere ghost of her other smiles as she looked up at the mantel arrangement. 'Took her rowing once, on Windemere. That's what his doctor thought Millie should do, go out on one of the lakes, she thought that it might help Millie get over her . . . obsessions. Not rowing on Wast Water, of course.' She smiled bleakly.

'Graham's doctor?' Jury thought back over Plant's report. 'Viner? Is that her name?'

'I think so. When it happened, she wrote me a long letter, just the once. I got the impression she felt very guilty, very , about her own patient killing himself. And she was concerned about Millie.'

'I'm surprised she'd write to such a termagant as Millie described.'

'Oh, I doubt the doctor believed all of that. Anyway, I never heard from her again.'

Wiggins was back with the tea, setting out the cups, being mother.

'Delicious.' said Tommy, as she sipped.

Wiggins beamed under her smile and returned to his notebook and pen. He had found a large mug for himself.

'Do you see Millie often?' asked Jury.

'I did. Until this.' She patted the brace. 'I haven't seen her in two years.'

'But I'm surprised she wouldn't come to you. If, as you say, she's so loyal.'

'Well, she doesn't know, does she?' said Tommy, briskly enough to hid the turmoil she was clearly feeling. 'I've never told her. And when she wanted to visit, I put her off. Millie still thinks I have my old, much larger flat; my old, much better job; my old, rather handsome fiancé. Now just an old flame.' Her smile was false.

For a moment, Jury was silent, sensing something he didn't much want to hear. 'What happened to the old flame?'

'This.' Again, she patted the brace. 'We were in an accident. He had to drive his brand new Alfa-Romeo at a hundred miles and hour, didn't he? He got out without a scratch. I didn't.' She shrugged. 'He left. His name was Ronnie.'

There was a drawn-out silence during which Jury felt ill.

Wiggins stared. 'Frankly, miss, I could kill Ronnie.' He dropped his eyes, then blushing for the unprofessionalism of it.

'If she ever found out, Millie *would*, Sergeant.'

And she laughed that exuberant laugh.

35

Wast Water couldn't begin to compare with Windermere in length, and yet about a mile along the road, with the giant, reddish screes rising above the opposite shore, Melrose wondered how a lake could be so long, or how mountains could look so close and yet be so far. Great Gable was probably a good two miles beyond the pikes of Scafell, yet looked as if it were wedged between. Had he been out for a view he would have admitted that, yes, this was one worth seeing, unprettified, desolate, grim and even creepy. The lake was not the inviting blue of Windermere but a cold, dark grey, the mood of which Fellowes had captured perfectly.

Melrose pulled the car over in a lay-by, braking beside some American car as long as a caravan — what was it? Cadillac? No, a Buick — and got out to stretch his legs in the chill wind and have a look at Fellowes's map, which he didn't know whether to trust or not. God, those mountains looked forbidding, yet they were as much for walkers as for climbers. More, really.

A couple strolled by the shoreline, hand-in-hand. Coming towards him was an elderly man with a stick. When he drew nearer, Melrose put him down as one of the locals; he looked hardy as the Swaledale rams. His face was so seamed from his pursuits in the open it was leathery.

The old man didn't smile (they didn't much, unless their glasses were empty) but politely touched his cap. 'Hoo do?'

'Very well, thanks. Just out for a walk.'

'Droppy day.' He looked up at the heavy clouds. 'Be gettin' reean.' He looked across the lake. 'Ya wasn't about to walk along scree side, was ya? Looks easy, but 'taint. Toorns from scree to boulders arf'ter bit.'

'I'm driving.'

'Smert.'

'Going up Scafell to Broad Stand.' He pronounced it 'Scawfell.'

'Doomb.' The old man pushed back his cap. 'Anyways, 'tis
"Scarf'l", 'tain't no ward "scaw"; 'tis "sca"; means "steep"
y'see; steep fell.'

Melrose was in no mood for a lesson in etymology. He poked
the map in front of the elder and said, 'Does that route look right?'

The old man studied it, nodded. 'T'Lard's Rake'll be hard after
two thousand foot. Ya cud go round by Rake's Progress, there.'
He stubbed his finger into the map.

'Thanks,' said Melrose.

Again the man put his finger to his cap. Then he got in the Buick
Le Sabre, revved the engine and drove off.

He had left the hamlet of Wasdale Head behind him over an hour
ago. He looked at his printed map − the one that pointed out
the rescue posts and kits − kits? Was it a do-it-yourself first-aid
station? Did you mend your own broken leg?

Melrose had purchased heavy walking shoes (which he doubted
he would ever use again) and a rucksack (about which there was
no doubt at all) in which he had stowed Fellowes's painting, Millie's
sandwiches and little compass, and binoculars.

He'd got past Brown Tongue to the Hollow Stones and he was
already picking scree from his shoes, pulling off a sock and
inspecting two toes for imminent corns and his heel for a blister.

He was sitting (masochistically, he supposed) near the cross that
marked a fatal accident to four walkers around the turn of the
century. He thought of that other one they'd told him about −
where was it? Red-something − the climber who'd fallen to his
death and was for weeks watched over by his faithful dog. If
Melrose fell off a precipice, he'd be watched over by a faithful
buzzard.

Rake's Progress, which he had given up on, was as apt a name
for the follies of walking as Hogarth had made it for the follies
of drinking. That route had cost him a good mile and an hour
and a half on his hands and knees (because of sliding stones) before
he'd retraced his steps and decided to follow his original route after
all.

What was annoying about this harebrained walk was not so
much that its object − a look at Broad Stand − would probably
reveal nothing to him, but there was all of this *physical* activity
involved. And even *that* wouldn't be so bad if, after he'd done

it, he could stride – brave mountaineer – into the Old Contemptibles and tell them he'd planted a flag on top of one of the Scafell pikes. Hell's bells, Wordsworth had picnics up there and Coleridge ambled up to write a letter. Coleridge had been an inveterate climber with little sense of danger.

Rain was coming down steadily in splinters, and he was sorry he hadn't got himself a cape. He was soaked through. He slogged on up the scree-gulley called Lord's Rake and was made a little happier by seeing two walkers slogging down it in rubber capes. As they passed, the other two greeted him, happy as clams, and calling the whole thing absolutely 'grand'. Melrose wished he had been a man for a view instead of a man for a fire, a snoring dog and a glass of Graham's port.

It took him two more hours to go up and over and up and over until he came, finally, to a fell and descended Scafell Crag. It wasn't easy, but at least it was near the end.

Finally, he came to it: one end of the Mickledore traverse and the steep pitch of rock where Virgina Holdsworth had gone over. Broad Stand did not look all that difficult as a means to get to Scafell Pike. But Melrose certainly wasn't going to try and find out. He turned and went east for several yards until he saw the cleft in the crag called 'Fat Man's Agony'. It was deep and could easily accommodate someone of his build. He only wished he could get Agatha up here and try her out.

Melrose went through it to a platform. The walls were smooth stone and there was no way up or out that he could see unless, perhaps, one were a real climber.

He went out and scrutinized the scene at the place where Francis Fellowes had sent up his easel; Melrose took the painting from the rucksack. Fortunately, the rain had let up so that he could see something of the play of light and shadow. When Fellowes had done this, there had been more light, more of a contrast of light and shade. Melrose took the Polaroid out and shot three pictures from different vantage points.

There was no question at all about it. No way out, no way down, no way back except by the dangerous Broad Stand or a retreat back the way one had come.

It was later afternoon by now. Melrose packed up his gear and retreated.

36

'Bootle?' asked the girl in the tourist information office in Grasmere. 'That'd be on the other side of Coniston Water.'

'No. Boone. It's only a hamlet,' said Jury. 'Near Wasdale Head or Wast Water.'

The girl, who had hair the colour of daffodils and eyes the colour of Ullswater, puckered her eyebrows over the map. 'Yes. It's here. But that means a longish sort of drive. On the ferry you could at least get across Lake Windermere to Hawkshead.' She looked up at Jury, smiling brightly.

'So where do we get the ferry?'

'It isn't working.'

'Then I expect,' said Jury, trying to be patient, 'we can't take it.'

Her smile dimmed. 'It's not in service till April. This is still March.'

Since her tone was imploring, as if he might think she was to blame for the order of months, he asked her kindly, 'How should we go to Boone, then?'

'Umm?' The pretty girl seemed to be memorizing Jury's face as she twisted a strand of daffodil hair round her finger.

'Boone. Wast Water. And we're in a bit of a hurry.'

One would not have felt any urgency from watching Wiggins, who was slowly moving the postcard turnstile, taking out a card, putting it back, taking another.

'Oh. Yes.' Again she bent over the map spread on the glass case that housed souvenirs of the Lake District. 'By way of Ravenglass, I expect. That'd take you along Windermere, down and up —'

'But that road goes north and we're wanting to go southwest.'

'It's the only decent road to take you most of the way. Wast Water is so isolated. Now, nearly all the other lakes you can get to on good roads.'

She clearly wished they'd go to some other lake. 'Then give me a *bad* road. There must be one that would cut off going so far out of the way.'

She had now pulled the lock of hair through her mouth and was regarding him deeply and mournfully.

Jury pointed to a lesser road that looked like a fairly straight run from Ambleside, a few miles north of Grasmere. 'What about this one?' It went right across to the area of Wasdale.

'Wrynose Pass, it says.'

'Oh, but you wouldn't want that.'

'Why?'

'It's awfully bumpy and twisty. And — ' She looked out of the window and checked her little watch. ' — it might be getting dark before you get off that road.'

Jury smiled, folded the map, and dropped a pound coin on the case. 'We're not afraid of the dark.'

He pulled Wiggins away from the postcards and turned and waved to the girl. She looked worried, perhaps thinking she was sending him to certain death.

By the time they were over Wrynose Pass, Wiggins was chalk white. 'Bumpy? *Twisty*? Is that what you said?'

'Nice view, though,' said Jury, who wasn't looking at it. It was too far down. He traced the road with his finger.

'Nice? We're surrounded by mountains — ' Wiggins looked up. ' — and ravines.' Wiggins looked down. He had pulled the car over to a lay-by. There were a lot of them.

'Never mind, Wiggins. You've always been a great driver. And it's only a few more miles.' True. But *what* miles. 'Right here, see, is a pub. We can stop there for a drink — a beer, a cuppa, whatever.' Jury proved it by showing Wiggins the map, directing his attention to the Woolpack, which stood at the end of this godforsaken road.

But he was careful to keep those innocent-looking sideways *V*'s overlying Hard Knott Pass hidden by his finger. The gradient was one-in-ten, ascending through high fells and deep gulleys.

The worst was yet to come

'Never again,' said Wiggins, mopping his forehead an hour later.

Jury squeezed his eyes shut. If he said it once more —

'Never again. You'll never get me on that road again.'

A coffee at the Woolpack hadn't mollified him at all. He wanted his nice hot bath and his dinner at the pub in Boone.

'For God's sake, Wiggins. Some of the drivers even smiled and waved at us.'

'Tourists, sir. Tourists don't care if they die, as long as they're on holiday.'

At the sign of the Old Contemptibles, colour returned to Wiggins's cheeks.

After leaving the Ford in the tiny car park, they entered the pub through a door on which was scrolled ENTRANCE in flaking white paint, and which stood opposite the door to the bar.

The hall was dark, quiet and bare except for a heavy mahogany chair, a few bird prints, and a writing desk on which lay a register. Beside the desk a tiny sign directed the prospective guest to push the buzzer below. Jury did.

The woman who flounced in from the back was carrying a mug of tea on a plate of biscuits and looking as hopefully at Jury as Wiggins was looking at the biscuits. They'd had no lunch and, except for the coffee at the Woolpack, no sustenance since leaving Penrith. And that had been more coffee and a stale and sticky doughnut that Wiggins had disdained, preferring to keep up his strength on charcoal biscuits.

Mrs Fish (as she introduced herself), Manageress, went very heavy on the makeup, the necklaces, the bracelets and rings. Oh, she'd be more than happy to offer them accommodation and appeared to be debating over the three keys hanging on a little board above the writing desk.

'You'll be wanting a private bath, I expect.'

Wiggins nearly snapped at her. 'Yes, indeed.'

'That's all right then. It'll be two pounds more a piece, of course. Have you signed? Good. Just follow me.'

Up the rickety stairs they went and into a narrow little hall, companion to the one downstairs off which debouched three rooms, two one side, one the other. A fourth door faced them at the hall's end.

'Here we are, then,' said Mrs. Fish, opening the doors to two rooms and placing the key in each lock. 'Bath's just there at the end of the hall.'

'But that's a *public* bath!' said Wiggins, hungry, dirty and indignant.

Well, there's no one else here, is there?' said Mrs Fish. She fairly twinkled with her improvisational scheme and took herself off after assuring the sergeant that she'd have a pot of tea waiting for them in the bar.

2

Out of the narrow window inset to the left of the front door to Tarn House stared a pair of eyes. The little girl was probably ten or eleven. Before Jury could raise the knocker, the door opened.

Not only had she large and beautiful eyes, she had lovely russet-coloured hair that fell to her shoulders and a fringe that nearly covered her eyebrows.

Jury told her who they were and added, 'I'll bet you're Millie.'

The little girl started slightly, yet kept her countenance, as if to show the world held no more surprises. Sucking the inside of her mouth she nodded, arms folded. For distraction, she looked down at the black cat at her feet and said something sharp; but the cat, too, was proof against surprises and sat its ground, staring up at the interlopers.

Jury asked if Mr Plant was about.

'Out. He went out to walk after lunch and he hasn't come back.' She made it sound as if she were worried he never would.

'If you could take me to either Mr or Mrs Holdsworth, and take Sergeant Wiggins here to Miss Galloway, I'd appreciate it.' Since Jury had already seen Madeline Galloway in London, they had decided Wiggins would talk to her and George Holdsworth; Jury, to Genevieve and Crabbe.

They were police. *Scotland Yard* policemen. Millie Thale kept the excitement in her eyes from glimmering in the rest of her face as she commanded Wiggins to 'stay here' and led Jury to a huge set of double doors.

The black cat stayed with Wiggins, who pretended not to notice.

'Virginia?' Crabbe Holdsworth was obviously surprised that her name would even arise. 'Deliberately *pushed*? What on earth makes you think *that*?' He rose from his chair with a jerk as if a puppeteer had pulled the strings. 'I thought you came about poor Jane!'

'I did,' said Jury. 'It's possible there might be some connection between your first wife's death and hers.' The man appeared genuinely shaken. 'Mr Holdsworth, I'm sorry if this upsets you, but there have been so many misfortunes in this family.'

Rather than reseating himself, Crabbe took a few steps over to the wall where hung the Ibbetson prints and a Gilpin aquatint. 'I don't need you to remind me of that.' For a few moments he studied the pictures; then he moved, hands behind his back, to the bookcases. 'That's why you find me here.'

'I beg your pardon?'

Crabbe turned. 'Amongst my books and my paintings. This library is my sanctuary, as Robert Southey's was his. They had their misfortunes too, you know, the Lake poets. Wordsworth seemed to escape, for the most part. Perhaps it was his temperament,' he added reflectively.

The man stood there, stiff and starched, and Jury waited for the inevitable lecture, the delving into personal interests that so often had to be got through before the witness, the suspect, or whoever he was questioning could be led to the point. Oddly, Crabbe Holdsworth stopped talking. But he seemed to be dreaming of that old century; he seemed altogether a dreamy sort of man, a man with little common sense, but one who could escape or forget.

He would be little help.

The dinner party had occurred only the previous night, and yet Jury had the guest list more clearly in mind after Melrose Plant's one report early that morning than Crabbe Holdsworth had after spending hours with these people. He could not recall what had been discussed (except for his own comments); could not remember (except that there had been such a woman), the lady that his father Adam had invited as guest; nor remember anything about the meal except for the excellent oysters and the hare his brother had killed.

It was interesting to Jury, as he watched the man's eyes move again amongst the prints and paintings, that Crabbe himself had no inner eye that could capture, in little views and vistas, the various scenes undoubtedly thrown up by that arrangement of guests round the dinner table.

To Jury it was almost shocking that a man whose best company included Wordsworth, Coleridge, and De Quincey was also a man utterly lacking in imagination.

She remembered.

'Maurice Kingsley was quite drunk. Well, you can imagine, having had his several run-ins with police. He was in London the night Jane died, I understand.'

She seemed unabashed pleased as she sat herself in her snug fitting rose-wool dress on the end of the chaise longue, which allowed her much more latitude for arranging herself than any chair would have done. She could lean forward and accept a cigarette. 'He was *there*.'

Jury was in a wing chair, reaching over to light her cigarette. 'So were you, Mrs Holdsworth.'

That caught her in the midst of holding back her dark hair from the flame. 'But *not* on a bench on the woman's door-step!'

Jury said nothing. He let her fiddle with her whisky and soda, let her go on.

'I can't understand why Jane's death is being . . . investigated so thoroughly. Of course, it was shocking.' She inspected a rosepainted fingernail. 'But she *did* kill herself.'

'Probably.' Jury thought of Pete Apted, not for the first time since they'd talked that morning. 'Probably.'

She shrugged. 'Then it makes no difference who was *where*.'

'The thing is, Mrs Holdsworth: in the past six years there have been two alleged accidents and two alleged suicides in this family. Doesn't that strike you as against the odds?'

'Why "alleged"? What are you saying?'

'A year after Virginia Holdsworth had her fatal fall, her son hanged himself in the gatehouse down there. Several weeks later, your cook, Annie Thale, took *another* fatal fall from the property here above Wast Water. Now, some five years later, Jane Holdsworth kills herself. Assume the suicides really were,' Jury said, sadly, 'and let's take these "accidents". Start with Virginia Holdsworth.'

She rolled her glass so that the finger or so of whisky made little waves. 'Talk to Francis Fellowes. He was there.'

'I'm talking to you.'

With a gesture of supreme confidence, she smoothed her hair. 'Mr Jury, the local police looked into that; well, I expect they had to, since it was a violent death. It was either Francis — who'd no

244

reason to do it — or it was no one. No one. People were quite satisfied with the *ob*-vious.'

She drew the word out, and Jury thought again of Pete Apted.

'For heaven's sake, accept it: a February day, with sliding rocks and ice and that tricky little prospect. Ginny *fell*.'

'I'm not accepting the obvious just yet. You call her "Ginny". Did you know her well?'

'No, not really.' Her slight shrug seemed truly indifferent. 'I met her *and* Crabbe — if that's what you're thinking — when I was up here six, seven years ago on holiday with a group of friends.' She sighed. 'Fatal holiday, that was. I prefer London.'

Jury almost laughed at the woman's priorities. 'Smoking your credit card through Harrods, that sort of thing?'

Genevieve *did* laugh. 'Absolutely.'

'It was fatal, certainly, for Virginia.' Jury was surprised that the implication elicited no heated response from Crabbe's second wife.

'I simply happened to be around, Mr Jury. Let's say I got him on the rebound.'

Jury smiled. 'We could say, but you don't look like the rebound type.'

'That seems to be a crazy sort of compliment.'

'Would anyone have had a reason to murder Virginia Holdsworth?'

Again she sighed, looked at the drinks table. 'Compliment rescinded. You mean me, don't you? To get me hands on the Holdsworth money?' She looked almost bored. 'I'd have done better to have tried for Adam.'

In a way, he found her chilly candour disarming. But candour was often the stock trade of villains. 'What about Graham Holdsworth and Annie Thale'.

She thought for a bit, making those little circling waves with what was left of her drink. 'Why do you mention them together, Superintendent?'

'For the obvious reason that that's the way they died. Very closely together.

This seemed to interest her. 'Well, I know that Graham and Jane were heading towards divorce. But I can't imagine Annie had anything to do with it. Or do you always think that another woman is waiting in the wings?' She knocked back the rest of her whisky in a gesture that was far more likeable than her earlier poses and mannerisms.

'Why were they having problems, do you think?'

'Jane was broody; Graham was spoiled. Neither one of them had ever done a stint at hard labour. Don't look at *me* like that. The uncalloused hands you are pointedly observing were once those of a shorthand-typist.'

'What about Annie Thale?'

'What about her? An extraordinary cook. Is cooking in the genes, do you think? Her daughter Millie is also remarkable. Sometimes, I wonder just how much Mrs Callow *does* in the kitchen.'

This little puzzle seemed to interest Genevieve more than the death of Millie's mother. Her memory was better than her husband's but her priorities weren't. He doubted she'd be much more help. Still, he asked, 'You're quite sure it was an accident, then?'

She rose, took a heaving breath, and headed once again for the decanter. 'I'm not *sure* of anything. But why in God's name would it have been anything other?' After a glance at the mantel clock, she said, 'You'll have drinks with us? Or dine, perhaps?'

Jury thought it was a very ingenuous invitation, in the circumstances. And she had already made an inroad on the cocktail hour. 'Thanks, but I'd like to talk to the others. Francis Fellowes, for one.'

'Francis? He lives in the gatehouse. You passed it. But since there's still a bit of light left, he's probably out with his paints. He's always painting Wast Water, for some reason. It seems to hold him spellbound.'

Genevieve gave Jury directions and seemed almost sad to watch him go. Even police made a change, perhaps.

'Not a very likable person, Madeline Galloway,' said Wiggins, removing the cap and pulling up a little plastic cup. It expanded in tiers. 'Cold-fishy sort.' From his back trouser pocket he took the sort of leather covered flask that was a staple, together with binoculars, at racecourses. Wiggins's held mineral water. 'I can tell you she didn't like her sister; I can also tell you she didn't like Virginia Holdsworth and doesn't − ' He took a drink of water, shook a two-toned capsule from a vial and popped it in his mouth.

' – like Genevieve Holdsworth.' He returned the paraphernalia to the individual pockets.

He went on. 'George Holdsworth wasn't much help. Had to compete with the damned hounds for an audience. He was fond of Virginia, he said. It's hard to tell his feelings for the others. He liked Jane Holdsworth, though. "A tragedy. Not surprised, though." That's what he said. *I* was a bit surprised. He thought she was driven. That was his word: "driven." And he uses precious few words.'

Jury was silent. They were getting into the car. 'The servants?'

Wiggins made a face. 'Awful pair. Hawkes was polishing silver and seemed by way of wanting to let his hair down, you know, for a good natter.' Wiggins nose was twitching. He yanked out his big handkerchief just as a sneezing fit came on.

'Let's go, Wiggins; a little lake breeze'll do you good.'

Wiggins just looked at him.

3

The surface of Wast Water was grey, ruffled and icy-looking, not a body of water to do his sergeant much good. Volcanic rock had thrown up a view at once awesome and somewhat threatening. At the far end of the lake rose the steely rockface of Scafell and Great Gable. On the far shore rose the screes, a totally different surface of reddish-brown scree, a huge fell disintegrated, crumbled in the rain.

What was left of the light was changeable. In the few moments it took Jury and Wiggins to leave their car and plod over the rocks and mosses, the lake colour had changed from grey to slate green to umber, depending upon the movement of cloud cover.

In anticipation of swift changes of light and shadow, the painter had set up not one, but three canvases and, as Jury and Wiggins walked towards him, he was hastily moving from one to another to another, imitating the action of the light.

'Mr Fellowes?'

The painter turned from the nearest canvas quickly, stared at them and turned as quickly back, crying out, 'Damn it all!' He slapped the brush down on the easel. 'That's done it!' he yelled, not to Jury and Wiggins but to the shifting clouds, the screes, and the lake itself. In this eerie, early spring light, it looked sinister. 'Thank you very much!' he bellowed.

This shout was probably meant for them, but he could as easily have been blaming Nature for refusing to sit for his painting.

'Sorry to disturb your work. You're Francis Fellowes?' He set about wiping his hands on a rag as he said, 'Yes, I expect so.' Just as indifferently, he muttered when Jury and Wiggins produced identification. He might not have cared who any of the three of them were.

Wiggins immediately went off to get a closer look at the paintings of Wast Water.

'We're here about your cousin Mr Fellowes. Jane Holdsworth.'

'Again? There was a DI here from London just recently.'

'Yes. Detective Inspector Kamir; he's in charge of the case. I just happened to be a friend of Jane Holdsworth.'

'Oh,' said Fellowes, noncommittally. Then he called over his shoulder, 'Sergeant! Be careful, there, will you?'

Wiggins had inspected each canvas and called back, 'I rather like this middle one, sir.'

Fellowes, who seemed to get emotional only when it came to his work, yelled back, 'Well, it isn't a question of what you or I *like*. It's a question of what we *see*.' He then looked about him at this once-expansive landscape that had offered such inspiration to his brush, as if the scene had turned traitor and shrunk to the size of a prison cell. He looked as if he could spit.

Wiggins was back again, still determined. 'I expect that's so, sir; but even with three different canvases, tomorrow or the next day the various lights might still never be the same. Have you thought of that?'

'No, Sergeant. I really am too busy trying to paint light to pay any actual attention to it, being as rank an amateur painter as there are amateur policemen.'

This was said utterly without malice. It wouldn't have bothered Wiggins, anyway. Fellowes might have riddled the words out as if they were bullets; Wiggins was bulletproof.

'How well did you know Jane Holdsworth?'

Fellowes was collecting his tubes of paint. 'Fairly well. Enough to think she didn't kill herself.'

Jury was surprised he'd come across this way. 'Why?'

He shrugged. 'I can't see any reason; she wasn't the type; she was too fond of Alex, her son.' He looked from Jury to his easels. 'Look, must we go through all of that "where were you on the night of" business? Because I really must get my canvases back to the house.'

'I know all of that from Inspector Kamir. But just for your impressions, Mr Fellowes, I'd like to talk to you later, if I could.' Jury was following him to an old van.

'Then you can find me at the Old Contemptibles. That's where I am when I'm not here or at the house.'

As Fellowes finished loading his gear in the back of the van, carefully wedging the canvases so that they wouldn't slip, Jury forestalled the comment about the middle painting he could almost see forming on Wiggin's lips by stepping on the sergeant's foot.

Fellowes drove away.

'You look knackered, Wiggins. Go back to the pub and have a kip. And some dinner. Drop me off at Castle Howe.'

Wiggins brightened, but said dutifully, 'You'll need the car to get to the pub, sir.'

'Don't worry about it. I want to see this psychiatrist, Helen Viner.'

'What about Kingsley?'

'I'd rather wait until I see those letters Mr Plant has. You know, I can't imagine Melrose Plant out all day walking. My God, it's all he can do at home to get from his front door to his garden bench.'

'Or down the pub, sir,' said Wiggins, smiling and rubbing his instep.

37

A stocky woman knitting what looked like an interminably long scarf sat behind a highly polished, hotel-like front desk, and a hotel-like register, above which was a large mahogany box divided into pigeonholes for letters. She looked at him suspiciously over the tops of her spectacles.

It was the dinner hour (she said, as if that hour were sacrosanct) and Mrs Colin-Jackson was not to be disturbed. She was doing the books. It was not this lady that Jury had asked to see (he reminded her); it was Dr Helen Viner.

It was, however, a rule that Mrs Colin-Jackson see any first time caller at the Castle. She did not bother looking up from the black wool or stop the click-click of the needles as she said this.

'Then get her.' Jury shoved the leather wallet with his identification right up to her spectacles.

She reared back in her chair. But at least she got out of it.

Nobody here could be short of money, Jury thought, as he looked at the luxurious carpeting, the antiques assembled round an open hearth in a large drawing room, the heavy curtains, the burnished wallpaper and fitted bookcases.

From somewhere down the thickly carpeted hall came sounds of shoutings and clatterings. He walked back to inspect. To his right was a lavish dining room of blue paint and white mouldings, silver and crystal (even running to wineglasses), white cloths and linen napkins, the latter of which one spare woman whose tan and muscle testified to her deep involvement with real or false suns, tennis courts, horses, pools — this woman was snapping her napkin at another fattish one who returned the snaps with her own napkin wetted in her wineglass. Droplets flew, napkins flashed. The guests, still brightly eating what looked like some creamy French concoction, had to divide their eyes and time between that little show and another on the other side of the room. A man with a palsied hand was taking aim with a piece of meringue at a woman who had risen with a piece of cutlery, set to strike.

Applause all around.

Jury stood there, hands in pockets, hoping for more.

'Yes?'

The thick voice came from a heavily jowelled woman, probably in her fifties, but looking older because of the tiny red lines that webbed her cheeks.

Mrs Colin-Jackson, her face overlaid with too much blush and peachy-coloured powder, brought with her the heady combination of L'air du Temps and gin. To all intents and purposes she was smashed. She could only *just* keep her eyes focused and her smile hooked up on one side as if her mouth had lost contact with muscle. He *bet* she'd been doing the books; he would love to know what an auditing of her books would disclose.

'Dr Viner?' Mrs Colin-Jackson adjusted her décolletage, tucked in a strand of hair highlighted to hide the grey and looked a little disconcerted that it wasn't she herself Jury had come for. 'I expect she'd be in her office — it's her quarters really, a small cottage at the end of the gardens.' She pointed. 'Down the hall, turn right, and go out of the side door.'

Jury could see her in the lighted window, her head bent over her desk, the green-glass-shaded lamp directly above washing that part of the face he could see in watery rivulets. From this vantage point, Dr Viner appeared to be a very attractive woman.

Up closer — after she opened the door at his knock — she appeared to be still more attractive, her face was mobile, expressive; her voice was warm. As a policeman, Jury wasn't used to a warm greeting. He told her he'd come from Tarn House.

Dr Viner had spent a long time learning how to mask her own emotions; therefore, it was difficult to take her by surprise. She merely opened the door wider, motioning him in.

'It's not much of a cottage,' she said. 'But it's private, at least. One does like to get away.' She nodded her head towards the main edifice and allowed herself a wicked little smile. 'We've a strange combination of "guests".'

Jury smiled. 'I was outside the dining room. I thought pie-in-the-face went out with vaudeville.'

She sighed. 'Are the Bannisters at it again? Husband and wife. Isn't it sweet to take up retirement together?'

'If you've the money, very sweet.' Jury sat on the other side of the green pool of light and studied her mouth and chin. The eyes were in partial darkness. She hadn't turned on any other lights. 'Are they all receiving treatment?'

She shook her head, laughed. 'Oh, my Lord, no. Actually, the minority. We're here − Dr Kingsley and I − for those who get a little out of hand. There is also a GP who lives in Boone and another near Wasdale Head; and we have very well-trained nurses.'

'Adam Holdsworth lives here, I understand?'

'Oh, Adam.' Her chair creaked back and her entire face was in shadow. 'He's one of my favourites. Definitely *not* one of my patients.'

'His grandson was, though.' There was a sudden stillness. Even the wavy, seawater light had stopped moving. 'Graham Holdsworth.'

'I know who you mean, Superintendent.'

'Tell me about him.'

'As a friend?'

'As a patient.'

'No.'

The word was not charged with anger but with melancholy.

'Dr Viner: you're surely not going to invoke the confidentiality of a doctor-patient relationship for a man who's been dead for five years.'

'There are other people still living.'

'Which tells me you know something painful.'

She exhaled a long breath, as if she'd been holding it for some time. 'Hell,' she said, hoarsely. 'I should learn to keep my mouth shut.'

'You're doing a pretty good job.'

She leaned forward then over her crossed arms, and her mouth, though tightly clamped, seemed still to want to smile. Creases showed at each corner, a woman much given to smiling good humour. 'I should do a better one. And I don't see what on earth this has to do with Jane Holdsworth.'

'You're assuming that's why I'm here?'

Her swivel chair creaked as she leaned back again. 'Well, that's why all the *others* − police − have been here. Though I'm

253

surprised a Scotland Yard detective would turn up, frankly. As a matter of fact, I was surprised the other detective from London came here.' The flat of her hand was rolling a pen back and forth on her blotter. 'I think you all think it wasn't suicide. You think it was murder.' She kept her eyes on the hand covering the pen.

'What do you think?'

For some time she didn't answer. She stuck the pen in a jam jar that held her collection of biros, old fountain pens and pencils. Then she laid one hand over the other flat on the blotter and bent her head as if she were studying the intricacies of the hand's faint bluish veins. She plucked out another pen, drew over a prescription pad, doodled a bit, shoved the pad aside. He wondered why she remained silent for so long. None of her movements came across as nervousness, or as any hesitancy in answering, but more as if she were taking stock.

Finally she sat, her hands in her lap, her shoulders hunched slightly forward, and looked at Jury. 'No.'

'No to which.'

'To both, really.' Silence fell again. Her silences were deep like the shadows gathered in the corners, reshaped by the movement of the branches of the large tree against the window. A wind rattled the casement, ruffled the papers on her desk, and set the smaller branches scraping the leaded panes. In his loneliness, Jury heard them as fingers tapping, someone trying to get in.

She shook her head as she spoke. 'That someone she knew would have given her an overdose is too hard to believe. She had no enemies I know of. But if I have to choose . . . and obviously it was one or the other — ' She looked up at him with an expression of great sadness. 'No to suicide. No.' She shook her head. 'I just don't think she could have done that, either to herself or to Alex. Her son.'

'You knew her well, did you?'

'Yes. We were good friends.'

Jury asked outright: 'Had she — was she having an affair with Maurice Kingsley?'

Helen Viner didn't seem shocked by the question. 'I don't see how. I can't imagine them together.' She seemed amused at the thought. 'I know he was there that night. The police were here yesterday. I can understand Maurice was in a state over that; he got quite drink last night at the Holdsworth's dinner

254

party.' She shrugged. 'But why, for heaven's sake? Jealousy?'

Jury was, for the first time, very glad he had seen Pete Apted, glad that Apted had convinced him that Jane had indeed killed herself. That was hard as hell to handle in and of itself; to think she might also have been seeing someone else − like Kingsley − would have been much harder, a different kind of loss, a wrenching disenchantment. 'I don't know. I don't see that Dr Kingsley would have a motive. Of course, I haven't talked to him yet, but police here have found no reason for him to have done it. I don't believe he did.' He paused. 'I don't believe anyone did.'

This, for some reason, *did* surprise her, and she showed it, whirling round from the window which she had risen to wind inward. She opened her mouth but no words came out.

Jury smiled. 'So you probably won't need that alibi.'

Back at her desk, she frowned. 'What ali − oh!' The smile returned. 'I forgot. I *was* dining with friends in Kendal.'

'Kamir − Inspector Kamir − checked that. You've known the Holdsworths for some time?'

She nodded, her gaze returning to the tree, whose tapping still persisted. 'Ghosts,' she murmured.

He was quiet, waiting for her to go on.

'Ten years. I've been here that long. I knew the first Mrs Holdsworth, Virginia. I must admit I liked her a good deal better than the second. Ginny was a pleasant, enthusiastic, quite lovely person. She liked the area; Genevieve doesn't. Not a true Laker, I don't think.' Her mouth curved in that slow, disarming smile.

'Ginny loved to walk. Unfortunately.' Her head dipped.

'Annie Thale?'

Her head came up quickly. 'Annie? What makes you mention her?'

'I would think that'd be obvious.'

'Sorry, you've lost me; it isn't.'

'Another accident. Very much like Mrs Holdsworth's.' When she didn't comment, he went on. 'Dr Viner: two suicides, two fatal falls.'

'Yes. It's tragic. Especially for Alex. Both parents . . . of course, Alex doesn't believe his mother took her own life. He can't believe it, can he?' Her head went down again.

'I want to know about his father. What *you* know.'

She shook her head.

Jury stood up. 'Okay. I'll subpoena your records, Dr Viner.'

She rose, splayed her hands on the table, leaned towards him. 'Dammit! Leave the poor man *alone*!'

Jury remained standing. 'Homosexuality isn't shameful, not anymore.'

She stared at him, her mouth slightly open, and then sat down heavily. 'Wherever did you hear that?' she asked, her voice soft, calm.

'Annie Thale. Or rather, her sister.'

Helen Viner looked totally taken aback. 'Millie's "Aunt Tom"? You're not serious.'

'Yes, I'm serious. You must have known Holdsworth confided in the cook, Annie, and that he was fond of her. But she was much fonder of him.'

The silence lengthened, the twig-fingers tapped the black pane. Helen Viner put her head in her hands. 'All right. Yes Grant had been tormented most of his life by his feelings. Homosexual, perhaps bisexual – he had, certainly, a sexual relationship with Jane. But he couldn't continue it.' Her hands came down.

'And Annie: was she so much in love with him that *she* couldn't continue living?'

'I'd have to have known her far more intimately to know that. It's possible, yes. Anything is. Tell me, what is she like?'

'Who? Oh, Miss Thale?' He thought of Millie's 'Aunt Tom.'

'Um, perhaps a bit stiff. A bit cold.'

'Really? I was convinced Millie'd made it up.'

Jury was watching the shadows now cast by the moving branches. His oblique response to this was, 'Adam Holdsworth's very fond of Millie, isn't he?'

'Very. And Alex. That goes without saying.'

'They should be watched over. The people Adam Holdsworth is fond of have a way of dying. I'll Let myself out.'

38

Jury and Wiggins had stopped at Cumbria police headquarters in Penrith to see what files they had on Graham and Virginia Holdsworth and Annie Thale. The suicide note written by Graham was authentic; there was no reason to believe that Virginia Holdsworth's death had been anything but an accident, Broad Stand being a notoriously dangerous traverse; yet every reason to believe that Annie Thale's death had not. That had apparently been suicide also.

Jury wasn't satisfied with the 'apparently', but he could certainly understand that out of kindness to her daughter, they had said it was most likely an accidental fall, although the written records stated otherwise.

Cumbria police did not object to Jury's making his inquiries, since Jane Holdsworth's death was not their case; it was London's.

In the Old Contemptibles, Francis Fellowes tapped the table with one of his brushes. 'I can't help you. Never detected anything in Graham's manner that would indicate he was gay. Never heard anything, never saw anything. Though I don't think he was a very passionate man; I mean, he didn't really have awfully strong feelings.'

'Apparently you're wrong.' Jury's tone was edgy.

Fellowes stopped the tapping, looked at Jury, reddened. 'Yes, well, I didn't mean —' He shrugged.

'Supposedly he'd been going to marry Madeline Galloway before her sister appeared, is that true?'

'Wishful thinking on Madeline's part. I doubt Jane broke up anything.'

'Don't you find it odd Miss Galloway would continue on at Tarn House?'

Fellowes smiled. 'I expect that money — or the hope of it — can offset these little humiliations.'

257

'Has she expectations?'

'They *all* do, Superintendent. Adam can't live forever.'

'In that house, people don't even live through middle-age. Were you a friend of Graham Holdsworth?'

'Yes. But not what you'd call a confident. You know the person he really seemed to confide in, oddly, was Annie Thale. She was cook; her daughter's still there, Millie. Graham talked to Annie when he wouldn't talk to anyone else. she was that sort of person.' He picked up his pint. 'I'd never really thought much about that before.'

'Did you ever think she killed herself because of him? His suicide?'

Fellowes had taken up his sketchpad and was making quick strokes on it, of the bar and the people there, doing it as some people doodle, in order to centre his thoughts. He shook his head. '*I* thought they were merely good friends. But I could be wrong.'

'What did the family think of that relationship?'

Fellowes frowned. 'I'm not sure they knew, or thought anything.' He left off the drawing and turned to Jury with a slight smile. 'And remember, when you speak of "the family" you're talking about two different entities. There's Adam. And then there's everyone else – Genevieve, Crabbe, George and even Madeline.'

'Alex? What about him?'

Fellowes was shaking his head before the question was finished. 'He's in a class by himself. He's the one who'll get the lot.'

'The inheritance.'

'Oh yes. Of course, there'll be bequests to everyone else, me included, though I'm only a distant cousin. Millie will come in for a very large chunk, more than anyone else, I'd say, after Alex. Adam doesn't believe that blood is thicker than water. He was very fond of Millie's mother, and of Virginia, and of Graham.' Fellowes chewed on the tip of his brush again, thinking. 'You see, these particular people aren't after his money. They are – were – genuinely fond of him. And Alex, well, Alex and Adam are two of a kind. They love schemes and scams.' Fellowes smiled. 'I'm glad the boy's back.' He looked at Jury again. 'And very sorry about Jane.'

Jury was silent for a moment, drinking his ale. Then he said, 'Don't you think, Mr Fellowes, this family is terribly accident-

or suicide-prone? To the point, really, that one begins to wonder if the deaths of people Adam was so fond of were precisely that. As you yourself put it, why kill them of piecemeal?'

Fellowes's pencil hung in midair as he stared at Jury. 'Who the hell told you that?'

'I did.'

Melrose Plant stood at the table, looking down at his friend Richard Jury. 'I'm sorry about – ' With Francis Fellowes present, he stopped. 'I've been out walking. It wasn't until dinner at Tarn House that I found out you'd arrived and were staying here. Where's Sergeant Wiggins?'

Jury had risen to shake hands. Now he smiled. 'Sleeping it off – the five-hour drive to Penrith and the far worse drive along the worst road I've ever seen.'

'Hard Knott Pass. I'm an old hand, if you ever need a chauffeur.' He finally plunked himself down. 'A pint of something. Where's our dear old Con? Ah, here she comes.'

Fellowes looked from one to the other, arms folded. 'You two know each other?'

'We do,' said Jury, smiling at Melrose. 'Have done for years.'

Fellowes laughed. 'I never did think you were a librarian.'

I wonder if anyone did. Thank you, Mrs Fish.' His tweed sleeve was torn, one of the elbow patches loosely sewn, and his face was scratched.

'You look pretty done in,' said Jury, pleasantly.

'I *am* done in, but never mind; it was worth it.' Briskly, he went for his rucksack, opened it, pulled out Fellowes's painting, which was carefully sandwiched between two squares of cardboard to protect it. Beside that he put the leather pouch, and beside that, a Polaroid camera. 'Now.' He shot his cuffs as if he were preparing for a little magic act.

Both Jury and Fellowes were looking at the table display and then at him.

'What's all this?' Jury nodded towards the painting, the leather pouch, the camera.

'*This* is basically Mr Fellowes's valuable contribution towards solving these crimes.'

'Crimes?' Fellowes's eyebrow shot up. '*I* solved?'

'One crime, and this one strongly implies at least one other.'

Jury was examining the mirror he'd taken from its leather holder.

'It's called a Claude glass,' said Fellowes. When Jury looked blank, Fellowes explained. At Melrose's further request, he explained how the painting had been done.

'You remember the picture of Broad Stand and Fat Man's Agony?'

Fellowes nodded. For Jury, Melrose pointed out the cleft in the stone through which a ribbon of light showed. 'And in this Polaroid shot: you see the light coming from the exit, or the entrance. As Francis told the story, Virginia Holdsworth had walked some way ahead of him. She was' – Melrose explained to Jury – 'determined to get to Mickledore by way of Broad Stand. That's here.' He pointed it out on the map. 'When he'd got up here, on this small plateau near Broad Stand, he didn't see her.'

'I assumed she'd done it, managed to get over to Mickledore, since she wasn't around.'

'She wasn't. My guess is that someone pushed her off Broad Stand.'

Fellowes stared. 'How? There wasn't anyone up there.'

'Yes, there was.'

'Go on.'

Fellowes was still objecting. 'But I was there for a good half hour or more. No one could have got past me. And I didn't see anyone.'

'But you had your back turned all of that time. You were using this.' He held up the convex glass. 'The person who sent Mrs Holdsworth over the edge didn't know it, thought he or she was safe if he merely waited you out.'

'I'd have seen him in the glass, wouldn't I?'

Melrose shook his head. 'Not if he was hiding in Fat Man's Agony, waiting you out.'

'But –'

'Look at the way you painted the entrance to the opening.'

Fellowes and Jury looked.

'There's a figure in there. You were painting, in the best picturesque fashion, exactly what you saw. Only the barest pinpoint of light is coming through. Whoever was in there thought he was safe enough since he must have assumed, with your back turned, you were simply doing a view of Wast Water. "Fat Man's Agony" is a good name; anyone with some pounds on him would have a hellish tight squeeze.' Another pint came; more thanks were given Connie Fish. 'I took my Polaroid shot from as near the same point as you painted with the Claude glass. All right, there wasn't any mist, but still you can see the difference. Even with the naked eye, you can make out something; with a magnifying glass you can make out the curvature of a human being. Not fat, obviously.' He handed over a small magnifying glass.

Both Jury and Fellowes looked from painting to Polaroid for some time. 'I'll be damned.' Jury had moved round to look over Fellowes's shoulder. 'You're right.'

'I know,' said Melrose. 'Your forensics people, or your sophisticated police equipment, could enlarge this to the point you could see the person couldn't they?'

Jury frowned. 'It's a painting, remember, not a photograph. Whether the figure's a man or woman might not be discernible.' He smiled over at Plant. 'Good job.'

Fellowes leaned back, let out a puff of breath. 'How do you know this person didn't *see* I was painting with a Claude glass?'

'Simple. You wouldn't be sitting here tonight drinking your beer.'

2

'Apted? You mean Pete-Queen's-bloody-Counsel-Apted? My God, you do have friends in high places. I know you're supposed to be valuable, but I'm surprised the Metropolitan Police would spring for Apted.'

'Thank you for that "supposed to be", and, no, the Met would hardly pay for him. But thanks to him, I'm back on rota.'

Melrose was on his third pint of Jennings, but finding it difficult to get drunk. He was too concerned about Jury. 'Sorry about that. And it never occurred to me for a moment that you were in any real trouble.'

'It occurred to *someone*. An anonymous someone. Who do you think?'

Melrose frowned. 'Trueblood's got the money . . . Who am I kidding? Trueblood being anonymous?' His face lit up. 'Vivian! Good Lord. It would have to be Vivian. Trueblood would have let her know *immediately*. It'd be a *far* better way than being hit by a lorry.'

261

'Better way? For what?'

'Private joke.' He hurried on. 'You'll want to read these.' From his rucksack he pulled the bundle of letters and tossed them on the table. 'I thought I'd better keep them with me. They were simply turned over to me − if you can believe it − at the dinner party last night.'

'Turned over by whom?'

'A Lady Cray.' He put his head in his hands. 'She's a patient, guest, take it as you will, at Castle Howe. She came with Adam Holdsworth. To the dinner party, I mean. She's quiet . . . unusual.'

'They're addressed to Jane.' Jury sat very still. 'What's in them?'

'They have the sort of . . . I don't know . . . sound of love letters, yet they're . . . well, first off, they're very short . . . second, they're typed. Word-processed.' He looked at Jury. 'Would you process love letters?'

'No.'

Melrose moved his nearly empty glass round in little circles. 'Ever written any?'

'One or two. How did this Lady Cray get hold of them?'

'That's even odder. She said she got them from Kingsley's office.'

'How?'

'Didn't tell me; the conversation was very brief.' Melrose scrubbed his hands through his hair. 'I assume she's in treatment with him, I don't know. It was all very − surreptitious. I mean, the way she *did* it. I felt I was in the middle of a spy novel.' He described the room, the mirror, the bag.

Jury said nothing.

'Look, I'm sorry about Jane Holdsworth.' Melrose wiped at the wet rings his glass had left with a screwed up napkin.

'I am too. Thanks,' Jury said gravely. Then he took the clip from the letters.

'Alex said Kingsley was outside the house that night. To retrieve these, do you think? But why would he take such a risk just to get them back?'

'Why are you assuming he wrote them?'

'I expect simply because they were in his office. Hidden, I take it. But look at them − they're so . . . oblique. You can't even tell what this "illness" that's mentioned is. The homosexuality, presumably.

'Why would Maurice Kingsley be writing about that? And why would he be concerned about the sate of their marriage if he wants her himself? Hell, you'd think he'd be relieved.

'They're so oblique they could have been written by anyone — Kingsley, Fellowes — even Crabbe or George. Or some man we don't know about. But who would *type* love letters?'

'If they *are* love letters. The writer didn't want the handwriting analyzed — if it ever came to that.'

'Typewriters have distinctive characteristics. But what about word-processing? If the software's the same? Madeline has an IBM and that's the same system Castle Howe has, she told me.'

'Even so, look how short each one is. Could have been typed on, say, Madeline Galloway's computer by someone at Castle Howe, or on one at Castle Howe by a person from Tarn House. Hell. Whoever this is must have thought of that. No handwriting, no signature."You know how I feel — but not to the point of doing damage to your marriage" could mean almost anything. the "feeling" could be resentment as well as love. And we don't know what *this* person means by Graham's "illness". Not necessarily what Tommy Thale told me, although I'd bet my life she's right — that her sister knew.'

Jury returned each letter to its envelope, restacked them, clipped them as they had been. He picked them up and turned them round. 'This is how Lady Cray gave them to you?'

'Yes.'

'The clip certainly isn't five years old. It looks new. I'm wondering who removed whatever was used to tie them?'

Plant frowned. ' "Tie"?'

'You can see the indentation at the sides; you can see a lightening of the typeface across the top one. They were tied with something. She didn't read them?'

'No, she said not. Neither did Adam.'

'You believe her?'

'Yes.' Melrose sat looking at the letters for a while and then said, 'I think we should talk to Alex; he said something was missing from his mum's room; I think perhaps this is it.'

There was a silence broken by Melrose's suddenly saying, '*Mon amour premier.*'

Jury leaned over, looked at him closely. 'What do you mean? You seem distracted.'

'Do you ever run into people, well, women, who remind you of other, well, women?'

'Yes.'

'Helen Viner. It occurred to me that women often remind one of one's mother. Sounds damned silly.' Melrose's laugh was embarrassed.

'Why silly? Is that the "first love" you meant?'

'I don't like my personal feelings getting mucked around in a case. For you, well, it's even worse. The whole thing must have been godawful.' He shoved aside his pint, said, 'Let's have some wine; it's more poignant. Chablis Contemptible. Nineteen-ninety was a good year for that. What do you say?' Melrose asked again, urging Jury. 'I'm sleeping here tonight; there's another room.'

'See Connie Fish doesn't charge you another two quid for the private bath.'

Jury sat there, turning the letters over and over while Melrose got the wine. He also brought back two wineglasses, fairly clean.

As Melrose poured the dubiously labelled white wine, Jury thought of that first afternoon, the flight of the swallows. ' "*Agnosco veteris vestigia flammae.*" '

Melrose took refuge in annoyance. 'I wish you'd stop *saying* that.'

'You were spouting French, weren't you? Anyway, I've only said it twice – ' Jury counted on his fingers. ' – in ten years.' He did not mention the third time, over two weeks ago.

'Do you *have* to say it?'

'Yes.'

Melrose looked up. 'Why?'

'It's the only Latin I know.'

The glasses clicked.

3

Grey light was bleeding through the cracks around the blind. Jury hadn't realized it was morning until he took his arm from his eyes and turned his head to the window.

The bed was littered with notes, documents, letters. He hadn't slept. He hadn't undressed. He had read and thought and thought and read.

Now he swung his legs over the edge of the bed and sat staring at the floor and the pot of coffee Connie Fish had supplied him with last night. Cold dregs looked pasty in the cup.

Jury walked to the window and raised the blind. Smoke rose from the chimney pots of the few cottages in a drunken line on the other side of the narrow road down which now a drover and his boy were steering a flock of Swaledales. On the corner at the T-junction was the post-office store. And that was Boone. In the distance he could see Great Gable shrouded in vapour.

Had he felt in a better mood, he imagined he would have seen it all as bucolic, peaceful, and that range of mountains as grand.

His mood wasn't good. He felt drained. It was strange to him how his rage at Jane had been extinguished in the course of one little day. She had used him, yes, but only in a sense. She must have suspected what had happened five years ago, and seen her own behaviour as compliantly evil, though Jury saw it merely as confused and complex.

Poor Jane. She had wanted him, and only him to investigate. Had her suicide been too obvious a 'murder', there would be no way of controlling the results — and the one that concerned her most was that Alex not be hurt any more than he would already be.

Probably, she had thought he could find the evidence to prove it all. Well, he couldn't; there was no hard evidence, not these letters, and not this painting. It was a figure without a face, and there could be no face if Fellowes hadn't painted one in.

Alex would suffer if the truth came out.

Millie would suffer if it didn't.

39

'For a psychiatrist, you seem to be in a muddle,' said Lady Cray. 'It's only nine; our appointment is for this afternoon.' Although she hated to admit it, she felt some trepidation, and couldn't help but rake her eyes again over those rows of books.

Maurice Kingsley laced his hands behind his neck, leaned back and smiled. 'I thought I'd like to see you now. Is this a problem?'

'Problem? Certainly not.' He was being a bit superior. From her black leather bag she drew the black Porsche lighter and lit her cigarette.

'Never did find mine,' said Kingsley, nodding at the lighter.

She arched an eyebrow. 'It wasn't on the bookshelf? Where you left it?' Her gaze shifted to the shelf behind him, the one that had held the letters. Might as well call his bluff. Proprietorially, she ran her index finger over the lighter, felt something on the bottom. Her glance slid to it, then straight back to the doctor. It was the first time she'd noticed it – a tiny gold band with the minuscule inscription *From A*. Oh, hell.

'I don't recall leaving it there.' His eyes held hers. 'I wouldn't care that much, except it was given to me by a friend. Sentimental value, you know.'

'Oh, I'm sorry. I certainly *do* know. My grandson gave me mine. You know, Andrew.' She fingered the inscription.

'Ah, yes, Andrew. Your favourite person.'

'Umm.' She smoked away. Was he suppressing a smile? One had to be careful with psychiatrists. They were tricky, untrustworthy. 'Well? Why did you want to see me this morning?' What, she wondered, was he up to?

'About last night –'

She shifted in her chair, kept her face expressionless.

'Does the sight of blood make you ill?' asked Kingsley, suddenly.

She stiffened. 'I don't know what you mean.'

He'd brought down his arms, was leaning over them, doodling on a pad. 'You went white at the dinner table when Mr Plant cut his hand. I thought you were going to pass out, really. What were you thinking?'

'Thinking? Nothing really.' She laid the lighter on the desk, nearly midway between them. 'Why?'

'That's what I'm asking *you*, Lady Cray.'

The trouble was, she didn't know. It had been more a feeling. A feeling-thought. As if the words were imprinted over a feeling, or run into it, the mortar that held the bricks together. One couldn't separate mortar from stone or the whole structure would topple — Oh, what the hell was she doing? Calmly exhaling a thin line of smoke, she said, 'You seem to be chasing some idea of your own.'

He sat back, smiled. 'I am.'

Did he know? Did he know *what*? Why had she thought of those letters . . . more precisely, the ribbon that lay hidden beneath her silk scarves. She'd wanted to throw it out but felt oddly bound by it. She felt, indeed, like weeping. 'Mirrors,' she said suddenly.

'Oh? Blood makes you think of mirrors?'

What she was thinking of was the mirror she'd been looking into last night over Mr Plant's shoulder and the doctor's and Madeline Galloway's reflection in it. 'Were you watching?' Her voice was edgy, nervous. She didn't like this at all.

He became very still. 'Watching what?'

'Oh, nothing.' Change the subject. 'My mother had a three sided mirror. I used to stand before it and preen.' This wasn't changing the subject. He was looking at her — *scrutinizing* would be a better word. 'I dislike looking in mirrors.'

'But you used to like it, apparently.'

She laughed. 'Well, I was a child, wasn't I? So conceited. Still am. I'm a preening sort of person.'

'No, you aren't. Just the opposite, I'd say. You're very, very clever. Canny, shrewd. I wouldn't want you, you know, on *my* trail.'

Oblique, she thought. Very clever himself. 'My mother was quite beautiful, you see. And my father —' She stopped and swallowed.

He was looking at her in that odd way. 'Go on. Your father.'

'Have you ever been married, Dr Kingsley?'

Silence. And he seemed to be humouring her when he answered, 'Yes. A long time ago.'

She glanced at the lighter. 'To A.'

Again he smiled. 'Yes to A.'

'I've often wondered about Dr Viner. Has she?'

'What? Been married?' He sat back. 'No. What's all this interest in the marital state of psychiatrists?'

'Both of you are so attractive. It seems odd that neither are married. Especially Dr Viner.'

He started his doodling again. 'And have you some fantasy about me and Dr Viner?'

'That would be rather − impudent.'

He laughed. 'Impudence isn't a word that has much coinage in psychiatry.'

She filled in her own thoughtful silence by taking out another cigarette. But she wouldn't use the lighter; she pulled out one of her monogrammed silver matchbooks. she like matches. Perhaps shc'd been a child arsonist. Yes, she'd mentioned that if the conversation got unpleasant again. But that wasn't at all what was chiefly on her mind. she said, 'A number of years ago I became rather attached to an exquisitely beautiful woman. Foreign type.' She struck the match, watched the tiny flame spurt up between them, watched it die. 'I don't recall my feelings as being of a sexual nature, but the experience did lead me to question my, well, latencies, shall we say. Now, she herself was one of those exotic, European women. Mind you, nothing at all passed between us. But I know she was drawn to me physically. I don't know *how* one knows that sort of thing.' She smoothed her skirt. 'She gave me boxes and boxes of chocolates.' She smoked, looked mistily at the light spangling the tall window.

'No, she didn't.'

'What?' She started.

'Give you boxes and boxes of chocolates.'

'And *how* do you know that?'

'It was an afterthought. You tossed it in to lend credibility to the whole story − this "foreign type " of woman.' He smiled. 'I know you nick chocolates. It's apparently a real obsession. Like the ribbons −'

'Let's not pursue that, thank you −'

'If you had been "enthraled" by this "foreign" lady, your description would be more precise. And you, Lady Cray, do not strike me as a person much given to "thralldom". You're too damned clever.'

'Next you'll be saying I'm a pathological liar, I expect.'

He laughed. 'Oh, no. You're definitely not that.'

Again, she was silent, thinking. 'Several years ago I was riding on the Underground behind a young lady with her hair tied up in a ribbon. It was pale blue; but I still remember. It dangled down to the top of the seat. I stared at it for some time. Then I pulled the end very slowly, absurdly thinking perhaps I could get it. Well, of course she felt the tug. She turned, yelled . . . rather nasty things. "You old *les!*" meaning, I expect, "lesbian". It was quite humiliating. Again, I wonder if one can tell — about one's self, about others.' The thin, upward swirl of bluish smoke might have been that ribbon.

'Yes, if one's extremely sensitive to the signals of others.'

'And was I sending out a signal?'

'To her?'

'Ah, you *believe* in this lady?'

'Yes. But you weren't signalling her. You are me.'

'Why would I do that?'

'I'm not sure.' Kingsley was chewing on the end of his pencil. 'You want to know something.'

'No. As I said, I was just wondering if some instinct could tell one of another's . . . sexual preferences.'

'Homosexuality, you mean.'

She shrugged, letting her eyes rest of the beam of sunlight.

'Me? Is it me you're wondering about?'

'Heavens, *no*.'

'Why does blood remind you of mirrors?'

She jumped. 'Good heavens, what's *that* to do with the subject?'

He smiled. 'But that *is* the subject. Much more than the chocolates. You thought I was watching you in the mirror last night.'

She didn't answer.

He leaned forward, his head jutting over the desk. 'Do you know what displacement is?'

Her eyes were fixed on the window. 'I daresay I could deduce the meaning if I wanted to. Which I don't.'

'Example: all of these ribbons of different colours. Pale blue, green, yellow, it doesn't matter. Except for red. *That's* the one that matters. All the other colours mean nothing, but if you see

270

red as only *one* colour amongst many, then it loses some of its potency.'

He must know about the letters. She felt in some sort of dreadful danger and thought of his watching her in the mirror. But was it him? Dr Kingsley? She tried to swallow; there was a stone in her throat. 'The hour's really up and I have to meet —'

'Sit down. Come on. Lady Cray: what does a red ribbon bring to mind?'

'Blood.' The word came out against her bidding.

'Was it really your mother's three-sided mirror? Or is that a screen memory? You standing in front of her mirror putting ribbons in your hair? Preening? You saw blood. But where?'

She really couldn't swallow. Her mouth opened, shut.

He waited.

She said nothing.

'What happened before your father died?'

'My *fath* —' And then she saw it. The little image pulled her from the chair. 'Shaving. He was shaving and I crept up on him. Surprised him. The razor slipped and cut him —' She ran her finger down her ear down her throat. 'He was furious.'

'Superficial. A purely superficial cut. How long after that did he die?'

She shook her head. Nothing came. She thought of the ribbon lying where she'd hidden it. It was no longer a treasure. It was no longer anything.

She felt a terrible sense of loss.

'It's odd, isn't it?' asked Kingsley. 'What plagues us is what we most desire. One of those needs has to go.'

After a few more moments, she rose and hoped her dignity was still somewhat intact. After all, she was an old lady. Terrible for an old lady to be driven by the terrors of a little girl. She walked towards the door, able now to swallow. To speak. She turned. 'I really think you've earned it.'

He raised his eyebrows. 'What?'

'Although it's of great sentimental value to me, do keep the lighter.'

She glanced at the desk where it lay and walked out.

271

40

'Faster, faster!' yelled Adam Holdsworth, arm raised like an officer commanding his troops.

Short of breath, Wiggins stopped. It was nine in the morning; Adam Holdsworth had breakfasted on scrambled eggs and four rashers of bacon, urging Wiggins to have something more than tea and toast. Wiggins was already exhausted. 'But you must understand, sir I *can't* go faster; there's too many twists and turns and blind hedges. He took out his big handkerchief and wiped his face as the old man mumbled something about 'sissy police'.

They were in the maze, privet hedges six feet tall, and Wiggins felt they'd been here for hours because of the similarity of every green corridor. Never mind, he told himself. He was only humouring Holdsworth in order to get him to talk about the family.

He refused to 'pick up the speed' again. 'I need to talk to you, Mr Holdsworth.'

'So? Talk and push, Sergeant.'

'If you don't mind, I'll just rest for a bit.' Wiggins slapped his handkerchief across the moistness of a white bench and sat down, ignoring the hugely exaggerated sighs of Adam Holdsworth, who was twiddling his thumbs.

'I should think you'd be concerned about your great-grandson's welfare, sir.'

Adam's head whipped round. '*Certainly*, I'm concerned! I've made every provision for Alex.' He lowered his head. 'It's rotten about his mother; you probably know my grandson – ' He looked away. 'Well, you know about Alex's father.' Wiggins nodded. 'Graham was a perfectly nice boy. A bit weak, perhaps, and much too impressionable. But . . . I expect psychiatrists can't work miracles.' He sighed. 'I expect depression and despair can hit any of us, correct?'

Wiggins wondered if Adam had guessed at the apparent source

273

of Graham Holdsworth's despair. 'Did the doctor ever indicate the cause of it to you?'

'Hmm? No. I wondered, though, about that troubled marriage. From what I could gather, it was largely Graham's fault – well, his wish to get out of it. I don't think Jane was heartbroken, but she wasn't pleased, certainly. Madeline, however, was.'

'Miss Galloway?'

'Well, she'd wanted to marry him. Expect she was jealous as hell. I think she's pretty colourless; of course, she's always nice as nine pence to all of us. Money. It's always love or money or both. You know, I wouldn't be at all surprised if she had thought she might just snag Crabbe after Virginia died.'

'What?'

'Why not? Happens all the time with employers and their secretaries. Then here comes Genevieve. *That* must have put the poor girl's nose out of joint.'

'You don't care much for Miss Galloway and Mrs Holdsworth?'

'Hell, Sergeant, I don't care for any of them now except Alex and Millie. The others are gone.' He squeezed the bridge of his nose tightly.

When Wiggins told him what they'd discovered about Virginia Holdsworth and what they suspected about Annie Thale, Adam sat there like a graven image. 'Good Lord.' He was silent for a long time, looking about, unable to see anything except row upon row of green hedge. 'Why not just kill *me* and be done with it, if it's the money?'

Wiggins didn't want to remind him that he, Adam, was eighty-nine. The old man hadn't that long to go. And, Wiggins thought, this killer was very patient. It had been five years since the grandson and cook had died.

After a few more minutes of kneading his blue-veined hands, Adam said, 'Move! I'm sick of all this talk of death and desolation. Come on, Sergeant, push!'

Obediently, Wiggins rose and spent another ten minutes pushing the old man at a fast walk.

Then he heard something like the sound of a death rattle. Immediately, he went round the chair to check for signs of life and discovered old Adam was laughing and tattooing the chair's arms with his small fists.

Well, he certainly found a joke in all of this that was lost on the sergeant. As Wiggins started to push again, the old man demanded to know the time.

'Just going on nine-fifteen, Mr Holdsworth.'

'What? *What* I need my medicine. Supposed to take it on the half hour, that'd be nine-thirty, and by God if I don't get it, there's no telling! I go into fits! I'll have a *seizure*. Happened once before. So get rolling and push me out of this damned place.'

Wiggins, thoroughly alarmed, pushed harder, and then remembered this was a maze and if he hadn't found the exit yet, he wasn't likely to in the next fifteen minutes. 'You'll have to point me in the right direction, sir.'

'What the hell are you talking about? *I* don't know where it is.'

Wiggins's alarm was turning quickly to terror as he trotted behind the wheelchair, going right, going left. Breathless, he managed to say, 'Good Lord, sir! I'm a perfect stranger! How would I know the entrance?'

Bumping along, his head tilting in the wind, Adam said, 'Because you're a copper! You're supposed to have some sort of deductive powers but you damned well don't seem to be using them. Do you think I'd've been fool enough to come in here with just *anybody?*'

Wiggins had his arsenal of drugs in his coat pocket. 'What's . . . the . . . medicine . . . for?' he asked between hard breaths.

'My insides.'

It wasn't that much to go on; still, undaunted, Wiggins reached in his pocket and brought out a charcoal biscuit, stopping just long enough to take another breather. 'This works like . . . magic,' he huffed.

His own lungs felt on the verge of collapse.

Adam bit it, made a retching noise and spit it out.

'I've an idea!' said Wiggins.

'First one today. What?'

'Crumbs. I'll drop crumbs along the path and that way we'll know if we've been on that particular part before. So's we won't be going round in circles.' Wiggins rammed a privet hedge while trying to manoeuvre round a corner.

'Help! HELP!' Adam shouted at the sky, or tried to. His reedy voice was growing weaker; he could barely get it out. 'Ah . . . ahh . . . ahhh. I feel it coming on.' Then his head lolled.

Wiggins had been dropping crumbs all along their way, which

prevented his going down several openings since he could see they'd already been there.

From the chair came heavy, stentorian breathing. Then Adam said, 'What I need's a damned drink.'

Wiggins was relieved that he seemed a bit livelier and bumped him over several large rocks, careening round a corner.

'Time?' demanded Adam.

'Nine twenty-two.'

Now the groaning began and Wiggins was pushing at a run, leaving new crumbs behind him at the same time he was avoiding the old crumb trails. Wiggins knew what this sort of exertion, coupled with all this tension, would do a nervous system. At last he saw it: 'The exit! Straight ahead'

No response was forthcoming from the lolling head of Adam Holdsworth. Wiggins stopped and gave him a gentle shake, felt the pulse. Still there, but for how long? He pushed faster out of the maze and across the lawn. He could see at a distance someone — yes, it was the nurse named Rhubarb. He hailed her. She glowered at him, but he ignored the look. Wiggins, despite his breathlessness, just managed to convey the message to her.

Miss Rupert looked totally blank.

'Mr Holdsworth's medicine! You can see he's ill.'

Miss Rupert studied Adam Holdsworth. 'Looks all right to me. A person his age, eighty-nine, isn't he? One expects a little slowing down. ' With this unarguable comment, she set off down the path.

'Mr Holdsworth is doing more than slowing down. He's coming to a dead halt! I *insist* you go find a doctor.'

'You needn't get shirty about it, Sergeant. I know him better than you.' And she continued on her way.

Wiggins sat down at the edge of the mildly sloping lawn and dropped his head in his hands.

A heaving noise came from the wheelchair. He looked at the old man through parted fingers. Adam Holdsworth was laughing and slapping his leg — or the rug that covered it.

'Got you running like hell, didn't I?'

Wiggins got up, his face set in stone. 'Are you telling me it was all an act?'

Wham went Adam's hand across his knee. 'Scared within an inch of his life, he was! But I'll give you this, lad; that crumb thing was a damned good idea. Hard getting out of that maze.'

'You've been in it before, is that it?' asked Wiggins in his strangled voice.

'Hell, yes. I know every bend and turn and there are clues left all over the place. Well, you weren't sharp enough to see the clues, but, still, no one else ever got out without help except Alex. So you're not such a bad copper, after all.'

During this little dissertation on the sergeant's competence, Wiggins had slowly walked round behind the chair, which was facing the long, sloping lawn, at the bottom of which sat the little stone cottage Helen Viner used as her office. 'I appreciate the compliment, sir. Now I must go and see if Superintendent Jury is here yet.'

With that, Wiggins pushed the wheelchair with his foot and sent it flying across the lawn, which had just enough incline to send the chair careering, but enough upward slope at the end to stop it.

Old Adam had his arms stretched out, bellowing to the skies: 'Hallelujah! I'm about to meet . . .'

Who he was going to meet was lost on the wind.

Wiggins chewed on a charcoal biscuit and smiled thinly.

Then he saw the wheelchair bump and twist, heard what could have been a scream or a wheezy laugh, and walked down the lawn.

Definitely a wheezy laugh. 'Brilliant, Sergeant! Let's do it again!'

'No more playing silly buggers, sir.' He knocked the old man's hand off the lever. 'Superintendent Jury wants to see you.'

'No joy there, I'm sure.' Then he put his finger to his mouth and whisper. 'Not a word; this is just between the two of us.'

'Depend on it,' said Wiggins, grimly.

More than was usual, Jury noticed, Sergeant Wiggins kept his eyes glued to his notebook. He was sitting in a black lacquered chair on one side of a long window.

In the companion chair sat a handsome woman, slightly built, beautifully tailored, and shrewd-eyed. Probably in her seventies, but looking sixty.

Adam Holdsworth told Superintendent Jury that his sergeant had given him a pleasant little push about the maze. He also said he found it difficult to believe that what had happened to Virginia and Annie Thale was anything but an accident.

'Who on earth would have pushed Ginny off those rocks? Not

that arse of a Fellowes. And if you're checking on poufs, check on him –'

'Oh for heaven's sake, Adam,' said Lady Cray, studying the ceiling. 'That stereotype of the artist is cretinous.'

'You don't know him,' said Adam testily. 'Painter and flamer, I'll bet.'

She shook her head as she rose and murmured something about leaving them.

'Please don't leave, Lady Cray.' Jury held up the packet of letters.

Adam smacked his chair arm. 'Jig's up!'

'You took these from Dr Kingsley's office, Lady Cray?'

'Yes, I happened to find them there.' She inspected a fingernail with blood-red varnish, then quickly folded her hands under her arms and tapped her foot.

'They were tied with something,' said Jury. 'String perhaps, or a ribbon.'

She cocked an eyebrow. 'Oh?'

Jury nodded. 'Find anything like that? Or were they clipped together the way you gave them to Mr Plant?'

Adam said to her. 'Tell him for God's sake. Does he care you're a ribbon fetishist? Better than heavy breathing.'

'I'll just fetch it, then.' She turned at the door. '*Was*, Adam, I now find ribbons boring.' She left.

'My daughter-in-law' – thinking of Genevieve apparently disgusted Adam – 'wouldn't get off the phone after you were at Tarn House yesterday. Clearly thought she was suspect number one in Jane's murder. *If* Jane was murdered. And who told you about Graham? Was it Helen Viner? She was treating him for depression.'

'No. She thought it would be unprofessional to comment on a patient. It was Millie's aunt.'

'*That* old battle-axe?'

Jury smiled. 'It was her sister, Annie, who told Thomasina.' Jury didn't want at this point to drag in Millie's tales of Aunt Tom.

Adam shook his head. 'Hell, I suppose it's possible. What isn't? But then why would he be fooling around with Annie?'

'He wasn't; they were friends. I think the point of this is who would benefit most by your will. And who would have?'

'God. Money.' He gripped the arm of the wheelchair, cleared

his throat and said, 'Alex is chief beneficiary. And then Millie. That probably surprises you, but she's all alone and she's only a little girl.' Again he washed his hand over his bald pate. 'Now, I'm pretty worried about them, I don't mind telling you.'

'I don't think there's any danger, Mr Holdsworth,' said Jury, mildly. *'Not for now.'*

Lady Cray made her entrance on that note, walked over to Jury and dropped a carefully coiled ribbon into his hand.

Jury handed both the letters and the ribbon to Wiggins . 'Work on this.' Then he turned both a smile and a question in his eyes to Lady Cray.

'They were in his bookcase — but, obviously, Mr Plant would have told you that. He has a particular little row of books, half a dozen, fourth shelf up, fake spines. They're hollow; he keeps them for booze. There was another out of place, I thought, on the shelf above. Dr Kingsley is undoubtedly an alcoholic, not that that's important, and it certainly hasn't blunted his powers of perception. Oh, his eyes aren't very good; but his mind makes up for them. *My* eyes however, are perfect. These are not grey contact lenses you're looking at; I could spot a raven in a flock of buzzards at a hundred feet, or a foot on a wheelchair from the ramparts.'

Jury noticed that Adam and Wiggins exchanged quick and half-hidden glances as Lady Cray poked her finger upwards.

'It looked, you see, like a little ribbon bookmarker that hadn't been pulled down completely to separate the pages. I happen to have a penchant for ribbons — especially red . . . *did* have, I should say. Now, I saw this ribbon during my ten o'clock appointment yesterday morning — an appointment *not* requested by me, incidentally. I didn't notice the book's ribbon until the very end of the hour; consequently, *I* requested the hour be changed and that Dr Kingsley see me thenceforth at three o'clock. Well, it didn't make any difference — two, three, four — but I chose the first hour that came to mind. When one wants something, one doesn't want to wait, don't you agree? Yes. When I returned to his office at three p.m. I naturally looked at the shelf to make sure the ribbon was still there. I had, naturally, made my plan to get at it. Getting to the shelf and purloining the fake book wasn't *precisely* as simple as nicking a pen; one can always do that, you know, with the pretence of reaching . . . oh, sorry, I'm sure you don't want to hear about all of that. The point was to get him out of the room.

So I asked for some chocolate, said I was feeling a dreadful anxiety attack coming on, and, of course, he knew about the problem with chocolate. Like ribbons. *But*! Do you know gentlemen, there's something I'd forgotten. I can see you don't. Alcoholics very often are fiends for sweets, especially chocolate. The good doctor simply opened his desk drawer, smiled and reached over a Wispa bar. Well, *that* was a setback. Until I realized that I myself had chosen this scenario, and that I *myself* had forgotten that I have no feelings at all for chocolate *bars*, only for boxed chocolates. I sometimes wonder if it has to do with the theatre . . . with that play at the Haymarket my father − do forgive me; that's hardly the point. Very well. I told him that to me, "chocolate" meant the small, rounded ones, each in its separate place, rather like − do you know what it's like? It only just occurred to me . . . like seats in a theatre. I'm rambling. But after all, Dr Kingsley *did* do me an enormous amount of good. Back to it: this quite decent man left his office to find a box of chocolates. Et cetera. And after he'd nicked − well, I like to think that − a tiny little box from someone's desk, he gave me them, hoped I'd feel better, smiled that absolutely ingenuous smile and then −' She looked at her audience. 'Is something wrong?'

There was a humming sort of silence, as if speech could have the sort of after image on the ear a camera's flash could leave on the eye. For a few moments none of them seemed to realize she'd stopped.

'*Then* what happened?' said Adam Holdsworth; and with small flicks of his hands urged, 'Go on, go on!'

'There's nothing to be going on *with*.' She placed a finger against her cheek, thoughtfully. 'Except, I'd certainly say that whatever you're investigating, I doubt very much he did it. I can't say the same for the other one. Did the letters tie up properly, Sergeant?'

Wiggins still sat with his pencil poised over his notebook, staring at her. 'What?'

'The ribbon. When I took it off I looked at the marks it had left. It didn't seem to fit.' She looked from Wiggins to Jury and back again.

His eyes still full on her, Wiggins tossed the packet of letters to Jury. At last, it was business as usual. 'I don't think it's the original ribbon, sir.'

Jury held the letters up at eye level, moved the ribbon, moved it back. 'It isn't. Too new, too narrow.' He turned his gaze to Lady Cray. ' "the other one," Lady Cray?'

'Psychiatrist. You know, Dr Viner. Well . . . I know you're very fond of her, Adam, as is everyone else here. She's awfully — plausible, isn't she? But, my instincts say she's definitely not quite the ticket.'

Jury smiled, still holding up the ribbon-tied letters. 'Meaning?'

She looked round at the three of them and sighed. 'Men.'

'Pack of cards.'

This new voice amongst them came from Alex, who had entered through a window, suddenly. Now he stood in the room very still, looking at the letters as he might have looked at a cobra.

Said his great-grandfather. 'Dammit, come in through doors once in a while. You always act as if you're on the lam. As they say in the States.' He sounded gruff; he was covering up other feeling, thought Jury.

Jury would have known him even without them. Alex Holdsworth had the colouring of his handsome father, but he had *her* expression, her mannerisms, her inflection. Even in the few seconds the boy stood there, Jury could tell this. He was overwhelmed once again by loss. If things had been different, this boy might have been his stepson. No, he thought. No. It wouldn't have worked even if she'd lived. 'Alex?'

The boy shoved back the hair out of his eyes and looked at Jury, vacantly. 'Sir?'

'I'm — we're — policemen. Scotland Yard. We're — rather unofficially — looking into the death of your mother.'

For a moment, Jury thought he hadn't heard, that he still had his mind on the letters.

Alex said, 'S-U-P-T. R.Jury. I know.'

Wiggins rose and put out his hand and, in an uncharacteristic try at humour, said, 'S-G-T. Wiggins. How d'ya do?' They shook hands.

Jury thought Alex looked awfully pale; his face had the pellucid look of a lake after a rain. 'What did you mean just then, about the cards?'

'Nothing.' He glanced at Jury, glanced away. Poor lie. 'I only came to see Granddad.' He shoved his hands into the back pockets of his jeans. Jeans and a rather ratty-looking Aran sweater was what he was wearing.

'I think I'll be going,' said Lady Cray, who had, throughout this entire meeting, remained standing. Now she appeared to feel she was in the way.

'Not you, Alex,' said Jury, stepping towards him as the boy turned and nearly had one leg over the sill. 'I'd still like to talk to you, all right?'

Alex seemed to be considering. Then he just nodded.

PART IV
DEATH PAST-POSTED

41

'You were a friend of my mother?'

'Yes,' said Jury.

'She didn't do it. She didn't commit suicide. She couldn't have.'

He sounded, Jury thought, ferociously defensive. They were sitting in the conservatory amidst the potted palms, the gloxinias, the hanging plants. Jury had collected two coffees from a side board where a silver pot was, apparently, replenished throughout the day.

Alex told him about the close check he kept on his mother's medicine. And then he handed him a small paper.

'What's this?' Jury set his cup on the quarry-tiled floor.

'A list of people who were at the house — up here, I mean — when Mum lost some medicine. Any of them could have taken it. And I thought — hell, doctors, nurses, they can get hold of Seconal in the time it would taken Fortune's Son to do a sixteenth of a mile.'

'That's true.' Jury looked at the list, feeling desolate, not knowing what to say to Alex. So he asked him about that 'pack of cards'.

'It's a dream. It keeps coming back, recurring.' Alex told Jury the details. 'I knew something was missing from Mum's room, but not what. She kept those letters in the drawer of her nightstand.' He stopped. 'I don't understand the Queen of Hearts. Dr Viner said that it probably had to do with feeling guilty about being expelled from school.' He looked over at Jury. 'I play poker. I got caught. I bet on the horses. I got caught.'

Jury wanted to laugh. 'You're pretty young to be getting into betting shops.'

'Betting shops?' His look at Jury was scornful. 'I wouldn't bother. I past-post.'

'What's that?'

'You wait until the race is run and you know the winner. You call your turf accountant and bet on the horse. But, of course, the turn accountants, they turn around and time the race, so they don't cover the bet until they've seen whether the horses left the gate before you phoned in your bet. They're not completely stupid. But they're greedy, like most people. Now, its obviously got to be done quick and you've got to set up the bookmaker, haven't you? So you phone in bets over a long period of time on long shots. He doesn't take the bet until he times the race, and since it's already run, he just phones back and says thanks, but no thanks. And thinks you're round the bend anyway because you're betting these long shots. You have to vary the size — some small, some larger — to prepare for the big bet. You're doing long shots, really long, but then you vary that a little, too. What he thinks he's got on the other end of the line is someone who's, one, dumb about horses; two, plain dumb, betting those twenty-and thirty-to-one shots. He always checks to see if the bet's placed late. Eventually, you wear him down. You wear him down because he's got a totally green face and there's nothing he'd like to see more than really tall money. I've got a partner, of course, because the calls have to go through *very* fast. I'm in the tree with my phone; he's on the ground in his car with *his* phone. The second horse hits the finish I call him and he calls the accountant. This time it took us about two months to set him up. It was a big bet on really long odds and he could see those fifty quid notes stampeding straight towards him. So the big bet he finally takes without timing the race and there isn't one effing thing he can do about it, not even when he finds out the bet went down after the horses had left the gate. Out of the gate? Mine was over the finish, the post, see, And the thing for Ned and me was, there was absolutely no way we could lose. If he'd taken a small bet earlier, well, we'd just've got less money. But lose? No way. That's past posting. If you ever want to try. I told the biology master I was doing a study of leaf fungus. That's why I was always up trees. The binoculars weren't suspicious because I told him too I was studying the migratory patterns of certain birds when I wasn't doing the leaves.'

Silence hummed. Jury shut his mouth, cleared his throat, said 'You and Lady Cray would make a good team.'

'Why's that?'

'Never mind. Dr Kingsley didn't recognize you last night at dinner?'

'Not unless he's a good actor.'

Jury rose. 'Let's go and find out, shall we?'

As they walked along the blue corridor and neared Kingsley's door, Alex said, 'Know what Millie thought about the Queen of Hearts?' He stopped. He smiled as if there were still some brightness left in the day. 'That it was the Red Queen from *Alice-in Wonderland*.'

Millie, thought Jury, might be right.

'Wait here, Alex, until I come for you.'

'Never saw them before.' Maurice Kingsley, looking gloomy, was turning the beribboned letters over and over. 'What the hell's going on?' Anger surfaced above the gloom.

'I thought you might help to answer that question,' said Jury. 'That packet was on your bookshelf.' Jury scanned the rows of books, thought he saw what might be fake spines. 'They were in one of those hollowed-out books you keep for whisky.'

Kingsley seemed stunned. 'How . . .? Who . . .?' He closed his eyes, leaned back. 'Lady Cray. Christ, does the woman have X-ray — ' Kingsley flicked the ribbon. 'This is it, isn't it? She saw the ribbon. Oh, my God. ''No, not a Whispa bar; I simply *must* have some *boxed* chocolates.'' '

Jury couldn't help smiling. It was a credible imitation of Lady Cray's inflection. 'Go ahead. You can read them.'

Kingsley quickly removed the ribbon and now stared at the top envelope. 'Jane? He spread them out, looked at the post mark. 'They're all to Jane. Five, six years old.'

Jury nodded.

Kingsley read through the letters in total silence. then he replaced each in its envelope, made a neat pile, and sat staring at the pile. Still, he said nothing.

After some moments had passed in this way, Jury said, 'Well?'

Kingsley shot him a hard glance. 'I'm thinking, Superintendent.'

'Good.' Suspects seldom did. Jury waited.

Finally, Maurice Kingsley said, 'Anyone could have told you I was going to London the day of her death. But then so were Genevieve and Madeline — and anyone else, except for Helen and Crabbe Holdsworth. And after police came here, a number of

287

people knew I was actually sitting outside her house the *night* of her death. Why would I do it? Why would I kill Jane?' He shoved the letters back with the tip of his finger. 'I Certainly didn't write these.'

'I know. I also know you had no motive for killing Jane Holdsworth. But you don't get the point.'

'Enlighten me.'

'I will, if what I'm saying stays in this room.'

Kingsley nodded his assurance of that.

I think she killed herself. I think she wanted me — I was a . . . personal friend — to find out what really happened to Virginia Holdsworth and Annie Thale.'

Kingsley stared at him, got up and moved to the shelf holding the hollow books. 'I'm having a drink on that one.' He pulled a pint bottle of whisky from one volume and held it up to Jury.

'Not at the moment. I'm sure the motive is money. For example, Genevieve would have a motive to kill Virginia Holdsworth in order to get into the family, to get next to Adam's millions. But "next to" can still leave a large gap. Madeline? Same thing. George Holdsworth is of the family, but he'd gain nothing more by killing his sister-in-law. Fellowes, even less. and he's out for other reasons. And the wild card here, the really wild card, is Annie Thale. The only reason I can think of is because of what she knew about Graham Holdsworth.'

'You mean she knew he was homosexual?'

'No. She was fairly sure that he wasn't.'

Kingsley drank off a finger of whisky and poured another. He said nothing, only looked at Jury

'Those letters are about Graham's problems; there's more than a hint that the writer thinks divorce is the best choice.'

'They could've been written by anyone. Typed on any number of machines here, at Tarn House, in London, on the moon, for God's sake.'

'Oh, come on, Dr Kingsley. You know — ' Jury inched his chair closer to the desk. 'I want you to talk to Alex.'

Kingsley snapped up eyes that had been staring into his glass. 'Why?'

Jury walked to the door, opened it and told Alex to come in.

Alex stood in the middle of the room, his head cocked slightly.

'Remember me?' He was staring at Kingsley.

'Of course I remember you. We had dinner together.' Kingsley's smile was strained.

Jury had dragged over another chair and Alex sat down. 'We warmed a bench together, too.'

'I don't know what you're talking about.' He squinted at Alex.

Jury asked him, 'Did you have a total blackout from the booze?'

Kingsley looked down and up again at Alex. 'Not total. I vaguely remember someone sitting next to me. I expect it was a bench; I expect — well, police *assured* me it was outside Jane's house. It always keeps coming back to me, doesn't it?' He exchanged glances with Jury.

Alex sat stiff in his chair. Finally, he said, 'Did you kill my mother?'

'No.'

'Why the hell should I believe you?'

'You shouldn't.' Kingsley shrugged. 'I'm lazy, I'm a drunk, I have a rotten temper.' His eyes met Alex's squarely.

Alex grew less rigid. He started to smile, caught himself, kept the line of his mouth thin as he looked at Jury.

'He had no reason to kill your mother, Alex. None.' Then Jury added, 'Why don't you tell him that dream?'

Alex frowned. 'Why? I already told Dr Viner and it didn't help.'

'You know more about it now. Go on. That Queen of Hearts thing is going to bother you the rest of your life. Kingsley's a psychiatrist.'

'Not much joy there,' said Alex, his eyes burning.

'Couldn't agree more, old chap.' He reached round to the shelf behind him. 'Valium? Librium?' He looked over a couple of vials and then up at Alex. 'Oh, go ahead. Tell me. Can't hurt. Queen of Hearts? I'm intrigued.'

One foot crossed over the other knee, Alex fiddled with the lace of his Reebok shoe and related the dream. And there was a flow of talk about his school, his betting, his ponies, his poker. Suddenly, he stopped, embarrassed.

Kingsley lit a cigarette. He held the packet up to Alex, and when the boy nodded, tossed it to him.

'Good looking lighter,' said Alex.

'I like it.' Kingsley looked at the bottom. 'Sentimental value.' Then he just sat there, smoking.

Alex squirmed. 'Well?'

'Sorry. I'm thinking.'

He kept inhaling, studying the smoke as he exhaled, saying nothing.

Alex blurted out: 'But I don't *feel* guilty. I mean, about the betting.'

'Why should you?' asked Kingsley. 'You were doing it to help out your mother. To help with expenses. To help keep Genevieve off you mum's back.'

Alex kept talking. 'The thing is, I know I cheated. But it was mostly bookies. Most of them are villains anyway. And the cards. I had the dollar in more of a recession than the Fed.'

Kingsley laughed, hard. 'Is it a secret?'

'What?'

'The trick. You didn't win, or hardly ever, but you always walked away with more than you went to the table with.'

Alex was silent, pulling at his earlobe. Then he reached in his back pocket and brought out a wallet. From this he extracted a twenty-dollar bill and laid it on the table.

'Well?' Kingsley didn't touch it, just looked at it.

Alex turned it over. It was a single. 'Pasted together, back to back. That's why I couldn't use sterling. The bills are different sizes.'

Jury was fascinated. 'I don't get it. I'm dim.'

'You say you want change. Put in the twenty, pull it out as a one with other bills.' He looked from one to the other then up at the ceiling. 'Okay, I'm not proud of it – '

'I'll bet,' said Kingsley, dryly. 'On second thoughts, no. Not against you.'

Alex looked dead earnest. 'It's poker, isn't it? That Queen of Hearts thing.'

'Sounds like it. What do you get from that?'

Alex slumped back. 'I don't know.'

Casually, Kingsley said, 'Well, you were holding hands with your mother.'

'Queen of Hearts.' Alex paused. 'And . . . another one in the deck .'

Kingsley nodded. 'Poker.'

'A pair.'

'You and your mother – I didn't know you, but she was a friend, and she did little but talk about you.' Kingsley smiled broadly. 'I can't tell you, Alex, you and Jane were a great pair.'

Again, Alex slumped back, but with what looked like relief. He covered his eyes with his hand. He made no sound. Jury could see tears sliding down his face.

Kingsley opened a drawer, got out a box of tissues. 'Catch.'

Reflexively, Alex put out his hands. 'Thanks. Thanks a lot.'

'Ha, me. I didn't do a thing. What did Dr Viner have to say about that dream? I want to know which of us is the cleverer.' He smiled.

Alex told him. 'It didn't mean much, what she said.'

'Free association has to go somewhere. It probably would have come round to poker.'

'It's funny, though, what I thought when she was walking away.'

'What?'

'Association. Pack of cards. Pack of lies.' He got up. 'I'm going back to see Granddad.'

Jury nodded.

'That was very good, very clever. Wrong pair, though.'

'I expect so. You know, I wondered why Lady Cray kept going round and round on that point. The "exotic" woman who gave her chocolates. The ribbon she started to pull from the hair of a woman in front her . . .' Kingsley picked up the letters again. He shook his head. 'Wasn't it taking a hell of a change that *I* would find them?'

'They were well hidden, except from the eagle eye of Lady Cray. And if you had, what'd you have done? Had a confrontation? Burned them? They might make it appear you were having an affair with Jane, but . . . ' Jury shrugged. 'Graham Holdsworth committed suicide.' He paused. 'Alex says he didn't read them.'

'It's possible. He strikes me as a kid who'd respect his mother's privacy. It's also possible he couldn't resist the temptation when he was younger.'

'I wondered why a kid with his memory − stuff sticks to it like flypaper − couldn't remember after seeing those letters again and again − like the pills − couldn't remember what was missing.'

'Because he didn't want to.' Kingsley blew a smoke ring, stuck his finger through it.

'You surely don't think he *knows*?'

'Half knows. A shadow on the mind. A cobweb he can't brush

291

away. Don't worry, it'll fade, disintegrate. But what wouldn't fade
is for him to realize his mother killed herself. He'd be in a tearing
rage for most of the rest of his life.' He stubbed out his cigarette,
looked at Jury over the rim of his glass. 'So what are you going
to do about *that*?'

'Have a drink.'

Kingsley parked another glass on the table.

'Make it a double. I'm going to see her.'

42

'You're back.' Helen Viner opened the door wider; she was smiling; she did not seem to be at all sorry that he was back.

'I'm back, yes.'

She was wearing a dress of some soft material that swung and lay in folds about her. Across the pale background was a patter of willow branches with delicate leaves that seemed to drift and sway when she walked.

'I hope you don't mind my making a comment that might seem, well, not terribly complimentary – ' But she was already shaking her head. Of course she wouldn't mind.

'You know, you're not absolutely pretty – '

She sat back and laughed. 'I hope I'm not "absolutely" anything.'

' – but you give the impression of being so. If I weren't already drained of emotion, I'd be very attracted to you.'

'It's called transference.'

'It's also called other things.'

Her eyebrows rose in question over her hazel eyes that looked the colour of that damnable lake. Liquid stone. 'Odysseus was afraid of the Sirens, the Siren's song,' he said.

'That's very flattering – '

'No, it isn't. If the ship had bashed into those rocks, he and his crew would be dead.' Jury had no idea why this image was so present to him, but it was. 'Like Virginia Holdsworth, the friend you pushed from that tricky passage between Scafell and Mickledore.' Jury pulled Plant's snapshots from an envelope and placed them on her desk. 'Study these, why don't you?'

Her composure was astonishing. She denied nothing, merely gave the impression she might be humouring a delusion and did as she was bid: she looked at the pictures and then at him. She said, with a small shake of her head, 'I'm not sure what you mean.'

'Yes, you are. This is Mr Plant's shot of that cleft in the rock wall called "Fat Man's Agony." He saw that tiny smile drift across her face as the willow leaves did across her breasts when she shifted her arms.

'So? If Mr Plant has been walking and snapping pictures, what's it to do with me?'

'Everything. The reason he took it was to compare it with a painting done by Francis Fellowes six years ago. When he went up Scafell with Virginia Holdsworth. Or, to be more precise, *behind* Virginia Holdsworth. The painting itself is at the lab at New Scotland Yard. No one seriously questioned that Mrs Holdsworth's death was an accident because, if it weren't Mr Fellowes or some highly experienced walker who could have got away by means of Broad Stand — then it wasn't anyone.'

'It wasn't anyone. Ginny fell.'

'No one took into account that someone could have hidden in that large crevice, waited until Mr Fellowes finished his painting. Then, after he'd left, the killer could go down.'

Her expression betrayed nothing. The smile stayed in place as she turned her head towards the window at the sound of the branches slight soughing in the wind and back to Jury. 'I don't know what on earth the police might have come up with for you to make such a — momentous accusation. But it isn't true; Ginny Holdsworth was a good friend.'

'So was Jane Holdsworth.'

Perhaps she had tensed, for now she visibly relaxed. 'I thought it was fairly clear by now that Jane's death was a suicide. I, at any rate, was in Kendal.'

She shouldn't have looked so smug, thought Jury; she really shouldn't've. 'Oh, I know where you were, and I know where Dr Kingsley was, too. It was his bad luck that he was in Lewisham and drunk, to boot. You would have been better to leave him alone rather than to go to the trouble of planting those letters in his office.' Jury tossed the little pile of her desk.

Now her expression did change. A tiny muscle twitched in her cheek. 'What's this?'

'Letters you wrote to Jane Holdsworth. You were being careful, five years back, not to incriminate yourself. You didn't even sign them.'

Her frown deepened. She had loosened the ribbon, had removed one page from its envelope. 'Then what in God's name makes you think that *I* wrote them'

'Because Graham Holdsworth was your patient. And all the supposed "patient-doctor" confidentiality game you've been playing, as if you really meant to *protect* the poor man, has really been more of a trick. Let's put it this way, Dr Viner: we all have our latencies; none of us is totally heterosexual, and perhaps Graham Holdsworth leaned a little more in that direction. But as far as I'm concerned "latent homosexuality" is a meaningless term. But it's a highly charged term to many people who aren't practising homosexuals. I think you manipulated Graham into thinking his "latent" feelings were manifest ones that he was too frightened or straightlaced to express. He wasn't gay.No one person I've talked to ever had any reason to think that; just the opposite, really. The idea was totally surprising to them. Your purpose in all of this was to control both Graham and Jane Holdsworth because the person you really wanted to control was Alex. The way to control Alex was to control Jane.' Jury lit a cigarette with shaking fingers. 'And the way to control Jane was to have a love affair with her. You know who has your number, Helen? Lady Cray. In her rather clever and roundabout way, by telling Kingsley stories about her self and pondering her own "Latencies." she was trying to find out about you. "She's not quite straight", "not quite the ticket". Lady Cray's words.'

Helen Viner rose from her chair and walked to the casement window, staring out.

'Jane . . .' It stuck in Jury's throat. 'Jane was either bisexual or perhaps she was experimenting. But not a lesbian; *I* know that. It makes no difference how long- or short-lived her relationship was with you; in the end she couldn't live with whatever part it had had in her husband's suicide, couldn't probably, live with the thing itself. And certainly couldn't live suspecting it might have had to do with Annie Thale's murder.'

Her hand was on the casement latch, pushing it open — possibly for reviving air — when Jury said that; it froze. 'Annie *Thale*?' Her back was turned, her hand still on the window against which the branches lashed as they'd done the previous night. She spoke the name again, shaking her head. Then she turned. 'That's insane.'

'That isn't; you may be. Annie Thale was the only person

295

Graham confided in; she might have been in love with him herself. At any rate she knew he was straight as an arrow, and she suspected that arrow was being deflected by you. Annie Thale was like her sister: a good, stable, even steely woman. Not they type to kill herself. I've talked to the sister. Tommy Thale is one person you overlooked.'

Helen Viner pulled the window to with a furious little tug and latched it. 'Superintendent —' She came back to her chair and leaned towards him. '— I think Jane's death has affected your ability to think clearly.' Her tone was maddeningly sympathetic.

'If my ability to think clearly were impaired, your whole presence would convince me you couldn't possibly have done all of this. You're so — what was Lady Cray's word? — "plausible". What is it you want? Control of Castle Howe? Or control, full stop. You're a regular puppeteer. That was a particularly adept touch you used with Mr Plant, suggesting that Alex might need therapy but *not with you*. That, of course, would allay any suspicion you wanted to influence him. But you already do, and you know it. And *that's* what counts. To control Adam and Adam's money all you need to do is control Alex. But Alex is much sharper than you think.'

Her laugh was strained. 'Believe me, I give Alex high marks for sharpness.'

'Not high enough. On some level of his mind he knows your whole persona is a lie. A pack of lies. Maurice Kingsley knows it too, though he's actually to honourable to say it.'

'*That's* amusing. Maurice is an incompetent.'

'Oh, no. No, he isn't. He's far better doctor than you are. Dr Kingsley might be a drunk but you're merely window dressing.'

She stared at him, then down at the letters. 'And so I "planted" these in Maurice's office?'

'Of course. It would pretty much cinch things, wouldn't it, if the police thought that Kingsley was Jane's lover? A jealous lover. And you directed Lady Cray to see *him* — thinking her obsession with red ribbons just might result in her spotting these letters.'

Helen Viner was turning a small dagger like letter opener between her fingers. '*That* would be taking a chance. What if Maurice had seen them first?'

'What if he had? What would he do with them? Take them to the police and say, 'Look, I found these in amongst my books, but I didn't write them?' Anyway, if it hadn't worked, you'd simply have gone back to his office and collected them.'

She smiled, as if Jury had made a genuine joke. 'No, I don't expect he would.' She laid down the letter opener, plucked a cigarette from a circular black box of John Players. When she saw Jury wasn't going to light it for her, she reached in a drawer for her matches. Then, her cigarette between her cupped hands, she leaned back and exhaled smoke towards the ceiling, thoughtfully. It was if she were considering the comments of a patient. 'Now. This all began with Ginny Holdsworth.'

That's right. Six years ago you knew about her planned walk up Scafell. You knew she'd always been determined to cross over by way of Broad Stand. You got up there before Virginia. But when you discovered Francis Fellowes had come along behind her – after you'd shoved her off – *that* must have unnerved even you, Dr Viner. There was no way down except past Francis.'

She said nothing. Jury waited. Her curiosity would force her to speak.

'Police questioned Francis because no one else could possibly have been up there, unless, of course, it might have been an expert climber. Which I am not.'

'You were there; Francis painted you into the picture.'

She laughed. 'Oh, my *God*! He couldn't have seen – '

It was the smallest slip. ' "Seen you"? Why? Because he had his back turned? Because you were hiding in that crevice called Fat Man's Agony?'

'No. He couldn't have seen me because I wasn't there.'

Jury tossed the leather pouch on the desk.

'What's this?' She picked it up, opened it.

'A Claude glass.'

'And – ?' Her smile was tilted. She tapped the ash from her cigarette.

'And he painted the scene behind him.' Jury nodded towards the little mirror. 'That's why painters of picturesque used a Claude glass. Fellowes painted the crevice in that rock face.'

She put it on the desk between them and a looking at him, still with the upward tilting smile. 'Superintendent, even *if* there were such a painting, I don't believe a face would be distinguishable. Not even with all your fancy forensics equipment. I take it you have nothing to show me to convince me otherwise.'

He didn't. 'I'm going to give you a choice.'

'Why, *thank* you. But am I going to choose?'

'Yes. You're thinking all of this is speculation on my part. But let me tell you this: out of the number of people who have a vested interest in Adam Holdsworth's money, you're the only one with a motive for these killings – and the manipulation of Graham and Jane. Because the only other people who could possibly come into a large part of that inheritance are Alex and Millie Thale. Adam wouldn't leave it to any of the rest of them. But as he's been donating to the upkeep of Castle Howe, its a fair bet he'd put the Castle in his will. And as he said, you really run the place. I said it before: you want to control Alex; you thought of yourself as the woman who might step into his mother's shoes. But you won't.'

'I won't? And how do you think you'll prevent me?'

'I'll ruin you. Here's your choice: either I'll make use of my "speculations" and these letters and the painting and pictures; or you'll resign your post here. And never come within breathing distance of Alex Holdsworth.'

She sighed. 'Don't be absurd. All of this' – she waved her hand over the pictures and glass – 'is pure conjecture'.

'The lawyer I have in mind will take this "pure conjecture" and have you down the Old Bailey before you can turn around.'

'If you're so *certain*, why give me a choice?'

The silence drew out as Jury looked at her. 'Because of Alex. He couldn't stand knowing his mother committed suicide. Better that none of this come out.' Jury got up.

At the door he turned and said, 'As far as I'm concerned, you ought to be shot, Dr Viner.'

He walked back towards the main building on legs that felt rubbery. On a white bench some hundred feet away he saw Lady Cray sitting, facing his way, now waving him over.

'Hello,' he said. Jury felt hollow as he looked at the older woman. Lady Cray was sitting upright, her leather bag clutched in her hands. Above the large sapphire on her ring finger, the knuckle was white.

'I'm not spying. Dreadful woman, isn't she?'

Jury couldn't help but smile. 'What have you got in there, Lady Cray? Ribbons? A gun?'

She sighed and relaxed a bit. 'I told you; I'm off ribbons. Thank God. And I'm not carrying, as they say.'

He laughed.

She opened the bag, shut it again. 'I do have a revolver *and* a licence for it. But Mrs Colin-Jackson thought it might be better if it were placed in the Castle Howe safe.'

Jury just looked at her for a moment. Then he said, 'You know what you remind me of?'

'I'd probably rather not.'

'Greek theatre. The *deaux ex machina*.'

'Ah,' she breathed, her fingertips tight along the top of her bag. 'I consider that a compliment.'

'It is. Did you want to see me?'

'I always want to see an attractive man. But the precise reason I waved you over is because Mr Plant wants to see you. He called from the pub. Not to me, but to Mrs Colin-Jackson. It sounded rather urgent.'

'How did you know where I was?'

She didn't answer.

Jury looked behind him, following her gaze. 'Why is her office set apart out here, and right amongst the flowers?'

'There was a similar situation in Eden, I believe.'

43

The girl in the tree shimmied down through the branches that blew and parted like wings, to drop the last few feet into a bed of flowers.

He'd followed her here and watched her get up from the same sort of stalks and petals he'd found her in long ago. She started off through the long grass and he followed, the grass barely separating over his head.

A rustle. Reflexively, he bellied down, tail twitching, tongue clicking. He was about to spring when he saw her ahead, getting away from him, and he sacrificed the smell nearby to the greater pull of the need to follow her.

This constant vigil was tiring, keeping her always in mind and nearly always in view. But she had been his business ever since he'd found her like a storm blowing over the vast lake, thunderclaps of rage, lightning flashes of terror. She was his business, and he'd better mind her.

A white stoat flashed across the line of his vision, catching him off guard. He nearly veered from his straight path and gave chase. No.

Flutters and shadows of wings glowed above him, lit atop the hedge nearby and he pulled up again. No.

Now she was small in the distance because of these stops and starts of his, and he ran faster.

It seemed to take forever, moving through these crowded fields and crowded skies, and he was late. Already she had been up the old tree and was down on the ground.

She was worse than hounds, her anger fenced in but swirling like a dark sea. Now there was a different smell, a different sound. He had smelled it before; he had heard it before — the sudden slap and ratcheting sound.

Then she turned and walked back and the seam of tall grass closed behind her like the wake of a ship.

Rushes, flights, runs. Mice, robins, stoats. Some day there would be time for all that, not now.

He raced towards the house.

Alex was standing at the sink, eating a tasteless sandwich, a lump of cheese between hunks of bread. No one was about. The only sound that registered was the tick of the long-case clock over by the hearth.

He was staring over the field and thinking of his mother. He was indulging in the most fatal of fantasies: what his life might have been like if only . . .

R. Jury, Supt. He chewed and fantasized. What if his mum had married him and Alex could have had a Scotland Yard superintendent for a stepfather?

He looked down at the sink, dropped the sandwich into it, ashamed of himself. That was the kind of wish some little kid would have.

Staring down, he tried to pull back the old, dependable Alex, the one that seemed to be getting away from him. He was not some little kid, the thought, furiously blinking his eyes.

Alex swallowed, looked up and out of the window and saw the cat streaking through the grass towards the kitchen.

Sorcerer? He opened the door, walked through the cramped cloakroom and outside.

Sorcerer darted towards him then turned and darted back. Back and forth, back and forth.

Alex followed.

Up the tree. Look around. Jesus *Christ!* 'Sorcerer?'

The cat nearly flew down the ladder of air and ran towards Castle Howe.

Alex followed him, stumbling through the long grass.

2

The car park of the Old Contemptibles was just about large enough for three cars. Nearly crowding Plant's Japanese car out was a Jaguar XJ10, this year's model, mirror-black, with a registration tag that in itself was worth a small fortune. It was personalised

FAN

having belonged, apparently, at one time to a 'Fan' or a 'Fanny' or a 'Frances'. Only this one had been recustomized — a G, intaglio — very professional, very illegal. Jury looked at it and slowly shook his head.

He didn't think anything could make him smile. This did.

'Superintendent!' called out Marshall Trueblood. 'She insisted; we called from Long Pidd; we're here; Agatha has tyre tracks on her back.'

The regulars were used by now to Melrose, the librarian. But the two new additions were something else. Wiggins was standing at the bar, apparently trying to convince O. Bottemly to mix him up some medicinal brew.

Except that her absence had doubled the beauty of her sometimes sharply etched, sometimes blurred memory-face, Vivian Rivington might never have boarded that train in January. She rose fluidly from her chair in the same cream wool dress she had been wearing the last time Jury saw her; even the large-brimmed hat was there, lying on the table by her glass of sherry. Jury knew she would have rushed towards him, but Vivian-like, checked herself and simply stood there.

If Vivian was a picture, Marshall Trueblood was a tableau: vicuna jacket, grey crepe de chine shirt into the neck of which was tucked a jade green ascot that matched his Sobranie cigarette, tasselled calfskin loafers. Trueblood had forgone Armani momentarily, thinking the Italian blood to hot, perhaps, for the Lakes.

'Vivian.' Jury felt the smile spreading through his body.

But she was wringing her hands as if she'd something to apologize for and saying, 'When they told me in Venice about your getting mar — '

'A drink, a drink,' shouted Trueblood, as if they'd all been stranded in a desert. He got up and shoved Vivian down — rather roughly, Jury thought.

She continued: 'When the three of us were in the Gritti Palace, they told me you — '

Melrose grabbed her hand, stroked it (also rather roughly, Jury thought) and said, 'Vivian, Vivian, let's not go on about it.'

303

She broke free of Trueblood's and Plant's holds, rose, took two quick steps and slowly wound her arms round Jury's neck. Her 'I'm so sorry,' came muffled from lips fast against his chest.

He could feel the small, shuddery sobs. 'It's all right, Vivian,' Jury said against her hair, his arms about her waist. 'It was wonderful of you to come.'

'Don't forget me, old sweat!' said Trueblood. 'I chauffeured! We came straight up from Long Pidd after Vivian drove hell-for-leather from Heathrow.'

Jury turned his face from Vivian's hair towards the window. 'That your Jag out there?'

Trueblood said, 'Actually, it's Viv's. Wedding present.'

Said Melrose. 'It's just what she needs in Venice.'

'It's not *for* Venice. It's for when she's home.' Trueblood was collecting glasses for refills. *Home* was, and would always be, Long Piddleton.

'Interesting registration number.'

Trueblood said nothing.

Vivian was blowing her nose. 'Registration number?'

'I didn't think you'd seen it, love.' He held her at arm's length. 'And incidentally, thank you.'

'For what?'

'For hiring Pete Apted, Q.C.'

She looked confused. 'Who?'

It wasn't Vivian? Who, then?

He said to Melrose and Wiggins, who'd left the bar with his hot toddy, 'We need to go back to Castle Howe.' Melrose was up in a flash. To Trueblood he said, 'You two stay here. We'll take Fang.'

'Helen Viner,' said Melrose. 'Why didn't I see it?'

'For the same reason Adam Holdsworth didn't. For the same reason Alex could look at her almost as a surrogate mother,' said Jury, as the Jaguar left the hamlet of Boone.

'What'll she do, sir, do you think?'

'I'll tell you exactly what I think she'll do, Wiggins: I think she'll try and bluff it out. She's convinced she has too much influence with Adam Holdsworth and that she's indispensable to Castle Howe − which she, not Colin-Jackson, runs − why give up now?'

'There's no hard evidence,' said Wiggins.

'None,' said Jury.

'She's ruined the lives of two children,' said Melrose, looking up at the scudding clouds that reminded him of 'Cristabel'. Clouds that 'covered but did not hide the sky'.

Melrose had always thought that line ominous.

44

Lady Cray was still sitting on the bench overlooking the deep lawn and gardens, watching many things.

She was watching the clusters of daffodils down there near the stone cottage swaying, but hardly 'dancing' (Wordsworth *would* exaggerate so) in a stiff breeze that made her grip the collar of her lightweight coat.

She was watching as Adam Holdsworth played his newest, silly-arse game (the one the sergeant had taught him) of flying his wheelchair down the grassy incline, whooping all the way, waving to her after he turned; he started buzzing up the lawn again, only to repeat the process. Once, he had come close to ramming into the doctor's cottage. She shook her head.

She was watching, with growing interest, the wide field on the other side of the gardens and the stone cottage, where a figure was walking along from the direction of Tarn House. Millie Thale. She could recognize the little girl even from this distance. Now Millie had reached the garden and was stopping, apparently oblivious to Adam Holdsworth's sideshow (that wheelchair was surely operating against the laws of gravity, coming up that incline as it did) and was stooping to pick a bouquet of daffodils.

She was *now* watching another figure, far, far in the distance coming from the same direction. Running.

Lady Cray rose so suddenly that her bag slipped to the ground. She retrieved it.

As she set off down the lawn, she returned Adam's wave.

2

'I brought you these,' said Millie Thale, her hands holding an enormous bouquet of daffodils.

307

Helen Viner, who had been sitting stock-still, frowning at the images in her own mind, rose as she changed her expression to one of smiling indulgence. 'Millie! But *daffodils*, Millie?' She started to come from behind her desk.

'I expect I'm cured,' said Millie, holding out the flowers with both hands.

'Well, thank —'

The daffodils fell away and fluttered to the floor.

The impact of the bullet flattened Helen Viner against the wall. Her body seemed riveted there, palms pushed to the wall, eyes staring, when Alex Holdsworth wedged himself through the window, yelling at Millie. Sorcerer jumped from the sill.

'She killed my mum and I'll kill her ten times.'

Alex grabbed the gun from her frozen, outstretched fingers. The second shot made Helen Viner lurch again; at the same time there was a thud, a whoop and a shout from outside the door.

Through the door came Lady Cray, who brought her small, neat hand down in a hard chop on Alex Holdsworth's arm, forcing him to drop the Webley.

Lady Cray pushed in front of Adam Holdsworth's wheelchair took careful aim and shot Helen Viner in the chest. The body that had been sliding down the wall hit the floor. There was little blood.

'*What the hell —*'

Lady Cray handed the gun to Adam. 'Shoot her!'

'If you say so.' Adam's hands wobbled the automatic up to some level or other and shot.

The four of them looked in one state of horror or another at the slumped form of Dr Helen Viner.

Briskly, Lady Cray removed a small revolver from her bag, walked over to Helen Viner's body, stood in the place where Helen Viner had last stood and shot carefully at the spot where Millie had been standing. The she pressed the gun into the good doctor's hand and let it fall away, quite naturally.

Millie was shaking and holding on to Alex.

Adam's mouth was working, but no words came from it.

Alex stood stock-still, staring at Lady Cray.

'She's quite dead,' said Lady Cray, 'for which we, and Castle Howe, should be thankful.' Then she looked hard at Millie and Alex, and said, 'But it's impossible to know which bullet killed her and one of them went right into the wall. So we're quite straight on that point, aren't we?'

They all nodded, Adam blubbering something about the law.

'Rough justice,' snapped Lady Cray. 'Now, we must get our story straight. Dr Viner obviously attempted to shoot Millie—'

'To shoot *me*,' said Alex. 'After all, it was *my* gun.' His face was flushed as he gripped Millie's hand. 'Millie grabbed the gun.'

'Very well. And clearly we had to shoot her in self-defence.'

'*Are you daft?*' shouted Adam. 'That gun you just planted on her is *your* gun, not hers!'

Lady Cray sighed. 'Of *course* it's mine. You don't think the staff of Castle Howe will allow their guests to tote revolvers about? She took it from me the first day I was here.'

'Oh,' said Adam, puzzled. He sighed and twirled his thumbs. 'Too bad, nice woman.'

'Nice? she was vile. That cat's a better judge of character.'

Sorcerer was sitting on the desk, blinking slowly.

'She killed my mum and she made Alex's dad kill himself. And other things. I was listening out there in the tree.' Millie's voice was high and shrill.

'But for God's sake, woman,' Adam said, 'we'll land up in the nick.' Then he whooped and thumped his fists on his wheelchair. 'In the nick at eighty-nine!'

'Oh, for heaven's sake, no one will land in the nick. With a good lawyer, what court would convict an hysterical little girl, a schoolboy, a kleptomaniac, and a crazy old coot?'

'Crazy old *coot*?' shouted Adam, indignantly.

'So we're agreed?'

They nodded.

'Then nothing leaves this room' – she whisked the Cadbury's box from the bookshelf – 'except these chocolates.'